LAUGH, CLOWN LAUGH

A Novel By

PENNY N. HAAVIG

Laugh, Clown Laugh

© 2018 Penny N. Haavig

Print ISBN: 978-1-54394-032-9

eBook ISBN: 978-1-54394-033-6

For anyone who wears a mask to hide a troubled heart

PART ONE

1930
BROOKLYN, NEW YORK

Chapter 1

I don't want to be here. Not now. Not ever.

"Violet Pearl, hurry up and get yourself together, you hear? Let's not stand around and gawk at the oddities of Vaudeville, okay?" My mama shouts as she scampers out of sight behind the curtain.

I don't know a lot of things. Why I don't scream bloody murder, when the voice from nowhere speaks to me. Why don't I tell someone? It's horrifying when it happens.

I quickly turn in wonder at the musicians tuning their instruments in the far corner of the stage and the acrobats flipping here and there, directly in front of me. *My, my, a person must watch where they're going around here.* If all the performers stood together in one place, it would look like one big colorful quilt with feet. My attention's drawn to the beautiful ballerina adorned in a flowing white tutu with blond hair pulled in a bun. *Someday, I'll be just like her.*

I'm dragged back to reality when I get a whiff of cigarette smoke, cologne, and a faint odor of whiskey blending together in an awful stench. The air's choking me.

Everyone has an eye on the stage manager and theater owner, Mr. Gruffly, who's an act all by himself. "Let's get cracking, folks!" He roars in a loud, grouchy voice.

Oh, dry up. I pull the lipstick out of the case and smear it on my dry lips. *This is the same routine every Friday and Saturday since I can remember. It's really getting to me.*

I turn to go and hunt for my costume items, the bright orange wig, and tambourine with ribbons. I pause in front of the full-length mirror that most people glance at before they get in line to go on stage. *I hope I didn't leave my bag in that disgusting lavatory. It's not only smelly, and the size of a telephone booth, but the voice from nowhere speaks to me there. Creepy.*

Looking around, I lift my dress and pull up my pantaloons firmly over the camisole. I put my hands on my slender hips and practice smiling with one odd grin after another. *How many twelve-year-old girls wear a brassiere anyway?*

I hear masculine voices. In an instant, I drop my dress, so it falls past my knees, but my attention's drawn to the dancers. Instantly, I find myself imitating their every move. Those Hoofer and Elocution lessons my parents made me take for the past five years sure paid off, but I don't look like a ballet dancer in this big polka dot, hoop dress. I almost want to laugh and cry at the same time.

Papa's just a few steps away, tuning his accordion. *I've got to talk to him.*

"Hello there, sweet Violet," Hans whispers in my ear as he brushes my shoulder with his, "You make a great clown, but I know what's under that costume." *He's sickening.* I told Papa that Hans is making passes at me, but he thinks it's all in my imagination. He uses dreadful language too. I want to haul off and give Hans a good swift kick in the buttocks. He'd better keep his distance.

Getting my father alone is tricky because he's either doing a gig with his band or practicing somewhere. *I've got to get out of here after the first act.*

I know they make lots of bucks when the band plays at Bar Mitzvahs and weddings for the high-society folks. Good thing, too. We wouldn't have food on the table if he didn't do that, I guess. Times are tough with the Depression and all.

A lot of people come to see Papa's band, The Domino Four. They're well known all over the five boroughs. Anthony wears a crooked bowtie and reeks of ugly cigar smoke. Then there's Marvin, the gentleman of the group who's always late. He's married with two loud, but adorable children, five and three years old.

Vaudeville days are numbered. At least that's what people are saying. Just a matter of time that the big screen will replace this form of amusement.

If I could pull Papa away from his group for a few minutes, I could ask him if I could skip the last act. My friends, Eleanor and May, are going to the movie theater. *I must go. After all, I'm going to be a teenager soon. Maybe, I should just write him a note and leave.*

"Places, everyone," Mr. Gruffly shouts. "Acts 1 and 2, get ready, and Violet Pearl Moretti, get moving, young lady! You know the drill. The first five acts must be ready to go. Zip, zip, zip!" He claps his hand with each zip. *I feel split in two.*

Now is my only chance to ask Papa if I can skip the Hobo duet. The girls are probably standing in the movie line now, and I can get there in ten minutes by taking the streetcar.

I spy the door to freedom. Should I go? *I can't disappoint Papa.*

Oh druthers, I do remember where I left that idiotic wig and that dumb instrument. I pirouette and leap across the stage and make a quick turn to the left. Right here. Whew. Not in the lavatory.

"I'm afraid for you, young Violet. The real world's a dangerous place for a girl with your face." The creepy voice whispers in my ear. I turn on my heels, but no one is in sight. I cringe.

No one will ever believe me if I tell about the voice. No one. Ever.

I reach my hands into the old ratty carpetbag, plop the wig on my head, grab the tambourine, and briskly twirl into place. Someone's right behind me. I turn and look. No one.

Suddenly, I feel a tug on my arm, and I'm afraid to look. After a few seconds, my eyes are fixed on the deep-dark-brown eyes of my talented father. Papa's the one I can always count on at home or on the stage. Although, he's somewhat peculiar in the way he dresses with the gypsy-like bandana wrapped tightly around his head.

"My little flower. Here, let me fix you up." He straightens my wig, reties the big red bow around my neck, and spins me this way and that. "There you be, my chickadee. You're ready to steal the show on this Vaudeville stage once again."

"But, Papa," I protest and scowl, "I have to ask you something. It's really important."

"No. Not now. No time for questions." He pushes me forward just this side of the curtain. He seems a bit more agitated than usual. I better not rock the boat.

I can hear the crowd applaud for Harry the ventriloquist, as the bumbling stage manager points to me and mimes, one, two, three, go.

At that moment, I look out of the corner of my eye to the spot where Mama always stands and waits for the finale. She's not there. *Where is she?* I feel an abrupt push on my back. Next thing I know, I'm at center stage, and Papa's playing "Yes Sir, That's My Baby" on his trusty accordion. My tap shoes click, and my hand hits the tambourine in perfect rhythm as I float from stage left to stage right. *I officially hate this day.*

Mama's probably chasing Daisy, that bearcat three-year-old sister of mine, because she's not in her seat in the front row.

I do a couple of hop shuffle steps and step heel turns. I scan the front row briefly. She's still not there. I stomp downstage to the last chords of the song and plop down in the big wooden chair as a floppy, old rag doll. The hooped part of my dress pops up over my head, and various tones of laughter can be heard throughout the auditorium. Mama taught me how to do this act perfectly. *Okay, now I've got to get to the movie house.*

"Bravo!" A man in the audience yells, and the applause grows louder.

Soon everyone is standing, with a laugh and a cheer. The curtain closes.

I run backstage toward the crowded dressing room. Now's my chance to corner Papa and ask him if I can go meet my friends. Perfect timing. He's there and alone.

I take a few giant steps forward, not looking where I'm going, and plow right into my mama. I stifle a giggle. "Are you okay? I'm so sorry, Mama." I grab her hands and lovingly squeeze them in mine. Her hands are very clammy. She remains quiet as I peer over her shoulder to see if Papa's still here. He's disappeared.

I smile at her, but she continues to look at me with those droopy puppy-dog eyes.

Always so sad. That glow of happiness has disappeared from her pretty face, and smiles rarely open her mouth anymore. I cringe at the sight.

"You look beautiful tonight," I manage to say affectionately.

She's in a lavender dress, and her long hair is pinned up in curls with velvet bows.

"I look ghastly, Violet. I wonder who that is when I look in the mirror. I missed your revue. Sorry," she utters quietly. She drops her head and stares at the floor.

I pat her shoulder. "Where's Daisy?" She slowly looks up at me, and we stand in silence.

"I'm not sure."

Why don't you know? What's wrong with you anyway?

"Great job tonight, Kiddo." I turn to see Papa holding my three-year-old sister in his arms. I'm perplexed as to how or when he got hold of her. She's wiggling like a worm on the end of a fishing line.

Daisy reaches her arms out to Mama and tries to grab her.

"No! Please, Daisy, not now!" Mama screams out abruptly. My head is light and cluttered with emotion.

Daisy starts to cry. Everyone within hearing distance turns and stares at Mama.

"What are you looking at?" she shouts. "Mind your own business!"

"Why Mommy, why?" Daisy whimpers.

My father puts Daisy down and reaches out to my mother. My heart pounds faster and faster. *What's going on?*

She pushes him away. "I need to be alone, Berto. Don't bother me!"

We freeze in place as she storms away to the large dressing room, a place where she can get lost in the chaos. She motions with her arms to get the gawkers out of the way.

Daisy curls up on the floor and sobs. I bend down to get her, but Papa beats me to it.

"Don't cry, little one. Please don't cry," he says softly.

Daisy hangs in his arms with her head on his shoulders as if glued to his jacket.

The small orchestra plays the Charleston, and the rhythmic sounds of the dancers come together in perfect concert sound. Loud applause follows. They file out through the center-stage curtain to the back area in a formed line. The ballerina dressed in white nods at me as she passes. I curtsy. My eyes follow her as she disappears. *She's so beautiful and graceful.*

"Berto, let's go. We're next. Come on!" Marvin waves Papa over.

"Just a minute," Papa says as he holds up a free hand. "Go on without me if you have to, okay?" He scowls as he speaks.

Papa turns to me. "Here, take your sister and get her ready to go home before we go back on stage. I want to talk to your mother." Papa throws Daisy into my arms.

"But, Papa, I want to ask…?" I'm trying so hard to keep the turmoil inside me, but it's not easy. "Papa." I shout.

He's already gone and can't hear me. I feel like I'm cracking in two.

"I lub you, Vi-Vi!" The words come slowly out of my little sister's mouth. Her face is wet with tears. We rub our noses together as we always do.

"I love you with a bushel and a peck and a hug around the neck," I chirp. I carry her to the coat rack and put her down and grab her wool coat. I push all negative thoughts deep within me.

"I scared, Sissy. Mama's acting nutty."

There's tension in the air, even though everyone around us is laughing. I can feel it.

The Domino Four, or I should say the three, are making their way on stage. How strange is that? Papa never misses a performance. Never.

Daisy starts to find a hiding place under the overflowing coat rack. I grab her. "I'm hungry," she announces. I hold her close to me and pull a sucker out of my pocket. She smirks at me, grabs the stick, unwraps it, and pops it into her mouth. "Yummy," she says playfully. It's amazing how a simple lollipop can pacify her.

"Violet Pearl," Papa says as he comes around the corner with my mother. "Get going and change your costume now. We have exactly six minutes to be in place before the next curtain."

In the few minutes since I saw her last, Mama's hair is half-up in tangles, the bows are gone, and she is sniffling profusely. She's not walking with straight posture. I bite my lip. Poor Mama. She's always preaching to Daisy and me to not slouch and to stand straight. Instead, she's slumped over and walking as though on eggshells.

"What's happening to my mother?" I ask. My heart feels like it will burst.

Papa folds his arms. "Humph." The tension's so real, I can feel it in my bones.

"Do as your papa says, Violet Pearl," Mama manages to say clearly but quietly.

"Do I have to?" I say as I hold back tears. *I never do the things girls my age do.*

"Yes, dear, you know this is our occupation," she says dismally as she stoops down and picks up Daisy with great effort. Papa holds out Mama's timeworn fur coat for her. Some dull flush crosses my face.

"I'll be okay, Violet. Please don't fret. I'll see both of you at home later," she says with a quivering voice, as they turn around and walk toward the door. I feel a little sting prick the center of my tummy. Papa and I stand in silence as we watch them disappear into the frigid dark night.

I know I must do this next act, but I would rather be on that streetcar with Mama and Daisy. Instead of going to Fifty-Third Street where our house is, I would jump off at Flatbush Avenue for the opening scene of the latest moving picture. Mr. Miller, Eleanor's dad, is meeting the girls in front of the theater when the movie's over.

I live in a dream world, I guess. Not going to happen tonight. Maybe never.

Papa plops the old fedora on his head and stands in front of me while I pull my dress off. I cleverly and without haste pull up baggy trousers and throw on a tattered shirt. Tears well up in my eyes. *Always a clown, nothing more.*

Chapter 2

The full moon lights up the jagged landscape, and it bathes me in irresistible sadness, as we step out of the theater. A street peddler's roasting chestnuts over an open fire on the edge of the cobblestones. The streetcar stop is on the corner in front of the vacant Christmas tree lot. The aroma of scattered pine needles fills my nostrils while we wait. *I wonder if the girls liked the movie.*

"Hey, why so glum, chum?" Papa pulls me to him with his strong arms.

My throat gets a little tight as I force a lie. "I'm thinking about Mama."

He steps back and drops his arms. "Here comes our ride. Do you have all of your belongings?"

"Yes, I do, Papa."

The streetcar makes a hissing sound when it comes to a stop. The clinking sound of nickels dropping into the fare box, people chatting, and horns honking make for a strange symphonic resonance. Luckily, there are two seats together in the sixth row. I always sit by a window, so I can escape into a world of make-believe on the ride home. I gaze out and look at the gothic shape of St. John the Baptist Episcopal Church and the grandeur of the Hotel St. George and try to imagine what the food tastes like at the

Superior Café. I count to one hundred in my head, trying to force myself to sleep. It's not working.

The bus is dimly lit so I seldom recognize anyone who climbs on after us. Tonight, is different. The giggling is somewhat loud and annoying as three people board at this stop. I know that laugh anywhere.

"Eleanor, you're so silly!"

Oh no, it's May.

"When you're feeling blue, call out to me!" Eleanor shouts back.

"Keep going, girls," I hear Mr. Miller say. "There're seats in the back."

I slump down in my seat and turn toward the window. *I hope they get off quickly and run all the way to Eleanor's to get out of the cold weather. This way, I won't have to talk to them.* My heart falls into my tummy. Good, Papa's snoring.

When I see the big Texaco sign, I know our stop is momentary. "Fifty-Third Street," the driver shouts. I nudge Papa.

He slowly gets up, and I follow him off the crowded car.

"Come on, Papa," I urge. "I'll race you home."

"Not tonight, Vi. Just not up to it." Pop. There goes another balloon.

Our footsteps crunch in the snow as we get off. Suddenly, my friends are running past us.

"Hi, Violet. Goodbye, Violet." Eleanor shouts.

"Slow down, Eleanor! I can't keep up with you," May cries out.

"Violet, is that you?" May asks as she slows down to look at me.

I keep my head down. I'm so broken.

They giggle some more, but Eleanor grabs May's hand and they sprint ahead, snickering loudly.

"Hello, Mr. Moretti. Violet, I thought you were going to meet the girls for the moving picture tonight," says Mr. Miller as he passes us. *Uh-oh, I'm in trouble now.*

"Hi, Mr. Miller," we say simultaneously.

"What's he talking about, Violet Pearl?"

I ignore him.

They're mere silhouettes in front of us now. May is obviously staying overnight at Eleanor's. That's the way the cookie crumbles, I guess.

I look quickly as we pass Eleanor's house. A big evergreen Christmas wreath with bright-red-cloth bows hangs on her front door. The tree in the big window is brightly lit with colorful radiance. Sounds from the player piano echo on to the street. I wish I could get close to this kind of happy.

"Did you hear me, Violet? Were you planning on skipping out on your performance tonight?" Papa growls.

"Not really, Papa. It was only a passing thought."

It's ten o'clock when we open the front door to our two-story house that stands side by side with a dozen others that look almost the same. The Tiffany lamp under the beautiful hand-painted mirror is dimly lit in the alcove. Mama likes to dabble in art. She painted a delicate design on the woodwork and glass of this wall hanging, which makes it a personal masterpiece.

We hang our wraps up on the hall tree coat rack, and before I know it, Papa disappears into the kitchen calling, "Blossom. Blossom. Where are you?"

He sounds worried about my mama.

The sparse Christmas tree stands in the corner by the front window, looking dark, spindly, and eerie. *Why didn't Mama plug in the lights? Christmas is her favorite holiday.* I take it upon myself to plug it in, and the bright colors twinkle in the dimly lit room making my heart happy. It's only been two days since Christmas, so I'm still filled with the spirit of the holiday. But Mama isn't.

I stop quickly when I see broken records strewn across the old Oriental rug that covers most of our parlor floor. I gasp as I stoop down to read one of the labels—*if you know Susie*—by Eddie Cantor. Mama's favorite twelve-inch seventy-eight is broken. A chill runs over me.

As I bend over and pick up the pieces, the familiar sounds of argumentative voices come through the thin kitchen door. Nothing makes sense; nothing is the way it should be.

"Have you been drinking again, Berto? I smell whiskey on your breath," Mama shouts.

"Stop accusing me of that! It's getting tiresome, Kitty," he yells back.

Papa uses Mama's nickname when he's angry at her, which is quite often these days.

"Then, why do I smell it?"

"Just one small shot glass with the fellas tonight doesn't classify me as a drunk!" he shouts.

Only the hissing sound of the radiators can be heard for a moment.

"Kitty, you must eat. You haven't had anything to eat all day," Papa says.

"You're not my watchdog. How do you know if I ate or not?"

"Stop looking at me with those hostile eyes," he says.

I want to go in there, but I feel helpless, so instead I continue to pick up the broken record pieces. *I hope little Daisy doesn't hear any of this. Hopefully, she's sleeping.*

"You haven't been sleeping. You're up all hours of the night, and I'm worried about you, my dear," Papa says softly. "Goodness, you're trembling."

"I can't do anything right. I don't care if anyone comes over here anymore. I can't even think straight, Berto," Mama says.

"Come now. The house is always warm and inviting, and the girls are dressed neatly every day."

"I see the way you look at those dancers at the theater and the winks you give the blonde. You're such a flirt, Berto."

"It's your imagination running wild again. Stop talking nonsense, Kitty."

That's it! I pop up, take a few swift steps, and open the kitchen door slowly.

"Go to bed, child," Papa mutters as he moves away from her. "Let your mama be."

Mama's head is buried in her arms as she sits at the kitchen table. The teakettle whistles slightly on the stove, but no one makes a move to get it. So, I turn off the stove and pour three cups of water and add tea bags.

"What's wrong with her?" I ask.

"I'm not sure, but she's acting mighty peculiar. Keeps crying over absolutely nothing," he says as he rolls his eyes. "She won't eat or drink. She'll get sick if she doesn't take care of herself." *Why can't my mama be normal, like other mothers?*

Mama chuckles rather oddly, in between sniffles.

Clapping his hands together with great force, Papa says, "Kitty, snap out of it! Don't you know that your daughter's right here?"

Mama doesn't move a muscle, only groans softly. My stomach flip-flops.

"Come on, Kitty. At least drink some tea," he pleads as he tries to keep his composure.

Mama remains quiet, but her whole body's quivering.

"Violet, get your mother that wool shawl on her chair in the parlor. She's freezing."

I bolt through the door and leap across the floor, grab it, and within seconds I put it on my mother's shoulders. "Mama, I love you so much." I say warmly as I wrap my arms around her. Mama seems frozen in this position, so she doesn't respond to me.

I pull myself away from her, holding back the tears.

"Something's wrong with my mother, Papa. Help her, please," I mumble as tears trickle down my face.

Papa puts his arm around me and pushes me toward the door. "I know this is hard for you, daughter, but she'll be better in the morning."

"Please let me sit with her awhile longer, Papa. I can sing to her. She likes that."

"Let me take care of your mother. Please go and check on your little sister and make sure she's sleeping. Then get yourself ready for bed. It's late." He snarls.

I pull away from him and swiftly move to Mama's chair. I wrap my arms around her again in hopes that she will say something, anything, to me.

"I love you, Mama," I say one more time.

"Sure, sure," she mutters.

I pull the chair around, so I can investigate her eyes. It's as though she's looking right through me. My mother's a shell of a woman. *I hate being part of this crazy family.*

I couldn't stay there any longer, so I head upstairs to bed. Daisy's room is right next to mine. Mama left her little lamp on because she's afraid of the dark. I tiptoe in and gently pat her soft, curly-brown hair. She doesn't move. I pull the quilt over her small body and tuck in the sides under the mattress, so she doesn't fall out. She clutches her grungy, old, reliable teddy bear in her arm's embrace.

I sigh and walk quietly to my room.

The pretty lamp with the china figurines is dimly lit as it sits on the small marble top night table next to my bed. My aunt Flossie gave it to me for Christmas. We call her Auntie. She's so kind to Daisy and me.

My room is lifeless. I wish I could have some of that flowered wallpaper on the walls like my friend Eleanor. That way it wouldn't be so dark and dreary at night. I get on all fours and peek under the bed. Good, just dust.

"Are you looking for me?" Snarls the voice from behind me.

I feel like I am fighting my way through quick sand. "Leave me alone. I'm only a kid."

"Ha, ha. You know I exist. All you have to do is look at what's happening to your mother."

I gulp down my fear and turn around. "If you're real, let me see you."

This is ridiculous. A figment of my crazy imagination. I'm alone for sure. Or am I?

"Oh, I'll stop talking for now, but I'm still here."

I throw my bag on the floor and hurl myself on the bed face down on my pillow, and cry, hoping no one hears me. My poor mama has not been herself for days. She's so sad, troubled, and a real wet blanket if you ask me. Not long ago, laughter filled this house, and joy was written on the faces of those who live here.

I try to go to sleep, but my eyes won't shut. The events of the night somersault in my mind, and the imaginary voice might materialize again. I reach for *Little Women*, my favorite book. I love to read because I can pretend to live someplace else. As I turn to the place I left off, I spy a pretty envelope. I pull it out and read it. My name is written on the front. Violet Pearl.

I carefully open it up and pull out the invitation giving all the information about Eleanor's birthday party next Saturday night from 5:30 p.m. to 9:00 p.m. It's nifty because our birthdays are a little less than one month apart, but after tonight, I'm not sure I want to go.

I read the invitation again and bang my fists into the pillow. My mind is running in different directions. Of course. The party is right when I must be on stage. Papa will never let me go. Tears start to well up again, and I whimper. Why must I always be in the show? I might as well move into the storage room at the theater and call it home.

The floorboards on the steps creak several times, and I jump up.

Quietly, I go to the door and peer out through the crack to get a glimpse of my folks coming up the stairs. My room's dark enough, so they don't see me.

Papa's lovingly pushing Mama up the long staircase. "Tell me what's really bothering you, Blossom?" he whispers.

There are twenty-five steps to climb. It seems like a dog's age when they finally reach the top. His arms are wrapped tightly around Mama. My goodness, she's shaking, like there's a thunderstorm under her skin.

Their door closes and so does mine.

Chapter 3

"Oh, what a beautiful morning," I sing as I wake up to the sun radiating through the flimsy curtains on the one window in my room. Silence fills the house, and all I can hear is the winter wind howling outside. I don't have to worry about that voice because it's never here during the day. I must investigate and find out why it's so quiet. I sneak a slide down the banister.

The smell of toast and Chock-Full o' Nuts Coffee always sparks my appetite, even though the Java bug hasn't bitten me yet. I love Sunday mornings because we can take our time and enjoy a nice family breakfast together. These days, we're lucky if we have eggs, butter, or milk.

"There you are, my Petunia!" I say as I spy my cat. "Come here and give me some loving, my soft one." I gather her into my arms and curl up on the high-back chair with the velvet cushion that's right by the door to the kitchen. A surge of warmth happens through my chest as I stroke her soft fur. "You leave me no choice, Kitty," Papa's voice wafts out to me.

"It's best if I go stay with Anthony for a few days. Everything seems to upset you. I simply can't stand it anymore and stop that ridiculous whimpering."

"Anthony?" Mama belts out. "Can't you do better than that? Honestly, Berto. He isn't the best influence on you. Such a goon, with the drinking habit he has."

I jolt off the chair, and the cat leaps out of my grasp. My heart starts to kick my chest. This isn't right. I attempt to push the kitchen door open, but something is preventing me from it. I push harder, and this time it pops open with a great deal of effort. I squeeze through and look down at my father's accordion case.

He picks it up, along with his traveling bag, and steps away from me.

"Where are you going, Papa?" I glare at him.

He doesn't respond and walks over to look out of the window.

"Vi-Vi!" Daisy shouts with her arms out. A small field of yellow puddles under her high chair.

"Oh, little girl, what a mess. Let Auntie clean this up," Aunt Flossie utters as she stands and heads to the sink.

"Aunt Flossie! Oh, my goodness." I barrel over to her, nearly knocking her over, and wrap my arms around her tiny waist. She strokes my hair tenderly. Her soft voice is music to my ears.

"I was wondering when you were going to get up, my Violet. I thought you were going to sleep the day away." She motions me over to the chair near Mama while she grabs a dustpan and broom.

Papa remains glued in the same position, not uttering a word.

I reach my hand out and grab Mama's hand. She barely looks at me but tenderly squeezes mine. *Why can't she be the normal, happy-go-lucky mother she used to be?*

Aunt Flossie is Mama's only sibling and five years older. Her real name is Florence Thomas, but everyone calls her by the nickname. I often look at my aunt with amazement because she's not only attractive but an excellent pianist and opera singer. Churches pay her to play and sing. Will she ever marry? Auntie Flossie hasn't courted anyone since Grandma died last year.

She brings me some toast and orange marmalade. *Why is Auntie here?*

"What are you doing, Papa?" I ask.

No answer.

"Papa!" I shout.

He groans loudly.

I get up and walk over to him.

"Where are you going with that bag?"

He lifts his arm out and draws me close to him and rubs my back. "I have to go away for a few days; your aunt will be staying here to take care of things."

"Where are you going? What about the show on Saturday?" I ask. *Maybe it's cancelled.*

"Flower, I just need time away from this house. I'll see you at the theater. Aunt Flossie will bring you there, so don't worry."

"I don't understand."

"It's better this way. You'll understand in time." He stares out of the window.

I pull away from him, turn, and look at Auntie. She shrugs her shoulders and shakes her head.

Mama just sits there, statue still. My mind feels crowded.

Papa turns and puts his belongings by the back door. He walks over to Mama and puts his hands on her shoulder. "Just go, Berto," she says. "Go get loaded to the muzzle with your friend. I don't need you here anyway." Mama cries as she pushes his hands away.

One minute she's here and the next in outer space. My brain is buzzing with exhaustion.

"Papa, hold me. Hold me." Daisy raises up her hands to him. He pulls my sister out of her high chair and holds her in his arms. A few seconds later, he passes her to Auntie like a basketball and then grabs his bags and stomps to the door. In an instant, he's gone. I'm getting a headache.

Daisy screams, "Papa, Papa, come back!" She squirms and kicks Auntie. "Put me down; put me down!" Auntie just holds her and rocks her tenderly while softly humming, *All the Pretty Little Horses.*

I start to follow him, but Auntie releases one hand to stop me.

Feeling rejected by my own father, I shout to the door, "Papa, why did you leave me?"

Muffled whaling sounds arise from my mother.

I stand there wondering what I should do next. I fall into the nearest chair. I don't let anyone see what's going on inside of my head.

Mama's drifting away from herself and Papa's gone. *How much more can I take?*

Auntie is the only relative in my life. Everyone on my mother's side of the family died or we never see them. Papa's family still live in Italy, except for Aunt Lucy.

"Alright, everyone. Time to go upstairs and get ready for the day," Auntie utters calmly.

"Come, my dear sister. I'll help you." She helps her out of the chair. Mama staggers to the door, giggling mysteriously. She looks so messy.

For some reason, we congregate in my parents' bedroom. This is the biggest room upstairs, and because of Mama's ability to sew, it's elegantly decorated. The full-size brass bed is adorned with a light-green brocade bedspread. Two large throw pillows that are stuffed into bright-red cases brighten up the room.

I mosey over to the old secretary desk and sit on the wooden chair in front of it. I find a small stack of lavender notepaper with matching envelopes. Scrawled out on a scrap piece of paper are the words: *Come to Violet Moretti's Thirteenth Birthday Party on January 31 from 5:00 p.m. to 8:30 p.m.*

Oh no! I forgot about Eleanor's party this Saturday. She'll be thirteen before me, and I must be there. How can I ask for Papa's permission now? I can't be in the show. I won't.

Holding the paper in my hand, I scrape the chair on the hardwood floor as I scoot around so I can get a good visual of the rest of the room. Visions of my big party swirl inside my brain.

"Mama, wear this dress. Please. Pretty, please." Daisy says. She's dragging a blue dress on the floor with the hanger attached. She drops it at

Mama's feet, runs to the dressing table, and grabs Mama's long blue necklet. She throws it over her head, picks up the dress, and piles it all on Mama's lap.

Mama weeps as she brings the dress to her face.

"Don't cry, Mama. You be alright," Daisy stammers as she puts her head on Mama's lap.

I watch Aunt Flossie putter about picking clothes up off the floor. I love her long light-brown braids she carefully pins up on her head. Such beautiful blue eyes and perfect skin too.

"Auntie? Do you know about this?" I ask as I walk over to her with the note I found on the desk. "I think this is Mama's penmanship."

Auntie stops what she's doing and reads. "Yes, Tootsie. Your mother wants me to help you get these out to your friends since the date is drawing near." I always get a warm, fuzzy feeling when she calls me Tootsie.

"But, but…she is supposed to do it with me. We have been planning this for months."

"Violet, come here," Mama mumbles.

I turn around and dash over to her. "You're speaking clearly."

"Of course, I am, silly dilly," she says with confidence.

I'm puzzled by the instant change in her but thrilled she's talking to me.

"Let your auntie help you with the invitations; so, they will be ready to hand out at school next week."

"What do you expect me to do about Eleanor's party this Saturday? I'll be the laughing stock of the whole class if I don't go."

Silence.

Stamping my foot enough to make Daisy jump, I demand, "Someone say something!"

Mama stares at the dress in her hands. She's gone again. *Darn it, anyway.*

Auntie grabs my hand. "Don't you worry, my dear Violet. You'll go to the party."

I sit down next to Mama and put my head on her shoulder, "I want you to help me with the invitations. You have perfect penmanship and original artwork to make them shine."

She rocks back and forth. My mother's slipping away from me again.

"She's having a difficult time, Tootsie."

"I wish I could help her." Prickles of sweat break out on my neck.

"Be patient with her. Hopefully, she'll come out of this miserable state."

"Alright, I will. But I must go to that party this weekend. Please?" I look at Auntie and back to my mother. Once again, no response.

"I really, really want to go to Eleanor's party. Mama must give me permission since Papa's not here. What am I going to do?"

"Violet, you'll have to ask your father if you can skip the performance at the theater." My aunt finally says as she flutters about the room.

"He's not here, or haven't you noticed?" I growl. I stand there with my arms folded in front of me, my jaw clenched tight as I glare at them both. I feel mad at no one in particular.

"Your father should be back here in a couple of days. You can ask him then." Auntie says.

I fall on my knees before my mother and look up into her dark eyes. "But, Mama. I can't plan my thirteenth birthday without your help. I just can't."

Mama stares at me with a blank look as though her heart is made of stone. I start to tremble but hold back the tears.

"Violet, please take your sister into her room and get her dressed at once," Auntie commands. "I'll help your mother wash up and get dressed."

"Are you mad at me, Auntie?"

"Just do as I've asked, dear. Your mother and I need some time alone."

Chapter 4

I grab my sister in my arms and hold her tight. "I love you, my little Daisy girl," I whisper in her ear. She wiggles and turns. "Let's rub noses, like the Escimoses." She giggles.

"Vi-Vi, what should I wear? Can I wear the green jumper?"

We both jump off the bed and race to her closet.

"Why's Mama sad?" Daisy asks.

"She's not getting enough rest. Auntie will take care of her. Now, is this the jumper?" I ask as I gently remove it from the hanger.

"Yep." Daisy replies.

"Here, put this blouse on first, okay?" She plops on the floor and fiddles with the buttons. Thankfully, there are only five, just right for small fingers to manipulate. Soon, she jumps up, climbs out of her nightwear, and disappears under the blouse. "Boo! I'm a ghost," she says as she turns around with it draped over her head.

"Funny girl." Laughing quietly, I pull it down as she puts her arms in the sleeves.

"Okay, done. Let's skip to my Lou over to my room so I can find something to wear."

Mama made my bedspread out of scraps of material, and the deep-red pillows on my bed make me feel like Greta Garbo from the moving pictures. Auntie gave me her old armoire since I don't have a closet. I absolutely love it because it has a full-length mirror on the door.

I open the big door, peer inside, and grab the navy-blue sailor dress.

Daisy mills through my hair ribbons as though she is uncovering some buried treasure. I smile at her antics.

"Here, Sissy. Wear this ribbon today."

"Alright, I'll wear it for you." I giggle and tickle her under the chin. She laughs uncontrollably. I love to hear her laugh.

We have an old Victrola, but there's a real knack to spin a record smoothly. I carefully take out the 78 from its brown paper sleeve. Nutcracker Suite by Tchaikovsky is a family favorite. I wind up the crank carefully but steadily. Soon, the room is filled with melodic sounds of a huge symphony. I twirl gracefully on my toes, and soon I'm swaying, turning, and bending like a ballerina. I feel like I'm floating on a cloud.

"Daisy wants to dance too, Vi-Vi." She grabs my hands. We curtsy to each other, and we move this way and that in a somewhat polished manner.

Suddenly, a door upstairs slams shut. It's so loud that the record makes an awful screeching sound as the needle slides across the surface. My sister and I run to the bottom of the stairs. We look up, and Daisy starts to climb the stairs. I pull her shaking body into my arms.

"Get out of here, Flossie! Leave me alone! I don't want to hear any music not now. Not ever!" Mama shrieks.

"Stop it, Blossom. The children will hear you," Aunt Flossie says.

"Who cares if they do? Way too loud anyway," Mama belts out.

"Mama, Mama. I want my mama," Daisy wails loudly, as she thrashes about. "Put me down. I want Mama, now."

"It's okay, little one," I say as I struggle getting her to the big rocking chair. "It's going to be alright." She leans into me and sucks her thumb as I rock.

The floorboards on the staircase squeak as Auntie descends to the main floor of our house. Our aunt always lights up our lives with her presence. What would we do without her?

"Come on, girls, let's get on your outer wear and galoshes so you can go outside and build a snowman, okay? Your mama needs to rest for a while."

"But I want my mama," Daisy whimpers. Before I can control it, my eyes fill.

"I'll race you to the back hallway." I say eagerly, wiping my eyes.

My sister wiggles her way out of my arms and bolts ahead of me through the kitchen door. "You can't catch me. I'm the Gingerbread man."

The snow is perfectly moldable, and it feels good to be outside doing a kid thing for a change. We make snow angels and pour syrup on clean white snow for a tasty treat. We form a snowman with a corncob pipe, a button nose, and an old top hat of Papa's.

We don't even pay any attention to the cold wind blowing in our faces because we're having a whale of a time. I'm overcome by a feeling I don't know how to hold. It's the opposite of trouble and gloom.

"Girls, you need to come in soon, so you can change out of those drenched snowsuits," Auntie calls from the door. We play a bit longer and head inside for lunch.

Much to our amazement, Mama's sitting in the kitchen when we get back inside. She's clutching a thin white leather book that says, *The Shepherd Psalm. Why is this book so special to her?* Her hair is tousled, and red lipstick is smeared all over her mouth. Red rouge is smudged on her cheeks in huge circles that makes her look like a circus clown. This is not my mother. Her undergarments are showing because the buttons on her dress are not fastened.

"Did you have fun in the snow?" she slurs with a slight lift of her head.

"We did, Mama. Yes, we did," I say as I wrap my arms around her.

Daisy leaps into her lap. "We ate snow sundaes too."

Mama manages a grin of approval.

She's holding her book as though it is a rare jewel and stares down at it in undivided attention. "The Lord is my shepherd," she whispers. *Is she talking about God?*

After wiping the excess lipstick off Mama's face and teeth, Auntie serves us creamed chipped beef on toast for lunch. Mama picks at it as she plays with her fork and then looks up at me.

"Violet, I've been thinking. Since your father is who knows where, I'm going to let you go to your friend's party tomorrow. That's if you still want to."

I look up at her in total shock because she's speaking clearly. "May I?"

"Yes, you may."

"What about the show?" I ask.

"Your papa can find a replacement," Auntie says.

Mama slowly stands, "He's going to have to understand, and that's all there is to it."

I feel contentment engulf me, like a warm wave. *Is this real?*

"There, Eleanor will love this book especially wrapped in a pink headscarf." I quickly take a glimpse in the mirror, straighten my dress, and grab my purse. I fly down the stairs and grab my wrap off the hook. Good thing Eleanor lives only two doors down.

"You look beautiful," Auntie says. "I will walk you out to the sidewalk, dear, so I can watch you go to Eleanor's."

"Where's Mama?" *She was fine a few minutes ago.*

26

"She said to have a good time, and she will see you later."

"Okay, better get going. I don't want to be late." I know I sound shaky, even though I'm trying to control my quivering voice.

Auntie grabs her wool shawl, wraps it around her, and opens the front door. "I'll stand outside and watch you walk over there."

On the threshold stands my father, bigger than life.

"Berto! What are you doing here?" Auntie says.

"I'm here to bring Violet to the theater. That's what." He replies with a frown.

"Come on, Violet Pearl, we don't want to be late for the show," he says.

Auntie puts her arm around me. "She's going to her friend's birthday party tonight."

He grabs my arm. "Baloney! She belongs on stage with me!"

"Please, Papa. Just this one party. I simply must be there for Eleanor's thirteenth." Tears well up as I throw my arms around him, sobbing unceasingly.

"Honestly, Berto, let her be a girl for once, and let her have some fun with her friends," Auntie says in a soft voice.

"Who do you think you are, Florence? She'll go with me. Do you hear?"

"Berto, please be reasonable. Violet needs her friends. You know full well that your band can replace her act."

He holds me with a tight grip, so I don't bolt away. I feel shivers go down my spine.

"Please, Papa," I whimper.

"I came all the way over here to get you, Violet Pearl. Come on." He pulls me to the sidewalk. I can see kids arriving at the party. *Thank goodness, they don't see this charade.*

"I won't be able to concentrate on the act. My mind will be someplace else." I cry.

"Your place is on stage."

"Look at me, Papa. I'm in a dress, not a costume. Please let me go to Eleanor's."

He looks at me and smirks. "Humph. It's against my better judgment, but I guess this once won't hurt." Warmth floods over me.

I take a few steps back and look up at him. "Thank you, Papa." I turn on my heels.

I walk up the steps to Eleanor's house and turn to wave at Papa. He's gone.

Chapter 5

The Christmas tree's gone, decorations are put away, and I'm back in school. Papa's still at Anthony's. There's a heavy feeling on my chest, and lightness in my stomach. I miss him so much.

My desk is attached to my chair, and it can be quite uncomfortable at times since it's the hardest wood ever. Eleanor sits to my left, May to my right, and Skeeter is right behind me. He's fiddling with my braids again. I hope Mrs. Rulon doesn't catch him in the act. He'd be sent to the corner for sure. Arithmetic and English are done for the day. I don't think I passed the fractions test. Drat it anyway.

The teacher rings the hand bell, which indicates lunchtime. The sound of crushing paper bags and the whiff of overripe bananas and peanut butter fill the classroom.

"Violet Pearl, please come here for a moment," the teacher says. *Uh, oh. What did I do now?* I stand in front of her desk. My legs get restless, like they want to carry me out of here.

"You can mail your invitations now, but don't take all day." She scowls over her glasses. I breathe a sigh of relief.

"Yes, Mrs. Rulon." I glance at a few curious girls, staring at my every move. In the entryway, besides hooks for coats, the teacher has placed a long string with our names on clothespins. I'm having such a hard time with this. I want to invite the twenty girls in my class, but I can only ask twelve.

"Our house is not big enough for more than thirteen girls, Violet." Mama said a few weeks ago. I hope the other girls will understand.

I live two blocks from school, so my feet are the only transportation I need. The ugly slush covers the sidewalks today, as I propel toward home. I move swiftly, paying close attention to the busy traffic, on the one street I must cross.

I smell bread baking when I open the door. I unload my stuff and dart into the kitchen.

Mama's staring into outer space as though someplace else, and Auntie is pulling the bread out of the oven. Adrenaline rushes through my veins.

"Sissy. Sissy." Daisy scoots over and hugs me tight. I lift her into my lap and grab Mama's hand. "Mama, I gave out the invitations at school today."

She stares straight ahead and nods her head, which indicates some type of approval.

"They have two weeks, Violet," Auntie says as she serves the warm bread and butter.

"I know, but I'm so excited that I can hardly think about anything else; I want it to be the best party ever."

Mama scarfs down the bread as though she hasn't eaten in days. "Very good, Flossie," she manages to say. I don't want to change her face; it's already wrinkled with frustration.

Auntie pats her shoulder and smiles. "I'm glad you like it, Blossom. It's good to see you eat something."

It's so hard to understand why Mama acts normal one day and the next, positively odd. Life is like a rollercoaster ride with no end in sight.

A loud knock at the back door startles us.

"Who comes to the back door? Good thing it's locked. Stay here while I check." Auntie disappears into the small porch.

"Papa!" I run into his arms, with Daisy at my heels.

Mama's shoulders start to shake. "Get out of here, Berto."

"Don't worry, Blossom. I'm not here to stay. I came to talk to Violet."

"Come, sit down, and have slice of homemade bread. I'm sure you can spare a few minutes with your daughters." Auntie says.

"Thanks, Flossie."

I pull my chair next to his. "I miss you, Papa. Won't you please come back home. It's too quiet around here, without you."

He looks up at Mama. She's a shadow, a lump of darkness in a bear's cave.

"Only if your mother wants me to, but from what I can see, she doesn't."

Auntie rubs Mama's shoulders. "Give her time, Berto. Now, why did you come here?"

"The band is playing at a wedding this Saturday, and I want Violet to sing with us."

I pull away from him. "What are you talking about?" I wonder if there's a limit to how many questions a person's brain will hold.

His brow is all bent out of shape already. "I let you skip a performance, so you could go to your friend's party. It's payback time now."

A cold hand closes around my heart.

"I think it's time for you to leave, Berto." Auntie motions to the door.

"That's funny, Florence. How can you ask me to leave my own house?"

"Can't you see you're upsetting my sister?"

Sobs rack Mama's body, coming from someplace deep inside of her.

He makes his way to the door. "I'll be by to get you at two o'clock on Saturday, Violet Pearl. Be ready. Come give your papa a hug, goodbye girls."

Daisy wraps her arms around his legs, "Don't go, Papa."

There's a fist in my chest, bang, bang, banging. I try to calm down, but I flee to my room instead.

Chapter 6

Manhattan, Upper East Side

I feel so out of place, in this childish pink dress with the big bow in the back. All the ladies are elegantly dressed in gowns of sequins and chiffon. The array of fragrances that adorn them fills the room like a beautiful garden of roses, lilies, and gardenias. The men are visibly attentive to the ladies as they watch the bride and groom waltz across the vast chamber.

The Domino Four are dressed in timeworn white dinner jackets and black pants. Their red bowties add a dazzling touch to the outfit of white. It's an evening set apart from the turmoil and sadness filling the city streets, a few blocks away. The folks attending this event are fortunate to be well off, despite the misery others are going through. I cross my arms and let out a huff of air.

"Let me call you sweetheart; I'm in love with you," Hans's voice floats from the microphone, as he winks at me. I blush. He has a charming voice that the ladies swoon over. My inner voice is going full speed.

He's too old for you. He winks at anything wearing a dress. He does make me smile though.

The band pauses as Papa takes the microphone. "Let me introduce ourselves to you." He points to his right. "This is Marvin on the piano,

Anthony on the sax, Hans is playing the violin, and he is the one that sings most of the time. This cute young lady is my talented daughter, Violet Pearl. I'm Berto Moretti. We all live in Brooklyn." Applause breaks out everywhere.

"Now, Ladies and gentlemen, it's time for everyone to join the bride and groom on the dance floor," Papa announces. I press my hands under my thighs, with anticipation. My job is to play the tambourine for fast numbers, but who knows when that will happen? I sink back in my chair.

The melody of the *Vienna Waltz* fills the entire residence as many couples spin stunningly in one direction. Waltzes and fox-trots bring joy to couples dancing cheek to cheek. I'm mesmerized by the bride and groom as they take center floor. She has such beautiful black hair and stunning blue eyes. His eyes are on her every minute as they glide by. The next hour is unbearable, with two songs needing a tambourine and my pip-squeak voice. My knees grow weak and turn to rubber.

"We are taking a break, everyone. The Domino Four will be back in fifteen." A few folks applaud as we head down the hallway.

The smoke-filled dwelling is big enough to have a nice den for the group to hang out in between sets with a small washroom in the corner. The men sip on small glasses of brandy while I guzzle a glass of Coca-Cola. *Why do men smoke? I wish there were some kids my age here.*

Anthony puffs on his third cigarette, "Those people are so high and mighty in those fancy clothes. Did you see some of the jewels those dames are wearing? They have no idea the turmoil there is, only a few blocks away."

I study him carefully.

"Calm down, Anthony. They're paying us good money for this event." Hans says.

"Listen, Bud, I can complain. I have every right to. Leave me alone."

Papa pats Anthony on the back, "I'll give you my share, but keep your voice down, okay?"

"Berto, you always do that. No, I won't take any more from you. I'll figure something out. Maybe, I need to pick someone's pocket. I don't think

I can handle much more of these high and mighty individuals." He turns on his heels and staggers out of the door.

"I'll go get him before he makes a scene out there," Marvin says.

"Let him take some time to cool off. We must go out in five minutes anyway. How are you doing, Violet?" Papa says as he puts his arm around me.

It's funny how you don't know you're in a clump of pieces, until someone cuddles you together. "How much longer, Papa? I'm bored."

"Oh, probably two more sets. You better try the bathroom before we go back out."

I open the door of the washroom and peek in. *It reeks in here.*

"Papa, I'll meet you out there. I'm going to find a bathroom fit for ladies."

There are so many doors. I feel completely bewildered.

"Are you looking for a powder room, young lady?" The bride's mother asks.

"Yes, Ma'am."

"Go down the hall and take a left. It's the first door on the left."

I curtsy, "Thank you."

I bolt through the door, lock it, and beeline to do my business. *Wow, look at that vanity with gold legs.* I plop down on the velvet cushion and primp my hair with my fingers. Why do I feel like someone's in here with me? I'm alone, for crying out loud.

A breeze sweeps past my face. "Ha, so you think you're by yourself, little girl?"

I leap off the stool. I can't breathe. I tug at the top of my dress, pull it away from my skin, and take a deep breath. *Calm down, Violet. Look around.*

"Someday, I will make you a famous movie star. You've got the looks and the talent to make it big."

I throw my hands over my ears. "Stop it. Leave me alone. You're not my keeper."

A knock on the door causes me to jump. "Can you come out soon? There's a line out here." I hope no one heard me talking. I shrug my shoulders and open the door.

I run around the corner and don't look back.

My mind's still churning when I find my seat next to the stage. *What's up with the imaginary voice, I keep hearing?* I must get my mind on something else.

The band plays on as I watch the guests mill about chatting with people from other tables, while others are taking last puffs on cigarettes. Waiters are collecting plates from the tables, with a cling, clang, cling. The bride and groom are cutting the mammoth wedding cake.

Papa plays a few notes on the accordion to get the crowd's attention. "Have you had enough giggle juice, folks?" He chuckles. A few folks laugh. Most are mingling among the tables or taking in the sights below on the balcony.

Suddenly, loud, earsplitting screams echo throughout the palatial space.

"I think Anthony's going to jump!" A woman from near the balcony hollers to the crowd.

People rush closer, but it's too crowded to get through to see anything. I start to move in that direction, but Papa holds me back.

"You arrogant, pompous people." Anthony's voice is overbearing enough that he can be heard throughout the dwelling. "You're so caught up in your fancy jewels, expensive hideaways, and stashes of dough hidden under your mattresses that you don't even care about us poor folks who have to scrape up your scraps to pull together a meal." I perch on a chair and watch him climb on the cement ledge of the four-foot wall. My tongue fills my mouth, and my thoughts are muddled.

"Come on down from there!" the father of the bride shouts.

"Let's talk about this, buddy," another man says.

"Stay away from me, you, jerks."

"Stay right here, Violet." Papa says as he moves toward the balcony. The lump is back in my tummy, and it's hard as a rock.

Papa manages to push his way through the crowd and hollers at the top of his lungs, "Anthony, what...!"

Gasps and screams fill the air.

He's too late. Hot tears begin to fall down my cheeks.

The ride home is awful. I keep the ugly scene in my mind as it plays over and over. Papa's silent as he looks straight ahead. I want to fly to the front door and into my mother's arms when the car stops at our house. *I hope Mama sleeps with me tonight.*

The house is dark, except for the hall light at the top of the stairs. I'm shaking all over with fear. *I want my mother.*

Papa pats my shoulder, "Go right to bed, Violet. It's almost midnight. Be quiet, so you don't wake anyone." I turn to hug him, but he's already gone.

Chapter 7

The wind's howling outside my bedroom window, as I snuggle under my warm blankets. I witnessed a living nightmare last night. I'm a girl, just a kid, who never should've watched someone kill themselves. I take a deep breath as I remember Mama and Auntie, holding me into the wee hours of the morning. I tried my best to be quiet, but those creaky steps won. I might as well get up, even though it's only six o'clock.

I tiptoe downstairs to the kitchen where I find Papa sipping on a glass of water.

"Papa, you're here." I run over and wrap my arms around him. He pulls me on his lap, holds me tight, and weeps loudly. This is the first time Papa cried in front of me that I can remember. A wave of turmoil washes over me. He's home to stay because his suitcase and other belongings are just inside the doorway.

"I'm sorry you had to witness such horror last night, Flower. I wish I could've stopped Anthony." Silent tears consume me.

"I'm so glad you're home, Papa." A strange happiness settles inside me, as we lean on each other for support. The kitchen clock ticks rhythmically to our beating hearts.

"Papa!" Daisy calls as she flies through the door.

Mama and Auntie are right behind her.

"Berto," they say in unison.

He motions with one arm to Mama to come to him. She does. It's been great the last few days because my mother seems perfectly fine. I hope she stays this way.

"I'm so sorry for the tragedy that struck your band," Auntie says solemnly.

"Oh, it's so sad about Anthony. Really it is. So sad," Mama whimpers.

"I need you, all of you, right now," Papa says softly. "There's no place I'd rather be than right here, right now. You're all I have, you know."

"How about some pancakes?" Auntie says and heads to the stove and puts on a pot of coffee.

Berto smiles. "Sounds wonderful, Flossie."

Maybe everything will be fine. My birthday party should bring joy and excitement back into this house. Mama looks better, and Papa's back. Look at them, so much in love.

It's been a week since Papa returned home, and we're going to Aunt Flossie's house in Queens. To get there, we take the bus part of the way and then the elevated train, commonly called the "L."

Aunt Flossie's house is so interesting and adventurous. Although, I've never been in the attic because it is always locked. I love to imagine ornate trunks filled with old hats and dresses. I would gather the neighborhood girls together to put on a play, where I'd be the director and the star. The long staircase coming down would be the perfect entrance for center stage. Auntie would play her grand piano as the accompanist. Oh, it would be divine.

Until then, I take out the old porcelain child-size dishes from her curio cabinet and play with them on the round dining room table, which is covered for protection with a hand-crocheted tablecloth.

"Daisy plays too." She says running from the kitchen. "I be careful, Vi-Vi," she says.

"Let's have a tea party. We're fancy ladies in a mansion that overlooks the ocean. You pour the tea, Ms. Daisy, and I will pretend to serve some warm tartlets." Her legs swing rhythmically under the table.

Mama dropped us off here today, so she can shop without distraction. She's happier these days. She loves the second-hand stores. It's a quick way for Mama to make some cash by putting old clothes on consignment. The shop owner called and said she sold several items. With that money and the five dollars Papa gave her, the shopping spree should last for hours.

My aunt's crystal clear, harmonious voice catches my attention and gives an immediate feeling of being in a concert hall such as the great Carnegie. Daisy picks up her head too, and we stop what we're doing to listen to our Aunt Flossie sing and play her piano.

I grab Daisy's hand, and we tiptoe into the front room and stand in absolute awe of her as she makes beautiful music. Her hands touch the keys superbly but with marvelous style.

The back door to Auntie's house slams. Daisy and I jump because we're so mesmerized by the lovely music that Auntie is serenading us with. I'm curious, so I move into the dining room, peering out of the window on my way.

"Auntie, that strange man is outside your window again," I whisper in her ear and then hide behind the sheer curtains that don the bay window. I bite my lip to keep from screaming.

Auntie moves swiftly, but cautiously, to the window and peers through the curtain. She gasps for air.

"You-hoo, where is everyone?" Mama shouts. Daisy runs to greet her, and Mama picks her up with a big squeeze. "Mama, can we go home now? Please?" she asks.

"Just give me a few minutes with your aunt, my precious. Okay? Then we'll bundle up and head out to catch the three o'clock bus."

"Okay," Daisy said as she slides out of Mama's arms.

"Did you see any good deals out there today?" I ask her. "I don't see any bags, Mama."

She either doesn't hear me or is ignoring me. She pulls her sister away from the window and all but drags her into the kitchen.

"Daisy, play quietly for a few minutes. I'll be right back." I whisper.

Good. I can hear everything now. "Flossie, that sinister bimbo of a so-called fella is standing right in front of your house again. You need to call the police from the precinct right away. He scares me," Mama pleads nervously.

"I keep all of my doors and windows locked all the time, especially during these cold winter months. He comes, and he goes, dearie. I'm not the least bit concerned. So, don't you be."

"Well, okay, but watch your back when you leave your house alone." Mama tells her.

"See, I told you that he comes and goes. He isn't there anymore. Look for yourself." Says Aunt Flossie.

Mama moves cautiously to the window and peers out from the corner of the curtain, so she won't be seen. "He's gone. We better get going before he comes back, Flossie."

I beeline over to play with my sister.

"Girls, let's get a move on," Mama calls to us. "The next bus leaves in ten minutes, but we still have to walk one block. We can't miss it, or we may have to stay here tonight."

We grab our coats and pull on our galoshes, give Auntie hugs, and before we know it, we are standing at the bus stop. I look up at Mama for a split second to see her staring intently at a very creepy dude who's also getting ready to get on our bus. It's that man!

The bus tires screech as it veers up to the corner. A few folks get on ahead of us, and we climb on board the crowded bus. The doors close. The man is left on the sidewalk.

"Who is that, Mama?" I whisper. "He looks so scary. He was standing outside Aunt Flossie's house."

"Don't worry, Violet Pearl. He's a bit out of sorts but harmless," she assures me calmly.

I'm still worried all the same. I tremble at the thought of seeing him again.

After rolling over the city streets and gliding over the Brooklyn Bridge, we arrive a few blocks from our house. The air's still nippy as we walk home, but it feels good.

It's early evening when we finally step inside the warmth and safety of our house.

"So, there're my girls. I never thought you would get here. Come and give your papa a hug."

"Papa, Papa! I'm hungry," Daisy says as she runs and jumps into his arms.

"What is that wonderful smell?" Asks Mama.

"Yummy. I smell onions and garlic for sure," I say, licking my lips.

"Your papa's a great cook with that Italian background of his," Mama declares. "He and Aunt Lucy should open a restaurant. The aroma sure makes me hungry."

Daisy and I break away and race each other into the kitchen, plowing through the door as we go.

"I saw that peculiar hoodlum again today. I tell you, Berto, he's following me. I thought he was following Flossie, but now I'm convinced it's me."

"Oh, come on, Blossom. There's a lot of his kind around these days due to the difficult economic downslide we've been experiencing."

She pulls away from him. "He was standing right outside Flossie's house one minute and at the bus stop the next. If the bus wasn't full, he would have gotten on right after us. Don't you even care?"

Chapter 8

I can't believe it's the last night of Vaudeville—on this stage anyway. The big screen is taking over, and those who want to see live acts will have to go elsewhere. The smell of incense is filling the entire area, even though there are no animal acts. Good popcorn at five cents a bag.

"My dear daughter," Papa said as he puffs out his chest in pride. "In a few years, you'll be going to the performing arts school in the big city. I can't wait to see your name, Violet Pearl Moretti, on the marquis outside the Erlanger Theater on Broadway. You'll knock 'em dead, my dear."

I look at him with a slight scowl. *No way!*

"Oh, Berto. She's still a kid," Mama says as she powder's Daisy's face. "There's plenty of time to decide what Violet will do with her future. Right now, the show must go on, and there're only a few minutes until curtain time."

"Mama, can I please wear that really short dress with all of those crinolines under it, please, please?" my sister asks. Warmth floods over me, as I marvel at her cuteness.

Mama goes over to the overcrowded clothes rack, pulls out the bright-red satin dress, grabs my sister's hand, and moves with urgency to the small changing cubicle.

"Okay, Morettis. There's five minutes until your last act. Let's go out with a bang," shouts Mr. Gruffly.

I glance at myself in the big mirror and am astonished that my make-up's on perfectly. I did it by myself too. I put the big top hat neatly on my head and straighten my short tuxedo jacket that neatly complements the red jumper. I force a smile and get in place.

"Now, for our next to last act on this Vaudeville stage in the Gotham Theater. Introducing Berto Moretti and his two girls, Violet Pearl and Daisy Mae. This is Daisy's debut performance. Let's give them a big hand, folks."

Papa walks on stage first playing his accordion to the tune of, *If I Had a Talking Picture of You*. We follow. Daisy's in my arms. I sit down and sit her on one leg. Instantly, she becomes my puppet, and I'm the ventriloquist.

"So, dear Daisy, what's new with you today?"

She nods her head up and down.

"Come on now, you can do better than that."

She opens her mouth very wide.

Words are on the tip of my tongue, but I'm completely dumbfounded as I look at the audience. Mama's in the front row and smiling from ear to ear but sitting directly behind her is that scary hoodlum who was hounding Auntie last week. My heart begins to pound like it will pop out of my mouth. It's up to me to keep us on task.

"Ah, ah, ah," Daisy utters with her mouth still wide open.

The audience laughs; Mama smiles while the creep slumps down in the seat behind her.

"Say hello to the people," I say. With great effort, I control my feelings.

"Do you know that this is the last night that we can perform on this stage?" I ask her.

She nods her head profusely up and down, so much that her great big bow falls over her eyes.

"Oops. Upsy-Daisy." she squeals.

The audience roars with glee.

44

"Here you go, bow." She reaches up with one quick motion and throws it into the audience.

I must laugh because everyone else is.

Papa runs to our side with the accordion and plays a peppy tune. A few people in the audience start to clap to the rhythm of his music. He gets close enough to give me a nudge, and I quickly release Daisy. Luckily, we have our tap shoes on and begin dancing our way out of a disaster and off the stage. The audience must love us because the applause and laughter echoes throughout the theater for at least five minutes.

Mr. Gruffly sprints to center stage. "Now, Ladies and Gentlemen, your favorite band from your home town of Brooklyn, New York. The Domino Four."

As soon as we remove our tap shoes, I take Daisy's hand, and we quietly make our way down the narrow hallway that brings us to a side door to the auditorium. Mama always saves two seats for us in the front row. Oh good. Aunt Flossie's here too. She must have arrived a few minutes ago. I hope that goon is gone.

I stop short.

Daisy tries to pull from me. "Let go of me, Vi-Vi." she whispers. "I want Mama."

Since we're only two rows away, I let her go. I don't want to cause a fuss.

The man behind my mother turns slowly, and our eyes meet. I'm frozen with fear.

He stands up slowly and grabs the corner of my jacket. A shiver runs up my spine, and I feel like I might wet my pants.

"Sit down!" a man yells.

"You're blocking my view," another grumbles.

Auntie and Mama turn around simultaneously. He looks at them and glares at me.

They squeal in unison.

"I know where you live," he whispers in my face as he gets up.

In an instant, he's gone. My stomach fills with a mass of bees. I freeze like an ice sculpture.

Mama motions to me. I run and sit on her lap. My mind's a jumble.

A few nights later, Berto wakes up with a start. It is two thirty in the morning, and Blossom's not in bed. "Where's my wife?" he says out loud. "She's been sleeping through the night without a toss or turn."

He creeps down the stairs and into the kitchen. There he finds his beloved Kitty washing the floor on her knees while the kettle is whistling out of control.

"What in the world are you doing, my dear? Do you know that it's almost three o'clock in the morning?"

She keeps scrubbing the same spot profusely and does not answer him.

Berto goes to the stove and removes the kettle from the burner and turns it off. "Kitty!" he shouts.

She looks up, stares at him a moment, and starts laughing in an uncontrollable, high-pitched cackle.

He goes to help her up, but she lashes out at him and scratches his face, nearly missing his eye. She gets up on all fours and hisses like an angry tomcat. Once again, he tries to assist her in getting up, and he achieves his goal.

"Well, Berto. You always call me Kitty. So that's how I should act, right? Meow," she says as though everything is normal.

He isn't amused. "Come to bed and turn the radio off."

"I'm not tired."

"You come with me this instant. You know I have that big engagement in a few days in the Catskills. You need your sleep."

"Did Violet tell you about the sinister character and what happened in the theater the other night?"

"Yes, she did. I gave a description of him to the police. Don't you remember? They said they will be on the lookout for him."

"Flossie had to stay with us that night because she was frightened out of her wits, and I think I saw him looking through the backdoor window just a little while ago."

"How would he know where we live? It was a good thing our neighbor, Sergeant O'Malley, was at the show and escorted us home. The depraved stranger was nowhere in sight, and O'Malley has the precinct on the lookout too. So, don't worry. No way could he be looking in that window." Berto walks to the window and looks out into the dark backyard.

"Flossie's petrified. She doesn't want to go out of her house, you know."

"Okay, I'll ask O'Malley to call the police department in Queens tomorrow and see if they can watch her place. Now, let's get some sleep. Daisy will be awake before you know it."

"Go on up, Berto. I will be there shortly."

Berto pulls her to himself. "I'm not going without you."

"Violet, I have a few things you can have to decorate for your party on Saturday. Do you want them?" Eleanor asks on our way home from school.

"Sure. I want to set the stage for a splendid party just like yours. Go get the things and bring them. I'll ask if you can have dinner with us."

I run into the house and into the kitchen. "Mama, Mama! Where are you?" The smell of gingerbread tickles my nose.

"How was school today, dear? You didn't hang up your coat, Violet. Please do," Mama says. *She's acting so normal. Maybe, she's all better now.*

"Eleanor's coming in a few minutes to share her decorations with me." I take a few breaths. "Can she stay for dinner, please? It means so much to me to have our parlor oozing with joy for my birthday party."

The doorbell rings.

"Of course, Eleanor can have dinner with us. Go get the door, Violet, and hang up your coat!" Mama yells after me as I bound into the parlor.

"Wow. That's a big box. What's in there?" I ask my friend.

"Why is Sergeant O'Malley always walking back and forth on our block?" Eleanor asks. "The other day, there were two cops."

"Can't be too careful these days, I guess. My mother said you can stay for dinner."

"Thank you, Eleanor, for the decorations."

It's the day before my party, and I can't concentrate on what the teacher is saying about my English lesson. *Will I look pretty like the other girls?*

The handbell suddenly rings out in the hallway, indicating recess.

Good.

"What are you going to wear, Violet?" Eleanor giggles.

"I can't decide. Either the pink and white satin dress or the plain white one that my mama made for me."

"I have your present all wrapped and ready to go, Violet," Eleanor says.

"I'm sure it will be just perfect if it comes from you. I have the records in a row next to the Victrola, so the music will be continuous. That way we'll have a great time."

"I'm so excited because my sister's letting me borrow her red feather hair clasp for the party," May says.

"Really? You're so lucky. Some of the older girls at the Gotham Theater wear those. That'll look so nice in your blond hair, May."

"Well, we're no longer little kids, Violet," Eleanor states with enthusiasm. "It's time to get out of the Shirley Temple dresses and step into the sleek, sexy look of the roaring twenties, even though that era's almost behind us."

"My mother doesn't like me to say that word, *sexy*," I whisper. "It's not proper talk for a young lady."

My friends laugh merrily. "Oh, fiddlesticks. That's not a cuss word, silly."

Three more hours of school, and I'll be on my way home. Mama and I are making the cake tonight. I'm so happy she's feeling better, but it was only weeks ago that she acted peculiar.

I giggle at my sister's frosting covered mouth, as I tousle her hair. Mama's scurrying around faster than a jackrabbit, cooking beef stew, cleaning the kitchen, and boiling eggs for the tea sandwiches we'll serve at my party tomorrow.

"Mama, you didn't make the cake without me? You said you and I would make it when I got home from school."

"Calm down, Violet. Yes, we'll bake right after supper. The frosting is the only part I made."

"Are you going to put those little violets around the top?"

"I think I can. Not sure. So much to do with your father leaving for The Mohonk Resort in a few hours."

The back door in the enclosed porch outside the kitchen slams. We all turn to look with some trepidation. Mama grabs a broom quickly and heads to the door.

It bursts open. Daisy hides behind me, and Mama squeals.

"I'm home, everyone! I don't know what you're cooking, Blossom, but it sure smells wonderful," Papa says.

"You really frightened us, Berto. You rarely come in this way. Will you be eating with us? I know you and the fellas have a train to catch at seven-thirty and you still have to pack."

"You look as white as a ghost, Kitty. I came in that way to reassure you, there isn't anyone out there. Joseph will be picking me up soon."

"You can't go. You just can't," Mama pleads.

I play *Patty Cake* quietly with Daisy to drown out Mama's voice. "Patty Cake, Patty cake bakers man…." I feel like a fluttering sparrow.

"I told you last week that you could come with us. I've voiced my opinion many times that you could be a lead singer with the band. It would be nice to have a female touch to make us a more varied group."

"I can't leave my girls for that long, Berto. Violet's too young to watch Daisy all by herself. Besides, the guys in the band act like they don't like me. So, how can I be a part of the group?" Her voice is louder at the end of her rant.

Mama starts dishing up the stew into a big serving dish while I set the table.

"Please don't worry. I'll be back before you know it. I'm going to gather my things, while you put the food on the table." Papa says as he rushes to the door.

"Violet Pearl, will you please come and help me with my luggage and instruments?"

"Yikes. You are taking a bunch of stuff with you. That's for sure. How long did you say you were going to be at Mohonk?" I ask as I help him pack.

He pulls a small gold velvet sack out of his pocket.

"Happy thirteenth birthday, my flower. Here's something special for you to wear for your party tomorrow."

"But my birthday's tomorrow. Not today."

"That's okay because I won't be back until late Sunday night. Open it, please, honey."

I take the pouch, pull the strings open, and reach inside. I pull out a pink pearl necklace.

"Oh, Papa. It's beautiful. Can I wear it now? I want to show Mama and Daisy."

Papa nods his head in approval, and I bring the necklace over my head, so it falls gently on my neck.

"I'm glad you like it."

I'm thoroughly disappointed when neither Mama nor Daisy notices my new piece of jewelry.

The front door bell rings.

"That's probably Joseph. I'll let him in." Papa mutters.

"Hi, Mrs. Moretti; hi, Violet. Hey there, Daisy."

"Hello, Mr. Finnegan," Mama says.

"Those are mighty fine pearls you're wearing, Ms. Violet."

"It's a present from my papa. Thank you. I don't think I'll ever take them off."

"Sit down, eat something, my friend." Papa motions to an empty chair.

Joseph sits down across from me. Mama puts a bowl of stew in front of him.

He closes his eyes, folds his hands, bows his head, and speaks softly. "Holy God, thank you for this food before me. God bless those who prepared it. May you protect this house while Berto is gone. Amen."

We stare at him with curiosity because of the sincerity in his voice.

"This is mighty good, Mrs. Moretti. Berto is right. You are a marvelous cook." Joseph says between bites.

"Thank you, Joseph, but please call me Blossom." Her face twists, and I know she's going to cry.

We dig into the meal before us, but Mama putters around the kitchen, stopping to glare out of the window into the dark, shadowy night. Then I see her walk over to the back door, open it, peek into the porch, and quickly close the door. She must be scared to death that someone will come in uninvited. *I hope that creep is far, far away from here. The thought of him brings goose bumps up my arms.*

"Blossom, aren't you going to eat something?" Papa asks. "What are you looking for out there?"

She turns around, sprints over to the table, and sits down. Her hands are trembling.

"We better go, Joseph. We can't miss the train, and we still have to pick up the fellas."

"Come give your papa a hug, girls."

I pick up Daisy and carry her over to Papa. He hugs us with a bear hug embrace. It makes me feel peacefully warm all over.

"Blossom. I'm going."

Mama blows her nose and waves her hand, "Just go, Berto."

He goes over to Mama, adoringly grips her hand, and pulls her up to himself. She immediately wraps her arms around him. "I love you, and you will be alright for two days, dear. Be sure to latch that new lock I mounted yesterday, okay?"

She smiles up at him but stays attached with all the strength she has in her. "I must go, darling." He pries himself away from her, as he plants a kiss on her head.

"Violet, take care of your mother for me, and happy birthday too." He winks.

Mama rushes to the door, latches the lock behind them, and pulls down the flimsy shade.

Chapter 9

The house feels so empty when my father is away but even more so tonight. My lamp is going to stay on every night, so I don't have to stare at the ghostly ceiling. It's odd that Mama didn't want me to clean the kitchen. She insisted that we all come up stairs and go to bed. Daisy fell right to sleep, but I'm not sleepy at all.

I get up and saunter over to where my birthday dress is hanging. I take it off the hanger, press it to me, and soon I am gliding gracefully over the small open space in my room. Quietly, I open my door, tiptoe across the hall, and lean into Mama's bedroom door. Not a sound.

Back in my room, I smile as I clutch the pearls that Papa gave me a few hours ago.

They'll always stay around my neck, so I can keep him close to me. A peculiar happiness settles inside me.

Funny thing is, the mysterious voice is leaving me alone.

Cozy in bed. *In a few short hours, I'll be a teenager.* I smile, close my eyes, and drift off to sleep. Darkness encompasses me.

"Wake up, Violet Pearl! Wake up!" Mama screams. She pulls the covers off me and yanks on my arm. I can feel anger building inside of me. I hate this nightmare.

I feel a grip on my arm, firm and solid.

"Ouch! You're hurting me!" I say, trying to open my eyes. I try to free myself.

"Get up child. Now."

My body hitting the floor, wakes me up. Weeping Daisy is in Mama's arms.

"What are you doing, Mama? It's in the middle of the night."

"We have to go, now. Come on, this instant." Mama cries.

"Go where?" I cross my arms and turn away.

She yanks me up. "Come on. Do you hear me?" She says forcefully as she bolts out of the door and down the steps. I feel like I'm sleepwalking.

I manage to get on my slippers; pull on my robe; literally run down the steps after her; and grab my sister's hat, coat, and boots on the way.

No one is around, but I quickly glance at my mother. She's in a slip and barefoot. I turn to run to Sergeant O'Malley's house when she grabs my hand.

It's cold and damp, and the smell of heaping garbage on the curb turns my stomach.

"I need to go to the store. We need food. The bus will be here any moment." Mama says loudly, clutching hysterical Daisy with all her might.

In the distance, I can see a figure standing under the lamppost. Breaking away, I run full speed ahead, hoping it's not someone bad. My eyes fill with tears, and I swallow hard.

Screams and sounds of crying can be heard behind me as I move closer.

"Sergeant O'Malley, something's wrong with my mother! Help her, please!" I cry in desperation. The panic spins up, like there's a hurricane in my belly. I don't let it show on my face.

"Where is she, Violet Pearl?" He asks as he takes my hand.

Mama's screams are getting louder and louder.

A few lights come on in the neighbor's houses. Someone comes out, "What's going on out here?"

"Call an ambulance, please." The sergeant blows his shrill whistle as he wraps Mama in his arms. My mama explodes into a monster, right in front of us. I helplessly watch as she kicks, screams, and thrashes about.

"What's going on with my mother?" I cry.

Mrs. O'Malley rushes out of her house and picks up my wailing sister. "Hang close to me, Violet. Help's on the way."

Mama falls limp in the officer's arms.

Siren sounds are getting closer as three policemen scurry across the street. "O'Malley, what can we do?"

"Keep Mrs. Moretti warm until the ambulance comes. Can one of you spare a winter coat?"

I try to get to Mama, but firm hands keep me in place. The cold air's biting my nose, and my hands are so cold. This is like a scene in one of those moving pictures. They're lifting my mother into an ambulance. I'm utterly petrified. Tears roll down my face. I hold my sister in my arms as we are ushered into the police car. Silent sobs are rocking her chest up and down.

"Mama. My mama. Where are they taking her?" I ask.

"I want my mommy," Daisy hollers.

"They're taking her to Bellevue Hospital, Violet. Your father told me he would be upstate this weekend, so we'll get hold of your aunt Florence," Sergeant O'Malley says calmly.

"Oh, Papa!" I cry as I grasp a hold of the pearls.

Three other people I don't know are waiting in this clean white room in the hospital. The big clock on the wall reads three o'clock in the morning.

Daisy's asleep with her head on my lap. Sergeant O'Malley is directly across from us with his eyes closed.

Where's my mother? What happened to her? This has been the longest two hours I've ever spent. My throat is closing. The room is spinning and swaying.

I don't know if I fell asleep or not, but suddenly Aunt Flossie is at my side with her arms around me. She's weeping, which is very unusual for her.

"Mama. My mama," I whisper in her ear. "I want to see her," I manage to say in between tears.

"They're doing everything they can to help her, Violet. She's very sick with pneumonia," she murmurs.

I'm wrapped in her warm embrace, but in a state of confusion, crying uncontrollable sobs.

It's a wonder my sister's asleep.

The door to the emergency room opens, and a man dressed in a long, white coat steps into the room. He looks so serious with his wire-rimmed glasses and a clipboard in his hand.

"Sergeant O'Malley," he calls out.

"Yes, Doctor." O'Malley rises to go talk to him. The doctor's mouth is moving, but I can't hear what's being said. O'Malley removes his hat, and I see him rub his eyes.

"Miss Thomas, can you come here, please?" The sergeant calls.

"I'll be right back, Toots," my aunt says quietly and gives me another quick squeeze.

The men talk to her, but I still can't hear a word. Until…"I'm so sorry, Miss Thomas," the Doctor says.

My resilient auntie buckles into the sergeant's arms and cries loudly.

"Mama! Mama!" I scream.

Daisy wakes and immediately bawls huge crocodile tears. An elderly nurse comes out of nowhere and scoops my sister onto her lap. I propel my feet forward and bolt through the big double doors. Each moment bites. I want the nipping to stop.

A nurse tries to grab me, but I manage to escape her reach. I spot a bed on wheels and what appears to be a body under a white sheet.

I freeze in place.

Aunt Flossie, now at my side, grabs my hand, and we walk together to the bed.

She nods at the doctor with tears running down her face. He pulls back the sheet.

Mama's laying lifeless with her eyes closed as though in a deep sleep.

"Wake up, Mommy. Please wake up. Please!" I cry.

No response.

Chapter 10

The heavenly aroma of coffee brewing and the soothing smell of logs burning in the colossal brick fireplace in the hotel lobby welcome the weary travelers. Berto and the band members walk across the marble floor. It's midnight, but people dressed in their finest attire are sitting around the fire conversing and laughing, while others are climbing the winding staircase to guest rooms on one of the ten floors.

"Can I help you, boys? You look lost," a bellhop says.

"We're The Domino Four. We're your band for tomorrow's wedding in the Victorian parlor." Berto affirms.

"Of course. How was your trip here?"

"It was okay, but we need to check in and find a place to practice before we call it a night."

The front desk clerk squints his eyes and says, "So, you must be the band for tomorrow's event?"

"Yes, Sir."

"Here are the keys to the cottage, outside the front door to your right. You can practice in the staff lounge in the basement, so you won't disturb our guests."

They drag themselves to the cottage.

"Bunk beds?" Marvin says with a snarl. "Are you kidding me? Look at these mattresses. Kind of thin, huh?"

Berto laughs and shakes his head. "You can handle it for two nights. Really you can."

Looking at his pocket watch, Hans says, "Guys, it's one o'clock in the morning. We better practice before turning in."

Soon the rhythm and harmony of accordion, saxophone, guitar, and piano fill the small room in the smoke-filled basement. The boys are caught up in their own music for over an hour. No one appears to be tired.

"Hey, Berto. Thanks for making a pot of coffee. I can probably play until the sun rises now." Joseph smiles.

"Let's take a break, fellas, for ten minutes," Berto says. "Go up on the patio for some fresh air, and I am going to take a few minutes and unwind. We can sleep in tomorrow because the reception doesn't start until four in the evening."

Berto lays down on his bed, hoping he doesn't fall asleep.

I hope everything's alright in Brooklyn. They're probably sound asleep. Violet is probably gripping the pearls with all the strength she has.

Marvin bursts into the room from the porch. "Berto! A telegram came for you!"

To: Berto Moretti.

Please come to Bellevue Hospital as soon as possible.

There is an emergency.

Your family needs you.

From: Sergeant O'Malley.

"Good Lord! What has happened? We just got here." Berto collapses in the nearest chair and brings his hands to cover his face.

"What is it, Boss?" Marvin asks. "What does the telegram say that has you so upset?"

"Here, see for yourself." He tosses it to him. "I don't know what to do."

Marvin reads it. "You'll have to turn around and head right back to the city. Someone is in Bellevue. Sounds like you're needed, buddy."

"I'll be right back after I check with the front desk on when the next train leaves for New York from New Paltz." Joseph runs out of the door.

"I can't leave you fellas like this. We're getting paid big bucks for this engagement."

"Here, take this shot of brandy. It'll relax you, my friend." Hans says.

Joseph bursts into the room with superfluous energy like he's at the starting gate for a big race. "Berto. The next train's at noon."

"Give me another brandy, would ya?" His eyes are wide, and his lips pressed in a thin line.

"Hey. You may or may not agree with this, but I would like to pray for you and your family right now, if it's alright." Joseph offers.

"Come on. Are you joking? What can God do?" Hans snickers. "Pick Berto up and fly him to the hospital?"

"Don't be so hard on Joseph, Hans. What harm can it do?" Marvin says.

Berto sits on the edge of the bed. "Go ahead, Joseph. Do your thing. It's fine."

Joseph pulls up a chair next to him and folds his hands. "My Father in Heaven, may you watch over the Moretti family right now. Allow my friend Berto some rest and a safe trip back to the city. Amen."

"I don't know if there's a God or not, but I thank you for that prayer," Berto mumbles as he fades off to sleep.

"Let's all get some sleep. The show will go on with or without Berto," Marvin whispers as he turns off the only two lamps in the big room. The ceiling light in the tiny lavatory beams into the room so the three men can get ready for bed quietly.

In two shakes of a lamb's tale, everyone's cutting zees in melodious fashion except for Berto who is tossing and turning.

The sun shining through the windows wakes Berto from a deep sleep. The boys are sitting at the little kitchen table munching on hard rolls and sipping coffee.

"It's morning. I must have slept some. How long have you boys been up anyway?"

"We've been up awhile," Hans said. "We just got back from a walk around the lake."

"Wow. It's nine thirty! I did sleep," Berto exclaims as he pulls out his pocket watch.

He sits down, and Joseph pours him a cup of coffee, but Berto is rapidly distracted when he spies the telegram once again. "I really shouldn't be sitting here, fellas. I must get back to the city."

"The train doesn't leave until noon," Hans declares. "And it takes only twenty minutes to get to the station, Berto."

"I know, but I'd much rather wait around there than here."

"I don't know what to expect back home. It could be anyone in that hospital. That's why the sooner I get there, the better it is. Blossom seemed to be fine when I left. Someone must have fallen on the ice or something." The tears are trapped behind his smile.

He grabs his jacket off the hanger and places his overcoat over that. Adds his brown muffler and black beret. "Okay, Marvin, you're in charge of these kids. Can you pack my things and drop them at my house? I'm going to wait at the front entrance to see if I can hitch a ride to the station," he moans.

A few hours later, the train screeches to a halt at Grand Central. Berto runs full speed to the ticket counter in hopes of making a phone call.

"I'm not at liberty to tell you anything over the telephone, Sir," the doctor tells him.

"What do you mean? Someone sent me an urgent telegram saying there's a family emergency. Surely, you can tell me who and how serious it is," Berto speaks firmly into the receiver.

"Please, Mr. Moretti, keep it down, will you? It's your wife."

"My wife? Tell me; is Blossom still there?"

"No, she's not. Listen; I must go. I suggest you call Sergeant O'Malley or your sister-in-law. Good afternoon."

Berto stares at the receiver for a few seconds and then puts it on the hook. He's fuming on the inside.

Grand Central Station is massive, and one must be knowledgeable in finding their way around. *My Kitty. My Blossom girl. I hope you're alright. Violet, Daisy. My little girls.*

"Sir, can I please ask you to call my home? Something has happened to my wife, and it will take me at least an hour to get there."

"I really shouldn't do this. I could lose my job," the clerk behind the counter replies.

"It's an emergency."

"What's the number?"

"Murray Hill, 555-1212."

"Here. It's ringing."

"Hello. Flossie?"

"Berto, is that you? I can barely hear you."

"Blossom, how is she? I was on my way to Bellevue but decided to call you first. The doctor wouldn't tell me anything."

"I think you better come right home, Berto. Get here as soon as possible," she says and hangs up.

Chapter 11

"He leads me to rest in green meadows, and He leads me beside peaceful streams," the Reverend Nicholson's voice resonates through the quiet winter air.

"Blossom Thomas Moretti can rest in peace with the saints who went before her. May God bless her husband, Berto, and daughters, Violet Pearl and Daisy Mae."

This frigid day in January, we gather around my mother's grave. The trees look like tall skeletons with many scraggly arms; some move to the slight breeze while others stand in place.

I'm shaking not only from the cold but scared to the core of my being. I know Mama's in that big box, and I'll never see her again. All the breath leaves my body in a rush, and I feel like I've been whacked in the tummy. Good thing there are a few chairs for us to sit.

"Peace to all of you who are here today in memory of this young mother plucked from this life too soon. The family invites everyone back to their house for some refreshments immediately following the service," the reverend says.

I fall on my knees, on the hard-frozen ground as the tears roll down my chilly face and pull two red roses out of an arrangement. It's so cold, but I don't want to go anywhere. I can't fix it. Any of it.

Suddenly, someone's pulling me up to my feet.

"Violet Pearl, you can't stay here any longer. Look, it's starting to snow."

The voice isn't familiar, but everything she says is in broken English.

Who is this?

I turn and look up into the face of an angel.

Tamara Romanova, the beautiful dancer from the Gotham Theater is standing right in front of me with her hand reaching out to mine.

As we walk to the waiting car, I look back at the casket sitting on the ground and realize we were the last two to be at Mama's side. I'm a ball of electricity, shaking from head to toe.

On the way back home. Papa squeezes my hand and says, "Tonight, after everyone leaves, we'll work on your audition for Little Bo Peep. You know the character in the story, Babes in Toyland?"

I look out of the window and wish I was anyplace else but here.

My mama is cold in that awful box, and I'll never hear this woman's voice or feel the warmth of her embrace again. *How can Papa talk about an audition now?*

I've never seen so many people in this house at one time, and they are all dressed in black. The jumbled whiff of coffee, hot cocoa, egg salad sandwiches, and Italian meatballs infiltrate the whole house. A few old ladies with lots of wrinkles are sitting in the corner by the fireplace, eating cake. They look ancient. One of them looks up at me and motions for me to come to her.

"You must be Violet Pearl. Your father tells me you want to be an actress?" she comments.

"Not really, I want to be a ballet dancer."

"Let me introduce myself. I'm your aunt Lucy, your father's sister. I haven't seen you since you were a baby. My, you're growing up fast and so beautiful. Did your father tell you I'm staying here for a few months?" *I can hardly understand this woman. She must have just gotten off the boat.*

I curtsy. "No, I didn't know."

I look down at the cake, and I recognize it's the same one that Mama and I so intricately made a few short days ago for my birthday. Putting my hand over my mouth, I gasp loudly. *This isn't right. Not one bit.* "Please excuse me. I must look for my sister."

Darting through the throng of folks standing near the kitchen door, I plow through to find Aunt Flossie cutting gingerbread into squares. The back of my throat burns, blazing paths into my memory.

"Violet, my dear girl, are you okay? Here, help me arrange these on this platter with the cake. Will you, please?"

"Auntie, that's my birthday cake! Mama and I made it. They can't have it. It's mine. My thirteenth birthday came and went, and nobody out there knows or cares," I say amid another barrage of tears.

She stops what she's doing, wipes her hands on the apron that covers her navy-blue dress, and hugs me close. I melt into her arms as we cry our hearts out. *How can I go on without my mother?*

Papa bursts into the kitchen. "Violet, have you seen your sister since we came home?"

"Not since I brought her teddy bear to her, and that was about an hour ago. Why? Isn't she out there?"

"She must be hiding in her room, Berto. Did you look under her bed?" Aunt Flossie asks.

"We looked everywhere that she could possibly be in this house, and it's too dark and cold to go outside." He looks around the kitchen as if it held some secret hiding place, but it doesn't.

I run out of the door, wiping my eyes on the way. Weaving in between all these people reminds me of a maze.

"Violet, what's the matter?" Tamara asks.

"My sister, Daisy, is missing," I whisper to her, so no one panics.

She takes my hand, and she pulls me into the foyer, away from the crowd.

"Let's think. Does this house have a basement or an attic? Sometimes, little girls like to hide where there are interesting things around."

"Our attic is very hard to get to. Papa must get a ladder and climb through an opening in his closet, but the cellar door's over there. Daisy never goes down there alone."

Tamara smiles and gently pulls me over to the door. Everyone is so busy talking to each other or gazing at photographs of my mama that they don't even see us.

As we go down the dimly lit creaky stairs, I pause. "There's no way Daisy would come down here by herself, let alone at night. It smells so old and musty down here, Tamara. Let's go back up. She's not down here."

Faint whimpers come from the far corner. The only other spot in the entire basement that has a light.

"Daisy? Are you down here?" Tamara calls out.

Petunia, the cat, leaps out from behind the old leather trunk and darts up the stairs.

I almost push Tamara over, so I can be the first to see if my sister's here.

"Vi-Vi. Vi-Vi! I so sad. I want Mama. No Aunt Lucy. Pewees." She cries.

We're amazed to see that she has three old quilts piled high for a bed, her pillow, bear, and even a few books, and she's sucking on a lollipop.

How did she sneak down here without anyone seeing her? Pretty amazing.

Tamara and I sit down on the comfy bedding, and I pull her on my lap. The footsteps above sound like a herd of cattle heading out to pasture.

My new friend starts to hum a tune I don't recognize. She sings in a soft beautiful voice:

"Little Children, come to Jesus. Hear Him saying 'Come to me';

66

Blessed Jesus, who to save us, shed His blood on Calvary

Little Tongues to sing His Praises, Little feet to walk His ways."

Hmmm, another religious person.

"What's your name?" Daisy asks as she looks up at her with admiration and wonder.

"My name's Tamara. You're a cutie pie, Daisy girl." She smiles widely.

I pick Daisy up in my arms, and we venture upstairs.

Papa grabs her from me. "Oh, little one. You scared me half to death. Don't hide like that again."

"I sorry, Papa. Please let Aunt Flossie stay with us?"

"Violet, take your sister in the kitchen and get her a glass of milk."

"Do you need a ride, Tamara? I'll be leaving shortly, if you don't mind waiting that is. I'm just going to clean up the dishes." Aunt Flossie asks.

"Thank you. It's getting late, and I don't want to be waiting at the bus stop alone."

Aunt Flossie heads to the kitchen.

"Tamara, I'm so grateful to you for coming today and for finding Daisy. She's so distraught without her mother," Papa says. I feel anger building inside of me.

"My pleasure. She's a precious little girl. Violet and I found her, Berto."

The house seems so empty and still, now that all the guests are gone. I look up the stairs with hopes that Mama will be down any minute. I know in my heart she won't.

"I see you have some records and a Victrola, Violet. Can we listen to some music while I wait for Flossie?"

"Pick one out. We used to have a lot more, but my mama smashed some a few weeks ago." I let out a long, slow breath.

The lovely melodic music fills the parlor as Tamara gracefully performs a lovely dance in front of me. Her body stretches and turns as though the music lives inside her.

"Do you know the five positions of beginning ballet, Violet?"

"Not really. Can you show me?"

"This is first position with heels together and legs straight. You try it."

I wiggle a bit with my behind sticking out. "Like this?"

The kitchen door bursts open, and Aunt Flossie rushes out and grabs her hat and coat. "I'm ready to go, Tamara. Now! I can't be around that brother-in-law of mine any longer!" she roars.

"You better turn the music off, dear," Tamara says as she nods to me.

"Flossie. You can come by any time you want to. The girls love you," Aunt Lucy remarks as she comes through the door. Papa's right at her heels mumbling something in Italian.

"I should be staying here, Berto," Aunt Flossie says, her face red and a frown on her forehead. "That's what my sister would want!"

"You talk nonsense with my daughters. You let them do what they want. My sister will have rules."

I cling to Aunt Flossie and sob uncontrollably. Tamara pulls the hair from my eyes and rubs my back. *I can't believe I'm this close to a ballerina and she smells wonderful too.*

"Tamara, I'm sorry you have to witness this," says Papa.

She stares at him and shakes her head.

"I'll see you soon, Tootsie." Aunt Flossie hugs me with tears in her eyes.

Papa goes to put the records away. "Good night, Tamara."

He has not shed one tear yet.

I watch Aunt Lucy go upstairs to Daisy's room. This will be *her* room while she stays here. I'll have to share my room with my sister from here on in.

Tamara slips a folded piece of paper into my hand and puts her finger to her mouth. "Shush."

I put it carefully it in a pocket on my dress. "I hope to see you again sometime."

I watch her go out of the door knowing the chances of seeing her again are unlikely.

"Good night, Papa."

He doesn't turn to look at me but manages to say, "Good night, daughter."

As I climb the stairs, I wonder if he'll ever shed a tear of grief for his wife, my mother.

"Papa?" I turn and run back down in hopes of giving him a hug, but he's gone.

As I approach the top of the stairs, I notice a cardboard box wrapped with string. *What's in here?* I do exactly what any other thirteen-year-old girl would do. I scamper into the bathroom with the box, close the door, open it, and examine its contents. Quiet tears roll down my cheeks as I pick up my birthday party decorations, one by one, and when I get to the bottom, I find an extra invitation to a party that never happened. I sink my head into my hands.

Chapter 12

Ten days have passed. Eleanor brought my homework to me every day after school. Papa thought I needed time to mourn my mother's death, so he let me stay home. I don't know if I can face my classmates after this long absence. Aunt Lucy, the drill sergeant, is still here, and she insists I return to school tomorrow.

Darkness is all around me; thick impenetrable darkness is everywhere. Somehow, I drift off to sleep.

Mama and I are running through an immense field dotted with beautiful black-eyed Susans. We're dressed in flowing, lavender chiffon matching dresses, and we aren't wearing any shoes or socks. Words are not exchanged, but we laugh uncontrollably as we move in unison. She grabs my hand, and we fly gracefully over the beauty beneath us.

"Vi-Vi! Wake up!" I hear Daisy's voice in the distance.

Mama lets go of my hand, and I start to fall into a tall patch of flowers.

"Come on, Sissy. Pweeze wake up!" I feel a pull on my arm and a sudden cold sensation over my whole body.

My eyes are mere slits, but soon they focus. Daisy's breathing heavily and staring at me two inches from my face. I nearly jump out of my skin.

"Violet Pearl, are you out of that bed? You better be. You have exactly forty-five minutes to eat breakfast and get to school," Aunt Lucy calls from the base of the stairs.

"Daisy, go tell her I'm on my way down, okay?"

As I approach the kitchen, I smell the overwhelming aroma of apples, cinnamon, allspice, and cloves. *What is she baking anyway?* Upon opening the door, I see Aunt Lucy cutting up cake and putting it on a plate.

"It smells great in here."

"Good morning, Violet Pearl. I made Depression Spice Cake. Come, sit down, and eat. You don't have much time." Her voice cuts into my thoughts.

Last night was so freaky with the keeper's piercing voice in my ears. "Your mother is gone. Your papa never talks to you. Trust in me. I'm your keeper now."

Aunt Lucy grasps my shoulder, "Violet Pearl, go fix your hair. It's a mess."

"The bell will ring in fifteen minutes, though."

"And don't forget to wear a sweater over that flimsy dress," Aunt Lucy says.

Good grief, she's like a drill sergeant. I shove the cake into my mouth, take a slug of cocoa, throw on my coat, grab my bag, and head to the door.

"Goodbye, Daisy. See you later, Alligator."

"Here's your lunch sack," Aunt Lucy says as she hands it to me. "Be sure to eat your lunch, be on the lookout for strangers, and pay attention in school, Violet Pearl."

"Are you all set for the audition at eleven o'clock today?" Papa asks when I arrive in the kitchen for breakfast the next day.

He looks a bit agitated as he rushes around the kitchen grabbing a cup of coffee and some toast.

"Yes, Papa. Should I change my dress?" The heat is creeping up my neck.

"The dress is fine, but you must do something with your hair."

"Can I come too, Vi-Vi?" Daisy asks.

"No, no, you can't, little one. You must stay here with Aunt Lucy. We won't be gone long."

Papa and I walk past the stinky fish market, Mrs. London's bakery, and Luigi's Italian restaurant with its pungent garlic smell. *I love living in Brooklyn.*

Papa doesn't utter one word during the forty-five-minute journey. I try talking to him, but it's useless. Disappointment washes over me.

We finally arrive at the building where the audition is. "Okay, Violet Pearl. I'm going to walk you in the front door, but you're old enough to take the elevator to the second floor, aren't you?"

"Yes, Papa. I can do that."

"Your aunt Flossie will be picking you up at twelve thirty. She won't come looking for you, so please be waiting right here, inside this building. Now, go on up."

I move to give him a hug goodbye, but he turns around abruptly and heads out of the door. I watch him cross the street and disappear into the crowd of people moving about on the sidewalk.

Pulling the folded piece of paper out of my coat pocket, I read:

Romanova's Ballet school, 1500, 53rd Street, Brooklyn, New York

My goodness. I think that's one block down from here. I wonder if Tamara's there now. I start to push the outer door open but step back with fear. *What if Papa sees me leave here? He'll be furious.*

I start toward the elevator, but the male attendant looks me up and down. "What floor, Miss?" The door opens, and I realize that no one else will be going up with me except this freaky guy. My hands are trembling. I squeeze them, trying to make myself calm.

Immediately, I turn and race out of the main door, make a left, and sprint to 1500, 53rd Street.

I enter the building. The piano can be heard all the way down the hall, and it draws me closer. I reluctantly look through the open door and see three little girls, barely five years old standing with their hands overhead and feet in first position.

Tamara doesn't see me because she has her back to me, but the girls freeze in place, stare at me, and start giggling.

Their instructor turns. "Violet."

She runs over and gives me a big hug. "You must be disappointed. I know you're expecting something pretty and feminine with butterflies, flowers, and dance pictures all over the walls. The landlord let me have this place for a real song. Does your father know you're here?"

"Not really."

"Why not? Where are you supposed to be right now?"

"Tamara, I hate this acting on the stage stuff. My father wants me to star in the big theaters of New York, but I want to be a ballet dancer like you. I'm supposed to be at an audition this very minute."

The little girls are running everywhere, pushing each other out of the way so they can see themselves in the floor-length mirror. One knocks another on the floor. "Girls, girls, girls! Come here, Mary Jane. Now, now. You will be fine." Tamara hugs the little girl in her lap, and the other two kneel in front of her.

I glance at the old clock on the wall and see that it is twelve fifteen.

I start to leave. I let my face relax. My cheeks are sore from smiling.

"Violet. Please wait! Girls, please do the exercises I showed you last week, okay?"

"I should go." *In my heart, I want to stay.*

"You need to have a heart-to-heart talk with your father."

"He's never home long enough to talk to, and he wouldn't understand anyway."

"I can try to talk to him," she offers.

"That's alright. You don't have to. Sooner or later, he'll find out that I never went to the audition today. I'll be in big trouble for sure." I rub my eyes but hold back the tears.

"I miss my mama so much. She always made sure I went to Dramatic Dance Lessons. She would have loved it if I became a ballet dancer."

I look at the clock again.

I have exactly ten minutes to get back to the audition location.

"See you, Tamara." I rush out of the door, run down the hall, and out to the busy street. In viewing distance, I can barely see Aunt Flossie getting closer and closer. She's busy looking in the store windows, so she doesn't see me bolt into the foyer of the building.

I catch my breath, fix my hair, and plop down on the bench by the door. Close call.

"How are you, Honey?" she asks.

"Oh, Auntie Flossie. I'm so glad you're here." I swallow the lump in my throat.

"You look a little flushed, Tootsie. That must have been quite the audition."

"It was very interesting, to say the least."

"I have a surprise for you, Violet. Can you guess?"

"Um, you brought me some chocolate from Shrafts."

She giggles. "No."

"You're going to come and stay with Daisy and me. Aunt Lucy is leaving!"

She laughs. "Do you give up?"

"Tell me, please do."

"You, my dear niece, are coming home with me today, and you can stay overnight too."

"Really? Did Papa say it's alright, Aunt Flossie?"

"It took a little convincing, but he finally gave in. He said that you have been through a lot and you could use a change."

"I don't have my nightclothes or a change for tomorrow."

"Your father, my brother-in-law, can be one tough brute, my dear. One must have a sense of humor to deal with him. I know he loves you girls with all his heart for sure."

"What about Daisy? Aunt Lucy scares her."

"Your father has the night off and will be home until Monday. You can change your mind if you want to, Toots."

"I want to go to your house." A smile tugs at my lips.

"We have to get some groceries at the market first." She laughs.

I wonder if I'll get a chance to tell Auntie I never went to the audition. She does love classical music, so maybe she'll be alright with the ballet thing.

The smell of highly seasoned pastrami fills the meat market from wall to wall. Auntie is buying kosher frankfurters, mouthwatering salami, and a few cheese blintzes. I guess being a single working woman has its advantages.

"Let's hurry a little, Violet. I always feel better when I'm in the house before dark and all the doors are locked."

"Do you ever see that odd man, Auntie? You know, the one who followed you—the same one I saw at the bus stop a few weeks ago with Mama?"

She grabs my hand and cradles the bag with the other. "No, actually, now that you bring it up. No, I haven't seen him around at all. Must have moved on."

I certainly hope so.

Chapter 13

The moon glitters through the sheer curtains in the dining room, and the street lamps glow through the film of smog that embraces the street in front of my aunt's house. We had frankfurters, sauerkraut, and carrots for supper. The cheese blintzes for desert were the perfect finale to a scrumptious meal.

"Let's relax a bit before we turn in for the night," Auntie suggests as she sits down at the piano.

I briefly gaze out of the big window with apprehension to see if anyone is out there, but the fog is too thick to see clearly.

"Violet, your pastel chalks and sketch pad are in the bottom drawer of that chest."

The time rolls away as I listen to her play Moonlight Sonata as though she is playing for a full house at the Metropolitan Opera. Art is a favorite pastime, and it clears my mind of any negative thoughts. Drawing people is very difficult, so I decide to use my aunt as a model to sketch.

"It's getting late. It's almost nine thirty," Auntie says. "We better get ready for bed, my dear."

"Look at this, Auntie." I show her my drawing of her sitting at the piano.

"Honey, this is superb. You're so talented for a girl who's only thirteen."

I smile up at her. She holds a special place in my heart.

As I lie on the narrow bed in the guest room next to my aunt's big bedroom, I jog my memory of the events of the day and allow the distant dream of dancing with a pink tutu across the grand stage of Carnegie Hall to permeate my thoughts.

Auntie checked on me a little while ago to say good night and said she would leave the hall light on in case I needed her for anything. She must be asleep now because the house is very quiet.

I roll on my side, pull the covers up to my neck, and gaze out of the one window to see the stars sparkling like diamonds in the night sky. I always feel safe in this house, even though I don't know what's in the attic.

My eyes won't shut. I can't sleep. Darn.

Maybe, if I count those foolish sheep jumping over the fence again, I'll drift off. Closing my eyes, I count. One, two, three, four…one hundred, one hundred and fifty.

A sound of glass shattering jolts me out of my near-slumber state. *What was that?* My eyes pop open, but I lie still. I catch a glimpse of someone tall whiz by, and it's not a woman. Oh, no! The hall light's out. Panic shoots through my inside.

The only light glittering through the window comes from the moon.

Now, there's an eerie, rhythmic thunk-tap of boots striking the hard wood steps going to the attic.

I start shaking and break out with a cold sweat. My tummy's doing pirouettes.

Does Auntie hear any of this?

Thud and another thud echoes through the floor above me.

Should I get up and run to Auntie's room or stay here? It's possible the intruder doesn't know I'm here. Why won't this headache go away? My pillow's sopping wet because I'm sweating so much. I can't move. I strongly sense that I'm not alone.

It's quiet above me now.

Someone is touching the blanket over my foot.

I want to scream, but nothing comes out. Tears of terror silently roll down my cheeks.

I see a figure next to my bed but try not to move. My heart's in my clasped fist.

I feel a tap on my foot; I hear a whisper. "Shush. It's me, your auntie. Move over."

We cuddle together under the covers, trying not to make a sound.

The sounds of the boots now are descending the stairs.

"Hey, I know you're in here somewhere!" the raspy voice shouts out from the dining room. "But I'm not going to bother with you this time. I'll be back to get you. So, watch out!"

Auntie hugs me close to her and gently strokes my hair. I'm frightened out of my wits.

A cold sensation comes over me, and I realize that I wet my pants.

"Violet. Stay here. I think he's gone," she whispers.

I try to pull her to me, but she slips out of bed. The silence is overwhelming.

A flicker of light from the dining room opens a path for me to follow.

"Hello. Hello. This is Florence Thomas at thirty-five West Jamaica Avenue. Someone broke into my house." I listen, but silence prevails for a moment.

"Yes. He's gone."

"No, my niece is here with me."

"Okay. Good. We won't go anywhere until you get here, Detective."

Auntie lights up the house like a Christmas tree with every light shining brightly.

"Be careful, Tootsie. There's broken glass on the floor. That creep smashed the light. Did you see anything at all?" she asks me. I'm flooded with feelings I don't have words for.

"Kind of. A tall figure of a man but hard to see as he went by so fast."

"Detective Marlowe is on his way, and he has his boys out on the beat looking for this fella now. So, don't worry. I know this is scary for you, though. Can I get you anything, dear?"

"I'm so embarrassed. I wet my pants."

"Oh, honey. Come with me. Let's get you cleaned up before he gets here."

"But the glass in the door is shattered, Auntie. What if the bad guy comes back?"

"Not with those sirens heading this way and the house lit up like this."

She grabs the heaviest frying pan, my hand and we flee to her room.

"Help yourself to some clean underwear and nightie. Here's an extra robe."

"Thanks, Auntie. I feel like such a baby."

The doorbell rings, and I jump.

"Come in, Lieutenant," Auntie calls out, heading to the front door.

"I have some good news," he says. "It looks like we have a suspect. I have in my possession something that you might recognize."

He unwraps two very old coins.

Auntie gasps. "Those were my grandfather's. I stored them in an old chest in the attic. How would he know they were there?" She takes them and sits down and weeps.

"My boys are bringing him here for you to identify. It might be the same fella that has been stalking you and your late sister. Are you up for that, Miss Thomas?"

"Yes. I can handle that."

Detective Marlowe looks at me with furrowed brows. "And who are you, young lady?"

Auntie grabs my hand. "This is my niece, Violet Pearl."

"Don't worry. You won't have to go outside to identify him. They'll have him stand on the sidewalk, right under that streetlight, so you can see him. I suggest you turn out your kitchen lights."

The detective looks at me and shakes his head. "Must have been quite an ordeal for you, my dear?"

I nod and stare out of the window. The siren's coming closer, and I see a few lights come on in the houses across the way. *Somehow, I'm reminded of the night Mama died.*

"They're here," the detective tells my aunt.

She grabs my hand, and we peek through the sheer curtain.

"That's him. That's the guy at the bus stop, Auntie."

"Lieutenant, this is the same man who's been following me for a while now," she said.

He knocks on the window, and the cops load the hoodlum into the paddy wagon. The sirens sound off as they disappear in the distance.

"I called your brother-in-law, and he knows a crime has taken place. He wants the two of you to go to his house immediately. Pack a bag, and I'll take you there myself. A repairman is on his way to fix the window in your door. Don't worry about your house because it's now under twenty-four-hour surveillance until the repairs are done. I'll send some men upstairs to check it out."

Papa's standing in the doorway when we arrive home. It's 3:30 in the morning, the excitement has worn off, and all I want to do is plop in bed. I'm exhausted. My palms are all sweaty too.

"Oh, Violet Pearl," Aunt Lucy utters as she rises from the couch to greet me. "I'm so sorry you had to go through this awful night."

"Flossie," Papa says, turning toward Auntie. "I'm glad you're safe. I'll take the couch, and you can have my room."

"We did get the scoundrel, Sir," Detective Marlowe says. "Miss Thomas should be able to go back home in two days. Try to get some rest, folks." He tips his hat to us and leaves.

I follow my aunt upstairs. I try to quiet the pounding in my chest.

"Violet," Papa says as he reaches for my arm. "I need to ask you something. It'll only take a minute. I promise."

"She's positively drained, Berto," Aunt Flossie's face twists, as she wipes her eyes.

"Go get some sleep, Florence," Papa says. "And please be quiet. We don't want to wake Daisy." He pulls me into the foyer.

"I stopped by the Fox Theater building earlier tonight and found out you never showed up for the audition. You have some explaining to do, young lady."

"I'm so tired, Papa. Can't this wait until I get some sleep?"

"No, it cannot."

"I don't want to be in that silly play or any other play. I'm sick and tired of playing nutty characters in ugly clothes. Enough already!" I shout.

His face turns shades of red and his dark eyes squint at me. He starts to raise his hand to slap my face but grabs my shoulders instead. "Nasty girl. I'll tell you what you'll do. Remember that."

I burst into tears. "But I want to be a ballet dancer."

"Go to your room this once."

I run away from him and trip on the first step. I turn and glare at Papa. "I miss my mama." *I feel my mother's absence all the time.*

"Sure, you do. Oh, by the way I booked you for a clown gig at a Bar Mitzvah. So, brush up on your act."

Hot torrents of despair course down my face as I climb and sit on the fourth step.

Papa looks up at me and smirks, "You know what I always tell you to do at times like this. Right?"

"Yeah, laugh, clown, laugh."

I feel like I'm sleepwalking. I wish I were, then tonight would be a bad dream.

PART TWO

1936

Chapter 14

"Come on, Daisy. Hurry up!" I shout. "The bell's going to ring in twenty minutes. You're going to be late for school if we don't leave in two minutes."

Daisy comes barreling through the kitchen door with her hair down and all askew. She's huffing and puffing as though she ran a long race.

"I'm ready. Okay. Let's go." She grabs her schoolbag and bolts out of the door ahead of me.

I turn to see that all the lights are out and check my bag for the key to the front door.

Door locked.

As we walk to the elementary school, I take a brush out of my bag and brush her hair. Kind of a hard task but at least she'll look somewhat presentable.

"We're finally here! Now, remember, don't leave these front steps after school under any circumstance; do you hear?"

"I know what you're going to say, sis. There are strangers everywhere," she replies.

Looking back on the past few years, I realize a lot of changes have taken place. Now, that I'm sixteen, I spend most of the time a housekeeper and mother figure to my little sister. My father's still entertaining at night and sleeps during the day. Aunt Lucy went back to Italy a year ago, and my auntie Flossie works for the New York Telephone Company in Manhattan, and I mainly see her on weekends.

"Hi, Violet. I like your dress. Did you get new shoes?" May asks me as we walk into school.

All Girls High School in Brooklyn is a prestigious place for teenagers to get a good education. My eighth-grade teacher pulled a lot of strings to get me in this place, but I don't like the idea of no boys.

"Thanks, May. I got the dress and shoes at Woolworths. The shoes are a bit small, but they were cheap."

"Do you like working there?"

"I do, but it's a long walk. Twelve blocks to and from isn't exactly a stone's throw from my house. I stand for four hours straight. My feet hurt something awful by the time I get home. Luckily, I work two weekdays. If I find someone to watch my sister, I add one Saturday a month."

"Hey, Violet. I'm having a shindig this Saturday night. I hope you don't have to work at Woolworths again." Eleanor says as I go to my locker.

"I don't have to work this Saturday, but my father does. I can ask my aunt Flossie if she can come over to watch Daisy. Thanks for asking."

I'm one of the writers for *The Record*, our school newspaper. Sylvia Finkelstein, the editor-in-chief and a senior, gave me the assignment to do cartooning and posters because she likes my artwork. That's pretty good coming from her as she is the most popular girl in the whole school. It was a pleasant change but unexpected.

"Oh drat. First period today is the wonderful world of calculus," I whisper to Lucille standing at the next locker.

She laughs. "I still don't understand why you have such a hard time with this, Violet. It's so easy."

My heart skips a beat of jealousy, but I manage to chuckle a little. Then we go into class.

If I get another F on my homework; it will be the second one in two weeks. I hope I don't get left back. I must graduate with my class next year. If Papa finds out I didn't pass this test, he'll put me on house arrest for the weekend which will mean no party.

The bell drones out its shrill ring, and everyone quickly jumps out of their seats and heads to the hallway. I find my way to the student office to work on *The Record*. I submit a joke for the "Anything Goes" column.

"Oh," said the fisherman's daughter upon being congratulated on her new husband. "You should have seen the one who got away."

My job might be in jeopardy when the principal finds out about my bad grades.

I wish I didn't have to go to work today. I ponder on the bus ride from my school to Daisy's.

It is such a hoop-da-la getting her home and hiking twelve blocks back to the five and dime. If Papa were home tonight to take care of my sister, I could call in sick.

"Sissy! Can we go to the park on the way home?" Daisy asks as she runs to me.

"Not today. I must work. Papa's expecting us at home in a half hour. Maybe, tomorrow. Okay?"

"Papa's always glued to the radio. He never wants to play with me."

"You want that new dress, don't you?"

"Yep. I do."

"Then, I don't want to hear anymore." I pull out a small sack of Lorna Dune cookies.

"There's our bus. You can eat these on the trip back home."

It's 4:30 p.m., and the sun is starting to set in between the tall buildings, but the shadows from the elevated train block most of it from full view. Goose bumps break out all over as I pass the soup kitchen and see poor souls waiting in a long line to get some grub.

I get a quick whiff of vegetable soup and fresh baked bread, and my tummy starts to grumble. Men are in shabby clothes, unshaven, and awful body odor oozes from them.

No more appetite.

What was that?

"Hey, Girlie, do you have a little cash for me?" A man shouts as he pats my bottom.

How positively disgusting. That never happened before, and I have traveled this route many times.

I don't look back but run as fast as I can toward my workplace, which luckily is one more block.

F W Woolworths is a decent-sized store that does a wonderful job displaying a variety of items to please young and old alike. The best part is most things are priced at five or ten cents. People stop on their way home from work to get incidentals they might need. I'm kind of a jack-of-all-trades and a master of none when I work here, but it generates spending money for Daisy and me.

"Hey Ho, Violet," Marty, the fella working the fountain counter calls to me.

I giggle with my hand over my mouth, "Hi, Marty."

He's so handsome with his blond wavy hair and dark eyes. Sometimes when I'm stocking shelves and happen to glance up in that direction, I find him staring at me. When our eyes meet, he smiles and waves. I let the strange feeling wash over me, enjoying it while I can.

Mary Frances, from Catholic High, nudges me, "He likes you. I can tell by the way he looks at you."

"Why do you say that?"

"Last week, after you left, he asked me if I knew where you lived. Don't worry, I didn't tell him."

"Violet." Mr. Hamilton, our manager, says as he comes up to where we are standing. "You go to the register tonight, and Mary Frances comes with me. There are some boxes to unpack."

The store closes at seven on weekdays and five on Saturday, but we teens can only work a few hours a week. I'm amazed Papa allows me to work because it's always dark when I leave. I suppose he thinks it's safe because the walk home is well lit by streetlights and policemen always are walking the beat.

"Will you be going to Eleanor's party on Saturday?" Mary Frances asks as we prepare to leave.

"Yes. I hope so."

"You sound unsure, Violet."

"My dad has to work, but I'm going to ask my aunt Flossie to come over to watch Daisy."

Mary Frances is a little stout with short, brown, curly hair that matches her coffee-colored skin. Her mother sings with The Domino Four occasionally. Last October, St. Mary's Catholic girl's school had a fundraiser for their new gymnasium. It was on a Saturday afternoon, so I went because the band was the entertainment. Mary Frances and I have been good friends ever since.

"Okay, maybe I'll see you there," she calls to me as she climbs the stairs to the train above.

I can walk fast when I must, and now is that time. Five blocks. Good. The soup line's gone.

Four blocks. *I hope supper's waiting for me.*

Suddenly, a passerby puts his arm around my shoulder. I start running, but the arm stays right with me.

I don't dare look. I see a cop just ahead, and I open my mouth to scream.

"Violet? It's me. Marty from Woolworths."

I hit him in the gut. "You scared the wits out of me, you dumb cluck."

"Oh, come on. I only want to walk you home. I'm the great protector, you know."

I start walking away from him, but as I see, the policeman is almost in front of us now.

Marty takes his arm off my shoulder, and I can see his smile now under the street light.

"Good evening, officer," Marty says.

The cop glances at Marty and then at me. "Are you alright, miss? It's getting late for you to be walking these streets."

"I live only three and a half blocks from here, Sir. I walk this route a couple of times a week."

"I can walk her home, officer. If she will let me, that is," Marty offers.

I look at Marty, who's beaming from ear to ear. "Yes, that's fine."

"You kids be careful; you hear?" he calls to us as we walk on.

After a few quick blocks, "This is my house. Thank you for walking me home. Please don't scare me like that again though."

He laughs and shakes his head. "I promise I won't. Now, how about a date?"

"I don't think so. My life is too full of activity."

"Wait a minute. Do you know Eleanor, the gal in that house?" He points to it.

"Yes. Why?"

"Are you going to her big shindig on Saturday?" he asks.

"Maybe, why?"

"Well, *maybe* I'll see you there." He gives me a quick peck on the cheek and disappears into the dark night.

I stand in warm bubbly amazement for a few seconds. *What just happened, and how does he know Eleanor?*

Upon opening the front door, I get a strong whiff of garlic and onions. I drop my purse on the bench in the foyer and take giant steps into the kitchen.

"So, there you are," Papa says from the kitchen table. "I was starting to get worried when you didn't come home at the usual time of six o'clock."

"I'm ravenous. Can I help myself, Papa?"

"I actually had time to make spaghetti sauce today. It was so much fun sautéing the ingredients in olive oil and then adding that to the simmering tomato sauce on the stove. It's been cooking all day."

I scoop out the rolled-up beef braciola that is stuffed with the garlic mixture and pour some sauce over that.

"Yummy."

"Luigi brought over some homemade bread. I know how much you love bread, daughter."

I sit down at the table and start eating. "This is so good, Papa."

"I know how hard you work with school, Daisy, and everything in between."

We haven't had a conversation like this since Mama died.

I smile at my papa.

"Violet, there's something I must talk to you about before you go to bed."

"What's that?"

"The musical *Roberta* opened on Broadway last week, and there's a small part for a teenage girl. I met the producer at The Vogue Club and told him all about you. Usually, an audition is announced and then callbacks, but he asked if I thought you would be interested. Of course, I said yes."

I drop my fork on the plate and jump out of the chair. "You did what?"

"He's expecting you at the theater at three o'clock on Saturday for a rehearsal. The show's at seven."

"No. No. I won't do this, Papa. How could you?"

"You don't have a choice, my dear. You owe me. Call your aunt Flossie to watch Daisy. It'll be great to see you on stage with the professionals."

"I'm going to Eleanor's get together on Saturday, and that's all there is to it!" I yell as I storm out of the door and up to my bedroom. I don't look back to see if he's following me. I lock my bedroom door, fall on the bed, and scream into my pillow so the noise is muffled.

"Peace my child. You have only a few faults left. They stand between you, achievement, and all you desire." The eerie voice of the keeper hovers over me.

I cover my ears with my hands, "I was just fine without you all these years. Why are you badgering me now?"

"Fear not, my doll. You are blessed beyond your dreams. You have all the talents. They only await your call."

I roll on my back and scan my surroundings. "It's so hard to grasp what you're telling me, keeper. People will think I'm crazy and lock me up in an institution for thinking such things."

"You will see that all things will connect from now on. Be still. Wait."

Sweat covers my hairline, "Leave me alone!" I yell.

Chapter 15

I haven't seen my father since the big blow up two days ago.

Tamara expanded her dance school a year ago and asked me to teach the five-year olds. I knew I could handle once a week without my father finding out about it. Daisy's in this class, and she absolutely loves it. Will my sister be able to keep a secret?

The six little girls are dressed for class in black leotards and black ballet slippers. I help Daisy change as quickly as I can. "Okay, everyone to the barre for your warm-ups."

"Left hand on the barre, right hand out to the side, and feet in first position. Very good."

They do the five positions in perfect unison. I'm so proud of all my students and thrilled that Tamara saw potential in me after only a year of taking lessons. She's on a high these days because George Balanchine, the choreographer from St. Petersburg, Russia, is starting a ballet company in New York City. Tamara auditioned yesterday.

"Okay, children. Go to the middle of the floor and practice *Adagio*. Stay together; stay focused." They copy my every move as I perform the movements designed to help develop balance and control.

"Let's step up the pace and *allegro*." The children now do the fast steps that increase speed and exactness.

Tamara runs into the small classroom, grabs my hand, and pulls me aside. "I have some great news."

"What?"

"I'm on the first callback list. I'm so excited!"

The girls keep dancing to the music as we talk.

"What about all your classes here at the school?"

"I didn't get into the company yet," she says. "There'll be two callbacks, but if I make those, then I'm in the company. A formal invitation in letter form will be sent out to the winners."

I hug her with tears in my eyes. "Tamara, that's swell."

"I don't want to close the school. I'm hoping you could take over."

"My father will never let me."

"Let's not jump the gun. I may not make the second cut anyway."

I secretly hope she does, and at the same time I dread it.

A typical Saturday morning. No Papa. His half-filled cup of coffee is still here so I know he came home last night. Daisy's still sleeping which is a real switch.

I open the fridge door to see what I can wrestle up for breakfast when I hear the pitter-patter of tiny feet and a pint-sized voice say, "Vi-Vi. Are you down here?"

"I'm in the kitchen, Daisy," I call out.

"Ta-da! Never fear, Daisy's here." She dances a pirouette and into a plie.

"Sit down; I'm making poached eggs on toast for us."

"Only one, please."

"Aunt Flossie's coming to stay over tonight so I can go to Eleanor's party."

"Goodie. Does Papa know you're going?"

"Yes, but he's not very happy about it."

My first coed party is exciting but different. The music's blaring; a few girls are dancing with each other; a couple of fellas are looking the girls over; and others are sitting on the floor in groups chatting rapidly. Cakes and cookies are laid out on the dining room table with a punch bowl near the baked goods.

There must be at least twenty teens here. Eleanor sure knows how to party.

"Violet, I'm so glad you came," Eleanor yells over the hullaballoo. "Help yourself to some goodies, okay? Oh, look there's May."

I smell something peculiar. *What's that?*

"Violet. Do you remember me?" Someone says from behind. The voice sounds familiar.

I turn around and am face to face with Marty.

"Here, have some punch." He hands me a glass with a pinkish concoction in it. As I bring the glass up to my mouth, I smell that strange odor again. "What's that smell?" I ask.

"I saw Eleanor put apple cider in this. It does smell odd, doesn't it?"

I sniff the drink again, shake my head, but reluctantly swallow the beverage. "Not too bad."

"Can I get you more, my fair maiden?" Marty asks.

"Please."

Before long, we're dancing a waltz, but he's a little closer to me than he should be. He presses into my body. I feel something happen inside of me that I never experienced before.

All I know is I feel like I'm floating above the floor beneath us. Marty kisses my cheek, then my neck, and now our lips are touching. I'm hot and sweaty.

"Let's go outside for a bit," he whispers in my ear. I shiver because I'm not used to being this close to anyone.

He takes my hand, and we walk out of the back door, down the steps, and then we sit on the soft grass under a big oak tree. "It's a nice night out here, isn't it?" he asks quietly.

"Yes. It is." I look around and notice that we're completely alone.

I start to get up. "I think we should go back inside."

"Not yet." Marty pulls me down on the grass, kissing my cheek. "You're so beautiful. I want you all to myself."

I giggle, not knowing what to expect. "I guess it's okay for a few more minutes."

Before I know it, he is on top of me. Something inside of me knows this isn't right. I squirm and try pushing him off me but to no avail.

"I want all of you, Violet." Our lips touch, and unlike the kiss earlier, it brings a strong tingly sensation within my deepest being. This fella's roaming hands are touching places on my body they shouldn't.

I wiggle to get myself free. "Get off me now, or I'll scream."

He's smiling at me, and I can't escape.

Slurring his words, he says, "You won't scream, and even if you do, no one can hear you because of all the noise inside the house." His breath smells like the alcohol my father drinks.

I push with all my God-given strength and manage to sliver from under him. Marty grabs my arm, but I pull away and jump up as he tears my blouse in the process.

I bolt down the driveway to the street. I look up at the back porch briefly and see Eleanor. "Violet, is that you?" she asks.

I stop for an instant and dart into the night.

Don't look back. Don't look back. Don't go back.

I run all the way home and open the door slowly and quietly, so no one hears me. My face is wet and stained from the uncontrollable sobbing that I experienced in the short distance from Eleanor's house to mine. My beautiful white satin blouse is torn from one sleeve to the next exposing my heaving chest under my brassiere. The parlor is dark except for the glowing in the fireplace.

As my eyes focus, I see Auntie fast asleep on the sofa, covered with the quilt Mama completed before she died.

I take off my shoes and dash up the stairs, skipping the squeaky steps as I go.

Looking in the mirror on my dressing table, I'm horrified to see how destroyed my blouse is as it reminds me of what took place just moments ago. Undoing the last two buttons, I take my favorite top off and stuff it under my sweaters in the bottom drawer of my bureau.

It's only nine o'clock. Too early to go to bed, but I should at least try.

I can't sleep. I toss and turn.

"So, your beauty got you in trouble. Ha. I knew it would."

I bolt upright and glance around the dimly lit room. Shadows play havoc on the walls as my heart pounds aimlessly within.

"You thought you were rid of me, didn't you? I'm always around, even if you can't see me."

I dig my nails into my palms. "Go away." I whisper.

"Now, now my dear girl. No need to be afraid. I won't harm you, if you'll do what I say."

"I can get past this. I'm stronger than you think, keeper."

"No, you're not."

I pull the quilt tight beneath my chin and close my eyes for a few moments. Maybe, it's all a bad dream. *After all, if he is real, why can't I see him?*

The April breeze blows through my open window, and I look at the twinkling stars in the darkened sky. I start counting the stars, but my eyes stay open. Reality rushes over me like an avalanche.

Marty. That creep. I hate boys. I learned a painful lesson about the opposite sex tonight. I don't care if I ever talk to another fella again. I punch my pillow over and over.

Finally, I roll over on my side and close my eyes. I hear my bedroom door open.

I hear Auntie breathe heavily as she stands nearby. I know it's her because of the beautiful fragrance, she always wears.

Chapter 16

"Violet, what happened to you on Saturday night? I looked everywhere for you. Someone said you went in the back yard with Marty." Eleanor asks on Monday.

"He's a revolting, nasty fella dressed in sheep's clothing."

"Oh, come on," she says, giggling. "He's a sweetheart. So kind and thoughtful."

I look in disgust at my best friend, "What did he tell you, Eleanor?"

"He was laughing as he came up the back steps."

"Of course, he was."

"He said that you asked him to go outside, and you were all over him."

"You don't believe him, do you?"

"Well, you were dancing cheek to cheek, and you didn't stop him from kissing you in front of everybody."

"It wasn't like that at all, Eleanor." I feel my face getting red as my imaginary arms reach out to grab her by the neck.

May and two other girls who were at the party are staring at me. A few others are giggling and miming kissing.

"You are supposed to be my best friend. I can't believe that you even listened to Marty's dim-witted portrayal of what happened that night."

"Honestly, Violet. You're sixteen. Act like it." She joins the other girls.

The bell rings, and the girls head to their classes, leaving me behind, feeling betrayed and alone. I tamp down the tears and anger threatens to overtake me, but I gain control of my emotions. On to American history and a long day at school.

"Where were you? The principal asked if he should call Papa. You're supposed to be here before three o'clock." Daisy yells at me from the front steps of the school.

I point my finger at her as I walk up. "Don't you ever yell at me like that again? Do you hear me?" I grab her arm and pull her off the steps. She falls, skins her knee, and wails.

"Come on, child. You're fine. Stop your crying this instant!" I scream.

A few people glare at me as they walk past, but I scowl back, "Stop your gawking!"

Daisy tries to resist, but I continue to drag her to the bus stop.

"Let me go. Let me go!" she shouts.

"Not until we're on the bus. Now calm down, will you?"

"I have to go to the bathroom."

"Hold it in. I must be at Tamara's. She's expecting us in twenty minutes. You know I can't be late." For some reason, this is the first day, dance doesn't interest me.

"Violet, are you alright? You seem distracted," Tamara asks.

"I'm fine." I nod blinking back tears.

"Daisy ran in here by herself, and usually you're on her heels or holding on to her."

"You know what it's like when a six-year-old has to go to the bathroom, don't you?"

A surprised look crossed her face. "I sure do, but you need to brush your hair, Violet. It's a mess. Oh, I have some great news to share with you after dance class today."

After primping a bit in the tiny, dingy lavatory, I return to my small class of six eager little girls.

"Everyone to the middle of the floor," I say. "Let's begin with the five positions. Show them how it is done, Daisy."

"Good job. Now, second position."

Daisy complies.

"Now third, please."

She executes perfectly, and I praise her for it. "Good job."

I look for a record to put on for them to dance to. I choose *But Not for Me* by George and Ira Gershwin, and soon the music fills the small dance studio as the girls up the tempo to their ballet positions in precise but vigorous movements.

When the music stops, I go to my sister. "Thank you, Daisy." I hug her with all my heart and soul.

"Okay, girls, now let me see some graceful butterfly walks and let your arms flutter gently like wings. Feel the rhythm of the music. Emily, you lead this time."

I don't know if I want my private ballet class with Tamara tonight. I wouldn't be able to pay attention. Papa doesn't know about my ordeal at Eleanor's or that I am pursuing my dream of dancing ballet. Daisy pleaded with him to let her take one ballet class. He has no idea; I'm the teacher.

"Gather your things, girls. It's time to go. See you next week."

"Come on, Daisy. Tamara wants to talk to me before we go."

Tamara's so-called office is a small cubicle halfway down the hall toward the front door. On the wall are two pictures of ballerinas dressed in short white tutus standing in perfect formation. A small desk, an old file cabinet, and two chairs are the only furniture in the little room. Her newest addition is a telephone.

I sit down and pull Daisy on my lap. "Sorry about before, honey."

She turns and throws her arms around me.

Tamara drops into her chair. "Violet, I'm in the second callback for the Core de Ballet in New York City."

"Wow! That's wonderful. What'll happen if you get in?"

"That's what I want to talk to you about. You're such a fast learner, and you're a superb teacher. The children and parents are very pleased with you. You'll graduate from school next year, and by that time The School of American Ballet will be in full swing. Hopefully, if all goes well, you'll be the one trying out." She gives me a huge smile.

"Papa will never let me. The only reason he lets me come here is because of my sister. He has no idea I'm teaching here."

"I'll talk to him…invite him for supper."

"I'll keep my ten advanced students and won't take on anymore. Violet, you would be the manager of the dance studio. I'll give you a private lesson on my day off."

"I don't know, Tamara. Woolworths takes up my spare time. You better get someone else." I shrug.

"This is where you belong. It's here where you can fulfill your dream of becoming a ballet dancer. I see you put your heart and soul into your dancing and teaching."

Standing up and grabbing my bag, I say, "I don't think so."

"I'm so excited for you, Violet. You're one class away from putting on those toe shoes. Speaking of which, it's time for that lesson now."

"No, I can't. Not today." I burst into tears, grab my sister's hand, and dart to the door.

"Violet. Come back. Please tell me what's wrong," she follows me to the door, but I don't look back.

Chapter 17

The Marty incident plagues me on the bus ride home, but I hold back the tears, so my sister doesn't see the inside of my heart.

As soon as her feet hit the cement, she sprints ahead of me to our house.

"Yummy. Something smells scrumptious," Daisy squeals.

"Papa must be baking again. Let's go see. The last one in the kitchen is a rotten egg."

"Catch me if you can," she shouts back at me.

The perfectly shaped fluffy baking powder biscuits are stacked attractively on a platter in the middle of the table. There are three place settings. Papa pulls a square pan out of the oven.

"My girls. Glad you are home safe. Come sit. We're having an early supper tonight because I'm working on a new song."

"Smells great in here, Papa," I say. "What else are we having tonight?"

"Tuna noodle casserole. I got the recipe from the newspaper today."

Crinkling up her nose, Daisy says. "Ugh. Fish."

"Try it, my little bambino. It's good."

"Daisy. You'll love this. Come on. One bite. You can do it." I say.

She takes a small bite off my fork and gags. "Yuck. Please give me a biscuit."

He dishes out a small portion on her plate. "You can have a biscuit when these noodles are gone."

"But, but the biscuits will get cold."

Papa and I give her a look that triggers her to eat the noodles.

"How was dance class today, Daisy girl?" he asks.

"Violet let me teach the other girls. We had fun."

He looks at me. "Where were you?"

"I was right there, Papa."

"I see. Mary Frances called today asking for you. She wants you to call her tonight."

"How was that gathering at Eleanor's last Saturday night?" he asks.

I freeze in place not knowing what to say to him.

"Violet Pearl. Did you hear me?"

I place the dirty dishes in the warm sudsy water thinking about that ugly event that took place.

He turns me toward himself. "Did you have a good time?"

"Yes. Papa. It was very nice. She had friends from different schools. Eleanor follows in her mother's footsteps with hospitality."

"Say, were there some boys too?"

I start scrubbing the dishes with vigor. "Yes."

"Can we play Parcheesi after you do the dishes?" Daisy asks.

"Sure, we can, Princess. Glad you had a good time, Violet."

I feel a stab of pain at hearing Saturday night being touted as a good time.

I join Papa in the parlor two hours later. "Daisy's asleep," I inform him.

He's sitting in the large chair by the unlit fireplace as though in deep thought.

"Papa. Thank you for a fun night. The dinner was good, and game time with you was very special." I spurt out a loud chuckle.

"Violet Pearl. Blessed are they who can laugh at themselves, for they shall never cease to be amused."

We both laugh and hug.

"You go on up to bed. It's probably too late to call Mary Frances. I'll be up shortly."

I smile as I climb up the stairs with my cat in my arms. *I'll get past this Marty thing.*

Papa and I have not conversed like this in such a long time, in fact I can't even remember when he spent a whole evening at home with us. I get ready for bed, grab a book, and plop on top of my bed.

Oh Mama. Where are you? I wish you were right here, so I could talk to you about boys. Where is that illustration I'm putting into The Girl's High Record?

I remember.

I reach under my bed and pull out a brown portfolio. I open it and leaf through it. Here it is.

Don't take yourself so seriously.

Lighten up and laugh with me.

You have me on your side, so what are you worried about?

Signed, God.

Thank you, Mama. Or is it God that I thank?

All day Wednesday I contemplate whether I should go back to Woolworths or not.

I do like my job and my friend Mary Frances, but I don't want to see Marty ever again. I'm so happy I told her everything because she's trustworthy. I get paid tomorrow, so I better go.

"Don't you worry about that Marty; you hear me?" Mary Frances nudges me as we walk to work.

"I'll stay clear of him. That's for sure."

We walk into the store and get our smocks on. "I don't see him. Do you?" I look back at Mary Frances.

"No. Maybe he's off tonight."

I'm so relieved when the hours roll on and no sight of Marty.

There's only a half hour left.

"I'll take over for you, Violet, so you can get ready to fly the coop." A familiar voice offers. It isn't Mr. Hamilton.

I quickly remove myself from the small area by the cash register, turn, and glare at Marty.

There are no customers in view, and Mary Frances is loading counters with sale merchandise in the back of the store. I don't have any idea where the manager is.

"You. You. Big brute. I never want to talk to you again." I hold back the tears.

"Violet, I want to apologize."

Looking around. I step closer to him. "It's too late for that; don't you think?"

"I was the one who put a little whiskey in the punch. I found a small bottle in my parent's cupboard."

"You what?" I scowl at him.

"I got in big trouble with Eleanor's father. He suspected something when a few of the girls started to dance on the dining room table after you left."

"Eleanor did mention that fiasco to me, but you're still a jerk."

"Please forgive me, Violet. I got carried away, and I'm sorry I ripped your blouse too."

"Do you want me to punch his lights out now or later, Violet?" Mary Frances asks walking up to us.

"He apologized. I don't know if I accept it or not."

"You should be ashamed of yourself, Marty," she scolds.

"Look, I learned my lesson that alcohol is bad news. Come on, what do you say? Can we be friends now?"

"Okay. Friends. That's it," I say as I walk away shaking my head.

Chapter 18

I'm looking forward to a weekend at home. I don't have to work at the store, so I think I'll pull out Mama's old Singer and sew something. Not having a place to go, sounds good to me.

"Are you scrambling eggs, Papa?"

"Yes, do you want some?"

"I'd love some. Thanks."

"I want you to take your sister to the Brooklyn Botanical Gardens tomorrow. It's supposed to be a real nice day. I have to practice some new tunes with the fellas."

"Do I have to? I was looking forward to staying home, Papa. Can't you take her?"

"I can't this time, even though I want to. You're going on seventeen, Honey. I have great confidence in you that everything will be fine. I know how much you love the Japanese gardens."

"That place is so big."

"Daisy loves all the unusual fish ponds located throughout the gardens. Have lunch there, and spend the afternoon enjoying the extraordinary flowers and plants."

I let out a long sigh, "Okay, I'll do it."

It's so nice to live near the Botanical Gardens. I love roaming through the fifty-two acres of lush gardens and a medley of spectacular landscaping right in the middle of Brooklyn.

The lilacs have a fragrance like no other this time of year, and they line the walkway all the way to the Japanese gardens. My favorite place. The Japanese Hill-and-Pond Garden portion displays the most delightful trees fully dressed in shades of pink cherry blossoms. "Look, Daisy, aren't these cherry trees absolutely beautiful? This is the perfect time of year to come here."

She starts to run ahead of me.

"Don't run ahead of me. Stay close, please."

"Look, Vi-Vi. There are big orange fish in this pond." I smile at her delight.

"Those are carp. Look, there are some that are orange and white."

"Bridges. Little bridges everywhere. Look close, sometimes fairies hide under them."

"Really? I don't see any?"

"They're very fast."

"I'm hungry," she whines.

Rolling my eyes. "You're kidding. Let's see. We walked in the main entrance exactly twenty minutes ago. You can wait at least one hour, can't you?"

"Okay. Let's race. I'll beat you to that red thing over there."

"Do you mean the arch?" I chuckle and pat her on the head.

"Ready, set, go." She takes off, and I sprint to catch up.

"Ha. Ha. I beat you, slow Violet Pearl."

"Not by much." I grab and squeeze her.

We sit for a few minutes on the bench under the architectural wonder above us.

"Daisy, they're planting vegetable seedlings in the Children's Garden today."

Already up, she starts running away from me. I don't want to make a scene, as there are so many people heading in the same direction. I run as fast as I can and manage to catch up with her.

Nonchalantly, I grab her hand with a firm squeeze and pull her to me. "Don't run ahead of me again, or we'll leave. Do I make myself clear?"

"Yes, Ma'am."

"Line up right here, children," the garden educator says loudly enough. "And I'll give each one of you a vegetable seedling of your choice. I have tomato, cucumber, green bean, and pumpkin plantlets. We'll direct you on where and how to plant them."

At least fifty children between the ages of five and ten scramble to be first in line. Daisy manages to get into second place. She has a gait of a peacock.

The education assistant points to her left. "Pumpkins out that door, tomatoes and cucumbers directly to my right, and green beans directly outside the entrance door."

I know my sister's delight is carving pumpkins in October. Sure enough, I see her weave in between the other children and their guardians into the sunshine to my left.

I stand behind her as she digs into the dirt with bare hands and watch her gently take the two seedlings, one by one and place them in the holes before her.

Patting the dirt to complete the task, she jumps up. "All done. Nice job, huh?"

I smile and give her a big hug. "Let's go wash those hands and have some lunch, okay?"

"Sorry, folks, but we don't have a lavatory in this building." The education director says. "There's one right over there in the café building. However, you can rinse the dirt off your hands in this bucket if you wish. Please be sure to come back this summer to the progress of your plants."

The smell of coffee and freshly baked doughnuts fills the air as we walk into the café. There are big windows everywhere, and many trees in humungous pots decorate the vast space. The souvenir shop is nestled in a nook right in front of us with a display of different kinds of stuffed animals and colorful wooden toys in a barrel on the floor. Daisy's eyes bulge out of her head when her hands pick up a white bear.

"Miss, where are the lavatories?" I ask the cashier.

She points to the far corner past the lunch counter.

"Daisy, put that down. Maybe you can get one with your money after lunch."

She puts it down and once again moves ahead of me.

"You go in that stall, and I'll go right next to you."

She shuts the door, and I hear it latch.

"I can't believe it is two o'clock already," a lady outside the door says.

We did cover a lot of territory and saw many interesting things in two hours. I wish I took Papa's suggestion and brought the wagon. Daisy's way too fast. I wish she wouldn't constantly take off. The wagon would keep her entertained and close.

"What do you want to see next, Daisy?"

Not a sound.

Daisy?" I call out into the quiet restroom.

Pulling myself together and opening the door to the stall, I look around and see I'm alone. *She must be right outside the door.*

"Daisy?" I look in the three stalls. No Daisy.

I wash my hands in a hurry and fly out of the door into the room filled with people sitting at tables or checking out the fascinating displays.

Where's that child? I bet she's looking at the white bear.

I see a little girl Daisy's height and same hair color with her back to me.

"There you are." I grab her shoulders and turn her around. The kid looks at me in horror.

"I'm so sorry, honey. I thought you were my sister." I must look like a ripe tomato because my face is glowing.

Looking to my left and to my right, "Did you see a little girl this high with brown curly hair, wearing a red dress?" I ask the cashier.

"I remember you two from before. Yes. She bought that white bear a few minutes ago. I don't know where she went after that."

Scanning from corner to corner, I ask anyone in my view. "Did you see a little girl about six years old with brown curly hair?"

Negative nods. I feel like I'm on a runaway train.

"Daisy. Daisy Mae!" I scream as people turn and glare.

An elderly lady with snow-white hair taps me on the shoulder. "Are you looking for someone, my dear?"

"Yes. My little sister. Can you help me?" I say frantically.

"Calm down, dear. She must be in here someplace. What's she wearing? Her name's Daisy, right?"

"She's wearing a red dress and carrying a white fluffy teddy bear. Yes. That's her name."

"I'll check everyplace from here to the lavatories, and you look in this vicinity. Meet me back here in ten minutes." She scurries away, calling my sister's name.

Pretty soon I hear the name Daisy being called by several people in the building.

I'm trying hard not to panic as I continue my search. Tears well up as the storm surges within.

"Daisy. Daisy Mae. Can you hear me?" I yell as loud as I can.

A gentle embrace warms my shoulders. "I don't think she's here. What's your name, dear?" The elderly lady asks.

"Where can she be?" I cry as we head outside.

"I asked the manager to send the word out that there is a lost little girl in the gardens. I am Mrs. Barker, by the way."

"Thank you so much for helping. My name's Violet."

"I'm a volunteer here, and I was on my way home. However, I'm staying with you until Daisy's safe in your arms. Okay. Let's take the same route you took coming over to the café."

"Daisy, Daisy!" we call as we go.

No sign of her anywhere. Certainly, she would stick to the paths and not deviate into the thick foliage, but then my sister would chase a beautiful butterfly anywhere. "Daisy." I scream.

Looking at her watch, Mrs. Barker sighs. "The gardens close at five o'clock, so the main gate will be locked soon. The guard will hold a lost child in the front office until a relative claims him or her."

I'm shaking with fear and feeling very irresponsible too. A stranger may have lured her away from here. I may never see my sister again. The sobbing becomes uncontrollable now, and dampness seeps into my underwear.

Where's my sister? Where's Daisy? I can't leave without her.

A few attendants on bicycles ride past us.

"Jack, did you see the little girl in a red dress?" Mrs. Barker calls out to one of them.

"No sign of her. We've examined every place in this entire park," he said as he rides by.

My legs buckle underneath me, and I start to fall to the cement. Mrs. Barker catches me in time.

"Sit down here, and we will decide what to do next. I'm so glad there are park benches everywhere. Listen, honey, we never have any incidents of crime in these gardens. Don't fret."

This never would have happened if Mama were here. A river of feelings flows over me when I think of Mama.

I bury my face in my hands and cry hysterically. A cool breeze blows around me, and I'm scared to my deepest being. Why is this happening to me?

"Violet Pearl Moretti! How did this happen?" I look up and see my father standing before me with Daisy in his arms.

"What? Where did you find her?" I cry out to him.

"She was in Magnolia Plaza, the new building in the center of the gardens. I looked there for you and her when I arrived an hour ago."

Standing up slowly in bewilderment, "Daisy, how could you do this to me?"

"It's not her fault, Violet Pearl," Papa says with a scowl.

"She kept running away from me and then disappeared, Papa. I couldn't find her."

"I'm very disappointed in you, daughter. I gave you this responsibility, and you failed."

"I sorry, Sissy." Daisy whimpers.

"Darn you, Daisy Mae!"

"You are to blame! Stop blaming this little one, Violet!" he shouts.

"Why do you believe her over me? She's only six years old, Papa."

"In my book, she's one smart cookie." He takes a deep breath. "It's getting late. We must get home for supper." He snarls.

"Sir, please excuse me," Mrs. Barker says as she walks up to us. "But I was in the café when this all happened. The cashier said the little girl bought the bear and headed away by herself."

"I don't know who you are, but this is not your concern," Papa snarls.

She puts her arm around me. "Violet was worried sick over all of this. It isn't her fault at all."

"This is a family affair. Good day, Madam."

She looks at Papa with a pitiful look. "I'm going to include you and your girls in my prayers." Her eyes are wide, and her lips are squashed in a thin line.

"Thank you so much for your help, Mrs. Barker," I manage to say.

"You're so very welcome." She gathers her belongings and walks away out of sight.

Putting Daisy down and grabbing her hand, Papa turns to look at me with anger and disappointment in his eyes. "Everyone has the right to be stupid, but you're abusing the privilege."

I look at the clouds and fancy myself drifting away.

I sob as I follow him like a wounded puppy. *How could he treat me like this?*

Chapter 19

Weekends are over way to fast, and before I know it, the same old routine kicks in again. School, dance lessons, housework, and Woolworths. At least that's the game plan most days.

I must get some comfortable footwear to replace these tight-fitting shoes. Not only do I have to stand on my feet for three hours straight, but I must walk to and from work in them too.

Upon arriving home after work, I put my purse down and look around the dimly lit parlor. I realize it's way too quiet. "Hello?"

No answer.

Daisy's probably sleeping, and Papa must be in the kitchen reading the newspaper.

I push the door open and go into the dark kitchen. I flip on the light switch and see a sandwich waiting for me on the table. Good. I'm famished. As I take a bite, I spy a scrawled note on a wrinkled piece of paper tucked under the plate.

Violet, I took Daisy Mae to see Babes in Toyland on Broadway. Don't wait up for us. Papa

How could he do this to me? He must have bought tickets for this a while ago. Pretty sneaky. Did he surprise Daisy, or did she know about this all along? Talk about feeling left out.

I pour myself a glass of milk and devour the sandwich as though I haven't eaten in two days.

"They were dressed up when they left here. Look at it this way, girlie. There's no need to be afraid because I'm here to protect you." The keeper blurts out from behind me.

I want to smash my head through a wall, to get the demon-keeper out of my life. Goose bumps are creeping up my arms.

"Oh, by the way, they have front-row seats too. Now, how does that make you feel, Miss Violet?"

I fold my hands around my head, "Why won't you leave me alone, why?"

Some chill passes over me.

"I come and go, but I seek to comfort you when you're alone."

I try to soothe the goose bumps along my skin. "Well. You're not really here; my brain's conjuring up all this."

"Ha, ha, ha. I like the name you gave me. It truly fits. Do you remember what it is?"

I know I should say something, but I'm lost for words.

"I promise to leave you alone, if you call me that name."

I press my lips together and cringe, "Go away, keeper. Go away this instant."

Everything feels normal, but I can't stop shaking. "The show is about to start, and I won't be there to applaud." Now, why did I say that out loud. There's no one else here.

It's a bit creepy without another person in the house. My confidence is completely shaken after the encounter with the keeper.

I better be sure that all the windows and doors are locked. I'll turn on all the lights.

Maybe, Eleanor or May can come for a sleep over.

I dial Eleanor's phone number.

The phone rings three times when Mrs. Muller answers. "Hello?"

"Hi, Mrs. Muller. May I speak to Eleanor?"

"I'm sorry, Violet Pearl. She's at May's house tonight studying for the algebra test."

"I see."

"You could call her there."

"No, that's alright. I'll see her at school tomorrow. Thank you. Good night."

"Good night."

Well, that takes care of that plan.

Just then, I hear a banging noise outside. I jump up from the kitchen chair. I put my plate in the sink and stand frozen in place as the banging noise outside the kitchen window gets louder. Sprinting over to the back door, I double lock it and draw the shade over the glass.

I hear the banging again. This is unbearable. Where's the keeper now?

Moving slowly toward the window, I glance out and see branches on the oak tree dance in the wind. Then the shutter flaps into the window, repeating the same sound.

What's to be worried about anyway? I might as well get ready for bed and study for that ridiculous algebra test. As a matter of fact, I'll sleep on the couch tonight and leave every single solitary light on too.

I want to see Papa's face when I tell him how disappointed I am.

"Violet, Violet. Wake up. It was out of this world." Daisy says and then twirls around the living room.

"What? What time is it? Where's Papa?"

She giggles. "Papa went to the store but said to wake you up to get ready for school."

Throwing the quilt off me and moving myself to a sitting position on the couch, "It's morning already?"

"Yep."

"Did you have fun?" I'm ringing my hands. My stomach's in knots.

"Yep."

"Look at you. You're all ready to go to school. Oh, dear. It's seven thirty, and you have to be at school in forty-five minutes." I jump up and run up the stairs. Within a hop, skip, and a jump, I'm bounding down again all dressed and ready to go, except for a quick bite to eat.

"You should have seen the dancers, Vi-Vi. They were dressed like big wind-up dolls," Daisy says, smiling.

"Really?" *My head feels like its been clobbered with a baseball bat.*

"Papa wore a suit and a white shirt with a red tie too."

"I see. Come on. You can tell me more on the way to school."

As we walk down the sidewalk to the bus stop, I get a glimpse of Papa walking on the other side of the street. He doesn't look our way, so I don't get a chance to send him my disappointed face. I must go to school with a heavy heart because we're drifting further apart each day.

Chapter 20

Memories of the summer of 1933 will always stay with me because I was able to have the time of my life. Good Ole' Camp Sesame's a camp for girls set in its little corner of the world in the majestic Catskill Mountains. Papa let Daisy and me go for two weeks this year—my second year as camp counselor and Daisy's first camp experience. The smell of s'mores and frankfurters cooking over open camp fires add to my suitcase of delightful recollections.

Papa was away a lot during the summer, entertaining at the huge resorts in the Catskills or the magnificent mansions of the Hamptons. Auntie came and cared for Daisy, so I could go to work. She'd stay overnight to give me the freedom to hop into someone's jalopy with friends and head to Coney Island. She always says I missed having fun as a child because I was a permanent fixture on stage. My favorite ride is the Wonder Wheel, a 150 ft. tall glorified Ferris wheel with enclosed passenger cars.

Communication with my father is estranged now, and if we talk, it's brief.

"Hey, Violet, did you have your senior photograph taken yet?" Eleanor asks as she catches up with me in the hall at school.

"Does it look like I'm dressed for that today, Eleanor?" I look down my old dress.

"Well, aren't we grouchy today?"

"Sorry, but I grabbed this dumb dress off the hanger in such a hurry this morning. It dawned on me a bit ago that I wore it on the last day of school too."

"So, what? It looks nice. Who cares anyway?"

"You look beautiful today, Eleanor. Pink surely is your color, and with your hair down, you look gorgeous." Life is so unfair.

"Thanks, my dear. See you at lunch, okay?" She disappears into the auditorium where the photographer's set up.

Drat. I look like a rag a muffin today, and all the other girls look like models. I want to run out of the door and go home to change. The school bell sounds off over the intercom to remind me where I am. I have an appointment with the guidance counselor.

"How are you doing today, Violet Pearl?" Asks Ms. Jones, the senior adviser.

I shake her hand and sit down on the hard wood chair in front of the big metal desk.

"Okay, I guess. Ma'am."

"Graduation is in a few months, and you've had ample time to consider what you want to do after school is over. What are your thoughts?"

I straighten my dress and glance down at the floor. Then I look up at her. It's hard to tell how old she is with her graying hair slicked back in a tight bun and horn-rimmed glasses. Yet, her skin is smooth and free of wrinkles.

"Well, my friend Tamara who's a ballet dancer wants me to audition for the American Ballet Theater."

"I know you come from a long line of entertainers, Violet, but there are many other opportunities to consider."

"I want to be a ballet dancer, Ms. Jones."

"You're an average student, Violet Pearl, but you have all A's in type-writing and English. There are a few business schools in Manhattan that I think you should apply to."

"Business school?"

"Yes. A one-year course can land you a lucrative career as a secretary or receptionist for a growing company."

"Oh, my father will never let me do that."

"What does he want you to do after graduation?"

"To be another Katharine Hepburn. Perform on the great stage theaters of the big city, of course."

"Doesn't he know that many theaters have closed their doors due to lack of patrons?"

"I have a hard time talking to my father these days. He's hardly at home because of his affluent customers. He seems to be more interested in my kid sister than me."

"I do wonder how he makes a living at merely entertaining."

"I do think about that often too."

"He'll have to come to All Girls School College and Career Night. I encourage parents to work with students on their future goals. I have individual sessions for each student and their parents."

"He might come if it's during the week."

"How do you feel about business school, Violet?"

I shrug my shoulders. "It beats dressing up like a clown." My leg starts to jiggle. I rest my hand on my thigh to make it stop.

The remarkable echoes of a violin fill the hallways of the building where Tamara's dance school is located. It's beautiful, but I wonder why it's so loud. Daisy and I move toward the music. We sneak a quick investigate in Tamara's studio and see her doing a series of graceful arabesques across the wooden floor. Her beautiful hair is pulled on top of her head in a perfect bun, and she's wearing a short white tutu. The most amazing thing is she's dancing in her toe shoes with precision to every move she makes.

Tamara smiles at us as when she turns a few polished pirouettes and then two jetés toward the Victrola.

Daisy and I applaud. "Bravo!"

She takes the record off the turn style and then smiles at us. "Thank you, girls. You're my best audience."

"You're so polished and graceful, Tamara," I say.

"Come sit for a few minutes. Our classes don't start for another fifteen minutes. I'm so glad you came earlier today, Violet Pearl."

"Where did you get that record, and who's the violinist?"

"Mr. Balanchine gave it to me a few days ago. It's called *Sonatas and Partitas* by Johann Sebastian Bach. Did you like it?"

"It's okay, I guess."

"Sissy, I have to go to the bathroom," Daisy blurts out.

"Go ahead and go, Honey. You know where it is. I have to talk to your sister."

I nod in approval. "It's okay, Daisy, but come right back, you hear?"

Tamara grabs my hand and looks at me with her blue eyes wide open. "Violet Pearl, guess what? I start dancing with School of American Ballet Theater next week. I'm so excited."

"You got in?"

"I hope you can come watch my debut at the Wahlberg Estate in White Plains on July 1."

"I doubt it, but I can dream about it, can't I?"

"Hope it works out, but I have to tell you something else."

The giggling sounds of little girls trotting down the hall interrupt our conversation.

"I better catch them before they go crazy."

"I have to close the school, Violet." My hearts desires are broken.

"Miss Violet. Miss Violet. I have new ballet shoes," Emily says as she sticks her head in the door.

I force a smile. As I greet the parents and usher the children into my classroom, I realize Daisy isn't there.

"Emily, did you see Daisy?"

"No, Miss Violet. I didn't."

"She must still be in the lavatory. Girls, please practice your five positions at the bar for your warm-up."

Knocking on the bathroom door, I call out to her, "Daisy, are you in there?"

Not a sound.

Slowly, I open the door and find an empty room. I try not to panic.

The four girls are concentrating on the job I gave them to do so they don't see me go into the hall.

"Oh, Mrs. Brown, I'm so glad you're here. Can you please watch the girls for a few minutes? I have to look for my sister."

"Sure, I can."

"Daisy Mae?" I call as I walk down the hall to Tamara's studio.

Tamara's students are sitting on the floor, putting on their pointed shoes and tying the satin ribbon around their ankles.

"Did anyone see Daisy?"

"She isn't in the lavatory?" Tamara asks.

I turn on my heels and run down the hall out of the door. She's not anywhere to my right or left.

Then I remember seeing a peddler with a monkey standing on the corner one block over. The sidewalk is once again packed with people heading home from work. I'm on a mission as I zigzag this way and that. My insides feel like they're on fire.

Daisy's standing directly in front of the crowd of people and on the edge of the curb. She is absolutely mesmerized by the entertaining monkey dressed in a miniature red- and yellow-striped jacket and matching hat.

"Daisy Mae!" I yell.

A few ladies scowl at me as I grab my sister's arm. The peddler stops playing and gives the monkey to Daisy to hold. I'm out of control. I have no direction over anything in my life.

"You're in big trouble. Give back him his animal right now. We have to go."

"Why are you so mean to me?" she wails, giving the pet back to his owner.

"You ought to be ashamed of yourself, Miss," a mother yells at me.

"Come on, Daisy. I have a class to teach."

"Boo. Boo." The crowd chants as I walk away, pulling the kid behind me.

Daisy's crying with big crocodile tears rolling down her face as we come back to the studio.

"Where did you go, Daisy? Shame on you for leaving here without your sister," Tamara remarks.

"Do you want me to take the girls in to observe Tamara's class for a few minutes, Miss Violet?" Mrs. Brown asks.

"Thank you. I would like that."

Daisy runs into a corner of the room and falls on the floor into a full-blown tantrum. I lean over to pull her up, but she thrashes about and gives me a good swift kick on my kneecap. "Leave me alone!"

"Okay. We'll stay here until the cows come home as far as I'm concerned. Papa will be furious with you after I tell him what you did."

"Go ahead. Tell him. I don't care."

I had all I could do to keep my sister close to me on the bus ride home. I finally got up and switched places with her, so she could look out of the window.

I'm sure Papa will be angry when he finds out she took off without me again. She's so disrespectful too. I might not find her next time. When we get home, Daisy runs ahead of me and screams as she bursts through the front door. "Papa, Papa."

"What is it, my little buttercup?"

Papa's dusting the furniture in the parlor but stops what he's doing and pulls Daisy into his arms.

"Violet Pearl is a monster." She sucks on her thumb, glaring at me with furrowed brow.

"What happened this time, Violet Pearl?" He asks with an angry tone.

"She asked to use the bathroom but took off down the street instead, Papa."

"I only went to the corner to see the man with the monkey," Daisy says.

"But you didn't tell me. You just disappeared. I was frantic and worried. Anything could have happened to you. Tamara was worried too."

Daisy bolts out of her father's arms and pushes me.

"Oh, yeah. Tamara, Tamara. You're not even getting any money to teach my dance class, but I guess taking private ballet lessons from her is all you need to be a perfect ballerina."

"What is she talking about, Violet Pearl?"

"Aren't you concerned that she ran off alone again?"

"Not as much as you not getting paid for your efforts for a class you shouldn't be teaching."

I glare at Daisy for tattling on me. "Tamara is helping me prepare for the auditions at the School for American Ballet after graduation."

"You will stop talking nonsense immediately. Do you hear me?" he shouts.

Daisy covers her mouth and giggles. "Papa, I'm hungry."

"I made some biscuits. Go and get one, Honey. We'll be right there."

I wait until Daisy's in the kitchen. "Papa. I want to be a ballet dancer. Please give me your blessing. That's all I want."

"You can't make any money doing that. I know so many wealthy people who have connections to the film industry. All you need to do is graduate from high school, and the opportunities for you to be a rising starlet will happen."

"No. You can't make me do that. You won't; I tell you."

"I'll pay Tamara a visit tomorrow and tell her you are finished as a dancer. Daisy can learn to play the clarinet instead of dancing around in a hideous tutu."

I melt into a heap onto the Oriental rug and cry in pain of losing the dream that was almost a reality.

"Your mother pushed and pushed this dance thing. She went overboard with it, dressing you up in revolting costumes. It's her fault that you want to do this."

I look up at him as if he were a total stranger. "My mama loved me more than you ever will."

Glaring at me like he was ready to strike, "Supper's ready. Time to eat, Violet Pearl."

He turns away and goes into the kitchen. I'm left alone in tears and with a shattered heart.

I flee to the safety of my bedroom. My stomach's permanently dotted with anxiety.

"Ah, ha. Once again, I'm right here to comfort you, dear Violet. Wipe away those tears and trust me." The creepy voice of the keeper murmurs in my ear.

"If you're so great, why would you choose the likes of me?"

"I do not see what you are. I see what you can be."

"Oh, as if you can fill my mind with peace and my heart with joy?"

"Be still. Be quiet. For perfect reception, listen."

"This is ridiculous; you're a figment of my outlandish imagination. Go away, keeper. I don't need you in my life."

"Hail Violet-full of charm and beauty." Nauseating sounds of bizarre laughter fade away.

Maybe this keeper can be the secret to the turmoil within me. My thoughts grow hot in my gut.

Looking around, I'm reminded of all the loving touches from my mother that still exist. The paintings on the wall, the pillows, and quilt on my bed. Sometimes, I imagine her brushing her hair at my dressing table and looking at herself in the mirror.

It's been an hour since the big blow up with Papa. I hope he's happier now because I'm very hungry.

As I creep down the stairs and notice no one in the parlor. Roars of laughter and my sister's piercing voice can be heard as I make my way to the kitchen. *What are they laughing at anyway?* I sit down in the chair by the door and listen.

"Daisy, your eighth birthday will be the biggest and best held in Brooklyn."

"Will we have pony rides, Papa?"

"Yes. You will. I already made arrangements with the pony man."

"Yippee. How many friends can I have over?"

"As many as you want, Daisy. How about everyone in your class?"

"There are twenty-five kids, Papa."

"That's okay. I'll rent a tent, and we'll turn the backyard into a circus."

"Balloons. Lots of Balloons. Oh, Papa can we have a clown come and do magic tricks too?"

"I already have one in mind, my sweet girl."

"Who is it, Papa?"

"The great, Violet Pearl Moretti. The best clown in the state of New York."

I frown. *Why is he doing this to me?*

Chapter 22

Late spring

It's Monday after the big party, and I'm so glad to be on my way to school. Alone.

Hooray. Poor Daisy's home sick. What a shame. Papa wants her to recover from the big circus. So ridiculous. That was two days ago.

I stop to smell the beautiful roses in front of Sergeant O'Malley's house. I left fifteen minutes earlier today in hopes of forgetting the dumb clowning event.

"You are one good clown, Violet," the sergeant shouts as he picks up the newspaper from the porch.

Startled as if caught doing something I shouldn't, I say, "Oh. Thanks, Sergeant."

"Please call me Mr. O'Malley when out of uniform, okay? My Jackie is still talking about the magnificent clown at Daisy's party. I got a glimpse of you, when I picked him up."

"Didn't he know who I was?" I ask with a disappointed heart and a smile on my face.

"No. I had to tell him. He keeps talking about it. You looked like you really enjoyed dressing up like that. I give you credit; it must be hard to do."

If only he knew how I really felt.

"Violet Pearl, what are you going to do after graduation?" Eleanor asks as we put our belongings in our lockers. "I've been accepted into New York University for the teacher's program."

"Well, Ms. Jones has scheduled a meeting tomorrow with my father to talk over my future."

"Are you going to audition for the American Ballet Theater? I know you have been working hard for that."

I sigh and scowl. "My father won't let me. He gets very angry if I mention it, Eleanor."

"What are you going to do?"

"Business school. Yep. I'll be sitting at a desk for the rest of my life, I guess."

We, of The Record staff, feel very sad about Dr. Rogaland's retirement. With his helpful advice behind us, we are inspired to carry on our efforts to make this paper befitting the school it represents, and one of which he may be proud. The senior class passes the baton on to the juniors.

Submitted by: Violet Pearl Moretti, Senior Class President

Good. My last article for the school newspaper will be published on Friday. I should have written a topic like, *what do you really want to do after graduation?*

I can't believe that the senior dance is this Saturday and Graduation is a week from Friday. I must keep reminding myself that a high-school diploma is a gateway to a successful life.

Who will I ask to the dance? Some of the girls are going together because they don't know any fellas. I have someone in mind to escort me. He probably isn't the best choice.

Good thing Eleanor is staying over tonight. We must finalize plans for decorations and refreshments. I'll talk to her about my idea for a date.

"Hi, Violet. Are you and your father still meeting with me tomorrow?" Asks Ms. Jones as I walk into my English class. She looks so radiant today with her hair curled and dressed in a dark blue suit.

"Um, yes. Four o'clock, right?" I shiver at the thought.

It'll be nifty spending some time with Tamara today without my demanding sister. I know she'll add an extra fifteen minutes to my private session. Dancing on pointe is getting easier, now that I learned how to pack more cotton in the toe section of the shoes. Last week, Tamara remarked how I have improved in the gracefulness category and that I will be more than ready for the audition on July 1. It should be a piece of cake convincing Papa that ballet is the core of my being. I plan on going to the dance studio after graduation every day to practice. It's seems like such a good plan.

I step into the studio. "Tamara? Are you here?"

"I'm in here, Violet." Tamara calls out in a quivering voice.

Something's wrong. I drop my bag under the office desk and sprint toward her studio. A masculine voice can be heard at this point and then a giggle I can recognize almost anywhere.

I stop dead in my tracks as I investigate the room from the threshold. Tamara is sniffling with a hankie in her hand, Daisy's twirling as she looks at herself in the mirror, and my father is pacing with a dreadfully angry look. I freeze in place.

I really want to run away forever.

"Violet Pearl Moretti. Come in here and sit, this instant!" Papa shouts, waving his finger.

"Yes, Papa." I walk with fear and trepidation and sit next to Tamara.

Daisy spins her way over to me. "Ha, ha. Violet's in trouble."

My frown deepens. "I thought you were sick."

"Precious one," Papa says to Daisy. "I want you to go sit on the floor over there and look at the picture books. Here's a treat for you too." Papa pulls a small paper bag out of his pocket.

Daisy unwraps it. "Goody. Licorice. My favorite. I love you, Papa." She skips over to her little corner.

Sniffling, Tamara starts to speak. "Please, Berto, try to understand what I am saying here. Violet's a fast learner, very talented, and she yearns to be a ballerina."

"Her talents are to be used to entertain people through live theater or on the big screen. She has what it takes to be a star."

"What does she want? Did you ever ask her, Berto?"

"It doesn't matter what she wants. I know what's best."

Now, the adrenaline is bubbling inside of me, and I can feel my heart pounding faster than usual. I jump to my feet and stand face-to-face with my father. "If my mother were here right now, she would want me to pursue my dream."

"Don't bring your dear mother into this; do you hear me?" He scowls.

Tamara gets up and puts her arm around my waist. "Berto, she will make you proud one day when she glides across the stage of the great Metropolitan Opera House."

He stamps his foot and grabs a hold of my arm. "Tamara, this is not your concern."

He turns back toward me. "You will not embarrass me. I have several auditions lined up for you after graduation. Important people are expecting you on July 1, and you will be there."

I pull away from him. "You cannot make me. I will run away and live with Aunt Flossie."

"You wouldn't do that. Your sister needs you."

"I don't care. You will not destroy my dream of becoming a ballerina." I burst into tears, run out of the door, and plunge into Tamara's office chair.

Tamara follows and stands behind me. She starts to massage the back of my neck.

With Daisy in tow, Papa stands in front of us with disappointment written all over his face. "I'm anxious to see what Miss Jones has to say at our meeting tomorrow. I'm sure she will sympathize with me and put you in the right direction, young lady. Right now, I'm tired and hungry. Come on, Daisy."

I drop my head on top of my hands, lean on the desk, and cry hysterically for as long as the tears flow from my heart.

"Father in Heaven. Please visit my young friend and heal the hurt in her heart. Amen!" Tamara softly says.

Does she really believe God can hear her?

Eleanor is the only reason I'm going home tonight and not getting on the next train to Aunt Flossie's house. Ever since the Marty episode, we are best of friends. We have a bond that no one can sever, and I know this will continue for a very long time. Besides, the keeper won't show up if I have company.

I sure hope Papa has calmed down and that supper's ready to go on the table.

Okay, Violet, bury the deep wounds and cover them up once again. Joke around. Make them laugh. Remember, you're a clown.

Things must be relatively normal because the aroma of onions, garlic, and beef lingers throughout the house as soon as I open the door. I know from experience that Papa cooks only when he's in a good mood. I run up the stairs to the bathroom and check my hair and slap cold water on my face. My little porcelain clock reads 6:30 on the dot. Eleanor should be here any minute. I grab two blankets out of the hope chest in my father's room and proceed to make a bed on the floor in my room for my friend and me.

Back downstairs, I check out the records for something fun and fast. *Piano Rag Music*, by Igor Stravinsky. This will do the trick.

"Where is your sister, Daisy?" I hear Eleanor say from the kitchen.

"I don't know," Daisy says.

I burst through the door. "Eleanor, you're here. What time did you come?"

Papa spoons the smothering beef and onions on top of slices of homemade bread and serves each of us.

"I was sitting on my front steps waiting for you, Violet. Your dad and Daisy saw me, and they asked me to come inside. This looks so good, Mr. Moretti."

"I hope it tastes as good as it looks," he remarks as he sits down.

The conversation around the supper table is light and steady. Eleanor shares a full description of her dress for the senior dance and how she'll wear her hair in full detail.

"Violet, what does your dress look like? I hope you will model it for me tonight." Eleanor says as she takes another bite of her supper.

I need to avoid the question. "This was delicious, Papa."

"You girls must have been famished. There are no leftovers. Don't worry about the dishes. Go ahead and plan your dance." Papa smiles.

What a switch he's made.

The three of us dance to beat the band and then play a round of Chinese checkers.

"Okay, Daisy girl, time for bed." I say as I put the game away.

"Do I have to?"

"Yes, you do. You know how early you get up in the morning?"

"Yeah, I know. Before the roosters." She giggles.

Turning the little lamp out, I say, "Good night, Daisy."

"Are you both going to bed now too?"

"In a little while," I respond. "See you in the morning."

Clutching her tattered teddy bear, she closes her eyes and is fast asleep by the time we get to her bedroom door.

In my room for the night with the door closed, Eleanor speaks softly. "Your father didn't say one word about you or what happened at the dance studio, Violet. He did ask me what I was going to do after graduation, though."

"He was so angry. He will never let me fulfill my dream of becoming a ballet dancer."

Hearing the floorboard's creak, I put one finger to my mouth. "Shush." I point to the door.

"Girls. Don't stay up all night," Papa's voice whispers through the door.

Hearing his bedroom door click shut, Eleanor leans close to me. "Miss Jones will set him straight tomorrow, Vi. Don't worry."

"She wants me to ditch the ballet thing too and go to business school in Manhattan instead."

"Well if it were me, I would go with the business-school concept because the film-star idea is absurd. You can pursue your ballet dream during spare time."

"You might be right, my friend."

"Relax. Lets' talk about the color scheme for the dance now."

"Let's pull aside the junior-class decorating committee at lunch tomorrow. Purple and green streamers and tons of white balloons through-out the gymnasium. The PTA mothers offered to bake and decorate cakes. Should we serve any other food?" Eleanor asks.

"The senior class has forty dollars in slush money. We might as well spend it on nuts, mints, punch, and a few door prizes."

"Who did you ask to the dance, Violet?"

"No one. How about you?"

"Harry Whitaker is my date. Don't get any ideas. We're just friends."

"Actually, I do have someone in mind."

"Do tell me."

"Promise you won't scream at me?"

"Please tell me. The suspense is killing me."

That warm cozy feeling from within comes alive, as I fan myself from the hot flashes, "I'm thinking about asking Marty."

Eleanor's wide-open mouth and bigger-than-life eyes are priceless as I turn off the light by my bed.

Chapter 23

Everyone is buzzing about the upcoming dance. I'm ashamed to tell anyone that I still don't have a dress. I won't ask Papa for any money because he's always complaining we barely have enough to pay the bills. My job at Woolworths is strictly for incidentals for Daisy and me. *Never anything left over.*

All the final exams are scheduled for Monday and Tuesday of next week, but no one is interested in studying. The day is rolling by so quickly.

The bell rings out loudly in the hallway. Lunchtime already. Good ole Eleanor quickly gathers the junior girls at a cafeteria table for our mini decorating-committee meeting.

"You two oversee the balloons." I say to Teresa and Gladys.

"Jacqueline, will you hand out roses to the escorts?"

"Sure, Violet."

Everything is delegated by the time the bell rings for the next class. *Senior dance, here we come!*

Two hours later, I find myself sitting in the hall outside Miss Jones's office.

Glancing at the front door to the school, I see Papa enter. At that precise moment, Miss Jones opens her door. My vision's a blur as I see Papa enter the main door. *I don't think I can survive this meeting.*

"You can come in now, Violet."

I sit down, facing her desk, trying to speculate on what's about to happen.

"Hello, Mr. Moretti. How are you today?" Miss Jones asks.

"Fine, thank you."

"Please sit down, Sir."

I meet with all graduates and their parents at this time every year, Mr. Moretti. I like my students to have a well-thought-out game plan of what they're going to do after commencement."

"I want my daughter to be an actress on the big stage and eventually the silver screen. I have connections, and I know many influential people." Papa says with wrinkled brow.

"Yes, she told me. Have you asked her what she would like to do?"

Looking at me and back to Miss Jones, he replied, "She has a crazy idea of being a ballerina."

"Violet loves to dance. She told me that she has been preparing to audition for the first ballet company in New York City."

"I didn't come here to listen to this garbage, Miss Jones."

"Calm down, Sir. Violet knows that I have a productive idea that will provide a more lucrative future."

"And what might that be?"

"Your daughter's very intelligent and is at the top of her class in typewriting and diction. She would do well in business school after she graduates."

Papa bolts to a stance. "That's even worse than being a ballerina. My daughter was born to be an actress. That's it."

"But, Mr. Moretti. Violet does have a say in this. She's almost eighteen."

Turning to the door, he looks back. "This meeting is over, Miss Jones. Let's go, Violet."

"Papa. Miss Jones is right. Business school is a good idea. It's only a six-month course, and I will be placed as a secretary right away." *Did I really say that?*

"You are looney, daughter. In other words, you would give up this whacky idea of being a ballerina for sitting at a desk?"

I drop my head in disillusionment. "Yes, Papa. I would."

"Tsk. Tsk. I'll see you next week at graduation, Miss Jones." He turns on his heels and leaves the room without me.

"He'll never agree with anything I do." Overwhelming tears drench my face.

Miss Jones gives me a clean handkerchief. "Take all the time you need, dear. Why do you think he treats you so unfairly, Violet? I shouldn't say this, but he doesn't seem to be a very happy man."

Grasping hold of the pink pearl necklace he gave me for my thirteenth birthday, I look down at my lap. "He changed after my mother died."

"I'm so sorry dear. When did you lose your mother?"

"On my thirteenth birthday." I pick up my head and stare out the window in a complete daze as if lost in my own world.

I'm a big fat nothing. All my friends are bubbling over with excitement about the dance in four days, graduation, and college. They all have loving, caring parents who encourage them with plans to move forward. I can hardly open my eyes because they are burning so bad. "Violet, I have to go home. Are you coming?" Miss Jones gently touches my shoulder and startles me."

Getting up, I slowly follow her down the hall and out of the front door.

"I can see you to your house, if you think it's necessary," Miss Jones offers.

"That's okay, Miss Jones. I'm going to stop at Tamara's for a few minutes. She wants to know how things went today at the meeting." I force a smile.

"It was terrible, Tamara. Plain awful I tell you."

"Isn't Miss Jones on your side, Violet?"

"She is, and she isn't. She thinks ballet can be something I can do for fun but not for a career. Miss Jones is actually pushing a six-month course at a business school in Manhattan."

"How did Berto take that?"

"He had an anger attack again and was beyond reasoning."

The waterworks start oozing out of my bloodshot eyes. "It's hard for me to be in the same room as him these days."

"If things were different, I would invite you to move in with me."

I look at her, my interest piqued. "I'm eighteen, Tamara. I can move out and move in with you."

"I have to tell you something that I have been putting off for too long." She grabs my hands in hers and intensely looks at me.

"You can tell me anything. You know that, right?"

She puts her head down and squeezes my hands. "I have to close the dance school, Violet."

Pulling my hands out of hers. "What? No. You can't." *My whole world is caving in.*

"Two dancers from the company want me to share a flat in Greenwich Village with them."

"I can keep the school going for you, Tamara. I know how to do most everything now."

"Thank you, Violet, but my mind's already made up."

I have a pounding headache when I get off the bus and start walking home. I feel like a washed and weathered piece of driftwood buried in wet beach sand. I haven't eaten since this morning and that was just an apple. The funny thing is, I'm not the least bit hungry.

I open the front door; I look to see if anyone's in the parlor waiting for me. No one. Good.

I sprint up the stairs, avoiding the steps with the creaks. Quickly, I use the lavatory and slip into my room, my exclusive sanctuary. My room's the only one in the house that has a door that locks from the inside.

"Petunia, my pet. I'm so glad you are here with me." I whisper as I lie down on my bed with my furry friend.

I read a little and then draw a little, wondering the whole time why someone doesn't come looking for me? The dance is in four days and I don't have a dress or date. I might as well stay in my room because no one will miss me.

Then I hear the stairs creak as someone comes up.

"Her door is closed, Papa. She must be in there," Daisy calls out.

A firm knock sounds on the door. "Violet Pearl. Are you in there?" Papa shouts through the door.

I don't want to see him or talk to him. He doesn't care how I feel at all.

He fiddles with the doorknob. "Violet, I know you're in there. Answer me!" He shouts.

I roll over on my bed and stare out of the window. Petunia repositions herself at the foot of the bed. Anger rises inside of me.

He bangs on the door with a fist. "Come out of there, this instant. Miss Jones called to see if you're alright. She said you probably went to see Tamara."

My thoughts are my own, but it would be nice if I could share with an understanding parent. I hear nothing in the hallway. Good. Silence drowns the space between us.

I toss and turn. The sweat drenches me from head to toe. There's no way my life could get any worse.

"Maybe, you should do what your father wants. Go for those auditions; I'll make you a star." Moans the keeper.

Breathe. Just breathe, Violet.

"I know you can hear me, my dear. Don't be frightened. I'm here to help, not hurt." The keeper whispers.

My stomach flip-flops. "Leave me alone." I snarl.

"Now, now. Is that any way to treat a friend?"

My cheeks are burning. "Stop it. Stop it. That's enough, and by the way, you're not my friend."

"You can't get rid of me, no matter how hard you try."

I leap off the bed and start swinging my pillow. "Get out of here, you creep." I scream.

Loud banging on the door startles me. "Violet. Who are you talking to? Let me in." Papa says.

The last time, I looked at my clock, it said 11:30 p.m. It's 7:00 a.m. now. I roll over and pull the quilt over my head.

T he doorknob jiggles. "Vi-Vi, let me in. It's time to get ready for school." Daisy calls through the door.

I have no intention of going to school today or tomorrow, for that matter.

Come on, Daisy. I'll walk you to school today. Your sister needs a day at home," Papa says.

As time moves on, I manage to go to the bathroom, let the cat out-side, and crawl back in bed as a routine for two days. I sleep most of the time and stay in the same clothes.

On the second day, about 5:00 in the afternoon, a knock sounds on my door. "

Violet. It's Eleanor. The dance is the day after tomorrow. Let me in."

"Go away."

A little while later, I hear creaks on the stairs again. "Violet Pearl, you have to come out of that room." Papa pleads.

"Leave me alone." A wave of sadness and rage washes over me.

"You haven't eaten anything in days. You'll get sick."

"Not hungry."

The night rolls into the next day, but I only leave my bedroom when I know Papa and Daisy are gone. Sometimes, I stand on my chair and peek out of the window and watch my father and Daisy leave in the morning. If the house is unusually quiet, I venture out into the hall, peer down the stairs, run in the bathroom, and then quick as a fox I'm back in my bedroom with the door locked.

I stare at my mother's picture. "Mama, you look so happy in this photograph. What went wrong with you?"

I doze off thinking how much I miss her.

A sound on my door the next afternoon startles me. "Violet. Open the door. It's your aunt Flossie."

"What do you want?" I'm hiding because I'm still broken.

"You, honey. It's you I want."

"Where's my father and Daisy? I'm not coming out if they are still in the house."

"They're gone for the day. Your papa called me last night and told me about the argument you two had. He's very worried about you."

"He doesn't care about me at all. I don't even know why he called you."

"Everyone at school is concerned, and Miss Jones has been calling here twice a day."

Reluctantly, I throw the quilt off me and get out of the bed.

"Violet, I love you. Let me help you."

I turn the lock and open the door. Auntie grabs hold of me for a long time while I bawl my eyes out. No words are exchanged, but peace starts ascending through me like a quiet stream flowing gently through the woods.

"Here, my dear, is a new handkerchief just for you. I know how you love to collect them."

I smile for a moment as I study the colorful embroidery that forms an intricate design on the white cloth. "Thank you, Auntie. This is beautiful."

"You're so much like your mother, you know. I'll always be here for you; I hope you know that."

"I know, Auntie."

"Now, take a bath. You smell a little ripe. Then get dressed. We're going shopping."

"What about this messy room?"

"I'll take care of it while you are getting ready, alright?"

Out of nowhere, I get a spurt of energy, grab my robe, and head to the bathroom. I was able to find a few drops of lavender and drop them into the bath water. I stare at myself in the small mirror over the sink while the bathtub slowly fills. After two days in bed, my hair is a knotty mess. I pick up the nearest hairbrush and start grooming small sections.

"Violet, are you okay in there?" Auntie calls through the door.

I turn to answer her and see that the water in the tub is at the top. "Yes. Everything is fantastic." I step into the tub and sink down to my chin, as the water splashes all over the floor. My outlook on life seems to be returning to normal.

There are sales all over the place in Gimbel's department store. I don't see anyone in shabby clothes in this store. Auntie grabs my hand and directs me to a counter that displays several bottles of fragrances. She takes the top off one of them and sniffs.

It's nice. Here, Toots, smell this."

I bring the decanter up to my nose. "What's that? It's familiar."

That's gardenia. Your mother's favorite."

"Can I help you?" the clerk asks from behind the counter.

I place the container back on the counter and step back because there's no way I can afford this.

"How much is the perfume?" Auntie asks the clerk.

"It's fifty percent off today. I can sell it to you for three dollars."

Auntie looks back at me. "Do you like it, Violet?"

"Yes, but—"

"We'll take it. Wrap it up." Auntie hands the clerk the money.

We walk into the ladies' dress department on the second floor where the dresses are all color coordinated and hanging neatly in order on the racks. I whirl in every direction in awe of what I see. A small piece of lavender chiffon catches my eye, so I push the other dresses aside to be able to get a full look at it. It's a dress fit for a goddess. The dress is gathered at the waist with a thin rhinestone belt. I don't dare look at the price tag.

I turn to walk away; then all at once, Auntie's pulling the dress from the rack. "You have been looking at this for over ten minutes now. Let's see what size it is."

"It's too expensive, Auntie. Let's go to the worn-a-bit store."

"Hush, child. It is a size ten. Try it on."

I take the dress into the dressing room and hang it up next to the mirror. I smile at it as I undress and wonder if I can find something like it in a used clothing store.

"Come out and let me see it on you," Auntie calls.

"It's too expensive, Auntie," I say as I look in the full-length mirror by the cash register.

"You look absolutely beautiful in that color, honey," the clerk says with a smile.

I smile and twirl. All at once, I'm turning several pirouettes.

"You must be one of those ballet dancers from the American Ballet Theater." A lady comments as she steps out of the dressing room.

I freeze in first position, my heart suddenly crushed. "No, I'm not, Ma'am."

"My niece is graduating from high school next week," Auntie announces. "And her senior dance is tomorrow night. Go change, Violet Pearl. You have yourself a dress."

"Oh, Auntie," I squeal. "I'll pay you back. I promise. I never thought I would have a dress like this. Thank you. Can we have lunch at Horn and Hard art? I have lots of nickels in my purse to put in the slots."

"Of course, we can, but you don't have to pay me back. Consider this a part of your graduation present." Auntie says, looking at her watch.

Everything is falling into place. I can't wait to see the reactions of my friends when they see me tomorrow night in my exquisite dress. I sure have the best aunt ever.

Oh, goodness. Marty probably has other plans now. I'll have to make my grand entrance alone. I'm not good at letting go and moving onward.

Chapter 24

I'm so glad Auntie offered to meet Daisy at school and take my packages back to our house because I must be at Woolworths in exactly twenty minutes. The train coming out of the city this time of day is overcrowded with people getting out of work and boarding at various stops along the way. I'm lucky to have this seat so I don't have to stand and hold on to those nasty steel poles.

Who knows where those hands have been? Ugh. That fella sneezed into his hand and then grabbed the pole. Sickening.

It doesn't look like Marty's working tonight because Joseph's behind the lunch counter.

"Hi, Violet. Are you feeling better?" Asks Mary Sue as I lock my handbag in my locker.

"A lot better. Thanks for asking. My aunt took me out shopping today, and she bought me a dress for the dance. I'm so excited."

"Who are you going with? Please tell."

"No date yet. Might go alone."

"I know lots of fellas who would love to go with you, Violet. The dance is tomorrow, right?"

"Girls, the customers are waiting for your assistance," Mr. Hamilton says firmly.

Both of us walk swiftly on the squeaky hardwood floors to our designated areas. "See ya later, alligator," I say to Mary Sue as we head in opposite directions.

Tonight, I'm working in the hair-accessory department unloading bobby pins, scarves, barrettes, and bows from a huge cardboard box. I pull out a lavender silk bow and stare at it longingly because it will go marvelously with my dress.

Looking up for a second, I see the boss looking right at me.

I get engrossed in my work. Okay, the Bobbies are done.

"Do you need help?" Marty says from behind me.

"You scared me."

"Sorry, but you look frustrated, Violet."

"I didn't think you were working tonight. Joseph's at the lunch counter."

"I'm not. Came in for my paycheck."

My knees turn wiggly. "Um, are you busy tomorrow night?"

"Saturday night? Mary Sue's having some friends over for a get together. Are you coming?"

"No, it's my senior dance at school."

"I bet you're going with some college hunk from St. John's University."

"Not exactly."

"Customers, our Woolworths store will be closing in twenty-five minutes," Mr. Hamilton's voice rings over the loudspeaker.

"I better get going, Violet. I don't want to keep you from your work. That box better be empty before you leave tonight." Marty does his best impression of Mr. Hamilton. He turns toward the aisle to the front door. "See you next week."

Not realizing the consequences, I dart after him. "Marty. Wait."

"Whoa. What's the matter, girl?"

Looking everywhere but into his eyes, I conjure up my nerve. "Um, um. I was wondering if you could escort me to the dance." My cheeks are flaming.

"You're kidding, right?" He laughs loudly. "A few weeks ago, you hated me.""Miss Moretti. This box is not empty yet?" My boss looks at me and then at Marty.

"Hey, Violet. I'll meet you outside after you get off work, okay?" Marty calls out as he leaves.

I smile at my boss, "Sorry, Sir."

"You have called in sick a lot lately and slacking off on the job here too. I need good, dependable employees."

"I promise to get this box emptied before I leave."

"This is your last warning, Miss Moretti."

The lights in the back of the store go out one at a time. The last customer is at the cash register checking out her goods. My heart pounds rapidly as I complete the last batch of barrettes.

"Violet. Are you almost done?" Mary Sue asks on her way to get her belongings.

"I'm coming."

We step out into the brisk windy night.

"What are you doing here, Marty?" Mary Sue asks.

"Waiting for Violet."

She looks at me and him. "Leave her alone."

I gently take her arm and pull her aside. "Mary Sue. It's okay. Really it is."

"I'm not leaving you alone with him." She stands near the newsstand and glares at us.

"Fine. So, Marty, do you want to take me to the dance tomorrow?"

"Wait a minute!" Mary Sue shouts "No. No. No. That's not going to happen!"

Marty grabs my hand and looks at me with a sincerity I never saw before. "I'll consider it an honor to go with you, Violet. What time should I pick you up?"

"Actually, could you meet me at the door? A lot of the girls know what happened at Eleanor's party. So, there will be gossip."

"Of course, I understand."

"My father's band is the entertainment, and I know he'll want to meet you."

"Uh oh. He'll probably want to bring me outside and shoot me."

"He doesn't know anything about that night, Marty. Don't worry."

"I'm real glad about that. What time should I meet you?"

"Six thirty on the front steps. Oh, and don't forget the corsage."

He smiles as he runs to the corner to catch his bus. "See you then."

I start walking while Mary Sue catches up with me. "Are you serious, Violet? I would think you'd want nothing to do with him after what he did to you at Eleanor's party."

"He apologized, Mary Sue. He has been so nice since then. I won't let myself be alone with him, so don't worry."

"You'll be the talk of the whole dance, Violet. I hope you know what you're doing."

Chapter 25

"You look beautiful Vi-Vi, but I think you should wear your hair down with this black velvet headband." Daisy says.

"Do you like this color on me, Daisy?" I take the headband and put it around my hair. "This does work."

"I love lavender on you, Sissy. Wasn't it Mama's favorite color?"

"It was. Now, you better run and get ready to go. Papa wants us downstairs at six."

Daisy bolts out of my door to her room. I can hear dresser drawers slam shut and hangers falling on the wood floor. I giggle and shake my head as I put on the silver strappy shoes that Auntie bought me yesterday. I'm not sure what I'm feeling, but I sure like it.

"Girls, we have to leave in ten minutes." Papa calls out from the bottom of the stairs.

I apply a little lipstick, dab on some rouge, and grab Mama's silver purse. Glancing in the mirror for one last look, I realize I need something around my neck. It looks so bare.

"Come on, Sissy. We have to go." Daisy pokes her head in the doorway.

Standing up, I walk to the small jewelry box on top of my dresser and open it. I pull out the pink pearl necklace that Papa gave me on my thirteenth birthday. I secure it around my neck. Perfect.

Marvin's rich uncle let his nephew borrow the Ford Tudor to take all of us across Brooklyn. The vehicle is big enough to carry six people, an accordion, a guitar, a saxophone, and a set of bongo drums. Good thing the school has a piano. The janitor moved it from the auditorium to the gymnasium yesterday.

The gymnasium looks enchanting with white balloons tied in clusters everywhere. Tables are covered with white tablecloths. Small bouquets of purple lilies complimented by green ferns form perfect centerpieces.

I'm feeling a bit guilty because I didn't lift a finger to help the committee do any of this.

"You look ravishing, Violet Pearl," Miss Jones tells me. "The color is perfect for you."

She looks lovely in her cobalt beaded gown and is accompanied by a tall, handsome gentleman with jet-black hair.

"Thank you, Miss Jones."

"This is Doctor Adam Carney."

We shake hands. "Nice meeting you. My name is Violet Moretti."

He smiles and nods.

The band starts tuning up as a few girls and two couples enter the room and scope out where they should sit. I look up at the big clock on the wall, and my heart jumps when I realize it is 6:25 p.m. I try not to be too conspicuous, so I walk slowly but fast enough to allow the chiffon of my dress to flow. Two juniors are sitting at the ticket table, and several couples are patiently standing in line as I pass them and proceed out of the front door.

Where's Marty? He should have been here by now.

I'm feeling like a fish out of water. People are staring at me, probably wondering why I'm dateless. I might as well go back inside. He'll probably stand me up.

Turning to go in the school, I hear a loud unflawed whistle.

"You who! Violet Moretti!" Marty yells.

I blush as I turn and spot him standing by the old oak tree next to the Girls High School sign. As I go down the steps toward him, my knees go weak when I see him.

How handsome he looks. My skin tingles, and I rub my arm.

He pulls out a small box from behind him. "This is for you, pretty lady." I open the box and remove a white orchid corsage. "This is beautiful, Marty. Thank you so much."

"Let me do the honors." He delicately pins it to my dress.

We walk hand in hand up the front stairs and into the foyer. A few girls turn and stare at us as we walk to the gymnasium.

"I can't believe Violet is with that creep, Marty; can you, May?" Sam whispers loudly to his date.

"Sam. Shush. He's only an escort, not her boyfriend," she whispers back.

"I want you to meet my father, the band, and my sister," I say, ignoring the whispers. "Okay, Marty?"

"No time like the present. We're certainly the talk of the night already."

I take him by the arm and lead him to the stage. "Papa, this is my friend Marty."

Reaching out his hand and shaking it, Papa smiles. "Nice to meet you, Marty. I hope you kids are planning on cutting the rug tonight."

Daisy scampers off the stage and steps between us. "Hi, I'm Daisy."

Marty politely bows to her. "Daisy. I like that name. Please save a dance for me, okay?"

Daisy giggles and grabs Marty's hand. "I'll introduce you to the rest of The Domino Four."

Eleanor appears out of nowhere and pulls me into the locker room. "Violet, what are you doing? Marty? I thought you were kidding about asking him. Everyone is talking about you two and what went on at my party."

"Eleanor, it's not what you think. He apologized. We're just friends."

She raises an eyebrow. "Even the guys are mumbling about what a jerk he is."

"The dance is going to start. I must go and welcome everyone. Don't worry about me."

I leave her standing there and make my way to the stage where Papa hands me a microphone.

"I would like to welcome everyone to Girl's High School of Brooklyn Senior Dance. It's so nice to see all my classmates in attendance for this special occasion. In one week, we will be utilizing this room for our graduation, where we will bid farewell to our beloved alma mater. Now, without further ado, I would like to introduce tonight's entertainment, The Domino Four."

Loud applause and cheers rock the whole place. Marty's waiting for me as I step down from the stage. Taking my hand, he says, "Nice job, Violet. It shouldn't be too hard to find a table to sit at since you're so popular."

Looking up, I realize that all eyes are on us. I spot two seats at an empty table in a far corner.

I lead him away from the center of attention.

As the enchanted evening rolls on, folks realize how nice Marty really is. He's so polite to everyone, and dancing with Daisy made him look like a shining knight. She certainly thinks he is.

I don't know all my classmates' dates, which is not unusual for an all girls' school. A few of them look like men instead of boys.

I feel an urge to exit quickly to the girl's room after several glasses of punch, two slices of spice cake, and a few jitterbugs. "I'll be right back, Marty."

The hallway is dimly lit as I make my way to the rest room. Two giggly girls burst out the door almost hitting me. "Sorry, Violet," they say simultaneously.

"That's okay," I call out to them as the door closes.

I hear the door open and close as I am doing my business in the stall. I wonder why I don't hear any voices or running water. I take care of myself, flush the toilet, and unhook the latch.

Upon opening the door, I realize that I'm not alone.

"Is there someone in here?" I can't see beyond the four stalls because there's a small alcove there.

I go to the sink to wash my hands and dry them on the clean hand towel.

I must be imagining things again.

I look in the mirror and see two men standing a few feet behind me.

"Pretty girl. How about a little fun right here, right now?" One says as he steps closer.

I scream and bolt to the door. The second guy steps in front of me and pushes me down.

"Aww. Didn't mean to do that," he says as he reaches out his hand.

The dark-haired one laughs obnoxiously. "She's right where I want her." He starts unfastening his belt.

I start crawling away, but he grabs my legs and pushes me down, so I'm flat on my back. I open my mouth to scream but he stops me with his hand. He starts to push my legs apart with one hand, but I manage to exert all my energy and give him a swift kick.

He doubles over. "You're a bad girl. I like that."

I pull myself to my feet, leap toward the door, and let out a blood-curdling scream. Then I kick the guy standing in front of the door, and much to my surprise, I manage to get him right in the shins, and he falls to the floor. I fling the door open and fly right into Marty's arms.

"Let me at her!" yells one of the hoodlums.

Marty stands in front of me. "Don't lay a hand on my girl, you big brute."

The second blockhead appears. "Come on, Billy. Let's get out of here before they call the cops."

154

"I was just trying to have a little fun. What are you going to do? Call your mommy?" The one called Billy laughs.

Marty pulls his fists together. "I can knock you down, see?"

The janitor comes running down the hall, waving a metal snow shovel in his hands. "Are you alright, Miss Moretti? I thought I heard screaming."

I nod as I hold back the tears. I might be smiling, but on the inside, I'm in agony.

My screams must have been loud enough because several couples are congregating here.

The two sinister men try to weasel their way out, but the crowd forms a tight circle, so they can't escape.

"Will someone get Violet's father?" Marty yells.

The janitor hands the shovel to May's date. "Whack them with this shovel if they try to take one step."

He disappears around the corner.

I'm trying hard to keep my emotions private, but they are burning inside of me like a volcano waiting to erupt…. I'm not a very strong person, so where in the world did the strength come from I used moments ago? I could have been raped.

Miss Jones and Mrs. Barker, the school principal, followed by Papa make their way through the throng of onlookers.

"Violet, what happened?" Papa asks as he moves closer to Marty and me.

"Marty saved me from these ugly men, Papa."

"What's going on here?" Mrs. Barker asks as she glares at the two men.

"These men tried to molest Violet in the girl's bathroom, Mrs. Barker. She was able to break away from them," May says.

Mrs. Barker steps in front of the creeps, "You're no longer welcome here."

Billy laughs louder than before. "We won't leave without our dates. We'll have our time with them instead."

"Oh no, you won't!" Miss Jones said, narrowing her eyes at them. "We'll see to it that they get home safely and that their parents are told all about how awful you two are."

The man called Billy turns and eyes Miss Jones up and down.

"Okay. Break it up, folks. Step aside. What's the problem here?" A harsh voice shouts from outside the ring of people.

The flock of onlookers moves apart in perfect unison to create a visible path to the front door. Three policemen dressed in dark-blue uniforms with matching caps move in perfect formation and stand directly in front of the hooligans.

"You two again, huh? It seems like you were at the Brooklyn High School ball last week, hitting on a girl who was sitting by herself. I think a little jail time is right up your alley. Handcuff them. The paddy wagon's waiting."

Everyone applauds and shouts hooray as the law takes the bad guys into custody.

I'm bewildered as to what just happened, but Marty is still has his arm around me, and that comforts me more than I can say.

"Okay, students, let's go back in the gymnasium and try to have some fun," Mrs. Barker says.

Papa stops us before we could follow the crowd into the gym. "Wait, kids. I have something to say." A strange feeling takes over me.

Marty looks at me with concern and then to Papa. "Can it wait, Mr. Moretti? I think Violet needs to dance a bit to help forget the gruesome experience."

"I want to thank you, Marty, for being right there for my daughter tonight. I don't know what would have happened if she ran out into an empty hall."

"You're welcome, Sir. Violet's very special to me. I hope I have your permission to see her again."

Papa smiles. "Why don't you come for dinner tomorrow night, son?"

Chapter 26

A few days have passed, and I've been extremely busy finishing my final exams and practicing ballet techniques for the pending audition. I only have a small window of time to use Tamara's studio, so I might as well take advantage of it. Of course, spending time with my boyfriend, Marty, seems to crop up someplace. He turned out to be a real gem. My senior dance could have been a horrific experience if Marty wasn't there to rescue me. Papa loves him, and that's even better. Maybe, Papa will mellow out about my ballet dream. A smile fills my face when I think about it.

When graduation day arrives, the weather can't be more perfect. The sun's radiating against a cloudless blue sky, and there's a slight breeze blowing through my window.

I place the pink pearls around my neck and pin my hair up on top of my head, leaving a few curls dangling down. With gentle care and love, I pick up Mama's white headband with the pretty white artificial rose attached to it and secure it around my fashionable do.

I have a part of her with me today. A jolt of happiness races up my spine.

I take the white eyelet cotton dress with flowing capelike sleeves off the hanger and slip it over my head.

I feel a rush of cold air behind me. "Ah, your beauty always amazes me, dear one."

"Not real. Not real. Not real." I flee to the door.

"I may not control you totally yet, but I know you'll follow my lead soon."

"Are you finished, keeper?" I grin despite my fear, at the thought of things being different.

"Graduation is a must for your success. I'll leave you for now."

I suck in a ragged breath. My heart's troubled and restless. The graduating class sits behind the podium on the stage in alphabetical order.

Mrs. Barker stands and goes to the podium. "Success after graduation depends largely upon what students have achieved during the four years leading up to this special day. Our graduates have proven themselves with integrity and ambition for what lies ahead. These virtues pave the way for life outside the walls of this school. It's an honor to present to you the All Girls High School graduating class of nineteen thirty-four."

"Hip, hip, hooray," one parent shouts as he leads the audience in a massive applause. "We did it!" Everyone in the class shouts at once.

As we step down off the podium in single file, each one of us is presented with a small bouquet of red roses.

The guests continue to applaud as we make our way out on the lawn where a reception area is set up.

"Vi-Vi. Congratulations," Daisy says as she comes up from behind me.

Papa grabs me and gives me a big bear hug, and it moves me to tears of joy. "My flower, I'm so proud of you."

Still cradled by his love and acceptance, I manage to say, "Thank you, Papa."

"Here's a little something from Daisy and me." He hands me a small package wrapped in white paper adorned with a purple ribbon.

Gently unwrapping it, I open the small box. "Oh, Papa. It's beautiful." I take the dainty imitation diamond watch out of the container and snap it in place on my wrist. "Thank you. I'll always cherish it, just like my necklace." My life can't get any better than this.

"My dear niece, I'm so excited for you!" Aunt Flossie exclaims as she rushes to my side. "I can't even contain myself."

"Auntie. I'm so glad you're here." I hug her tight. "Did you see Tamara or Marty?"

"Marty's still in the foyer talking to a few fellas from his alma mater. I haven't seen Tamara at all."

Auntie looks around her and over my shoulder. "Honey, this is a very special gift for you from your aunt Flossie," she says quietly. "Please slip it inside your purse and open it when you are alone in your room."

I take the light blue envelope with hesitation. "What's the big secret?"

She hugs me, "I want you to be alone for the surprise."

After all the excitement of graduation day is over and I'm alone in my room, I take the three gifts I received and lay them in front of me on the bed. I take the watch from Papa off and place it back in the container; I slip the dainty ruby stone ring that Marty gave me off my pinkie and place the unopened envelope from Auntie Flossie face up in front of me.

What's in here?

Ripping the envelope open, I pull out two tickets and read them. *American Ballet School's presentation of Serenade at the Wahlberg Estate in White Plains New York at 2:00 on Saturday, June 29, 1934.* My heart starts to pound to a fast-arrhythmic beat as I open the light blue folded piece of paper.

My Dear Violet Pearl, Congratulations! These tickets are for you and me to enjoy the ballet together. Soon, you'll be joining them. I love you. Aunt Flossie.

A chill overcomes me, and I know the keeper is in my midst. I shudder and hide under my quilt.

"Congratulations, my dear Violet. The world is at your fingertips. I'll make you as famous as Agnes DeMille."

"You mean, you'll help me achieve my dream?"

"Peace my child. At last you're willing to listen to me. Wait and follow."

Chapter 27

"Where are you and your aunt Flossie off to today, Violet?" Papa asks on Saturday.

"Auntie and I are invited for lunch at the Felix Wahlberg Estate in Greenburg near White Plains." A little white lie never hurt anyone.

"The banker Wahlberg?"

"I think so. She met him at one of her piano concerts. They became good friends after that. We're taking the train into White Plains, and someone will pick us up there."

"Well, this may be your big chance to land a promising job when you get out of business school. The Wahlbergs have connections all over the world."

Giggling softly, I say, "Papa, you must be okay with me being a secretary?"

"Do I have a choice? Or should I rephrase that? Would I rather see you behind a desk taking shorthand for some executive on Fifth Avenue or dancing in a tutu across some stage for peanuts? I choose the desk job any day."

I shrug my shoulders as I blink away the tears. "I'll be staying at Auntie's house tonight. See you tomorrow, Papa. Love you, Daisy."

The mansion sits on a sprawling estate that covers ninety acres of beautiful property, overlooking the Hudson River. The magnificent white stone, six-story mansion stands like a proud monument in the middle of huge blue spruce pine trees.

It's a beautiful day to be outside. We follow others along the cement sidewalk which winds its way to the back of the humongous house.

A huge wood stage stands in the middle, and I count two hundred white chairs surrounding it. Three tents are on the other side of the sidewalk, across from the outdoor auditorium. *I hope I can talk to Tamara at some point today. Oh, maybe they're in that tent over there.* The sunshine's on my face, and it's warm enough to make my heart sing.

We give our tickets to one of the ushers, and she shows us to two seats, in the third row, dead center. "Oh Auntie, this is going to be spectacular. I can hardly contain myself; I'm so excited. I can't imagine how Tamara's feeling right now with only moments before her debut."

She motions for me to be quiet, with a smile on her face.

A well-dressed couple takes center stage, "Welcome everyone to the first public appearance of the ballet theater. It's exciting to host this marvelous event. We could not have asked for a better day for an outdoor venue. We ask that you refrain from applause until the end of the performance. Enjoy the show."

My heart's racing as the musical introduction for the first dance encircles the entire area. Auntie grabs my hand and squeezes it. The twenty ballerina's bourrée on stage wearing form-fitted blue bodices covered by pale-blue tulle skirts hanging down to their ankles. The costumes flutter with each step of a dancer's leg. The six male dancers are dressed in white tights and white tuxedos of the shortest kind. *I wish I was up there with them.*

As the company spins in unison across the stage, I recognize Tamara immediately. Her blond hair shouts, *here I am.* We are fortunate to have front-row seats because she spots me right away. I smile so I don't distract her. I close my eyes and imagine doing a solo on center stage. Ten pirouettes and one grand jeté. *That will bring my audience to their feet.*

Opening my eyes, I realize my daydream is blocking the live performance in front of me. What am I doing? I could have missed a Pate do or something.

Oh, they're all so beautiful and each step is perfect. I'll never be that good. Time stands still as couples spin gracefully, with a few lifts here and there. They're getting ready for someone to do a solo. I want to leap to my feet when I see Tamara float to center stage. She whirls into two, three, five, oh, my goodness, fifteen pirouettes. A male dancer, comes from behind her and lifts her as she gracefully goes into an arabesque. My throat is so tight. I can't speak, even I wanted to. "Bravo, bravo!" the crowd bellows as the corps de ballet takes a bow. The dancers run to the back of the stage and down the few steps to their tent.

"Auntie, this was a dream come true. This is the best graduation present anyone could have ever given me."

"You're welcome, honey. Here comes Tamara and someone's with her."

"You were fantastic, Tamara. Bravo." I clap just for her.

She hugs me and gives me a beautifully wrapped present. "I'm sorry I couldn't be at your graduation, but I had to practice for today. Here's a belated present. Hope you like it."

"Can I open it now?"

The older gentleman with her is dressed in a long-sleeved black silk shirt and tan trousers. "Do you have someone you want me to meet, Tamara?" He says in a broken accent.

"Yes, Mr. Balanchine, I do. This is my friend, Violet Pearl Moretti."

He reaches out his hand to me. "Pleased to meet you, Miss Moretti. I understand that you have become quite the ballet dancer. Is that right?"

I shake his hand in absolute wonder and admiration. "I hope I am, Sir. I've been diligently practicing for the audition on Monday."

"We'll be expecting you then. There are three openings in the School for American Ballet. I hope you get one of them."

"Thank you, Mr. Balanchine."

"Good day, Ladies," he remarks as he goes to visit with the Wahlberg's.

Tamara hugs me. "Have to run and change, Violet. See you Monday."

I decide to take the train back home on Sunday to save Aunt Flossie a trip. I could call Marty to come and get me, but I need time to think about tomorrow. Yes, Monday. July 1. The big day.

"Did you have a nice time with your aunt?" Papa asks as I walk in the house.

I can't help myself. I beam from ear to ear. "It was fabulous. They have a magnificent place, Papa."

"I hope Mr. Wahlberg hires The Domino Four sometime."

"I told him all about you. I think he's very interested."

"Good to hear. Now go put your things away and come down for dinner. Tomorrow's registration day at Delahanty Business School."

In my room, I open the package Tamara gave me. I pull out a white leotard with matching tutu. A note is attached.

Wear this for your audition. Good luck. Tamara

As I walk down Forty-Second Street and gawk at all the weird people and odd billboards, I chuckle to myself how wonderfully different people can be. I'm only steps away from The Delahanty Business School. Registration lasts from eight to one. I look at the knapsack with the ballet clothes tucked inside. I stop, pivot, and look to my left. Madison Avenue is about a twenty-minute walk from here. The audition starts in exactly thirty minutes. I turn and find myself in front of the business school. I open the door, stop, close it, and walk away.

"What do you really want to do with your life, Violet?" The familiar voice causes me to jump.

I freeze in place. "Really, in broad daylight, on a busy New York sidewalk, keeper?"

A few ladies look at me, shake their heads, and move swiftly away.

I look all around. "Go away." I shout.

"It's not that easy to get rid of me. I will make you famous as a prima ballerina. You can make it on time. Move forward, girl."

I'm frightened, dismayed, and disillusioned. My decision must be mine alone.

PART THREE

1939

Chapter 28

I'm finally ready to go out into the workplace after attending the Delahanty Business School for six months. I still have my part-time position at Woolworths, even though I pound the pavement every day to fill out applications at every bank, store, and library from Brooklyn to New York. Typewriting and shorthand are my specialties. A girl Friday position would be perfect. I don't care if it's part-time either, if I can get my foot in the door.

I better get a move on because Marty's waiting for me at the Moneta Restaurant on Bedford Avenue at twelve thirty for lunch. It's ten minutes to twelve now. He usually has the *New York Times*. Maybe I can find something today.

"Hello, Sweetheart." Marty waves as I walk in.

He meets me halfway down the aisle between the tables, grabs my hand, and plants a kiss on my lips.

"Did you happen to check out the help wanted ads yet in the *Times*?"

"No dice, just the same old domestic jobs. You like to sew. Maybe that's what you should do, until the employment rate rises again."

"I spent the last six months in business school to work in an office not to sit at a machine all day long."

"What do you two want to eat today?" The chubby waitress dressed in a light-blue uniform asks.

Looking at her nametag, I respond, "What's the blue plate special, Gertrude?"

"Meat loaf for three bucks."

"Sounds good."

"Okay. Two blue plate specials and one more coffee," Marty orders for both of us.

"Coming right up," Gertrude says as she turns and walks toward the kitchen.

"I guess I'll be working in Woolworths for the rest of my life, Marty."

"Hold the phone. As I was running to catch the train today, I caught a glimpse of a girl Friday-wanted sign over on Flatbush Avenue."

"Get out of town. Are you sure, Marty?"

Gertrude puts the plates of food in front of us. "Here you go, you two love birds."

"I can't eat. I have to go and look for that sign," I say as I stand.

Marty grabs my hand. "Sit down and try to eat something. We don't have to be at the store until three o'clock. I'll go with you."

I look down at the meat loaf and start picking at it. "I guess I can eat some of it."

I should have followed my heart and gone to that audition months ago.

"My feet are killing me, and it's two o'clock. Where is this infamous place anyway?"

He points to a bench. "Sit here for a bit. I'll walk up a few blocks and come back. Okay?"

"Forget it, Marty. It's no use," I say as he sprints ahead, looking in every window until out of sight.

I take off my black patent leather high-heel shoes and rub my feet. My aching feet are in such agony that I don't even notice that I'm not alone on the bench.

"Hi there, beautiful. I can help rub those pretty feet of yours," a man I don't recognize says near me.

I grab my purse and hug it to me. "Leave me alone."

He starts to put his arm around me. "I'm trying to be helpful."

I give him a good slap across his face, grab my shoes, and start running in my stocking feet in the direction Marty went. I turn quickly to see if the creep is following me. He's not.

Two blocks later and out of breath, I stop and try putting my shoes back on.

Where's Marty? I squeeze my eyelids shut.

"Hey, Violet, I found the sign," Marty says loudly within hearing distance.

"Where?"

He grabs me and swings me around in his arms. "I went inside and asked a lady behind the counter about the position." He stands me back on solid ground.

"What did she say?"

"She said that Mr. Moskowitz stepped out for some lunch, but he would be back in ten minutes."

"I can't go, Marty. My stockings are full of runs, my hair's a mess, and I have to be at work in a half hour."

He glances at my legs and feet. "What happened to you?"

"Some jerk hit on me back there while you were looking for the sign. My feet were sore from these darn high heels, but I didn't want to take the time to put them on. All I could do was run with hopes of bumping into you."

He wraps his arms around me, "Oh, Violet, I'm so sorry. Where's this guy? I should punch his lights out."

"Don't worry, Marty. He didn't follow me. This city is filled with all kinds of riffraff."

"Will you be alright to go apply for the job?"

I gasp and take a deep breath, "I guess so. I better not lose this one opportunity, but I'll be late for work."

"Listen, Babe, you're talking to your shift manager now. Get to work when you can, okay? Now scoot."

He hugs me, runs to the bus stop, and shouts back, "It's number fifteen sixteen."

Bells jingle as I walk from the street into the small storefront office space. I'm greeted with a mixed aroma of coffee and old leather. The front part of the office has one tall receptionist desk, three leather chairs, a bookcase, and a unique table lamp.

I wonder where everyone is. Maybe, this isn't a good idea after all. I start to turn to leave.

"Can I help you, dear?" a croaky woman's voice says from behind me.

Doing an about face, I realize I'm looking at a sweet old lady who appears to be older than God.

"Um, yes. Ma'am. I would like to apply for the girl Friday position."

Smiling in a most pleasant way, she asks, "Do you have any experience?"

"Not exactly, but I'm a very fast learner. I have a certificate from Delahanty Business School."

She chuckles. "Did your boyfriend come in here and inquire about the job a few minutes ago?"

"Yes, Ma'am. He did. I'm sorry for that, really, I am. He's trying to help me find a job."

"Have a seat, honey. My son will be back from lunch in no time. Can I get you some coffee?"

I sit and smooth out my dress. "No, thank you."

I watch her putter about as she files several folders in the file cabinets and attempts to dust.

Picking up today's issue of the *New York Mirror*, I leaf through it. "Mam, do you have a lavatory I can use?"

"Please call me Mrs. Moskowitz, and yes right down the hall to your left. I wonder where Theodore is."

The old mirror has a light film over it, so it makes it hard for me to look at myself. There. A little lipstick and rouge should do the trick. *I'm sure there have been many applicants for this position, and someone with experience will get it for sure.*

I stuff my makeup in my bag and turn to walk back into the reception area. I'm checking out my runny stockings and scuffed shoes when I plow right into someone. "Excuse me." I look up and find myself standing face to face with the man who was on the bench minutes ago.

I jump back and try to squeeze past him down the hallway.

"Are you here for the position advertised in the window, or are you stopping by to say hello?"

"This is a mistake. You're a creep."

"Feisty, aren't we? I like that."

"Theodore, dear. I think this young lady has great potential. Look at her application," Mrs. Moskowitz remarks as she hands him the paper. He glances at it for a few minutes, then winks at me. *Maybe, she's hard of hearing and couldn't hear her arrogant son.*

A red head with glasses and a briefcase walks in the front door. "I would like to apply for the job."

The man called Theodore, looks me up and down and then directly into my eyes, "I'm sorry, but the position is filled."

"Then take the sign out of the window, would ya?" She storms out of the door.

He pats my shoulder and pulls the sign out of the window. "The job is yours, Miss Moretti, if you think you can handle it."

I keep my anger deep within as I race to the door. "I'll find something else. If I were you, Sir. I'd put that sign back in the window. It was nice meeting you, Mrs. Moskowitz."

She smiles. "Wait a minute, Miss Moretti. Please reconsider. Theodore is in court most of the time, so you and I will be running the office. You need a job, and we have been looking for help for weeks."

"How can you offer me a position here, when I wasn't even interviewed?"

I can't work for this man. No way. No how.

I grab the front-door knob, open it, and start to step outside.

"Okay, Ms. Moretti. You're right. Where are my manners? Come, sit with us, and have a cup of coffee. Your resume looks wonderful, but I would like to find out more about you. I apologize if I came on too strong."

I breathe a sigh of relief. "I do need this job. Please ask all the questions you would like to."

I don't know what relaxed me more, the conversation that followed or the delightful cup of hot coffee. We laughed and chatted for a half hour.

"You have yourself a job. I will see you Monday morning, nine o'clock sharp, Violet Pearl Moretti." Theodore Moskowitz says. I'm so overcome with joy; I can hardly breathe.

That night alone in my room, confusion overwhelms me. Should I show up for my first day of work, on Monday at the Moskowitz firm or keep on checking the want ads? My potential boss could turn out to be my worst nightmare. I have looked for days at newspaper ads and employment agencies only to find the only women's jobs to be had are the domestic kind. I spent the last five years since mother's death cooking, cleaning, and from time to time sewing a quick skirt or jumper for Daisy. That's enough of that.

I look up at the tutu that Tamara gave me for a graduation present. It's gracefully hanging on the wall like a beautiful work of art. Lonely tears well up in the corners of my eyes as they trickle down my cheeks. That was the most challenging decision I had to make. Ballet audition or business school?

I have a job. I'm a big girl so I can handle that flirty boss of mine.

The light bulb in my lamp flickers, and a cool breeze whisks over me.

"Yes, your thinking is correct. You and only you can give anything power. You are the master of your fate, the captain of your own soul," murmurs the keeper.

"Have you been following me, keeper?"

"You already know the answer. The cobwebs of your brain will gradually clear away, leaving only love, if this is what you so choose."

"Why do I have spells of rat-race thinking? Why do I keep sliding back mentally, when I want so much to keep a steady true course?"

"There are many evil spirits in the world. When you allow them power, they can control you?"

"Can I fill my mind with love and peace?"

"Do not try. Listen. Be still. You will be moved to do certain things. Do them."

Hot flashes encompass my body. The keeper is gone.

"Good morning, flower," Papa remarks as I come into the kitchen.

"Good morning, Papa. Hey there, my little Daisy." I tousle her hair as I sit down at the table.

"What can I get you for breakfast on this chilly Saturday in January?"

"Hmm. Do we have any oatmeal?"

"Yes. Ma'am. Oatmeal with raisons coming up."

Daisy's eating cinnamon toast and enjoying every little morsel as usual.

I slice off three pieces of homemade bread for myself, sugar, some cinnamon, and place them on the cookie sheet. "Do you have an engagement tonight, Papa?"

"Yes, the band is playing for a backstage party at the Paramount Theater. It's the premier night, and we are excited to get this job. A lot of famous people will be there. Good exposure for The Domino Four. I wish you could come, Violet, but I know you work today and will have to watch Daisy tonight."

I take the sheet pan out of the oven with a potholder. "I get off work from Woolworths at three thirty. What time do you have to leave?"

"Joseph's picking me up at four thirty. I'm making beef stew today, so you won't have to worry about supper."

"Good. I'll be home in plenty of time."

Papa scoops the oatmeal in a bowl and tops it off with raisins. "Here, sit down and eat before it gets cold. What time do you have to be at work?"

"Which job do you mean, Papa?"

He looks at me with squinty eyes. "Woolworths, of course. What other job would you have?"

Papa brings the toast over, sits down, and picks up the *New York Post*. "There are several jobs listed today in the classified section, Violet."

"I have a job, Papa." I say as I spoon some oatmeal into my mouth.

Papa chuckles loudly. "Are you trying to play a trick on me, flower?"

Pulling the paper down from in front of his face, I say, "I landed a nice secretary position for a small law firm on Flatbush. I start Monday."

"Well, well, how did you find that?"

I look at the clock on the wall. "I have to get ready for my sales clerk job. I must be there in one hour. I'll tell you later."

The bread line is a bit shorter today. A man whistles his approval as I hurry past the dwindling line. I'm wearing my mother's brown fur-trimmed overcoat with a grey cloche hat. A few heads turn as I pass by because I look like something out of the Roaring Twenties. I pay no mind to them and keep walking with additional energy as the cold air attacks my face. One more block and I'll be in the store, away from this bitter cold.

As I walk into the store, Marty's saying, "Okay, Ladies. Let's not fight over these socks."

There's a crowd of women around the display table, and socks of all colors are flying everywhere.

We exchange smiles as I scurry to the employee lounge to hang up my coat, change shoes, and lock my purse in the locker. I fuss over my hair a bit as I look in the mirror and apply another coat of lipstick.

"Hey, Violet. Your birthday's coming soon, huh?" Mary Sue comments as I walk past her.

"Yes, in two weeks, but how did you know?"

"Marty posted all employees birthdays in January."

"Where did he do that?"

"Up by the office where our schedules are located."

Several card tables are set up in the front of the store for the Saturday sales. It seems like people come out of the woodwork when the price is right. Two weeks ago, men's ties, last week, handkerchiefs.

"Hi, Sweetie," Marty whispers in my ear as I take over for Elizabeth, a new employee.

I study my boyfriend as he gawks at the very curvaceous Elizabeth walk down the aisle.

"Has it been like this all morning?"

He leans on the counter with one arm, his full attention on Elizabeth until she is out of sight.

"Marty," I say loudly into his ear.

He places his arm around my waist and pulls me tight to his side. "I hope we can find time to be alone tonight even though we have to babysit."

"I think I can arrange that." I smile at him.

"Marty, how many more boxes of socks do I have to unload?" Mary Sue asks.

Looking at his watch, he replies, "Unpack this one box, and I'll bring the other boxes back to the storage room. You can spend the rest of the night straightening merchandise."

"Whew. That works for me." She says.

A lady brings ten pairs of socks to my station. "That will be two dollars and fifty cents, Ma'am." I say to her.

The shabbily dressed lady digs in her purse and pulls out a handful of change. We count one hundred pennies, and ten dimes. Meanwhile, a line of patron's forms.

"Come on, hurry it up," a man yells from the back of the line.

"Yeah. My husband's waiting for me," a lady shouts.

The lady on the other side of the counter starts to cry. I put her socks in a paper sack, even though she still owes fifty cents. "Thank you for shopping at Woolworths."

"Thank you, miss." She walks out of the door with her head down.

"You people are awful," I say loudly. "Look what you did to that poor lady. You ought to be ashamed of yourselves." My mask is slipping, and any second now, Marty's going to see me, the real me, broken and floundering.

A sudden silence satiates the whole store. If someone dropped a hat pin on that hardwood floor, it would be heard loud and clear. I close my till and burst into tears, and I run away from my post.

"Mary Sue, take over for her this instant," Marty calls to her as he runs after me.

I slump in a heap on the floor in the lounge. A big lump is back in my tummy.

"Violet. What's wrong with you?"

I'm too embarrassed to answer him or maybe I don't know what to say.

He continues to stand over me. "You were totally out of line just now."

I manage to say, "I'm so sorry."

We didn't say one word to each other all the way back to my house. Mary Sue left rather abruptly before Marty and me, but I did see her face. She wasn't pleased with me.

She probably won't talk to me again.

"Hello, kids. Daisy's in the kitchen eating stew. I must run. You two be good, okay?" Papa remarks as he goes out of the front door.

We hang up our coats, and Marty leaves me alone to wallow in my self-pity.

"Hey there, cutie," I hear him say as he goes into the kitchen.

"Marty. Have some stew with me," Daisy offers.

Something must be wrong with me. I can't believe I acted the way I did at the store tonight. I'm so ashamed of my behavior.

Later that night after Daisy's sound asleep, I try to get close to my boyfriend who's sprawled out on the rug in front of the fireplace. I sit next to him and put my hand on his shoulder. He rolls away and escapes to the couch.

I sit upright and stare into the reddish orange blazes. "Marty, I'm so sorry about tonight. The customers made me so mad over their reaction to that poor soul counting out her last pennies to buy socks."

"The customer's always right, Violet. You should have kept your emotions to yourself."

"I know. I promise to control myself in the future, okay?"

"On the way out of the door, one of the customers commented that they were going to complain to Mr. Hamilton about your behavior. You will be fired if that happens."

I turn to look at him with overflowing tear ducts. "I forgot to tell you. I got the position at Theodore Moskowitz Law Firm yesterday."

"You did? That's great news. When do you start?"

"Monday at nine."

Marty smirks at me, "Come over here."

"Are you sure? I hope you forgive me."

"I do, but I want my girl close to me."

I'll never tell anyone about the fifty cents I knocked off for the price of the socks.

The couch is big enough for four people, but I decide to sit on his lap. "I'm so glad you're my boyfriend, Marty." I lean my head on his hard-muscular chest. My whole body reacts to his touch.

Marty strokes my hair, turns me toward him, so we are face to face. I kiss him gently on the cheek. He returns the favor. "I think I'm falling in love with you, Violet."

His lips touch mine. They're soft and inviting. In the six months of dating on a regular basis, we've exchanged cheek kisses only. I move my lips away from his and kiss his neck.

"Oh, my Violet. I have waited such a long time for this moment."

"I love it when we make up." I place a kiss back on his mouth. My cheeks are heating up.

I get up to move to a safer position, but he grabs my hands.

"Your father won't be home for two more hours, and Daisy's fast asleep."

He unbuttons the first two buttons of my blouse.

I grab hold of his hands. "I can't let you do this."

He plants his open mouth on my closed lips and kisses me again. My legs start to buckle, and I fall on the couch. Still holding my hand, he completely stretches out and pulls me to himself.

Things start happening that I can't explain, and fireworks explode deep within.

"I want all of you." He whispers.

The heat of the night takes over, and I'm lost in uncontrollable emotions. He plants kisses down my neck.

"Vi-Vi. I need you. I can't find my teddy," Daisy calls from the top of the stairs.

My eyes pop open, and I literally fall off the couch. "I'm coming, Daisy."

Buttoning up my blouse and fixing my skirt, I scurry up the stairs and find my sister sitting three steps down from the top.

Did she see us?

"Go back to bed, Daisy. I'll look for teddy." I hug her gently in passing.

She yawns and goes to her room.

After searching Papa's room and then mine, I spot teddy in the lavatory by the bathtub.

"Here he is, honey." She's fast asleep under the covers.

I think Marty and I should play checkers or something. We're very attracted to each other, so things could get out of our control.

"Marty?" I call softly when I don't see him in the parlor.

"I bet you worked up an appetite, huh?"

Bursting through the kitchen door, I find another empty room.

Where in the world did he go? I only left for five minutes for goodness sake. Probably outside getting some fresh air. I can use some of that.

I grab my coat off the hook when I spot a Woolworths's business card lying on the small table under the lamp. With interest, I turn it over.

I need all of you, Violet. You drove me crazy tonight. Love, Marty

Chapter 29

I always arrive at the law office fifteen minutes early, Monday through Friday. I can say that I love my job and can't wait to get here every day. Theodore has been swamped with court cases and is at the courthouse more than he is at his desk. Mrs. Moskowitz and I rearranged the office two weeks after I started. We got rid of the tall reception counter and replaced it with a nice-looking used wood desk for me to work at. Since I do most of the office work, I'm happy to be in the front office where I can greet people as they walk in the door.

The weeks roll on by without any catastrophes, bad weather, or undesirable advances from my boss at the law firm. I still work the part-time job at Woolworths, so I can have a little extra cash in my pocket, but the biggest reason I stay there is to see Marty.

It snowed last night, so I have my galoshes on and carry my shoes in a sack.

As I enter the store, I glance at my watch and find I'm thirty minutes early. Good. I can go grab a quick cup of hot chocolate at the lunch counter.

"What can I get you, Violet?" the new kid behind the counter asks.

"May I have a cup of hot cocoa?"

"Are you working today?"

"I am, but I'm here early for a change."

A few minutes later, he sets a cup on the counter before me. "Here you go, Violet. Fifty cents, please."

I reach into my purse and pull out two shiny quarters.

I look around the store from my stool, hoping to see my boyfriend. "Have you seen Marty?"

"I saw him go to the back of the store about ten minutes ago."

"What about Mary Sue?"

"I don't think she is on this afternoon. She could have worked this morning. Don't know."

I gulp down the last drop of hot cocoa. "Thanks. See ya later."

As I make way back to the lounge and lockers, I notice that the store is quiet with only a few scattered customers. No one's at the front register; that's odd.

Getting closer to the lounge, I hear giggling and muffled voices. Turning the corner and opening the door, my heart skips a beat and anger surges within my soul at the sight in front of me.

"Marty!" I yell. His back is to me, but his arms are around Elizabeth.

She peers over his shoulder. "Uh, oh."

"It's okay, Elizabeth. Violet won't get mad."

He pats her rump and turns to look at me. "We're having a little fun because there are so few customers."

"Marty. Get your hand off her behind. Elizabeth, go back to the register."

She gives my boyfriend a kiss on his cheek and giggles uncontrollably as she exits the small room. *I want to slap her silly.*

"Violet. It's not what you think. You know you're my girl, right?"

"I thought so until I witnessed this mess." I struggle to come up with something, anything to say.

He pulls me to himself and plants his open mouth on mine, and I completely forget where I am for a few fleeting moments. "Violet, my sweetheart. I still want all of you," he whispers in my ear.

"Not here. Not now, Marty."

"Then where. Tell me."

Chapter 30

"Marty, my boy. Are you sure Violet doesn't know about this shin-dig?" Berto asks.

"No, she doesn't have a clue, Mr. Moretti."

"Her boss has it all under control, right?"

"Violet was so excited last night when she told me he was taking her to meet some colleagues at an early business dinner tonight," Eleanor says.

"Mr. Moskowitz will bring her here at seven," May says. "The invitations requested that all guests enter through the back door by six thirty."

Marty looks at his watch. "Well, its fifteen minutes past six now."

"There are ten people in the kitchen, Papa." Daisy says as she comes into the parlor. "I'm having a hard time keeping them quiet. When will Sissy be here?"

"Daisy, go back there so we can greet everyone when they arrive." Berto stands with his hands on hips, scanning the area for something out of place.

"Tamara," Marty says, "be sure to tell us when you see Violet coming up the sidewalk, so I can give everyone a heads up."

"Sure, will. I can't wait to see Violet's face when she sees how festive this place looks. I'll knock three times when I see her."

"Thank you, Theodore, for such a wonderful evening," I say as I walk in the door.

He helps me with my coat and then hangs it on a hook. I wonder why he's not saying anything. Then, I feel a slight push forward on my back.

"What? Whoa. What are you doing?"

"Surprise! Happy birthday, Violet!" Shouts an energetic crowd pouring out from the kitchen.

Papa turns the lights on, and Elizabeth turns on the record player, releasing merry music into the room, and one by one my friends hug me. The whole parlor is decorated with lavender streamers, clusters of blue and white balloons, aroma of fresh coffee, and Entenmann's cookies fill the house as I make my way through the crowd into the kitchen.

"Vi-Vi. Happy birthday," Daisy says as she runs to me.

"Thank you. Did you know about this too?"

"Yep. Marty told me I better keep it a secret or else."

Wrapping his arms around me from the back, "Happy birthday, Babe."

I turn to look at him, "This is a great nineteenth birthday party. Is this your idea, Marty?"

Grinning from ear to ear and delivering the biggest kiss ever on my cheek, he says, "I surprised you, didn't I?"

Exuberant joy bubbles inside as I giggle with gratitude, "You're the greatest, but why is Elizabeth here?"

He pulls his arms away and shrugs his shoulders.

"I have to go, Violet," Theodore says. "But I hope you have a great time at your party."

"Thanks again, Theodore, but you're welcome to stay. Please do."

Theodore waves and slips out of the door, as the crowd disperses into joyous conversation.

I take Marty's hand and pull him through the back door and on to the small porch. It's chilly, but I wrap my arms around him. "Kiss me like you mean it."

He turns my mouth to his and pries it open with his tongue. We passionately kiss for a few minutes and then he pulls away and stops. "Violet, I want all of you. Kissing's not enough."

"You say this all the time. You know how I feel, Marty. I'm saving myself for my husband."

"Isn't loving you enough?"

"We better get back inside. My guests will be wondering where I am."

"You go ahead. I'll be there shortly. I need time to cool off."

I plop into Papa's cushy chair in the kitchen and cover my eyes to hide the tears. What am I going to do about Marty? He says he loves me, but I found him in a compromising situation with Elizabeth. When we're alone, he's all over me. I'm not like other girls who are way too intimate with their boyfriends. *Oh Mama, I wish you were here.*

Auntie rubs my back, "Are you alright, Toots?"

"Oh, Auntie. Men are so confusing at times. I'm afraid to be alone with my boyfriend because something dreadful might happen."

"You're a smart young lady, Violet. I like Marty, but he's a ladies' man. Always flirting with anything in a dress."

I pick up my head and scowl, "Whatever do you mean?"

"I just came back from checking out the refreshments, and he was dancing with Elizabeth mighty close."

I fly into the front room. A few couples are dancing a waltz while others play charades over by the fireplace. I wipe my eyes and paint a plastic smile on my face, as I scan the room. There's Elizabeth hanging all over Marty. I should go over and punch her in the nose and tell her to leave. This is my party. I can't let her ruin it.

Tamara motions for me to come over. "I finally get a few minutes with the birthday girl."

"I'm so glad you're here, Tamara. How long have you known about this surprise party?"

"For a month."

"That boyfriend of mine is quite the planner, but I do have my doubts." I whisper.

"How is that going, Violet? Are you too serious?"

In good spirits, I smile and say, "I love him, Tamara."

She pulls me close to her and whispers, "Be careful. Fellas usually want more than a few kisses from their girlfriends."

"He knows how I feel about that."

A week later, The Domino Four have a performance in the Catskills which means Papa will be gone for most of the weekend. I'm taking today, Saturday, off from Woolworths so I can have Mary Sue, Eleanor, and May over for a sleep over. Daisy's at Auntie's for the weekend.

"*Love in Bloom* with George Burns and Gracie Allen is playing at the Lyric Theater tonight," May says.

"What do you think, girls? Should we go?" I ask.

Mary Sue and I are sprawled out on the sofa reading magazines while Eleanor and May are playing Chinese checkers.

"Let's do it." Mary Sue says, tossing her magazine onto the end table.

"We better get a move on if we are going to go to the six o'clock show," I say as I run to check that the back door is locked. *So glad the keeper's leaving me alone lately.*

A few minutes later, we're on our way. "Good thing we're so close to the movie house," May says.

We arrive at the theater in a most joyful state. Several patrons are ahead of us, but we stand in line patiently, so we can get our tickets.

"This is supposed to be such a good flick."

"I love George Burns," Eleanor says. "He's so funny." We make our way through the glass doors and stop at the refreshment stand. "Do you want to share something?" Mary Sue asks.

"I have plenty of food at home," I tell her, not wanting to let them know I don't have money for snacks.

Eleanor abruptly covers my eyes. "Don't look until I tell you to, Violet Pearl."

I grab her hands to pull them off my face, but she is stronger than I.

"Oh, I can't believe my eyes." Mary Sue says. She sounds aggravated.

"That creep," May says under her breath.

Prying and pulling on Eleanor's hands, I ask, "What's wrong with all of you?"

One girl grabs my right arm, the other the left. "We better get inside and get our seats."

As we move onward, I break away from my friends and head toward the lobby. I scan the back rows of the theater and take a double look at a couple in the far corner of the back row. Something looks awfully familiar about them.

I take a minute and stare. They're wrapped in each other's arms and kissing without a break. If only one of them would turn around. The lights start to dim.

"Violet. Over here," May whispers and motions to me.

Squinting my eyes as the house gets darker, I see the man stand up and head into the lobby.

Okay, now I'm curious. Who is that guy?

Turning on my heels, I go back into the lit vestibule. Looking down at my shoes as I always do, I collide right into someone.

"Excuse me. I should watch where I'm going."

Looking up, I find myself standing face to face with Marty.

"Fancy meeting you here. Are you alone?" I ask. My innards are boiling.

"Of course, I am. Two chocolate bars and two sarsaparillas," he says.

I study him up and down.

My, he sure looks like that fella in the back of the theater moments ago. Why all the goodies if he's alone?

"Marty, what are you doing? Are you here with someone?"

"Just a buddy, Violet."

"The movie's starting, handsome," Elizabeth comes into view. "Oh, Violet. How nice to see you?"

I pound on Marty's chest. "You no good two-timing jerk."

Elizabeth wraps her arms around my boyfriend and kisses him on the lips right in front of me. "Come on, let's go. The movie's starting."

Are you kidding me, you floosy? You know Marty's my guy. Who do you think you are? I want to spout out these words, but they remain in my head as I freeze in place.

He looks at me and mouths the words, "I'm sorry."

Chapter 31

I'm so glad to be surrounded by my closest friends at a time like this. All thoughts of Marty and that witch, Elizabeth, vanish because we all got so enthralled with the moving picture and the brisk walk through town.

However, I step into a reality check as I unlock the front door and walk ahead of my friends into the same room where my boyfriend gave me a surprise birthday party a short time ago. I halt in place while the others hang up their coats and kick off their shoes. They head over to the fireplace where a few lonely cinders are still glowing.

"Don't stand there, girl. Come over here and sing to us, do a dance or something," Eleanor calls out to me.

I hear her, but I don't move. I clamp my mouth shut.

"You who! Violet!" May says loudly to get my attention.

A moment later, someone from behind takes off my coat and moves me slowly to the sofa. My body starts to shake as I fall into it and roll up into a ball.

"Rest a bit; you've had a rough night," Mary Sue says.

She takes off my shoes and covers my legs with the quilt that was made by my precious mother's hands. *Oh, my dear mama. I miss your warm embrace.*

I burst into tears. "What's going on? I'm Marty's only girl. At least that's what he told me."

"Marty's a creep," Mary Sue said, emphasizing *creep*. "You're not the problem. I have told you this before, Vi."

"He had the audacity to ask me if he should invite Elizabeth to your party," Eleanor says, shaking her head.

"Are you joking?" I ask. Was he planning on two-timing me at my own birthday party?

"She's telling the truth, Vi," May says.

"I don't like the way that girl dresses. Always wearing a low cut, revealing dress to work." I grit my teeth.

"She flaunts that perfect figure, and she gets away with not wearing a smock too," Mary Sue comments.

"Violet, we're among friends. You and Marty have been dating for almost a year now. Does he put pressure on you when you're alone and in the heat of the moment?" Eleanor asks.

"Uh, what do you mean, Eleanor?"

"Some fellas take every possible chance to get alone with their girl-friend, so she sleeps with them."

"Yeah, I have a cousin who lives in California," Mary Sue says then sighs. "She slept with her boyfriend, and now she's six months pregnant. She's only sixteen."

"Marty always says he wants all of me," I mumble with my head down.

"I knew it. That's why sexy Elizabeth is in the mix now," Eleanor whispers.

"Ditch him, Violet." Mary Sue advises me. "He's a louse. That lawyer boss of yours is a dreamboat and seems to like you."

Throwing the quilt off me, I dash to the Victrola and put on *Lullaby of Broadway*. "Come on, girls, let's dance." *I must take my mind off Marty, or I'll go crazy.*

"How was your weekend, Violet?" Theodore asks me when I arrive for work on Monday.

"Three of my girlfriends came over for an overnight, and we had a blast."

His eyes light up in response. He takes a seat in front of my desk, smiles, and winks at me. "You look beautiful today, as always. How serious are you with that Marty fella?"

With a half-smile, I reply, "Not serious at all."

"He came in here to talk to me about getting you to the party and the big surprise he was planning. He sure acted as though you two were crazy about each other."

I shrug. "We're not going steady, if that's what you are driving at."

"So, if I invited you out to dinner tonight after work, would you consider it?"

My heart starts thumping more rapidly than usual. *I don't know if I should be alone with Theodore. Oh, what's wrong with an innocent dinner?* "Um. Maybe."

He stands up and moves cautiously around to the back of my desk and grabs my hand. "Madam, will you kindly join me for dinner tonight right after work? I promise to be a gentleman." Butterflies dance in the pit of my stomach, as his scent envelopes me.

I feel heat creep up my neck. Now, I'm blushing. "Yes. Mr. Moskowitz. I will be honored to accept your invitation."

As quick as a wink, he brings my hand to his warm lips, looks me straight in the eye. "Okay. Good. Now get to work."

What just happened? I can't believe that I'm going on a date with my boss. It wasn't that long ago when he was overly flirtatious with me. Is it safe to be alone with Theodore? I take a few deep breaths and shake my head. Silly me. Of course, it is. He has been nothing but polite since I started working here. Marty really hurt me, and now it's payback time.

Lundy's Restaurant on Sheep's Head Bay is so picturesque even in the dark of night.

The streetlights create a glittering illumination across the water, bringing instant peace.He opens the car door for me. "Thank you, Mr. Moskowitz."

"Please Call me Theodore."

I smile and nod.

We're escorted to our table for two which has a fabulous view of the bay.

"It's breathtaking here, Theodore. Just lovely." I breathe a sigh of relief.

This is a very romantic place to come with a boyfriend. Unfortunately, I'm with my boss. There are dimly lit candles burning on each perfectly dressed table with a violinist going from guest to guest, softly playing pieces from great composers.

Back to real life. This is a business dinner for crying out loud.

We share Lundy's classic Shore Dinner which is way too much food for one person. We start with Manhattan clam chowder and then dug into lobster, roasted chicken, a potato-vegetable concoction, and dinner rolls. Huckleberry pie for desert.

"Wow, that was delicious, but I'm stuffed," I comment.

He chuckles. "Aren't you glad I suggested we share?"

I smile and glance at my watch. "Oh dear, my father's probably frantically wondering where I am. I thought about calling him before we left the office, but I plum forgot."

He snaps his fingers to get the waiter's attention. "I'll get you home in a jiffy as soon as I pay the tab."

Twenty minutes later, Theodore pulls his brand new 1935 Ford Model 48 in front of my house and stops. If it were daytime, people would be coming out of the woodwork to gawk at this exquisite vehicle. I wish it wasn't February because I'm sure the convertible top would be down.

I start to open the door.

"Please wait." Theodore gets out of the driver seat and walks around to my side and opens the door.

What a gentleman.

He escorts me up to the front door of my house. "Thank you for a wonderful night, Violet." He takes my right hand and brings it up to his lips.

A few goose bumps make their way up and down my arms.

"I will see you tomorrow at the office. Good night." I open the door.

"Pleasant dreams, Violet."

"Where have you been, young lady?" Papa asks as he ascends down the stairs.

"You startled me, Papa. I meant to call, but time slipped away from me."

"Do you realize it's eight thirty, and I have been worried sick about you? I know that you get off work at six and are always in the house by six thirty at the latest."

"I'm so sorry, but you do forget, I'm nineteen now."

"Do you know that Marty has been waiting for you for two hours?"

Looking confused, "Marty?" *What right does he have to come looking for me after that display at the movies? I can't believe he has the gall to show up here.*

Papa points to the chair by the fireplace. "Isn't that Marty over there?"

I remove my coat, hang it up, and stand in total shock as I stare at my estranged boyfriend. The audacity of some people.

Marty rises and makes his way to me. "Hello, Violet."

"What are you doing here, Marty?"

"Violet Pearl, he's your boyfriend. He's here to see you, of course," Papa chimes in.

"I'd like to talk to my girlfriend alone, Mr. Moretti."

"I can take a hint. I'll be in the kitchen if you kids need me." Papa yawns and heads for the other room.

As soon as my father is out of hearing distance, I come out of my trance as my broken heart becomes painfully awake. "The nerve of you coming over here after you humiliated me in front of my friends."

"I'm sorry I hurt you. Will you ever forgive me?"

"No. Never."

"But you are all I want. You're my only girl."

"Oh yeah, then what about sexy Elizabeth, huh?"

"I told her I'm in love with you, Violet."

"You did not."

He moves closer and wraps his arms around me. "I love you."

A tear traces its way down my cheek. "Do you really mean that?"

Right then and there with my father in the next room, "Let me show you." He places a soft tender kiss on my lips and picks me up in his arms.

I don't have any energy to fight him. "What about my papa?" I whisper.

"Hush."

Papa will be in there for at least an hour especially since he put a comfortable high-back chair with matching ottoman, small end table, and quaint little brass lamp in that room. Most likely will fall asleep right there too.

Marty strokes my leg and continues to kiss me as he puts me on the sofa. I start kissing his neck and then back up to his soft lips. "Fire Elizabeth, if you really love me."

His eyes pop open and he pushes me away from him. "I can't do that. There's no reason to do such a thing. It's not up to me anyway."

I squint my eyes at him. "Touchy, are we?"

"She's a dependable employee, and even Mr. Hamilton likes having her in the store."

"It's her or me. Which is it?"

"You know it is not my decision to make, Violet."

"Come closer for a minute, Marty. I want to tell you something, and I don't want my father to hear me."

He maneuvers himself right next to me. I take his hand and place it on my chest. "Okay. Is this what you want?" I whisper.

He starts kissing me on my forehead and down my cheek to my neck. Leaving one hand on my chest, he begins exploring with the other.

I slap him across the face and leap away from him. "Get out."

"What are you doing?"

"You're a sex maniac, Marty. We're through. Get out of here now, or I'll scream."

He gets up and darts to the foyer to get his jacket. "I'll talk to you at the store on Saturday after you have a few days to cool off."

"No, you won't because I quit."

That night in the quietness of my room, I realize it was a matter of time before Marty would have dumped me anyway. Good riddance to that low-down good-for-nothing ding-dong.

A knock on my door startles me. "Are you okay, Flower? I thought I heard you crying as I came up the stairs."

"I'm alright, Papa."

"May I come in?"

I pull on my robe. "Yes."

He sits down on my bed. "Are you and Marty all patched up now?"

"I broke up with him."

"What? He loves you so much, my dear."

"He has another girlfriend, and she works at the store."

"I see. What about your boss, Mr. Moskowitz?"

"What about him, Papa? Do you mean is he a gentleman? Yes. He's a gem and so mature."

"Remember that it's best not to mix business with personal relationships, Violet."

"Don't worry, Papa. Tonight, was just a business dinner—not a date."

He tousles my hair like he did when I was a kid. "Better get some sleep."

Chapter 32

The next day after eight hours at the law office, I decide to pay Aunt Flossie a visit. It's been months since I've seen her. It's time I share with her what has been happening in my life.

"Violet Pearl. What on earth are you doing here? Is something wrong?" Auntie asks.

"Yes. No. Kind of. I broke up with Marty."

"Let me take your coat, child. Stay for supper with me. Can you spend the night?"

I force a smile. "I didn't bring any extra clothes, and Papa's expecting me."

"I can fix that. Sit down, and I will make you some tea."

She fills up the teakettle and turns on the pilot light under it. Then she disappears into the front parlor.

"Watch the kettle, Violet. I'm making a phone call."

"Do you want tea too?"

I hear her say in a muffled voice, "Hello, Berto."

Now curious, I lean against the opening, so she can't see me.

"Yes. Violet's here. Yes. She will be having dinner with me. I haven't seen her in a long time. Be reasonable, Berto."

A bit of a silence.

"Listen here, she's my niece, and I have helped you out with Daisy over and over. Violet's having dinner here, and what's more, she's staying overnight too."

"No, you can't talk to her. You'll only upset her. Good night, Berto."

The teakettle whistles profusely, so I grab it before it sings too loudly. I pour two cups of water into dainty china cups with the tea bags in place.

"Let it steep for five minutes, Toots."

"Auntie, what did Papa say?"

"He's incorrigible and has no sense of compassion for you. He forgets that you're nineteen years old for heaven's sake."

"Does he know I'm staying overnight?"

"He knows."

We enjoy our tea together for a bit, and then she starts to get dinner ready while I leaf through the latest issue of *Life* magazine. The smell of bacon and ground beef fills the kitchen as I sit at the small table for two. She must be making beef patties wrapped in bacon. Yum.

After we clean the kitchen and turn out the light, we head into the parlor. Auntie puts on some classical music to set a relaxing atmosphere. She always does the perfect thing at the precise time.

"Violet, men are an odd breed. I have courted several from various backgrounds over the years, but for some reason, I still prefer living by myself."

"Oh, Auntie. Marty says he loves me, but every time we're together, he grabs parts of me that are completely private. Always saying, 'I want all of you, Violet.'"

"Uh, oh. You did the right thing breaking off with him then. Does your father know any of this?"

"No."

"You'll have to face Marty at the store, but I'm so glad you only work there one day a week now."

"Not really. I quit." My body starts trembling as the tear ducts well up.

"I hope you gave a notice, dear. You know it looks better on your resume if you leave a place of employment on a good note."

Standing up, I pace a bit. "I can't look at that fella again or his sexy other girlfriend. I have a good job at the law firm, and next week is my review. If I do well, Theodore will promote me to his personal secretary, which means a bigger salary."

"Theodore? Sounds like you're getting pretty chummy."

"He's such a gentleman, Auntie. He took me to Lundy's for dinner last night."

"Oh my, Tootsie. Please be careful. When a boss starts doing things like that, it spells nothing but trouble."

I yawn. "I'm getting sleepy. I must be at work by nine tomorrow. Can I rob your closet? I'm going to need undergarments too."

Wrapping her arm around my shoulder, she ushers me into her room. "Come on, let's raid my closet. It's wonderful we're the same size."

I smile from ear to ear.

When I arrive at the office the next day, I find the door locked. Darkness fills the inside as I press my face into the glass door. I knock and knock. I jiggle the doorknob. Folks passing by are staring at me as though I'm a burglar trying to break in.

Wait a minute. Theodore gave me a set of keys last week. He said a day may come when I'll have to let myself in. I dig them out of my purse and open the door.

Moments later, I flick on the lights and hang up my coat. This is positively weird.

"Sarah, Theodore? Hello. Anybody here?"

I walk down the short corridor into Theodore's office and look around. Everything's exactly the way we left it last night. The door that goes to the back staircase is closed which is unusual. Shrugging my shoulders, I return to the front office. I might as well start transposing the letters from shorthand to typewritten so they can get out in today's mail.

The morning slips past me, and I can't believe it's eleven thirty already. Almost lunchtime. Very unusual for me to be the only one here for this long. Good thing Auntie packed a lunch for me today. After placing the *out for lunch* sign on the door and locking it from the inside, I retreat to the back office and sit at Sarah's desk.

A few minutes later, I hear footsteps overhead and down the stairs. The door pops open.

"Theodore. You scared me. What's going on?"

"Oh, my mother's sick and in bed. The flu or something. I cancelled all my appointments today. I'm glad to see you let yourself in."

He comes over behind me and starts massaging the back of my neck. It feels good, so I don't stop him. Warmth radiates from my stomach; the tension floats out of my limbs.

"Did you have a nice time last night, Violet?"

"Of course, I did. Thank you so much."

Pushing myself away from the desk, I get up. "I better get back to work."

"The work can wait. I'm giving you a break."

Chuckling nervously, "Oh, Theodore. You're not paying me to sit around."

He takes my hand and kisses it. Why does this adrenaline rush happen whenever he's near me? I can't speak. The words won't come.

Before I know it, we're sitting together on the big couch in his office. He wraps his leg over mine.

He kisses my neck. "Finally, we're alone."

"This isn't right, Theodore. You're my boss."

He starts to move my skirt up with his hand and plants a huge open mouth kiss on my neck.

"Ouch. You bit me." I squeal.

I manage to flee the scene. He's fast at my heels.

"Come on, honey. I'll leave you alone to do your work now."

"No, you won't. You men are all the same. You only want one thing. I quit."

"I don't think you will because you want that job promotion. That happens only if you're nice to me."

I grab my coat, purse, and the few pencils I love, head for the door, and throw the keys at him.

"Goodbye, Mr. Moskowitz." I leap for the door and flee to the safety of the sidewalk. My heart's pounding as the tears flow from my eyes, and I find myself running. *From what? He has been such a gentleman. What happened?*

Despair rises inside me like bubbling tar.

Chapter 33

A few days later, I lay in my bed wrapped up like a cocoon with a wad of hankies in my hands. It's a rainy day, and I can hear the wind howling away. No need to get out of bed. I'm ruined and penniless. *I hate men. All they want to do is take advantage of me. I should let myself go. Get fat and wear baggy clothes. Why did Theodore have to ruin everything? I loved my job, and his mother was a fringe benefit I won't find anywhere. I was starting to enjoy secretarial work.*

I punch my pillow several times, and the tears flow like Niagara Falls as my anger mounts to a peak. I throw the covers off and stomp over to the full-length mirror. I pull my nightgown over my head and stare at my naked image before me. Touching my hair and wiping the tears from my face, I realize my beauty and perfect figure could be a ticket to modeling.

Nah, not now. Not me.

"Yes, I'll make you famous. You can be a star model. Designers will be standing in line for you to wear the latest fashions." The keeper mutters over me.

I cover myself with my hands and slump to the floor. "I'm stronger than my fear of you."

"I'm always here. Always ready to give you a lift. Trust me."

"No. No. No! You're not real. Only a figment of my imagination."

"Violet, open the door. You have been shut up in that room for three days now. Enough is enough. You hear me?" Papa shouts.

I pull my nightgown off the floor and fling it over me. *Did Papa hear the keeper?*

"Alright, Papa. Give me a few minutes?"

"I'm making some poached eggs. You must eat something. I'll see you in the kitchen in ten minutes."

"So, you think I'm not here, my dear? Always, remember. I exist, even if you don't see me." The voice trails off as I flee to grab my robe. A black cloud of despair surrounds my body.

"You get out of my room and life." I slam the door behind me.

"Did you slam your bedroom door, Violet Pearl?"

"It was accident, Papa. I'm famished."

"Here you go, daughter. When was the last time you had something to eat?" my father asks.

I pick up the fork beside the plate of two poached eggs on rye toast and paw at it.

"Violet Pearl, I asked you a question."

"Two days ago."

He looks at me and then at Daisy. "Honey, go get ready for school and be sure to brush your teeth. We leave in fifteen minutes."

She brings her plate to the sink, grabs the last piece of toast, and darts out of the kitchen.

I take one mouthful with hesitation because I know I'm going to get the heat from Papa.

He pulls up a chair right next to me and gently takes hold of my chin to turn my face toward him. "I don't like what's happening to you, girl."

Taking his hand away from my chin, I take a bite of my eggs. "Don't worry about me, Papa."

"You're starting to worry me, Violet Pearl. Not eating and staying in your nightgown for three days is not normal behavior. I think you should see a doctor." *I want to hide.*

Forcing a mouthful of cold eggs into my mouth, I gaze at the dreary sky outside. "I'm alright, really."

"Theodore phoned three times yesterday and is worried sick about you."

Wrinkling my brow and taking in another mouthful, "Did he tell you I quit?"

"He said you grabbed all of your belongings in a hurry and announced that you weren't coming back."

"That's it?"

"Why, is there more you wish to tell me?"

I hesitate, then look him straight in the eye. "He pushed himself on me, Papa."

He chuckles and shakes his head. "It's so obvious that he likes you more than his employee, Violet Pearl. So, what? After all, you have been out on two dates with him and you are very beautiful."

I push the plate away from me and stand up. "That doesn't give him the right to put his hands all over me."

"Oh, come on, he did this in broad daylight while you were at work? Really, Violet. This man is an attorney, not a lowlife from the dark side of the city."

I stomp my foot and pound the table. "I can't believe you! You're my father, for goodness' sake. I expect you to stand by me one hundred percent."

He stands and grabs my shoulders. "Get it together, Violet Pearl. Take the day off; it's Friday anyway. Clean the house and call Theodore. That's an order. There are rules as long as you're living under this roof."

Daisy bursts through the door. "Papa, I'm ready. What's all the yelling about?"

He drops his grip on me and moves to the door. "Remember to meet your sister at school."

I busy myself with clearing the table and sweeping the floor. The waterworks ooze from my eyes as I recall the last hour in the law office of Theodore Moskowitz.

A few hours later, I marvel at the burst of energy that hits me like a ton of bricks. I don't leave the kitchen until all the dishes are washed, dried, and put away; floors swept and scrubbed; windows washed; woodwork dusted; and trash disposed of and counters cleared.

After that, I fly up the stairs, taking two at a time, and draw a nice hot bath for myself. After my bath, I get dressed in green wide-legged trousers with a matching striped knit sweater, strip my bed, change the bedding, and organize my room.

Prokofiev's *Peter and the Wolf*, long-playing record, bellows as I dust and clean the front parlor. The grandfather clock chimes two o'clock with a reminder that I have exactly one hour to get to the elementary school two blocks away.

I start to sway and twirl around the room as I clean. Soon, the music takes me center stage on our oriental rug, and I turn ten pirouettes in a polished order. I can almost hear the loud applause and shouts of *Bravo, Bravo*. I smile as a lone tear rolls down my face. I take a bow and gracefully fall into a heap on the floor. My shattered dream will never be a reality.

The rain has stopped, and the warm sun is shining brightly on the few puddles that are left on the street. I grab the mail to go through on the way. A few mothers walk ahead of me as I reminisce about the accomplishments of the day.

Leafing through the mail while waiting for Daisy, I discover an envelope with a return address, Theodore Moskowitz Law Firm.

I reluctantly open it. Instead of my last paycheck, I find a handwritten note.

My Dear Violet,

Please accept my apology for the way I acted on Monday afternoon. I realize that my behavior was not appropriate in any way. You're an asset to this law firm, and your secretarial skills are a necessity to our growth. Mother's still not well. I didn't enclose your last paycheck in hopes that I could see you one more time. Please give me another chance. I promise to treat you with the respect you deserve. Sincerely,

Theodore

"Vi, the sun's out. Can we go to the park now?" Daisy comes barreling down the stairs.

I almost drop the mail on the wet sidewalk at her sudden appearance. "Sure, we can. Do you want to go now or after you change?"

"Let's go now, Sissy. Please?"

"Why not. We don't have to rush back for supper because Papa will be late tonight."

I feel like a little kid today, so I grab her hand, and we skip most of the way to a small park that is almost near completion. There are no paved sidewalks, so it is a bit muddy from the rainfall. *Oh well, shoes and socks can be washed.*

A few other children Daisy seems to know are climbing and swinging. "Daisy, over here," one yells.

I tuck the mail into my coat pocket and lay my sister's school bag on the edge of the bench closest to the swings. I position myself on the swing and push myself off with my feet. My hair blows in the air as I swing back and forth. I'm having a ball. Higher and higher I kick my legs out for momentum. My imagination starts to run away from me as I reminisce about my mama and the things she did to entertain me when I was little girl. No playgrounds back then. We would spend hours digging in the dirt in the backyard, either making mud pies or planting seeds.

A big boy of about twelve grabs my feet. "Get off the swing. Now."

I kick my feet at him. "Okay, okay. Give me a minute, would you?"

As soon as I get close to the ground, I jump off and fortunately land on my feet. Next thing I know, I get a slam on my back that thrusts me forward, and I land face down in the mud.

Roars of laughter can be heard from all around me. I'm humiliated.

"What did you do to my sister, Eugene?" Daisy hollers as she pulls me up.

The boy laughs obnoxiously. "She has no business on the swings."

With fury in my heart and dirt all over me, I go after this kid. "Listen here. There are no signs that say these swings are only for children. Look what you did to me."

"Oh yeah. What are you going to do about it?" he yells in my face.

Daisy steps in front of me and gives him a good punch in his stomach. "Get on your swing and leave her alone, Eugene."

My kid sister stood up for me. Wow!

As we approach home, I can see someone sitting on the front steps but can't make out who it is.

Daisy runs at full speed ahead. "It's Mary Sue," she calls back at me.

"What in the world happened to you, Violet Pearl? You look absolutely hideous." She asks me as I approach the steps.

"Some oversize kid pushed me in the mud at the new playground. Come on in. I must get out of these filthy clothes. Can you stay for supper and how about overnight too?""I was hoping you would invite me. I have two days off from the university and thought I would take a chance to see if you were available. As you can see, I have a suitcase with me."

Mary Sue and I cook up a storm for supper. She made the most delicious potato pancakes, and I prepared applesauce from the last few overripe apples that were hidden in the pantry. Luckily, we found some chocolate and managed to make a devil's food cake for desert.

After supper, the three of us do the dishes and then sit down in the parlor to play Parcheesi. Before long, I realize it's time for Daisy to go to bed.

I kiss her on the cheek and pull the quilt over her small body. "Good night, sweet pea."

She yawns as she closes her eyes, "Thanks for taking me to the playground today, Sissy."

"You're welcome. And thank you for standing up for me with that kid—Eugene. That took a lot of bravery to do that."

She throws her arms around me. "I love you, Vi."

"I love you too, Daisy." I turn out the light and close the door behind me.

"What time is your father coming home anyway, Violet?" Mary Sue asks.

"The joint in Manhattan closes down at one, but they won't be out of there until two because it takes that long to pack up the instruments."

"So, we have plenty of time to kill, huh?" She laughs.

"We're in our nighties, and the beds are ready for us to jump in at a moment's notice. Sure. Let's get started on the gossip."

"You're not going to believe the news I have for you, my friend."

"What? Come on. Do tell."

"It's about your old flame, Marty. You know how he has trouble keeping his hands to himself?"

I suppress my thoughts and feelings. "Oh, of course. You don't have to remind me."

"I warned you about him a while ago, Violet. I'm so glad that you broke up with him when you did."

"Mary Sue. Get to the point."

"Elizabeth is pregnant."

My mouth drops open, and I become instantly speechless.

"Yeah. She's four months along."

Tears well up in my eyes. "That no good, two-timing creep. We were still dating four months ago."

209

Mary Sue huddles close. "Sorry, my friend. I've always thought he was a great big flirt."

"Me too." I sigh and grab her hand. "I was alone with him so many times, Mary Sue. I could be the one pregnant. Are all men the same? I quit my job because my boss made a sexual advance toward me." I want to scream. Instead I bring my hands to my face and let out gobs of tears. "I may end up like my aunt Flossie, after all." I sob.

I wake up bright and early on Monday with great uncertainty about my upcoming reunion with Theodore Moskowitz.

If I want my last paycheck, I must do the inevitable. I slip my crinkled crepe floral dress over my head and slide into my glossy black patent leather shoes; I realize that now is as good a time as any.

When I approach the office an hour later, I get cold feet. I turn around and head in the opposite direction.

Oh, come on. It's 8:30 in the morning. What could go wrong? I'll grab my paycheck and leave. It's easy, besides I really need the money. I take a deep breath and push open the glass door.

"Violet. It's so good to see you. How are you feeling, my dear?" Sarah asks.

"Sarah. What a pleasant surprise."

"Sit down and let me get you a cup of coffee."

Reluctantly, I peer down the hall. "Oh, I guess I can have one cup."

"Theodore said you were very sick. Are you going to work a full day today, dear?"

I pick up the coffee cup and take a sip. "Oh, I'm not staying. I came to get my paycheck."

"I'm so sorry that you're still not well. Take all the time you need, dear."

She has no idea what her dear son is really like. Maybe, I should let her know what almost happened in this very office.

"Violet. It's so good to see you here," Theodore says opening the door.

"Thank you, Mr. Moskowitz." Memories of this place snatch my soul and I shudder.

"Your paycheck is on your desk. I'm running late. I should be in court right now."

"Violet's going to work a half day today, Theodore," Sarah comments.

He looks at her and then at me and smiles. "Perfect. You can work part time until you feel like handling more hours. I'll see you tomorrow."

Before I can get up enough courage to say, I could never work with a jerk like you. He's gone.

Sarah's a special lady and I wouldn't hurt her for the world, so I don't share with her the encounter her son and I had last week. Instead, I lie and tell her I'm still not feeling up to working yet. She gives me a hug and hands the check to me.

"Thank you, Sarah. I'll see you tomorrow. Okay?" *How can I lie to such a sweet lady?*

I'm ashamed I lied to Sarah. I can't go back there. That's all there is to it. I open the envelope and pull out the check for a hundred and twenty-five dollars.. *That should last until I can find another job.*

I purchase today's issue of the *Brooklyn Daily Eagle* at a nearby newsstand with hopes that a new position will jump off the page at me. My feet are killing me. I might as well get a bite to eat. Who knows? There might be a perfect job right around the corner.

"What can I get you, Madam?" The waiter asks me.

"Corned beef on rye please and a Coca-Cola."

"Coming right up."

Flipping through the newspaper to the classified section, I glance at the help-wanted category. Let's see, seamstress…nanny…seamstress…salesclerk…. Dance teacher wanted at Alex Murphy's, 222 Flatbush Avenue. *That's right around the corner.*

Chapter 34

Wow. That must be the longest flight of stairs I've ever climbed at one time. I lost count of the steps after twenty-five but so glad to find a bench on this landing before I proceed up the last few steps.

A tall slender brunette chomping on a large wad of gum plants herself next to me. "Hi. Are you going to take some dance lessons here?"

"Uh, no. Not exactly. I'm applying for the instructor position."

Looking me over from head to toe. "Aren't you a bit young for this, honey?"

I scowl and force a grin. "I'm nineteen years old and have a lot of dance experience."

"Calm down, sweetheart. You may work out after all. You would be replacing me if you get the job."

"You? I don't understand."

"I've been somebody's dance partner for two years now but not anymore." She puts her hand in front of me and flashes a big diamond. "I'm getting married and moving to Buffalo."

Since I never saw such a beautiful piece of jewelry in my whole life, I grab her hand. "This is spectacular. Congratulations. When is the big day?"

"Saturday."

"This Saturday?"

"Yep. Now, come with me." She pulls me up and practically drags me to the top of the stairs into the huge studio. "By the way, my name's Maureen. What's yours?"

I'm totally amazed at the size of this room, as it appears to cover one whole city block. The large shiny wooden dance floor is surrounded by several tables with white tablecloths. A few couples are sitting down and conversing while two couples are in the middle of the floor practicing dance moves.

An older lady with graying hair approaches us. "I thought you left, Maureen."

"I came back to introduce you to?"

"I'm Violet Moretti."

"She's here for the position, Mrs. Murphy. Look at her. She's perfect for the job. Petite and beautiful, and she has a dance background."

Smiling from ear to ear, Mrs. Murphy says. "I would love to see you dance before I say you have the job."

"Well, I have to run. I'll leave you two alone. Good luck, Violet Moretti." Maureen flees out of the door in a flutter.

Stompin' at the Savoy, a Fletcher Henderson arrangement, fills the vast room, and several couples break out into a swing dance on the floor.

Taking my hand, Mrs. Murphy leads me over to a tall distinguished-looking gentleman dressed in a gray three-piece suit. "Violet. This is my husband, Mr. Murphy. We are the owners of this establishment."

"Pleased to meet you, Sir."

He smiles, and even though he's married and quite a bit older than me, I blush.

"She would like to take Maureen's place, but I must see what her dancing ability is first. Will you be a dear and dance with her, so I can observe if she's a good fit or not?"

"It will be my honor to dance with Miss Violet. Come, my dear."

I put my belongings down on the closest empty chair and take his hand. Some have resorted to sitting, and a few single ladies are studying the couples moving to the music. The only time I ever danced the swing dance was at my senior dance with Marty. My thoughts go there by themselves. This is a disaster waiting to happen.

He gently twirls me around one way and then the other. He grabs both hands, and I move my feet to the music, cheating as I peer at a nearby couple. Before I know it, he grabs my waist and lifts me over his head. I try not to show my nervousness, so I land gracefully on both feet. Lucky move.

"You're so tense. Relax," he whispers when he gets a chance.

He spins me around, and we boogie across the floor.

When the music stops, applause fills the room. On an impulse, I curtsy and smile.

Let's Spill the Beans changes the pace, and now we're in a soothing promenade, but it's different. He's close to me with our hands around each other's waist and the other hand resting, palm to palm.

"Follow my lead, Violet. This is a fox-trot not a waltz."

I nod and smile. "I think I need to take a class not teach it."

"We'll do slows which are two beats per step. One, two. One two."

"I did this dance many years ago on the Vaudeville stage."

"Glide, Glide. One, two. You're so graceful. Ballet lessons?"

Smiling but with very sweaty palms, I manage to say, "Yes."

"You're a very fast learner, but you need a few private lessons. We dance six days a week from noon to seven. The pay is one hundred dollars a week to start. No paid holidays. You must be dressed in your Sunday best every day. What do you think?" Mrs. Murphy asks.

"You would give me a chance, really?" My stomach does a jitterbug.

Mr. Murphy reaches his hand out to me. "It's yours if you can fulfill the guidelines my wife laid out for you."

Looking around the room at some of the more experienced dancers, I falter. "I don't know if this is right for me."

"Once you get the steps mastered with the fox-trot, Lindy, and cha-cha, you will have it made. Can you be here the rest of the week at eleven?"

"I can do that. How long will I have to take private lessons?"

"Maureen's last day is Friday. Tomorrow is Tuesday. You'll have these conquered by the end of the week."

"What do you say, Miss Moretti? Do you want to give it a whirl?" Mr. Murphy asks.

"I do need a job, and I love to dance. Okay. I'll be here tomorrow for my first lesson." I snatch my purse and shawl and reach out my hand to Mrs. Murphy and glance at her husband. "It was so nice meeting you both."

"Looking forward to seeing you grow as a Murphy's dance teacher."

Moving to the door, I turn around and ask, "Do I get paid to learn?" I'm so excited; I'm about to burst. I must be dreaming because this could be the best job ever.

The couple exchange glances and softly chuckle, "Not usually, but we like you very much. So how does five dollars a lesson sound to you? It gives you cash to cover your transportation. If everything goes well this week, then you'll be on the payroll by Monday."

I laugh with them. It lightens my chest and warms me from the inside.

"Thank you for giving me a chance. I promise not to let you down."

"I'll give you a short application to fill out tomorrow. Oh, and be sure to wear comfortable but stylish shoes."

My heart's throbbing, and my legs feel a little wobbly, but I manage to smile. "Looking forward to tomorrow."

I'm so excited I could scream. I didn't want to work behind a desk anyway. Teaching people how to ballroom dance is the next best thing of fulfilling my dream as a ballerina. Papa should be very happy for me because I'll be getting paid to do something I love.

Chapter 35

"What are you cooking, Papa?" I ask as I hang up my shawl on the hook in the foyer.

He's reading the newspaper, and Daisy is sprawled out on the rug in front of him reading the latest issue of *Adventure Comics*.

"Spaghetti sauce with lots of garlic and onions. Are you hungry?"

"Famished. What time is supper?" Petunia crawls on my lap seeking attention.

"There's something on the table in the kitchen for you, Violet Pearl." Papa manages to say with his head in the paper.

"For me? What?" I get up with the cat in my arms.

"Flowers, Vi-Vi." Daisy looks up and smiles.

Bursting through the door, I observe twelve long stem roses in a tall pink-tinted glass vase. Smiling with wonder, I pull out the attached tiny envelope. It is addressed, *To: Violet Pearl Moretti.*

Who would send me roses? I pull out the small card.

Violet, I'm so happy that you have reconsidered coming back to work at the law firm.

These roses are a token of my appreciation for your hard work and to help you feel better.

Theodore

I rip the note in shreds, throw it in the trash, go to the stove, and stir the red sauce in the large kettle.

"So, who are these beautiful flowers from?" Papa asks as he comes into the kitchen.

He grabs another pot and proceeds to the sink to fill it with water.

"They're from Mr. Moskowitz."

"That's so nice of him, Flower. He must be delighted that you have decided to return to work."

"I'm not going back there, Papa. Not now. Not ever. Anyway, I found a new place to work."

He turns to me and grabs my shoulders as he always does when annoyed with me. "You have a future with that law firm. You'll go back tomorrow. Do you hear me?"

"I'm nineteen years old. I can make my own choices on where I work."

"Are we having spaghetti or not? I'm hungry, Papa," Daisy says as she bursts in the room.

I flee to the cupboard to get the plates and set the table. I can feel him glaring at me as I complete the task.

"So, how was your day today, Daisy?" I ask as I smooth out her hair.

"Auntie met me at school today, and she took me shopping at Gimbel's in the big city. I got a new dress with great big flowers, black patent leather shoes, and white ankle socks with ruffles. She said we are all going to church on Easter."

"We'll see about that," Papa grumbles.

"I want to see you model that dress for me after supper. Okay?"

Daisy nods and smiles. "Auntie wants you to call her to make arrangements to go shopping with her too."

"Oh, Daisy. You look beautiful in that new outfit. All you need now is a hat and look out Easter parade; here comes the best-looking ten-year-old who ever walked the streets."

"All the girls at school are talking about bonnets for church. It's all the rage."

"You know what? I can make you a hat."

She gives me a big hug. "Sissy, can you have it done by Easter?"

"I'm pretty busy, Daisy. When's Easter anyway?"

"In one month. I really want to go to church, don't you?"

"It would be nice to go as a family. I haven't been in a church since Mama died. Do you think Papa would go with us?"

"I hope so."

A few hours later, on my way upstairs, I stop in the parlor. "Good night, Papa."

"I'm sorry about before, daughter, but I would like to know about your new job. Come sit for a bit, alright?"

I walk over to the couch and sit. "Papa, I was very upset with you when I told you that Theodore made a sexual advance toward me. You made me feel like it was my fault."

"I'm sorry, flower. Tell me again, and I promise to be more understanding."

"Two weeks ago, his mother was ill and could not come down to the office. Theodore and I were alone."

"That's not unusual, is it?"

"It would be fine, but he tried to force himself on me, Papa, but I was able to get away from him."

He grabs my hand with a vastly concerned look on his face. "Did he hurt you, flower?"

"Not my body but my spirit for sure."

"That's why the roses and the phone calls."

The tears start rolling down my face. "I don't care to date ever again. Men are all the same."

"These are the precious times that I wish your sweet mother was still with us. She would know exactly what to say. I can only tell you that you're a beautiful and sought-after woman. You definitely turn heads when you walk down main street, Violet Pearl."

I open the small drawer in the end table and grab an embroidered handkerchief, "Thank you, Papa."

"I mean that, not just because you're my daughter either. Now, what really happened between you and Marty? I certainly liked that boy."

I wipe my eyes and blow my nose "Marty told me he loved me and then tried to take advantage of me. He kept apologizing, but each time we were alone, things would turn."

"I'm so glad we are having this talk, Violet Pearl. Maybe you should continue this conversation with your aunt Flossie. You don't have to tell me anymore."

"Don't worry. He never succeeded. I broke up with him before it did."

"Well, he better not come over here to lure you back to him. He'll have to deal with me first."

"He's moved on to another victim. This time he got what he wanted."

Papa scowled. "He got a girl pregnant, didn't he?"

No more words are uttered. Instead, he wraps his arms around me and holds me in his arms for a long time. This is the most tender moment I've had with my father in years. I'm overwhelmed by the warm atmosphere in this house right now.

The dance studio is empty of dancers, and the blinds are drawn as I peek into the dimly lit room through the glass door. I knock on the door, but there doesn't seem to be anyone in sight.

Did I get the day and time wrong?

I hear footsteps coming up the long flight of stairs.

Mrs. Murphy appears, huffing and puffing, with Mr. Murphy behind her. "You're still here. Good."

"This girl is early," Mr. Murphy said. "I told you she's the perfect one for the job." He pulls a set of keys out of his pocket and opens the door.

"Show Violet where the dressing rooms are, Gladys, and I will get the application." He smiles at both of us.

I suddenly feel like a movie star as I feast my eyes on the women's dressing room. It's painted a pale pink with dark-crimson satin drapes adorning the three large windows. The pleasant scent of lily of the valley fills the area designated for the ladies.

"Honey, this will be your dressing room." Mrs. Murphy opens the door and ushers me in.

"Wow. This is remarkable. Look at this full-length mirror."

"You can leave your dancing shoes here every night. Maureen likes to have several dresses to change into, especially during the hot summer months. Take a few minutes to freshen up. I'll see you on the dance floor in ten."

With that, I'm left alone. I sit down on the white brocade high-back chair in the corner and change into black strappy leather shoes. Auntie wants to take me shopping, so I'll wait and buy a couple of dresses off the sale rack.

Standing up and looking in the mirror, I practice smiling and curtsying as though a handsome partner is smiling back. Smoothing out my two-piece green knit outfit and brushing my hair twice, I exit the small room.

"You look beautiful, girlie," Maureen remarks as I walk out on the dance floor.

I blush at the compliment and smile at her. "Hi Maureen, it's nice to see you again."

"Always respond to a compliment. You'll get a lot of them for sure."

"I'm sorry. Thank you for your kind words."

She laughs loudly. "I'm here to train and help you, Violet."

Alex Murphy comes out of the office by the entryway. "Good morning, Ladies. Let's begin with basic steps to the fox-trot. Maureen, face me, and Violet, four feet behind her. Yes. Okay. Now, music please, Gladys."

Fred Astaire singing *Cheek to Cheek* fills the vast room.

Chomping on gum, Maureen looks at me. "Think of me as Fred and you are Ginger. Okay?"

"Violet, let's master the waltz today. Our guests will arrive in forty-five minutes." Alex smiles.

Maureen and I glide across the floor to *The Blue Danube Waltz*. It plays over and over with a few pauses. Two couples arrive fifteen minutes before the first class, but we keep dancing.

A very short older man with brown horned-rim glasses and an extraordinary amount of brown curly hair bursts through the door. "Hey, who's the new girl with Maureen?"

Blushing with embarrassment, I drop my arms and freeze.

"Now, look what you did, Arnold. You upset my friend, Violet." Maureen scolds him.

He reaches out his hand and leans close to me. "You must be Maureen's replacement? My name's Arnold, and I guess you can call me a regular around here."

I'm appalled at his atrocious breath. "Please, excuse me, Arnold."

"Honestly, Arnold. You must do something about your breath," Maureen announces as she follows me to the office.

"Don't pay any attention to Arnold, my dear," Gladys Murphy says when we enter the office. "He's been coming here for a year now in hopes of finding a wife. He couldn't care less about learning how to dance correctly. If he pays for his lessons…that's all that matters. Now, have a seat so you can fill out this application."

Maureen taps me on the shoulder. "I'll see you tomorrow, honey. I have to get to work."

"Thanks for all your help," I say.

"No problem," she answers as she rushes out of the door.

"Violet, you really have the Box Waltz pegged," Alex says. "So tomorrow, we'll learn the American swing. After you're finished with the paperwork, please come, sit, and observe how we conduct the dance classes. You can leave any time after that. We'll totally understand." My heart jumps with his honesty.

Alex Murphy's Dance Studio is obviously a popular destination for the office crowd. I park myself at a table in the corner by a big window, so I can see the entire dance floor.

At exactly ten minutes to twelve, Alex cranks up the phonograph with *Rhythm Is Our Business*, and Jimmie Lunceford's voice croons loudly as the couples explode into the ballroom.

They know swing dancing like it's nobody's business. I don't think any of these folks need lessons. I stand in amazement when one fella flips his partner over his head and then flips her from side to side.

When the song ends, Alex walks to the middle of the floor, "Okay. Dancers. Great job. Clear the floor please so that Mrs. Murphy and I can demonstrate the fox-trot. Music please, Maureen."

Everyone stares in amazement as the two floats from corner to corner in perfect rhythm and sequence. I'm in awe of them. Suddenly, two hands wrap around my waist, and I turn to find my chest even with Arnold's eyes.

"What are you doing?" I ask him.

"Please dance with me."

"I really must leave. I'm sorry, Arnold. Maybe another time." *Whew, good thing the Murphys said I could leave when I wanted to. I couldn't stand another minute with that guy.*

Closing the door behind me, I breathe a sigh of relief. Looking down at my feet as I always do, I proceed down the first set of stairs and plow right into someone of the male persuasion. I can tell by the shoes he's wearing.

I look up at a very debonair gentleman with the bluest eyes I've ever seen. He smiles.

We look at each other for a minute or so. "Excuse me, Sir," I manage to say. "I should look where I'm going." My heart's pitter-pattering.

Sounds of high heels can be heard on the steps below. "Henry. Why can't you wait for me? You know how hard it is for me to keep up with you when I wear these shoes." A tall, slender big-busted blonde brushes shoulders with me and nearly knocks me down the steps.

I start going down the stairs but can't help but look back up. The man called Henry is still smiling at me. I smile back, turn, and continue down the steps. I never saw this man until now, but there's something different about him. He's handsome for one thing, but I know there's more.

"Hey. You're with me, remember that. Don't two-time me, Henry. Who's that dame anyway?" The woman says loudly.

I exit, with a smile on my face, into the fresh, welcoming air. I'm excited about my accomplishment of the first two days of learning how to dance with the crème da crème. I must get myself some new dresses, so I look more professional.

I don't really want to go home tonight because I'm not ready to tell Papa about my newest place of employment. I'll detour over to Auntie's house and spend the night with her.

Things are looking up.

Chapter 36

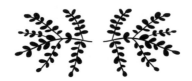

"There's so much to tell you, Auntie, but first I must call Papa and tell him where I am. He worries when I don't come home for supper. He knows you, and I need some alone time."

Auntie gives me a big hug when I hang up. "You're certainly a beautiful young woman now. The fellas must be standing in line at your front door to court you."

"Oh, Auntie. I'm on cloud nine right now. You must be the first to know about the new job I started two days ago."

"Please tell me while I rustle something up for supper. Hmmm. How about sausage, potato pancakes, and applesauce?"

She pulls out an onion from the pantry and grabs several potatoes. "Here, you can peel these while you tell me your news."

I get that warm fuzzy feeling when I am in this house but especially the kitchen.

"Violet. Talk to me, honey."

I chuckle and snort a bit. "I love your house, Auntie. Not only does it remind me of Mama, but I get such a warmhearted feeling whenever I walk through the door."

"Toots, I love you for that, but I want to know about your new place of employment."

"I have two days under my belt as an instructor at the Alex Murphy Dance Studio. I start full time on Monday."

She turns to look at me with excitement written all over her face. "Oh, that's simply marvelous. You have always had a heart for the dance, and I know how much you wanted to be a ballerina. The moves and steps are different, but your quick ability to learn will bring you up to par with the best dancers in no time."

"You always say the right things, Auntie." With that, I leap to my feet and hug her with all my might.

"What happened at the law office?"

"Mr. Moskowitz wanted favors for my advancement, so I quit."

She lets out a huge sigh. "That's a good reason to quit any job. Now, get back to peeling those spuds so we can eat before midnight."

After an amazing supper and making the kitchen sparkle once again, we head into the front parlor for an evening of relaxation.

"Auntie, can you play a waltz on the piano, so I can practice what I learned. I think I have it, but it's the fox-trot that troubles me."

She lifts the piano bench and pulls out a stack of sheet music. "Let me see what I can dig up. I know I have something. Here. How about the *Chopsticks Waltz*? That's nice and easy to follow."

I position myself as though a handsome man such as that Henry fella was right in front of me.

After an hour of doing the same thing over and over, Auntie stops playing and declares, "You have that down with perfection, my dear. Now, I do remember the fox-trot when I was in the courting days of my life. I will be your instructor, and all you must do is follow me. Okay?"

Auntie closes the piano and stands in front of me. "We don't need any music. The count and rhythm are all that matters."

One hour later, Auntie asks, "How are we doing, Tootsie?"

I turn her around, so she is facing me. "I think I finally have it. Thanks to you."

She turns on the Victrola, and soon we are gliding throughout the house.

She bows, and I curtsy.

"By George, I think you have these dances nailed, my dear girl. I'm sure your new boss will be very impressed. We better call it a night because we have a busy morning of shopping."

"Okay, see you in the morning."

I take a few minutes and wander around the house to check if doors are securely locked. Then I peer out of the bay window to see if any weird characters are gawking at this place. No one. Good.

Alone in my room, my thoughts are consumed with Mama. It's hard to believe six years have gone by since we lost her. I find myself doing some of the odd things she did leading up to the horrific night, like thinking I'm not alone in a room when I am or staring at myself in the mirror for an hour as I put on gobs of makeup.

Probably, a coincidence.

I burst into tears as I toss and turn in bed. *Why am I crying?*

Auntie's the only one who really loves me. Everyone just tolerates me. I'm nineteen and still living at home with my father and sister. All my friends are either in college or in their own places. The boyfriend thing is a lost cause.

Something must change soon.

"Oh, dear one. Don't you worry your little head. I'll take care of you. Don't you know this by now?" The cool, eerie voice of the keeper hovers over me.

I curl up in a ball on the floor and pull my hands over my ears. "You're not real. Not real."

"Listen to me when I speak. Do not try to think."

"You're not real."

"But I am. Remember this. I am a spirit. I live within. All is mine. Listen."

"Why can't others see this?"

The door bursts open. I leap off the floor.

Auntie pulls me in her arms. "Violet, I heard you talking to yourself. I'm worried about you."

I laugh, "I was practicing my dance moves out loud, Auntie."

She's not amused. "You better get to sleep. I'll keep the door open just in case you need me."

I'll be sleeping with the lamp on tonight. "Okay."

Hearing the clock in the dining room strike midnight, I crawl under the covers so the night can lure me to sleep.

"Yikes, don't you look snazzy, Miss Violet. That dress will get any man to swoon over you instantly." Maureen comments as I walk into the studio the next day.

I grin from ear to ear, "My aunt took me shopping."

"Well, you have a real nice aunt. I could use one like that," she says.

"Good morning, Violet." Alex says. "Let's see if you mastered the waltz yet. Find a record, Maureen, while Violet puts her things away and changes her shoes."

Music is bellowing throughout the dark studio when I return. Alex takes my hand. My palms are sweaty, and the nerves inside are striking their own beats.

Alex smiles, "Relax, my dear."

I take a deep breath; he takes the lead, and I amaze myself as we glide around the floor in perfect unison.

"I'm so impressed with you, Violet," Alex says. "You must have stayed up all night to master the waltz and the fox-trot the way you did. Do you think you are ready to dance with a student today?"

"Yes, Mr. Murphy. As long as we don't tango or rumba." I suppress the urge to burst out laughing.

He giggles discreetly and pats my shoulder. "You're a cutie, that's for sure, but please call me Alex."

Maureen tugs on my hand. "Come on, we'll take a break before the crowd surges through the door."

"Be back on the floor in ten," Gladys Murphy calls to us.

In my private dressing room, I gaze at myself in the mirror and smile with admiration at the yellow organdy tea dress I'm wearing. I must say, this dress accentuates my long black wavy hair. I wonder who my first student will be.

Someone knocks on my door.

"Come in."

Maureen, dressed in a red, flowing, midcalf-length dress is gleaming from ear to ear. "I'm so excited for you, Violet. In just a few moments, you'll be on that dance floor teaching your first student. You have come a long way babe in three days." She hugs me.

"I'm so nervous, Maureen. What if I get a real handsome hunk and I can't concentrate?"

"Listen, honey. If that happens, you'll hear a loud holler of the positive type from me for sure because the good-looking ones are always spoken for."

"It will be my luck to get someone like Arnold. Does Alex do the picking, or do we?"

"He does in the beginning. So be prepared to have a permanent grin on your face no matter who he picks for you. Take it from one who knows. We better get out there."

The instructors are asked to stand in a line near the front door, so they are available to greet folks as they enter the vast room. As soon as Gladys opens the door, couples of all ages push their way inside as if they are going to miss something. They find tables closest to the dance floor. One couple dances face-to-face looking starry eyed at each other while holding hands.

Oh, to be that much in love.

A few single ladies and gentlemen walk timidly into the room and stand across from us. Alex spots them.

Reaching out his hand, he says, "I'm Alex Murphy, and this is my wife, Gladys. These are our instructors. Find a table to put down your personal belongings. The first dance is a waltz, and it's on the house. All dance sessions are ten dollars, payable in cash before the second dance."

I'm teamed up with a young man who could be my little brother. He's a scrawny, freckled faced kid, but oh what a sweet smile. I take his hand.

"Hello, my name is Violet. What's yours?"

"Hi, Violet. I'm Johnny."

We never leave the place in which we start during the entire first song. He must have said "I'm sorry" for stepping on my toes at least ten times. Before the second waltz, Alex asks us to clear the floor, so people can pay, while experienced dancers do a demonstration dance.

Johnny bows. "Thank you, Violet. See ya later."

The *Shadow Waltz* fills the room as the dancer's glide across the floor in perfect rhythm and motion.

I'm so caught up in the music and the scene before me that I don't even realize a few new couples have entered the room.

As soon as the music stops, the couple I saw on the steps the other day is standing near the middle of the room. "Henry, you must teach me how to do that. Do you hear me?" the blonde wearing a skin-tight dress says loudly.

Everyone stops and stares at her.

Henry looks at her in a disgusted manner and leads her away from the center of attention, which happens to be right in front of me. "Shush up, Ruby. Must you be so loud?"

She pushes him in the chest. "You always say that, Henry. It's just your imagination. I'm not loud."

"Okay, Folks. Now we'll move on to a fox-trot." Alex announces. "If you don't know how to do this, then I suggest you team up with one of our instructors. I'll give you a few minutes to get organized before I turn on the music."

"I have to go to the little girl's room, Henry. You better be right here when I come back."

Ruby flits into the dressing room area where the lavatory is located. Henry shakes his head as he watches her leave the room.

"Violet? Please dance with Henry until his partner returns," Gladys says as she approaches me.

Reluctantly, I take his hand in the palm of my clammy one. "Yes, Mrs. Murphy."

Irving Berlin's, *Cheek to Cheek* fills the room, but Henry and I stand face-to-face holding hands. Some couples are dancing on the outside of the floor like they know what they're doing while others are counting out loud.

Someone taps my shoulder from behind me. "Back with the right foot," Alex whispers to me. "Slow. Back with the left. Slow."

As soon as Alex moves on to the next struggling couple, Henry says softly. "Follow me, Violet, but don't let on that I'm leading."

My, this man's so easy to follow, and I can't stop glaring into those blue eyes. This is amazing. I do have the best job ever. Our eyes are locked on each other as we float on the floor. Before I know it, we are gliding across the floor with the experienced couples and enjoying every minute of it too. I feel like I'm in heaven.

"Hey, what's the meaning of this anyway?" Ruby bellows as she pulls us apart.

"Honestly, Ruby. This dance is almost over," Henry says, evidently not affected by her rudeness.

She turns and looks at me. "Go on and beat it. Henry's with me."

Looking down at my black patent leather shoes, I say, "Nice dancing with you, Henry."

Most couples have stopped dancing and have decided that our display is much more interesting.

Henry takes my hand. "This song is still in progress. Let's finish it, Violet."

Ruby pushes me and then grabs my arm and flings me aside. "Don't even think about it, little girl." I can feel the blood flow bubble up inside of me; my heart races and I perspire all over. Not paying any attention to where I am, I grab the big blonde from behind, and with all my strength, I pull her down. Her skin-tight green dress splits up the front, exposing her black girdle.

She screeches in horror. "Look what you did, vicious girl."

I hear an applause from somewhere in the room.

I feel hands around my waist, pulling me away from the scene. "Come here, Violet," Maureen says.

Backing away, I see Henry extend his hand to help Ruby up. She gets up and then punches him in the gut. "Take me home this instant."

"Okay. Break it up, everyone. Let's take a ten-minute break," Alex announces.

Everyone scatters except for Ruby. "Fire her. That instructor of yours in the yellow dress is a flirt and a troublemaker."

Henry starts to come to me but turns to Ruby, "It's time to go, Ruby. Get your purse."

As she gets her belongings, she stomps over to me, but Maureen quickly stands in her way.

"You better leave my boyfriend alone. I'll carve up your pretty little face if you don't." Ruby says through clenched teeth.

"It's time to leave, lady," Maureen says. "We don't want any trouble."

Henry comes next to me and whispers, "Don't worry; she's all talk."

Ruby storms out of the door ahead of her date.

At first, I could've heard a pin drop in the Murphy's office, but I decide to speak first. "I'm so sorry that I let things get out of control, Alex."

"I should let you go, Violet. Your behavior was uncalled for. The customer's always right, regardless of the circumstances. However, I do have to look at the whole picture, because we are somewhat responsible."

"Yes. Alex. I asked Violet to dance with Henry because his partner was in the lavatory," Gladys chimes in.

Maureen's standing next to me with her arm around my shoulder. "That Ruby is one tough broad, Alex. Violet had to protect herself."

Peering out of the window to the dance floor, Alex finally says, "Okay, Violet. Pull yourself together and take as long as you need, but I never want to see that kind of performance again."

Chapter 37

"You're working where?" Papa asks as he opens the front door to leave for a Thursday-night gig.

"Alex Murphy's Dance Studio as an instructor."

He closes the door. "You went to business school to land a good office job as a secretary. Teaching people to dance for fun is not an option. Tell them to find someone else tomorrow. The boys are expecting me. I have to go."

"But, Papa."

He turns on his heels.

"I never expected him to understand or to be happy for you. Always a conflict. What's he going to do? Kick you out of the house? He has a built-in babysitter with you living here." The keeper whispers from behind me.

"Why are you here now? I thought you moved on to your next victim."

"Do you trust me, Violet?"

I look around the room, hoping Daisy's not hearing this conversation. "What can you do?"

"Be patient. Be still. I'm here for you."

I take in a deep breath, "How can I believe in something I can't see? You better shut up or leave, keeper. I think I hear my sister."

"Sissy, are you working in a dance studio again?" Daisy asks as she bounds down the steps.

"I sure am. Come on, you can be my student. Do you want to have some fun?"

The two of us meander to the record cabinet and peel through the various tunes. Time has no limit as we dance until bedtime. Daisy likes the Lindy hop. It's so easy to pick the little thing up and fling her around.

"I always have an arithmetic test on Friday. Will you wake me up an hour earlier tomorrow, Vi?" Daisy asks as I tuck her in bed.

"Papa or I will. Okay?" She's quite the little genius where schoolwork is concerned.

"I have to get an A. I won't settle for anything else," she mutters as she closes her eyes.

It's nice having the mornings to do any necessary housework or to practice dance moves. Of course, I do the latter if my father is out of the house, and today is one of those days. His Italian buddy, Victor Russo, opened a delicatessen over on Court Street a few months ago. So, Papa works a few days a week when he can. The deli's becoming quite the place to eat, and the locals are raving about Mr. Moretti's spaghetti sauce too.

The first week at Alex Murphy's went well, but I stay clear of Henry and Ruby on Friday. It's easy to do because Friday's are the most popular, and instructors are always busy. There are no lessons, but if singles attend, instructors are asked to seek them out and dance with them. The Murphys have declared this day of the week to be reserved for formal attire to draw the more sophisticated crowd. Flickering candles on each table add to the festive ambiance.

They surprise Maureen with a small wedding cake and champagne at the end of the night. Then to her utter amazement, her fiancé, Jack McIntire, arrives in time to celebrate with her.

"Congratulations, Maureen and Jack," Alex says as he raises a glass of champagne. "May you enjoy many, many years of marital bliss? We'll miss you, dear friends. Cheers."

To end the festivities, Alex plays *The Blue Danube Waltz,* so the happy couple can own the dance floor one more time. With hugs, tears, and two long-stem roses, it's time to call it a night.

My first Monday afternoon at Alex Murphy's is dullsville, to say the least. I've already been forewarned by Maureen that the first-time dancers are usually the only patrons who attend.

Oh no, here comes Arnold. Great. What's he doing here? Of course, looking for a wife. Oh no, he's heading this way.

I'll Dance at Your wedding Day, a slow waltz, fills the room.

"Come on, Arnold. Let's dance." I realize I have no choice since he's the only single male in sight.

"Violet, you look beautiful in that red dress."

I pull away from his grotesque breath but am happy his dancing has improved. We finish the waltz, and I curtsy to show my approval and slip him a breath mint.

Gladys comes to my rescue after three dances, so I can take a bathroom break. There are thirteen people in the ballroom today, including the Murphys and me. Three more hours. This is going to be a long day.

I brush my hair and place the black velvet bow back in my hair, straighten my dress, and head back out to the dance floor. A few more guests have arrived. Good.

As I make my way to the front, I realize one of them is Henry, and he's alone. My goodness. My heart's pounding in perfect synchronization. He's looking at me with that heartwarming smile too. *Get it together, Violet.*

I feel my mouth slip into a smile to match his. "Good afternoon, Henry. How are you today?"

"I'm doing great now that I see you in front of me."

"Are you alone?" I ask, moistening my lips.

"Yes. I am." He chuckles and takes my hand. "I suppose you're wondering about Ruby?"

Sing, Sing, Sing by Benny Goodman blares around us, and I see Alex give me a nod.

Henry and I evidently are going to be doing a demonstration swing dance for everyone because we are in the middle of a circle of folks clapping their hands to the music. A few lifts and quick moves later, he lifts me up in his arms and we strike a pose.

"Hooray! Bravo!" Everyone shouts with excitement. I'm smiling so hard, my cheeks hurt.

"You two kids take a ten-minute break," Alex says. "Wow. That was fantastic."

For some reason, we walk hand in hand over to an empty table.

Is it possible to fall in love with someone I barely know?

"Can I get you a cold drink?" he asks.

"That would be delightful. Thank you." I watch him saunter over to the small refreshment counter set up in the far corner of the room. Occasionally, I look at the door for that obnoxious Ruby.

"I hope you're okay with a Coca-Cola?" He hands me one and sits down beside me.

I take a sip. "This is just what the doctor ordered."

He grins. "How long have you been working here as a dance instructor? You're quite the little dancer."

"Actually, one week tomorrow."

"Well, you must have previous dance training because you hardly miss a beat."

"I appreciate you saying that, Henry. I love dancing with you because you're such an experienced dancer. You should get a job here too."

"Violet, you're so kind, and extremely beautiful I must add." His eyes lock with mine.

There's something different about this fella. He seems so sincere and caring. I feel my face blush when he leans closer to me. He takes my hand in his. "Will you have dinner with me tonight?" His touch sends currants from my fingers to my heart.

"What about your Ruby girl?" I look at the door and back at him.

"Forget about her. She went back to her old fling and is moving to Chicago as we speak. Ruby means absolutely nothing to me. How about that dinner?"

"If you don't mind hanging around until I get off at seven?"

"I got off work early, in hopes of seeing you. I have no problem wait-ing, if I can steal a dance or two with you."

Henry and I become the center of attraction because our dance moves are a good teaching tool for the new dancers. It's thrilling to see the expressions of approval on the Murphys' faces as we wiz past them.

Before I realize it, Alex announces, "Last dance is a waltz, everyone."

"I'll be right back, Henry. I want to freshen up a bit and change my shoes." I smile and walk toward the dressing room. *Am I really going on a date with a man I hardly know?*

As we head downstairs to the street, I look up at him. "So where are you taking me, and how are we going to get there? Bus or elevated train?"

Henry laughs as he approaches a black 1933 Buick Street Rod and opens the door. "Your chariot awaits." I take a deep breath. It all seems so real. Too sincere to be a dream.

My words are locked up inside of me as we drive over the Brooklyn Bridge and into China Town. He pays a dollar to park in a well-lit parking lot, and we walk through jam-packed streets filled with pedestrians. He doesn't let go of my hand as we stroll swiftly along, taking in the pungent smells of ginger, onions, and stir-fried meat.

After two blocks, we stop in front of a sign that says, *Wo Hop.*

"This is my favorite place," he explains.

We walk down several steps into a basement establishment.

"It's not a fancy place by any means, but they serve up the best Chop Suey in New York. I hope you like Chinese food."

Not letting on that I am ecstatic to simply be with him, I say, "I love it, but I must confess I don't have it very often."

We sip on hot tea, nibble on egg rolls, and share a generous portion of the main entrée. Conversation is minimal, but we seem so relaxed with each other. As though we have known each other for ever. The elderly Chinese waiter brings the bill with almond cookies and orange slices.

Henry looks at his watch. "I can't believe how long we've been here. No wonder we're the only customers left."

"Why, is it past your bedtime?" I chuckle.

"Not quite, but close. It's nine."

Frowning as I think about my father's reaction to me coming home late, I feel the need to not keep anything from Henry. "We better leave because I don't want my family to worry about me. I usually call if I'm not going to be home for dinner, but I forgot."

"I still live at home with my parents too, Violet, and I'm thirty-one years old."

On the ride back to Brooklyn, I realize that I don't know anything about this man, Henry. Other than the fact that he is twelve years older. So, I decide to be aggressive and find out a few things. "Say, tell me about yourself. Where do you work?"

He looks at me and nods, "You never know; I could be an escaped convict."

"Well, I don't usually date a fella unless I know a lot about him first. I'm surprised at myself for jumping in this car with you."

"I'm a Brooklyn boy but work as a file clerk for Metropolitan Life Insurance Company in Manhattan. I play the saxophone, clarinet, and piano for Lou Long and his orchestra. I have a dog, and I ride horses twice a week in Prospect Park. Oh, I have no siblings."

"I have a cat called Petunia, little sister nine years younger than me, and I grew up on the Vaudeville stage."

"How old are you, Violet? I hope you don't mind me asking."

Waiting a few moments to answer for fear of being rejected, "A lot younger than you."

I feel him glare at me with astonishment. "Hopefully, you're over sixteen."

"I'm nineteen. Turn left at the next stop sign."

We sit in utter silence as we pull up in front of my house. I proceed to open the door thinking that this is my first and last date with this great guy.

He gently reaches out and grabs my arm. "I'm a gentleman. I will get out and open your door so please wait."

"Thank you, Henry, for a wonderful evening. I had a swell time."

He offers me his arm and walks me to the door. "If you don't mind dating an old man, I would like to see you again."

Acting on a whim, I plant a kiss on his cheek. "You say the day and the time. I'll be ready."

We hug each other and part. I turn to go into the house, but my hand lingers a moment on the doorknob. I don't want this feeling to end. I finally sigh and open the door.

"Violet Pearl Moretti. Where have you been? I have been worried sick about you. This has got to stop!" Papa shouts as I walk into the house.

"Papa. Please keep your voice down. You'll wake up Daisy."

He storms into the kitchen, and I follow him as quickly as my feet will carry me, rolling my eyes all the way.

"I demand an explanation. You're still my responsibility as long as you live in this house."

"I know I should always call you, Papa. I'm sorry. I went out on a dinner date with a client from the dance studio."

"What? You're still working as a dance instructor?" He pounds his fist on the table.

"Yes, I am, and I love it too, Papa."

"You disappoint me, Violet. Who is this man you went out with?"

"Henry's his name, and you'll like him a lot, Papa, because he's a musician like you."

Chapter 38

"Vi-Vi, wake up. It's Easter Sunday, and Papa's going to go to church with us," Daisy says as she pounces on my bed.

I try not to wake up from a deep sleep and a beautiful dream of dancing with Henry in a magnificent ballroom in the Plaza Hotel. "What? Church? Where?" I mumble.

"The Little Church around the Corner."

I throw off my sleepiness, leap off the bed with a start, and fly to my closet where the newest dress to my growing collection of frocks is hanging. "Oh, I'm so excited to wear this one today, Daisy. Henry's meeting us at church, and he is taking us all to Easter dinner at Nicks. I'm thrilled for you and Papa to finally meet him."

"Does Papa know about this?"

"No. It'll be a surprise. You can keep it our little secret, can't you, Daisy?"

Papa looks dashing in his white summer suit, and to top it off, he's wearing a black fedora hat. A few single women turn their heads and smile as he walks ahead of us into the red-brick, Victorian gothic structure.

Daisy's beautifully dressed in the flowered dress that Aunt Flossie bought her a few weeks ago. She's wearing a hat adorned with soft, artificial flowers to match.

Auntie is waiting with Henry at the entrance for us. Papa tips his hat at her but keeps walking into the church as he doesn't recognize the gentleman in her company. I chuckle to myself because Aunt Flossie has dined with Henry and me two times now.

She absolutely adores him. *What will Papa think of my new beau?*

Henry smiles and takes my hand as we follow my family into the vast sanctuary. Luckily, we arrive early enough to find an empty pew for all five of us. As the organ chimes out a glorious tune, I get a glimpse of Papa gawking in our direction, and he isn't looking at Daisy or Auntie. I should introduce them now, but Papa looks perturbed. I'll wait.

Good thing there's an Episcopal prayer book in the back of the pew in front of us because we wouldn't have a clue what to do. Although, Henry seems to have a handle on when to stand or sit. The rector announces for us to turn to page eighteen of the hymnal, so we can sing, *Stand up for Jesus.* Okay, that's easy.

In unison, everyone stands. After the hymn, people start kneeling on the pads behind each pew. Henry nudges me, points to a prayer in the missal book, and begins to read it out loud with the five hundred or so people.

Daisy leans over to me and whispers, "Sissy, I have to go to the bathroom."

I motion for her to be quiet with my hand over her mouth. "Shush," I whisper.

She starts wiggling this way and that. "I can't hold it."

The people in front of us turn around and glare.

Henry pats my arm and smiles. "There's a restroom downstairs."

Reluctantly so not to make a scene, I take her hand and guide her out of the sanctuary where several ushers are waiting. "Can you please direct me to the ladies' lavatory?"

"Certainly, go down these stairs and straight down the hallway to your right." The older, more distinguished, gentleman replies.

"Thank you, Sir."

Daisy runs ahead of me, and I wonder if this hallway has an end to it. Good thing it's empty right now, knowing full well it will be inundated with women and a line a mile long in just a few minutes.

I decide to primp up a bit by looking in the full-length mirror. I just love this outfit. I hope Henry does. Auntie bought this midcalf-length silk dress from Gimbel's sale rack. I love the way it clings to my figure and these red, full-length elbow gloves bring out the shades of the red flower pattern that covers the fabric.

"What's all that noise, Vi-Vi?" Daisy asks as she flushes the toilet.

"Church must be over. Hurry up and wash your hands. I really want to walk in the Easter Parade before we have dinner."

"There you girls are," Henry announces as he sees us venture up the stairs.

"Henry, this is my sister Daisy."

"Nice to meet you, Sir." She smiles and sprints out of the door.

I can see Aunt Flossie and Papa sitting on a bench surrounded by cherry trees in full blossom. Papa's hands always move up and down and all around when he's disgusted about something.

Auntie shakes her head. "Be reasonable, Berto. You can't run Violet's life forever."

"What's going on? Papa, this is Henry, the man I've been telling you about."

Henry reaches out his hand, "How do you do, Sir?"

"Humph, Happy Easter. We better get going; the streets are going to be packed with people. Come on, Daisy." Papa grabs Daisy's hand and walks briskly away.

Why didn't Papa shake Henry's hand? My heart is breaking inside my body.

"Come on, kids. We better use some quick steps if we want to keep up with them." Auntie says.

Henry and I stroll hand in hand down the avenue among the throng of people dressed in their best attire. Hats of every color and size bob along the street; some look very peculiar with balloons, bird's nests, and colorful streamers blowing in the faces of those who are wearing them.

"Look, Henry, that white poodle is wearing a hat, and it matches its owners too," I comment as they pass by.

He squeezes my hand and laughs.

Aunt Flossie's dressed in a deep-purple cotton dress with ruffles around the neck and at the wrists. Her matching bonnet has a small veil that slightly covers her face.

She grabs my other hand. "This is so much fun and a gorgeous day to boot."

"It's lovely day, Auntie."

Papa and Daisy are walking together a bit ahead of us; I catch him stopping to look back at us occasionally.

"Henry, did you make reservations at Nicks?" Auntie calls out.

"Yes, for one thirty."

She looks at her watch. "We should head to the parking lot soon because it might be difficult getting out of the city."

"I'm not sure if Mr. Moretti knows where we're going or what time."

"Oh, he knows alright because I told him," Auntie responds.

I see Papa and Daisy walking toward us. "Let's wait over here out of the way until we are all together." *Good grief, he looks so perturbed, pulling my sister like that.*

He doesn't stop. "See you all at Nicks," he calls out.

Henry shrugs his shoulders but wraps one arm around my waist, "I don't think your father likes me."

"He'll be happier when he can sit, relax, and eat. How can he not like you, Henry?"

"Your father is a hard fella to read sometimes, Violet Pearl," Auntie declares.

"Don't worry, Ladies. In time, Mr. Moretti and I will be good friends. After all, we do have a lot in common."

The considerably large banquet hall is billed to seat five hundred patrons at a time. The heavenly aroma of homemade breads, muffins, and delectable pastries fill the large vestibule. The rumbling of my stomach and being lightheaded tells me I'm starving. I suppose I could have grabbed a bite this morning, but I wanted to look my best for Henry.

"Henry Funk, party of five. Follow me," the host calls out.

I look at Henry in astonishment because I never asked about his full name. *Funk? How positively odd.*

"This is perfect, Henry. How did you ever get this wonderful spot with this fabulous view?" Auntie asks.

"I came over here two weeks ago for lunch with some colleagues, and we sat in this very place, so I made reservations right then."

"I'm starving. I hope we get some bread right away," Daisy says.

Papa's sitting directly across from me, and if looks could kill, Henry would have been dead three hours ago. I smile at my father. "Papa, what are you going to have? The ham or turkey dinner?"

"Can we get a little of each?" he asks with a half grin.

"I don't think so, Mr. Moretti. I was told it is either one or the other, but they will serve the side dishes family style," Henry said.

"Tsk, tsk." Papa shakes his head.

A short time later, three of us are served ham with raison sauce while the other two get turkey and dressing on their plates. Servers bring us big serving platters of mashed potatoes, green beans, and fruit cocktail.

Someone else produces a basket filled with an assortment of baked goods and placed it in front of Daisy. There's nothing to her, but she eats like a horse.

Since we're all so famished, we dig into our food as though it's our last meal. As I chomp on my ham, I feel my boyfriend's hand on my left thigh, but as I look at him through the corner of my eye, I see him looking straight ahead. Chills run through me, but I keep myself composed.

I discreetly slide my left hand under the table and place it on top of his.

Water. I must have some water. All my senses are being bombarded at once.

Papa relaxes back in his chair, and with a forced smile he asks, "Henry, what kind of name is Funk anyway?"

"It's German, Sir." He slowly pulls his hand off mine.

Papa burst into laughter "I must say, dear boy, it's a name I never heard of until today."

Glancing at Henry, I see his face turn red. "I find the name Funk very interesting."

After the dinner dishes are cleared off the table, we are served individual portions of pineapple upside-down cake with a dollop of whipped cream.

"Henry, thank you for taking us to Nicks today," Auntie says. "It's so nice not having to cook on Easter."

"You're very welcome, Flossie. It's my turn to treat you to a meal since I have dined at your house two times now."

"Is that so?" Papa says in a loud tone.

A bit humiliated and not knowing how to respond to him without causing a scene, I get up and tap my sister on the shoulders. "Switch seats with me, Sis."

Auntie stands up, "I think this is a good time to go for a walk. Daisy. Let's go outside and get some fresh air. It is a lovely day. "

Sitting down next to my father, I say, "I love you, Papa, and I know you want what's best for me, but I honestly did not know how you would react to me having a new fella in my life."

"Humph. Tsk. Tsk." He folds his arms in front of him while glaring at Henry.

The waiter brings the tab to my boyfriend. "Can I get you anything else, Sir?"

"No, thank you."

"Please pay at the cashier's window on the way out. Happy Easter."

"Likewise," Henry says, then turns toward Papa. "Mr. Moretti, maybe you and I can get together sometime and make some music. Violet tells me that you have your own band and play a few instruments. I play the saxophone, clarinet, and piano."

"Good. I'm glad that you're a musician, but I am a very busy man. So, finding time to do such a thing will be difficult, to say the least. I'll leave the tip."

"Thank you, Mr. Moretti."

As we walk out to meet up with Auntie and Daisy, Papa turns to Henry. "How old are you, Henry Funk?"

"Papa." I scold.

Henry looks at my father and answers, "I'm thirty-one, Sir."

Papa pulls me away from my boyfriend, and in a loud unbearable voice, "You're too old for my daughter. Thank you for brunch, but you need to move on to someone your own age. My flower is still a kid."

Everyone in the nearby vicinity is staring, and I feel sick to my stomach. Right now, I don't like my father.

"Berto. That's enough. Take Daisy and go home," Auntie chimes in discreetly.

Papa steps in front of her. "Stop meddling, Florence. Let's go, girls."

I know Papa's fuming when he says Auntie Florence.

Daisy reluctantly takes his hand, but I take Henry's.

Papa turns around and glares at me. "Violet Pearl Moretti, I demand that you come with me this instant."

"No. Papa. Henry will take me home later."

He takes a few steps toward me. "In that case, don't bother coming home, Violet Pearl."

I can't believe what's happening. Why does Papa have to be in control of everything I do? I finally meet someone who's kind, sweet, and attentive to my needs, but Papa always has the last word. Auntie and Henry are conversing right next to me, but I don't hear them say a thing.

Chapter 39

It's difficult to keep myself from going hysterical in Henry's presence as we venture across the Brooklyn Bridge. My father always seems to find a way to humiliate me in front of total strangers, not to mention this one man with whom I'm falling in love.

"Ye gads, I am so sorry that you had to witness one of my brother-in-law's tantrums, Henry," Auntie blurts out.

"Is it the age thing, or I'm not the right fella for Violet?"

"It's not you, Henry. Berto's a hard man to please. He wanted Violet to be a major Broadway star, but that was shattered when her guidance counselor suggested business school."

I well up in tears, "That's only part of the story, Auntie."

"Violet's dream of becoming a ballerina was destroyed because of Berto's hostile attitude. He's been hard on my niece since then."

"I don't want to see him ever again," I cry out in frustration.

We pull up in front of Auntie's house, and Henry turns off the ignition.

Auntie pats my shoulder. "Oh, Violet dear, you know he'll get over it and eventually apologize to you. You can stay with me until he cools off."

Henry gives me a wink, "I was hoping Violet could come to my house for a few hours, so she can finally meet my folks. It's only five."

"Really?" I practically squeal but hold it back. "Oh, I would love to meet them."

Auntie positions herself in the middle of the back seat and leans forward so we can hear her better. "That is a grand idea. I'll wait up for you, Toots, so try not to be too late. Henry, thank you so very much for a pleasant time at church and at Nicks. Let's block out the bad part of the day, alright?"

"She's such a pleasure to be around, Violet," Henry comments as he drives away.

"Yes, she's a gem. Is this the way to your house?"

"Not exactly. I think we need a little diversion before we go over there. Do you mind if I take you to Rockaway Beach, so we can talk for a while?"

"Sure."

We drive to the beach in comfortable silence. When we get there, my heart jumps with joy as I see children digging in the sand, lovers in each other's arms, and women working hard to keep Easter bonnets on their heads while others ride bicycles built for two. We roll down our windows, so we can hear the splashing of the waves rush into the shore.

Henry pulls me to his side and wraps his arms around me. "I'm so glad we're alone."

I cuddle into his arms, "My father will like you in time."

"Violet, I think I'm falling in love with you." He kisses my cheek. My chest swells at the compliment. I can feel my face blush as I catch my breath. My knees are shaking, and I'm reminded of other times when alone with a man. *This is different. Isn't it?* I turn to look at him and place a kiss right on his smooth lips. He wraps a leg over mine, and we kiss passionately for a long time, as if we're alone on a remote island somewhere in the Pacific. My heart's beating faster and faster. My heart's so full I can hardly breathe.

Taking a breather, he looks at me as if he never wants to stop kissing me again. "Oh, Honey. I have to tell you something."

"What is it, Henry?"

"I don't live with my folks anymore. I finally moved into a little one-room apartment over on Sixty-First Street."

Gazing into his striking blue eyes, I ask, "Is it near your folks?"

"Not exactly. Do you want to see my place or go over to see them?"

Without flickering an eyelash, I pull him closer and scatter kisses on his face. With one hand, Henry starts the car. "I think I know the answer."

I'm so mesmerized by this man as we pull into the parking lot in the back of a high-rise apartment building.

"Wow, is this where you live? This looks like a big place."

"It is at that. The building's only two years old. I was lucky to get in here."

Henry fumbles with the brass skeleton key, and with a twist, the door opens. He steps behind me, takes my coat off, and hangs it next to his on the hooks in the entryway.

"Would you like some brandy or a cup of coffee?" he asks as he struts into the tiny kitchen. *I hope I did the right thing in coming here.*

"Um, do you have any tea?"

"Sure, I do. It will take a few minutes for the teakettle to boil. If you want to freshen up a bit, the bathroom's over there."

"Thanks." I close the door behind me and gaze at myself in the medicine cabinet mirror over the sink. *What are you doing, Violet? You're alone with your boyfriend in his apartment.*

Holding the pearls my father gave me and glancing down at my neckline, I realize that I'm showing way too much cleavage. *Oh, I can handle this. I'm a woman now.*

"There you are, pretty lady."

Still not sure what I'm doing here, I sit down in a high-back chair across from him. "I really shouldn't stay too long, Henry. My aunt will be worried about me."

He changed his clothes and is now wearing a striped shirt and baggy light-brown trousers. He's holding a glass that appears to be filled with an alcoholic drink. "Relax. Honey. The water's hot for your tea. Do you want me to get it for you?"

"I can get it," I say as I rise to my feet.

I check the water and wait for the tea too steep in the well-appointed kitchen. It's a piece of cake checking out this place from the vantage point I'm in right now. I glance around the small apartment and am amazed at how orderly it is for a bachelor's abode. There are two windows that over-look the Brooklyn skyline that are decorated with light-green full-length curtains with matching shades. *Obviously, some woman helped him fix this place.* The water finally boils; I pour myself a cup and drop in a tea bag. As I turn around, I discover Henry asleep on the couch.

I take my tea and sit at the small kitchen table for two, so I don't dis-turb him. Several photograph albums are stacked in perfect order in front of me. As I turn the pages carefully, I wonder if Henry is the photographer or if someone else took these marvelous pictures.

The Bronx Zoo and Barnum and Bailey Circus. Wow!

I love looking at photos. I can get lost in what I'm viewing as though I am right there.

"I'm the photographer, in case you are wondering," Henry whispers in my ear as he wraps his arms around me from the back.

"You startled me. I thought you were sleeping," I squeal as goose bumps and a fluttering sensation covers me from head to toe.

Taking my hand and pulling me to my feet, he says, "Come over and sit with me awhile."

"Only for a few minutes, Henry. It's getting late. I should go before it gets dark."

We sit on the couch, and he turns my face gently with his hands, so I'm looking at him. "Take it easy; the night's young. It's absolutely fine to spend a little alone time with my girl."

I've heard this line before.

He gently kisses me on my nose, "Turn around and allow me to give you a neck massage. You'll love it."

What the heck is he up to?

I do as he asks, and he caresses the back of my neck in soft, gentle strokes. I can feel the tension I was experiencing moments ago vanish, and I close my eyes in peaceful appreciation. Then he moves his soothing hands along my shoulders and continues in the same sequence.

"Ah, you're an expert at this, Henry."

Leaning his body close to mine, he whispers in my ear, "I love you, Violet Pearl Moretti."

My eyes pop open, but I'm too relaxed to move. He lifts my hair from my neck and plants warm, sporadic kisses all over the exposed skin. Chills run up my back. We kiss as he guides me gently to lie on the couch.

Not Henry too!

"Stop it! Get off me this instant!" I push him with all the energy within me.

Leaping off the couch, he says, "I'm sorry I brought you here, Violet. I have to admit it's hard keeping my hands off you."

I sit upright on the couch and fix my dress. "All men are the same. You all want my body. You don't care one bit about who I am."

Kneeling in front of me, he takes my hands, "Oh, my dear, sweet, innocent Violet. I'm in love with all of you. Your radiance, sense of humor, your inner beauty, as well as what's on the outside, and especially your out-going personality—these are a few of the many qualities I admire about you. I'll take you to your aunt's house, but will you allow me to take a few photographs first?"

I investigate those blue eyes, and I think I see that he's genuine—able to control himself when the others weren't. I smile. "I guess a few more minutes won't hurt."

"Alright, I want you to lie down on the couch. Don't worry, my dear. I promise not to touch you. Think of me as your own personal photographer."

This is weird.

"Let me brush my hair. It must be a mess."

"Not at all necessary. Give me your beautiful smile."

He points the camera and shoots "Okay. Good. Now sit up and with your legs apart and elbows on your knees. Of course, be sure to pull your dress over the knees. Look at me. Hold it."

The camera clicks as he takes another picture.

"Would you be so kind to slide your blouse down over your shoulders a bit? You have an extraordinary neckline."

At first, I'm reluctant, but then I think of a photo I've seen of Francis Farmer with her bare arms showing, and I figure it's nothing to worry about. I pull my blouse down over my shoulders just a bit.

"Great. Give me a serious look."

He snaps the picture.

I straighten myself to a sitting position. "I would love to see these photographs when you get them developed."

"Of course, you can. I have a few more shots to take on this roll of film, and then you can see how I develop them. That's if you can hang around for a few more hours."

"You have a dark room? Where?"

"Follow me, and I'll show you." This guy's getting more and more interesting by the minute.

He opens a door across from the coat hooks. It's a small shadowy room with a long table in the center. He flicks on a light that glows red. "This is a safe light to protect the film as it goes through the development process."

I grasp hold of my nose. "What is that putrid odor?"

"A chemical used to process the film from nothing to a brilliant photo. You do get used to it after a while."

Turning quickly to leave this odd room, my elbow catches an open container, and some of the strong-smelling liquid splashes all over my beautiful dress.

Screaming, I pull the dress over my head, flee to the kitchen sink, and fill it up with warm, soapy water. Tears flow freely from my eyes as I look down in horror.

I'm standing in my boyfriend's apartment in a slip!

Henry turns me around and holds me tight in his arms. "Don't cry, sweetheart. The solution will come out in a few minutes, if you let it soak. There's a nice breeze blowing through the window. Your dress will dry in no time."

He hands me a glass with something amber in it. "Here, drink this. It will warm you up."

"What is it?"

"Brandy. You'll l be relaxed and warm after drinking this. Trust me." His eyes are roaming over my body.

It tastes strange at first. I take short sips and before I know it, the glass is empty. He takes the glass and fills it up. It tastes so good, I drink two more.

"I'm chilly. Do you have a robe or a blanket?"

"Sure, I do. Come with me." I'm feeling a bit light headed and wobbly as I follow him with glass in hand. He pulls the green chenille bedspread off the bed and wraps it around me.

He pulls me beside him on the edge of the bed.

I kiss him tenderly on the lips and smile. "I think I'm falling in love you, Henry Funk."

I close my eyes, lean my head on his shoulder, and drift off to sleep next to the warmth of his body.

"Wake up, Sunshine. Your breakfast is waiting, and your dress is all dry too."

I can plainly see that I'm not in my little room at Aunt Flossie's. Not a chance. I'm under the covers of Henry's bed, and he's standing over me.

"What time is it?" I yell at him.

"It's seven in the morning." He smiles with a wink.

I jump up and push him out of the way, grab my dress off the hanger, and dart into the bathroom.

Bursting into uncontrollable tears, I cry out loud. "What happened after I fell asleep? Did he take advantage of me? *Of course, he did. I was under the covers, and he was in his pajamas when I got up.* How positively dirty and terrible I feel right now. How can I face him or anyone else for that matter? What will people think of me?"

He knocks on the door. "Open the door, Violet; I can explain what happened. Give me a chance."

"You got what you wanted. Go away and go to work, Henry." I manage to say through the sniffles.

"I'm not going to leave you like this."

All my past experiences with men crop up within me, and I crumble in a heap on the cold tile floor. It was a matter of time before I gave myself to Henry. I was attracted to him the minute I saw him. My eyes are burning with moisture from the tears as I contemplate how I'm going to explain to Auntie where I was last night. I can't lie to her.

Standing up as though in severe pain, I realize staying in here all day won't solve a thing.

"Please take me to my aunt's. Now!" I announce upon entering the room.

"Good. You're finally out of there."

I head to the front door, grabbing my coat and purse on the way. "I want to go, Henry."

The ride to Aunt Flossie's is a silent one.

I made a huge mistake, and in doing so, I lost my chance of marrying a man I love. Oh well, chalk it up to another bad experience in the life of Violet Pearl. How in the world can I explain to Auntie where I was last night? She must've worried sick about me. I'll never touch another glass of brandy.

We drive up to Auntie's house, and Henry puts the car in park.

He turns to me. "Violet. Nothing happened last night. You fell asleep, and I didn't want to disturb you."

"Leave me alone, you creep. Don't bother getting out." I slam the car door and walk as fast as I can up the walkway into the safe abode of my aunt's. I can hear the motor of Henry's car roar away as I open the door to the house.

"Where have you been? You look dreadful." Auntie says. "Let me get you some coffee."

I slump down at the kitchen table by the window. "I'm so ashamed of myself."

She sits down across from me and takes my hand. "Did you spend the night with him, dear?"

"Yes." I burst into tears. "Yes. Oh, Auntie, please believe me when I say my love for him got carried away."

"I find this very hard to believe, Violet. Henry seems like such a gentleman."

"He said nothing happened sexually, but I don't believe him. He couldn't keep his hands off me last night. Then, he got me drunk with brandy."

"I guess you didn't meet his parents after all."

"It was my decision to go see his new apartment instead of going over there." I sniff.

She looks at her watch. "Listen, I have to go to work, but you take all the time you need. Henry really loves you. It's hard for me to think that he would take advantage of you."

"It's over, Auntie. I don't think I'll ever date again."

"Your father called to talk to you last night. I told him you were sleeping."

Wow, she covered for me. I'm shocked. Henry's a thing of the past now. I don't have to worry about Papa's harsh opinion of Henry because I'll tell him we broke up. I flee to the safety of the bathroom, close the door, and sit on the toilet and cry.

A cool, body-chilling airstream hovers over me. "There are many lovely things in store for you. Tune in. Listen. Your spirit is mine, Violet." Whispers the keeper.

I can't speak because my sobbing consumes me.

Chapter 40

A week drags on and on without a word from Henry. He's probably taken up with a new bimbo by now. Adios. Cheerio. End of romance. Time to move on.

Papa seems happier now that Henry's out of my life. "He was too old for you, Violet Pearl. There are a lot of nice Italian men, your age who would love to court you."

Things are looking up. Alex Murphy rented the Grand Prospect Hall for a formal dance tonight from 7:00 p.m. to 11:00 p.m. Men must wear tuxedos, and women, full-length gowns.

I'm so glad I bought this soft and flowing ivory silk chiffon dress, embroidered with white and silver sequin butterflies. Just the right neckline too.

Alex expects all the instructors in place at 6:30 p.m. sharp, so we're available to greet single guests.

I hail a taxi and arrive in front of a dazzling place that looks like a French Renaissance-style palace. I make my way into a soaring and gilded marble lobby. There's a magnificent stairway that rises into someplace. I start to make my way up the stairs when I feel a tap on the shoulder.

"Violet, we're all over here," Alex comments quietly as he points to a room on the first floor.

"This place is splendid, Alex."

As we enter the side door to the main floor of the ballroom, I look around me in total amazement of the architecture and fascinating paintings that cover the walls. The orchestra is far away, but I can see the men on stage are dressed in white dinner jackets.

"Okay, Instructors," Alex claps his hands to get everyone's attention. "Please position yourselves at the main door in a unified line: ladies on the right and men on the left. Give everyone your biggest pearly white smiles and be sure to chaperone anyone who comes to the dance alone. Above all, have a wonderful time."

The evening moves swiftly along, and I find several single men to dance with. One fella is way too fat as far as I'm concerned; another is literally a giant with no hair on his head; and the last one is probably all of sixteen years old.

I need a drink.

There are two reserved tables to the left of the ballroom, in the front for the instructors. I make my way through the crowd to sit down. It feels good to be off my feet.

On the table are pitchers of red wine and ice water. I pour myself a glass of wine, sit back, and relax in the red cushion chair and look up at the twelve-piece orchestra led by Lou Long. I scan all the handsome musicians, but my attention returns to a familiar face.

It's Henry. He's playing a saxophone. I must leave.

I don't think he sees me because he's so engrossed in his music.

Trying not to be obvious, I skirt around the perimeter of the hall to find Alex. I'll tell him I feel ill and must go home.

As I approach the outer door to exit, Lou Long's voice comes over the microphone. "Attention, Ladies and Gentlemen. One of the members of this fine orchestra has an important announcement to make. Henry, please come."

I stop dead in my tracks and turn out of curiosity, must be another Henry.

It's my Henry. He steps over to the microphone and looks out at the crowd. "Is Violet Pearl Moretti in the house tonight?"

Now, I'm sick to my stomach, my face is burning, and I'm sopping wet with perspiration. I want to run, but I'm frozen in place.

The people are mumbling and looking around the ballroom.

"Violet, please take my hand, dear," Alex says as he walks me through the throng of people. "Henry has something to say to you."

Henry slowly walks down the three steps to the dance floor. Alex gives him my hand, and we walk back up to the stage together.

"What in the world are you doing?" I whisper with a slight smile.

He gets down on one knee, pulls out a small black velvet box, and looks up at me with a smile. Lou holds the microphone for him.

"Violet Pearl Moretti? Will you marry me?"

Horrified, shocked, and overwhelmed, I look out at the applauding crowd and then down at Henry. His blue eyes capture my complete attention once again.

Falling to my knees and holding back tears of unspeakable joy, I cry, "Yes. Yes. Yes. I will marry you, Henry."

Applause and cheers ring across the vast ballroom. The orchestra breaks out into "Let Me Call You Sweetheart," as we dance across the stage.

After the dance is over, we sit in Henry's car for a long time chatting about our courtship and our love for each other. The Murphys surprised us with twelve-dozen long-stem roses in a beautiful cut glass vase, and the aroma surrounds us. The diamond on my new ring is glowing brightly under the moonlit night.

"Oh, my dear, sweet Henry. This is by far the best day of my life. I love you so much." He holds my hand as he plays with the glittery ring. "Look at me, honey."

He takes my chin in his hand and gives me a soft, tender kiss, "I slept on the couch that night. I tucked you into the bed, and you never moved a muscle. I didn't have the heart to wake you up. You obviously can't drink more than one shot of brandy."

"I want to believe you; really I do."

"I kept thinking that you would wake up any minute. You didn't budge when the clock struck midnight, so I decided to let you sleep. I love you too much to take advantage of you."

"Did you really sleep on the couch?"

"Yep. I did. Although, it was a bit uncomfortable at times."

We both laugh.

"Now, let's go tell your father and Daisy the big news," he said as he starts the car.

Chapter 41

As we pull up in front of my brightly lit house, my heart beats faster. "Papa may not be as excited as you want him to be, Henry."

"I have to tell you something, Violet. Your aunt discouraged me from asking him for your hand in marriage. She knows how much I love you and was worried your father would discourage me from going through with the engagement."

I stare straight ahead into the night. "Once he sees the ring, he should be fine. Let's go find out." I'm feeling a bit light headed.

Papa is playing a medley of songs at the piano, and Daisy's stretched out on the Oriental rug, reading a book, when Henry and I enter the parlor. They couldn't care less that we are in their midst.

Holding Henry's hand, I lead him to the couch where we wait for the right moment to share our good news.

After a while, Daisy pops up and plops on the couch next to me. "You look beautiful tonight, Vi. How was the dance?"

Smiling, I wave the ringed hand in front of her.

"You got engaged!" she shrieks.

Papa pounds his hand on the piano, gets up, and leaps toward us. "What are you doing here, Mr. Funk? I thought you two were no longer dating."

Not able to contain myself any longer, I make my announcement. "We're getting married, Papa. Henry proposed to me tonight."

"What? He never asked me for your hand. This is not acceptable."

"Papa, I love him, and he loves me. Look at the beautiful ring he gave me."

"Give it back to him this instant, Violet Pearl. There won't be a wedding. At least not to a man so much older than you. Besides, you must marry an Italian."

Henry clears his throat, straightens his back, and stands. "Mr. Moretti, I'm in love with your daughter and want to spend the rest of my life with her."

Papa leans forward as close to my fiancé's face as he can get. "I don't care. It's not going to happen. Not now. Not ever. There's the door, Mr. Funk."

"You're impossible, Papa. If you don't give us your blessing, then we'll elope," I yell.

Daisy squeezes between us. "Stop arguing. Stop it!"

"Go to your room, Daisy," Papa orders. "You don't need to hear any of this."

"But Papa, I want to be a flower girl in my sister's wedding."

"Get going, child."

Daisy picks up the cat and darts upstairs, whimpering all the way, and slams her bedroom door. I'm horrified at Papa's behavior. He should be happy for us. *What's his problem anyway?*

Glaring at me and then at Henry, Papa says, "This conversation is over. Please leave, Mr. Funk."

Bursting into tears and leaning into Henry's embrace, I speak as distinctly as I can. "Give us your blessing, Father, or we'll elope." Everything hurts, but especially my heart.

"I can't do that, Violet Pearl."

Henry holds me in his arms, but I pull away from him, square my shoulders. "You leave me no choice, Papa."

My father turns away from me and heads to the kitchen.

"Papa, I'm leaving with Henry. I'll move in with Auntie tonight."

He stops but doesn't turn around. "If you do, then you'll never see me again."

I start to go to my father, but Henry holds me back.

"Papa?" I shout. I'm suddenly finding it hard to breathe. He disappears into the kitchen.

Henry hugs me tight, "Are you sure you want to move out of your house, honey?"

"Yes, I do. I'm going to move in with my aunt until we're married. I love you. I'm afraid my father won't change his mind. That's why it has to be this way."

"Maybe, I should wait in the car."

I look back at him. "I will be back in a few minutes. Don't worry. He'll stay in the kitchen all night and sulk."

Daisy's crying as I approach her door, and my heart aches for her. I enter her room and go to her. She's lying face down on her bed and sobbing uncontrollably, which is not like my ten-year-old sister. "Daisy, dear."

"Leave me alone!"

Sitting down on the side of the bed, I rub her back gently. "Not until you hear me out."

"Why do you and Papa always argue?" she mumbles as she turns on her back.

I wipe the tears from her face. "I'm in love with Henry, and Papa detests him, Daisy."

"I like Henry. He's such a nice man."

"He's waiting downstairs for me, so I can't talk too long. I'm moving in with Auntie until we get married. I'll call you every day, and I want you to be in the wedding. Okay?"

She sits up and throws her arms around me. "Do you have to go tonight?"

We rub noses. "Yes. It's the best thing for now. You do know I love you with all my heart, right?"

She blows her nose on an embroidered hankie. "I know, Sissy."

"Can you do me a favor and sit on the top step and keep an eye out for Papa. I don't want him to brutalize Henry anymore."

"Sure, I can do that."

She tiptoes and takes her place as a royal guard while I grab the largest suitcase I can find and head to my room. I hurriedly pack toiletries, undergarments, a few books, three nighties, several dresses, two pairs of shoes, and one pair of slippers. Good. Oh, I better take my robe. I throw it over my arm, turn out the light, and glance into the dark room. Nervousness tickles the back of my throat. *Maybe, this is the end of the keeper.*

I close the door.

Daisy grabs me at the top of the stairs. "I love you, Vi."

I squeeze her tight and give her kiss on the cheek. "I love you too, sweetie."

Everything is quiet in the house as I join Henry and he takes my suitcase. I turn to throw my sister a kiss, but she's gone. I love my fiancé with all my heart, but it kills me to have to move out of this house. I tack on a smile, hoping it's enough to mask my disappointment.

Chapter 42

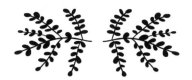

Two weeks have passed since I left the home where I grew up. Auntie and I managed to clean out my bedroom and pack several boxes of heirloom items of my mother's, as well as my personal things, when Papa was at work.

I wonder how Papa is. I haven't talked to him since I left. A flash of anger burns in my belly.

"Howdy-do, Violet. Hello. Are you with us?" Henry whispers in my ear.

I look at my aunt and him and smile. "I was thinking about Papa and Daisy. Hope they're alright."

"I was over there today, dear," Auntie says. "They're just fine. Daisy asked for you and Henry, but your father still needs some time. I gave them an invitation to your engagement party next week. I hope they come."

"That was a delicious roast beef dinner, Flossie," Henry comments as he takes a sip of wine. "Better than eating in a restaurant."

"Violet made the biscuits. She's becoming quite the cook."

"Most of what I know comes from you, Auntie."

"I bet you can't wait to set up housekeeping in our own place in a few months," Henry adds as he clears the table. "January 29 will be here before we know it, my love." *He's so comfortable here.*

"Are you going to live where you do now, Henry?" Auntie asks.

"Oh, no," he replies. "We've been looking at flats in Greenwich Village. We have to make a decision soon."

Henry embraces me tenderly from behind. "Do you remember what we're doing tomorrow, Ms. Moretti?"

"Off to the stables we go. My first horseback ride."

"I didn't know you're fond of horses, Henry," Auntie says.

"Those magnificent animals bring such joy to my life, and I get such a thrill when I'm riding a well-schooled mount."

"Well, you be careful, my dear niece. I want you looking perfectly beautiful for that party of yours. Okay?"

"Don't worry, Flossie. She'll be riding a very quiet old mare for the first few lessons."

"Henry bought me a riding habit. So, I must take this sport seriously." I giggle.

"Well, Ladies. I must be going, but I'll pick you up tomorrow at nine thirty sharp. Okay, Miss Violet?"

As soon as I step out of the car, I'm greeted with the atrocious odor of manure and filthy straw. Good thing Henry bought these riding boots for me because I can change before I go back to Aunties. I stay close behind Henry as we head into the dilapidated-looking barn.

"I want you to see something before your first lesson."

We stop in front of a stall with an iron grate that protects horse from human and vice versa. I peer in between the slats and see a dark-brown horse with the cutest little baby standing feebly by her side.

"How adorable. I never saw a baby horse before."

"She's a filly and only three days old."

Taking my hand and walking through the rest of the barn, Henry says, "I bet you're anxious to get on and ride."

"Kind of."

"I hope you're not afraid, Violet dear."

"I may look like an experienced rider in these clothes, but I'm scared out of my wits."

"Now Violet, breathe in and breathe out; then relax. Horses can sense when we're anxious about anything, and that makes them jittery as well."

"Do they have any ponies I can ride?" I giggle.

"Wait here for me. I will go and get Miss Royal."

"Who's she?"

He turns around and walks behind the barn but calls over his shoulder. "She's the mare you'll ride today."

I hope Henry rides the horse first. I can't remember if I ever touched one, let alone ride. Good grief. My eyes are riveted on the folks riding in the corral. Yikes, those saddles look like there's nothing to them. So flat.

"Honey?" Henry says from behind me. "Turn around."

As I twist my body to view my fiancé, I'm caught off guard by a beautiful white horse with dark eyes and black legs that look like socks to me. The fence separates us, and that's fine by me.

"There's a gate over there. Slowly let yourself in and remember to latch it shut, okay?"

Reluctantly, I do as he says, and within minutes I'm close and personal with a horse. My heart beats fast with hands sweating profusely.

"Come to the front and softly talk to her."

"Hello, Miss Royal," I say to the horse and then I look at Henry. "Can I pet her?"

"She loves her muzzle gently rubbed."

Smiling, I rub her and smooth out her pretty mane. "She's so calm, isn't she?" I hope she doesn't step on my foot.

"Lesson one, achieved. Now lesson two." He hands me the rope that is attached to the leather apparatus on her face. "Now, slide your right hand half way up the rope, hold the rest in your left, and start to walk her around the paddock."

Taking the rope hesitantly, I look at Henry and start walking. The horse stands still, her hooves frozen to the ground.

Henry chuckles. "Cluck like this." He makes a clucking noise and at the same time, tugs gently on the rope.

As my horse and I complete the fifth circle, a small man dressed in tan riding pants and tall brown leather boots joins Henry.

"Violet," Henry says as he waves me over. "Come here for a minute. I want you to meet my friend."

"Charlie, this is my fiancé, Violet Pearl Moretti."

He shakes my hand and says, "Pleased to meet you, Violet. I have heard so much about you."

"Henry tells me you're a horse lover too, Charlie?"

"Yes. We not only work for the same company but ride together at least twice a week. Henry, go and get the tack for Miss Royal because I'm sure this girl's anxious to ride."

Henry smiles and gives me a peck on the cheek, "I'll be back as quick as I can."

"Don't worry, he'll lead you around on the horse before he lets you go by yourself," Charlie says as Henry heads to the barn. "He asked me to stand by for your first couple of lessons. You'll do just fine."

I pet the white horse. "I feel better already. After all, Miss Royal and I became instant friends." The lie bolts out of my mouth before I can save it.

Henry comes alongside of me, arms full, with a saddle, blanket, and other necessary tack. In no time at all, the horse is ready to go. "Violet, stand on that wooden box over there and wait until I line the horse up to it. Charlie, hold Miss Royal while I help her into the saddle."

Charlie lines her up perfectly with me and the box. "Are you ready to mount?" he asks.

I take a deep breath. "Kind of, but where's the horn to hold on to?" I don't dare tell how I really feel.

"This is an English saddle, Honey. Okay. Left hand on this part of the saddle and the right here," Henry instructs. I grab hold as directed. "Good. Place left foot in stirrup and swing yourself up."

"There's nothing to hold on to. My legs are wobbly, Henry."

I take a deep breath as I'm somewhat comforted seeing a man on either side of the horse. My dancing has paid off. I pull myself up and on top of the horse.

"You did it." Henry smiles proudly.

"I feel like I am on top of a mountain. Wow." I smile. My heart's pounding a mile a minute.

"Charlie will walk alongside of you while I lead," Henry says in a comforting tone. "Tell us when you're ready. Try to sit straight, grip with your knees, and breathe in and out a few times."

I do as he directs. "I'm ready to ride." I'm terrified.

He hands me the reins. "Take these for something to hold on to, but don't kick the horse because I'm in control, okay?"

I nod, bite my lips, and take a deep breath.

We all move along at a snail's pace, and I'm amazed how quiet the horse beneath me is.

"Whoa girl." Henry says. He turns and gives the rope to Charlie. "You did excellent. We led you around ten times. How do you feel about riding one circle by yourself?"

"Do you really think I'm ready?"

They both nod as Henry takes off the rope. "Hold the reins loosely. I'll walk alongside of you."

The horse stands still. "She won't move." I complain with trembling hands.

"Cluck and gently kick." Henry says.

I do just that, and we move out around the paddock for the last spin of the day. Getting off is a lot easier than getting on.

"So, did you have a good time?" Henry asks as we pull up in front of Auntie's house.

I lean over and kiss him. "It was fun. Thank you for buying these terrific clothes for me. I'm sure Auntie will make me keep these boots on the porch, though."

He returns the kiss. "I'll pick you up at five for dinner. Tonight, is the big night you'll finally meet my folks."

"I hope they like me, Henry."

"My parents will love you almost as much as I do."

"See you at five, sweetie." I peck him on the cheek, turn, and head into the house.

As we walk into the Funk's house, the aroma of wood burning and the inviting scent of apple pie baking warm my soul. A terrier rushes out of nowhere, and plants two front paws on my black skirt. I bend down to pet him as I look around the cozy room.

Henry shoos the dog away. "Get down, Teddy. Leave Violet alone."

"That's okay. He's adorable."

"I wonder where everyone is. Wait here for just a minute." He heads down a short hallway and disappears to the right.

I decide to sit on the light-green brocade couch because the coffee table in front of it is adorned with *Life* magazines. Claudette Colbert's on the cover. *I love her.*

As I page through the magazine, Henry returns with two, stout, gray-haired people. Their most remarkable feature is that neither have any wrinkles on their faces. I quickly put the magazine down and stand. Sweat beads up on my back.

"Violet. I would like you to meet my mother, Gertrude, and my father, Harry."

I reach out my hand first to the one and then the other. "I'm so happy to meet you both. Henry has told me so much about you. You have a delightful home."

"Sit down, you two lovebirds," his mother orders.

"Something smells good, Mother," Henry says. "I'm famished so I hope we eat soon."

"Tsk. Tsk. Son. We must wait for your aunt Thelma. She'll be here shortly. Let me see that ring, Violet."

I smile and reach my hand across Henry's lap. "It's beautiful, isn't it?"

"I'm so happy my son's finally getting married. We were beginning to worry that he might be a bachelor for the rest of his life." Harry chuckles.

Gertrude shakes her head. "Oh poo, Harry. Henry was waiting for the right catch. The ring is gorgeous. Nice job, my boy."

"You-hoo," a voice calls from the front foyer. "Is anybody home?"

"We're all in here, Thelma."

"You must be Violet. I'm Emile's Aunt Thelma."

I smile, "It's nice to meet you."

Gertrude leads us into the sparkling white kitchen. The table's magnificently set with a light-blue tablecloth and the finest china I have ever seen. Mrs. Funk serves delicious corned beef and cabbage, potatoes, and all the fixings, with warm apple pie for desert.

After the last bite of the delectable pie, I jump up and grab a few dishes. "Can I please help you clean the kitchen, Mrs. Funk?"

She pats my shoulder gently. "Not this time because you're our guest. Once you're an old married lady, then you'll be put to work." She gives me a pleasant smile.

This house is so warm and inviting. No tension. Am I dreaming?

I'm basking in the comfort of true family love.

Chapter 43

A few days have passed since that wonderful evening with my future in-laws, but I've been unbelievably busy with working at the dance studio, riding lessons, and checking places out to rent in Greenwich Village. However, I'm distraught; I haven't seen or heard from my father or Daisy since I moved. The keeper hasn't been around since I left home, must be because there's no alone time. I breathe a sigh of relief.

"Violet, are you and Henry excited about your engagement party this weekend?" Auntie asks as I sit down for breakfast.

I spread marmalade on my English muffin. "I know exactly what I'm going to wear, and I can't believe that Alex is closing the studio early, so he and his wife can come. Have you heard anything from Papa?"

"I tried to call several times but never get an answer. Maybe, they'll be there."

"He can be so stubborn, Auntie. I don't think it's fair, if he keeps Daisy from coming."

"I know, dear." She rubs my back gently. "But I hope you'll have a great time anyway."

Henry snaps the camera as I sit on top of my beautiful steed once again, but this time I'm outside the fenced in area. Miss Royal is holding her head high, and I'm so proud of my accomplishment on becoming an equestrian in such a short period of time.

"Henry, are you sure I'm ready to go out on a trail?"

He mounts a bay thoroughbred. "Of course, you are. Remember to stay one-horse length behind me, and Charlie will do the same as he follows you."

The air's crisp and cool on this early November day. A few leaves are falling gracefully to the ground from almost barren trees, but the smell of the many tall pine trees along this manicured trail is magnificent. A squirrel scurries up a tree, and Ms. Royal stands at attention and looks at it. My body tilts to the right without notice, but I grab the horse's mane, straighten up, and continue.

"Keep two hands on the reins and grip with your knees, Violet," Charlie calls out.

Henry stops and turns. "Are you alright, honey?"

A fake smile crosses my face. *I want to get off right now before I fall off.* "I'm fine. It's such a perfect day to ride." I feel like I'm about to jump out of my skin.

A few deer can be seen in a distance, but Miss Royal continues moving forward without taking notice. Good. She's walking slower. Ah, it's time to relax and enjoy the ride.

Henry guides us to a clearing on the edge of a pond. "Let's give the horses a drink. Ms. Royal loves the water so keep a good grip on those reins. She stops well for you so hold back until I demonstrate how it's done."

"Good girl, good girl. Whoa girl," I say as I pat the horse on the neck.

The boys are having a ball sloshing their horses in and out of the water. Miss Royal starts to prance and my heart jolts too. "Whoa, girl. Whoa." I take a huge breath.

Henry arrives at my side, reaches out, and grabs my hand. "Are you ready for the induction into the water society?"

"As ready as I'll ever be. It's about time I join in the merriment."

"Slowly walk your horse toward the water."

Now, the water is up to the horse's knees. Getting caught up in the moment, I'm thrilled with the experience beneath me. "She loves this."

Miss Royal steps deeper and deeper into the pond. "Whoa, horse. My boots are getting wet."

"Turn her around, Violet," Charlie yells.

I pull the left rein to my left, but the horse stops suddenly. I fly off, hitting my chin on the stirrup as I splash into the water, bottom first. The murky water is ice-cold as it surrounds me.

All at once, Henry leaps off his ride, hands the reins to Charlie, plows into the water, and grabs my hand to help me up on my soggy feet. Miss Royal stands perfectly still in innocence.

Henry takes off his corduroy blazer, puts it around my shoulders, and points. "The stable's down the trail a bit. Can you walk, or do you want to get back on and ride?" He looks me in the face, and his eyes grow big. "My goodness, you're bleeding."

"What? Where?" I feel my frozen face and notice blood on my fingers. Then I remember hitting my chin on the way down. This is a disaster, and it all happened in front of two handsome men. How embarrassing. My mouth is dry. I don't know what to say.

Pulling a wet handkerchief out of his pocket, Henry places it on my chin. "Charlie, go get help." He grabs Royal's reins and hands them to me. "Do you think you can hold on to her?"

I sigh, "I guess so." I reluctantly take the reins and lead the horse out of the water.

Charlie takes off at a full gallop.

"Oh, I feel like such a fool. I should have paid attention to what I was doing instead of looking at the scenery."

We walk the horses to a fallen tree log, on the side of the trail and sit. "I have to get you to a doctor immediately, Violet. That's quite a cut. You may need some stitches."

I squint my eyes and shield them from the sun. "Is that someone coming toward us in a car?"

The car comes to a screeching halt and Charlie jumps out. "Henry, get her to the doctor right now. We'll take care of the horses."

My knight without the shining armor helps me into the car, making sure I apply tight pressure to my chin, and takes off down the road.

"There, there, Ms. Moretti. You needed only four stiches. It could've been a lot worse, you know." Dr. Smith says.

I try to hold back the tears. "But I can't look like this for our engagement party which is in two days."

"My nurse will give you some facial cream that you can start to use tonight. This will take down the redness considerably."

I place my hand gingerly on my bandaged chin. "Thank you, Dr. Smith."

"I'll give the news to your fiancé, but in the mean time you can get back into your own clothes." I pull up my damp britches and secure the button and put my lightweight dry blouse on.

Two hours later, we're on the way back to Auntie's house; I look up into the mirror in tears of horror as I peel away the bandage. "Look at this wound. The stiches are ghastly. We must postpone the party. I cannot be seen like this." I scream.

"Relax, honey, the redness will be gone by tomorrow night."

I can't wait to get out of this car. I'm freezing in this damp underwear. When Henry stops the car in front of Auntie's, I fling the door open and fly in the house.

"What happened, Violet?" Auntie squeals.

Uncontrollable wailing overcomes me as I race past her and flee into my bedroom.

"What happened to Violet? She seems distraught over something." I hear her ask as I close the door.

I fling myself onto the bed, in despair. "I hate horses. I'll never ride again as long as I live." I turn onto my back and gaze at the shadowy ceiling with my hand on my wounded chin.

"Get it together, Miss Violet. Move now and get out of these damp clothes. After that, march out there and tell them to postpone the party. You should not be marrying this man, anyway." The keeper murmurs in my ear.

A chill runs down my spine, one so frigid and alarming. "I thought I left you in Brooklyn, keeper. I love Henry. You don't know anything about love anyway."

"At least I found you and brought you to a point where you will listen."

"I'm going to marry him, and there's nothing you or anyone else can do about it. Now, go away."

Glancing at the clock on my dresser, I see it's 2:00 p.m. Breakfast was hours ago; no wonder I'm so hungry. I open the closet to grab my clean, red-striped sweater and a blush-pink jumpsuit. In doing so, I see a partial view of dark-green flowing satin. Out of curiosity, I yank the hanger off the bar and find myself holding the designer dress Auntie bought for my engagement. I hold in front of me as I dance in front of the full-length mirror.

There came a knock at the door. "Violet, are you talking out loud again? I made a late lunch for you. Come on out, honey." Auntie says.

"Coming," I call to my auntie as I carefully place the dress on the bed. I open the door, and my attentive aunt grabs my hand. "When do the stiches come out?"

"Monday. We must postpone the party, Auntie. That's all there is to it."

"Now, now. Come and have something to eat. Henry's relaxing with a cup of coffee. We'll talk about it together, okay?"

"People will understand, and love you more," Henry chimes in.

"Alex has already notified all of his patrons that the dance studio will be closing early," Auntie adds.

"But I look dreadful." I sip the homemade vegetable soup in front of me.

Henry smiles with that adorable grin I love so much. "I think you look kind of cute like that, sweetheart."

I start to laugh, but the stiches hurt too badly. However, it warms my heart to hear Auntie and Henry chuckle. "What would I do without you two? The party's on as planned."

Chapter 44

Henry, Auntie, and I arrive at Joe's Restaurant on Fulton Avenue on November 29 an hour earlier than the engagement party invitation states. Different shades of red brick cover the exterior of this popular eatery. Patrons know this place by the mahogany, larger-than-normal front door with its amazing sculpture. The aroma of steamed clams in melted butter and homemade meatballs laden with garlic, and fresh baked bread fill the air as we make our way through the main dining room to the stairs. The steps descending to the party cellar are carpeted in a rose tone with papered walls to match.

"You kids sit over here." Auntie directs us to a small table with a blue- and white-checked tablecloth and a single candle burning delicately on top.

I'm in awe of the décor in this room, but the pink chrysanthemums on the small bar catch my eye. "Auntie, did you get these for us?"

She buzzes around, checking out the place. "Yes. Aren't they lovely?"

Henry's all decked out in a single-breasted, fawn-colored worsted suit with chalk stripes. He looks positively handsome tonight. He takes my hands in his. "I love you, Violet Pearl Moretti."

"Are you enjoying the warmth of the fire?" Auntie calls out from across the room.

I look behind us at the floor-to-ceiling fieldstone fireplace, with flames dancing in the hearth. "Oh, Auntie. This is going to be an enchanting night."

"I knew this would be the ideal place for your engagement party, not only for the furnishings and food, but we can seat fifty-two people comfortably."

"Fifty-two? Who did you invite? All of Brooklyn?" Henry asks.

Pulling up a chair and joining us, Auntie answers, "Some family members and dance instructors from Alex Murphy's and a few of your friends and coworkers from the Met. I heard from everyone except Berto and Daisy."

"It would be just like him to show up," I say with a scowl, "even if he didn't respond to your invitation." *I don't think I can cope with this party, if they don't come.*

"You'll have a positively wonderful time without him. So, chin up, my dear." Henry says as he embraces me in his arms. I love it when he hugs me at the right time.

An hour later, the pianist is at the grand piano playing melodies from show tunes to classical while everyone feasts on fried half-squab chicken a la Maryland with bacon strip, corn fritters, green beans, and French-fried potatoes. Delicious and very filling.

Charlie stands and clinks his fork against his water glass to get everyone's attention. The room quiets down. "I would like to propose a toast to the happy couple," he says. "Violet and Henry, please come here to the seats of honor."

Charlie pours two glasses of burgundy wine for us and one for himself. "Dear friends, this is a special celebration in honor of two of my favorite people. Congratulations on your engagement. I wish you happiness, good fortune, and health as you prepare for your wedding day, in two months. God's blessings to you both."

"Here, here." Everyone simultaneously shouts as they clink glasses.

The tables are arranged around a small dance floor in the center of the room. The keyboard player hammers out his rendition of *In the Mood* by Glenn Miller, and soon a few couples are dancing up a storm. The place is jumping now. The single folks are hand clapping and foot tapping. There isn't a frown in the place.

When the piano player takes his last break before dessert and coffee is served, I look out at the crowd realizing my father and sister aren't there. I quickly escape to the ladies' room designed for one guest at a time. I feel like a lost child in the middle of Penn station.

I plop down on the toilet seat as tears flow down my cheeks. *My own father could not break through his pride to celebrate this happy occasion with me. Not only that, he kept my sister from coming too. Why can't he be happy for me? Why couldn't he at least let my sister come? What kind of person demands his own way of his grown-up daughter? Did Papa treat Mama this way too? Maybe that's why she was so upset before she died.*

The doorknob jiggles, and I realize someone is waiting to get in here. I glance at myself in the small mirror, put on a little rouge, and dart out of the door not paying any attention to who is waiting.

The one thing I learned during the Vaudeville years was to let my emotions hide under a joyful exterior. I twirl around my fiancé with a grin from ear to ear and plant a firm kiss on his cheek. He reciprocates back and everyone applauses.

"Thank you all for coming to share our engagement," Henry announces with his arm around me. "You're all so special to us. We hope to see you at the wedding." Henry and I place ourselves at the bottom of the stairs, so we can personally shake hands with each guest as they leave.

The party cellar is quiet now and most of the lights are off. I stop for a moment and glance back with an empty, cold feeling of gloom, realizing the two family members I wanted here the most never showed up.

The holidays were tough because Papa kept his distance, but somehow, I got through it without sinking into the pit of despair. Auntie was able to steal Daisy from Papa's clutches for two nights, and I will cherish those moments forever. His band had an overnight gig in Mount Kisco, and he needed someone to take care of my sister. I was a bit heartbroken when I learned he dropped Daisy off when I was at work, so he didn't have to see me.

"Your father did promise to be at the wedding on January 29, Violet." Auntie murmured in passing later that night.

"I have not spoken to my father in a couple of months, so I find it almost impossible that he would darken the doors of the church on my wedding day." My spirit is crushed.

Daisy's my only bridesmaid and Eleanor my maid of honor. *Maybe I should call Papa and ask him to walk me down the aisle. Then again, maybe not.*

Oh, how wonderful this warm lavender bubble bath feels tonight after dancing four hours straight. The place has been packed every night since the jitterbug became so popular. My stint as a dance instructor will come to an end after we get married. It would take forever to get from Greenwich to Brooklyn. Sinking deeper into the bubbles, I smile as I think about the new apartment in Greenwich Village. Small but perfect for two newlyweds to set up housekeeping for a couple of years. *The keeper has been quiet for a few weeks now.* I breathe a sigh of relief.

"Well, that's all you have to unpack, right?" Asks Henry after latching the last suitcase.

Sitting down on the edge of the new full-size bed in the apartment, I answer, "That's it, other than my wedding outfit I'm wearing tomorrow."

He sits down next to me, and we fall on our backs together, staring at the shadows dancing on the ceiling. He grabs my hand, "Can you believe it? This time tomorrow, we'll be Mr. and Mrs. Henry Funk."

I kiss him on the cheek. "The butterflies won't stop fluttering in my stomach. That's how excited I am. I was thinking about painting the bathroom a different color? What do you think, honey?"

"Well, it depends on what color?"

"How about a pale lavender?"

He wrinkles his brow. "Not very masculine, but if that's what you want, I will live with it. I love you so much, but you know that already." He rolls on top of me, we kiss each other generously and lock in a tight embrace. "We better get out of here before something happens we'll regret."

The sparks ignite within me. *So, what if we get carried away? We're getting married tomorrow.* I want to melt into him and never leave his side again.

He pulls himself off me and falls to the floor. "I promised myself, I would wait until after we're married for a sexual relationship with you. I better get you home because tomorrow night, there are no stops." We both let loose into a rumble of laughter as we scramble to our feet.

PART FOUR

1940

Chapter 45

The Little Church around the Corner is a huge early English structure built in 1849. Henry attended this church many times as a boy, and it's a perfect setting for a wedding. There's a small chapel on the far side of the property, a perfect place to say our vows of matrimony to each other. It's a cold, dreary day as we get out of the car and walk across the snow-cleared path into the tiny warm foyer.

"I'm so glad that you bought these warm tweed coats with matching muffs for Violet and me, Aunt Flossie," Daisy says.

Auntie walks into a small room and comes out with a box from a florist. She pins a pink rose corsage on Daisy's coat and a beautiful pink orchid on mine. "The ceremony is quite short, and it never gets warm enough in this place so leaving coats on is a good plan indeed. Everyone will be able to see your beautiful dress at the brunch reception at my house."

"Thank you so much, my dear sweet aunt," I tell her. "Mama would be so proud of you."

Auntie opens the door and peers outside. "The guests are starting to arrive. We must wait in the back room until everyone is seated." She ushers us into the little musty room where there are several wooden chairs, a small table, a tall bookshelf loaded with Bibles and books.

"But what about Eleanor?" I ask.

"She will find us. Don't worry, Violet Pearl."

Standing and scoping out the books on the shelves, my eyes focus upon The Book of Psalms. "Mama loved that little book entitled *The Shepherd Psalm*," I whisper to myself.

"Where's Eleanor? It's almost time for the procession to start." Auntie comments as she peeks through the door again. "Violet, do you know where she is?"

I keep reading. *He leads me in the paths of righteousness for His namesake.*

Oh, my dear mama. You should be here on my wedding day but somehow, I feel your presence. I'm glad we're getting married in a church.

The door creaks open and a frazzled Eleanor enters. "I'm here. So sorry I'm late."

"Does everyone remember when to go down the aisle?" Auntie asks.

We nod our heads in unison. The flutters in my stomach have multiplied.

Auntie heads out to play the piano; she glances over at us as we peek out of the door and nods.

When the music starts, Daisy begins the short walk to the front as a junior bridesmaid and ring bearer.

Eleanor steps out soon after.

I'm left alone. *Pull yourself together, Violet. You can do this.*

A few late stragglers are taking seats on the front left. It looks like everyone is here now.

I gaze to the front and scan the pews to the left first. Now to the right. My heart starts pounding, and tears well up in my eyes when I realize no one is here to walk me down the aisle.

What bride walks herself down the aisle to get married? My father should be right here by my side.

Henry and Charlie turn in unison and look at me. The Reverend Randall Roy raises his hands up, "Congregation, please stand."

The organist from above pounds out, *Here Comes the Bride.*

With trepidation, I step slowly forward with a painted smile on my face. I can hear those repetitious words of my father pounding in my brain. *Laugh, clown, laugh.*

"Henry Emile Funk, wilt thou have this woman to be thy wedded wife to live together after God's ordinance in the Holy Estate of matrimony? Wilt thou love her? Comfort her in sickness and in health, and forsaking all others as long as you both shall live?"

"I do."

The Reverend Roy repeats the vow to me.

"I do."

The reverend nods at Daisy. "May I have the rings?"

My beautiful aunt, all decked out in a pale-blue suit with matching hat softly plays *Jesu, Joy of Man's Desiring* by J. S. Bach.

Daisy does her job brilliantly as she carries the small pillow holding the rings to the rector.

We exchange rings and smile at each other with love and adoration. Looking past Henry, I see Auntie wink at me as she continues to play until the Rector gives a nod.

"By the authority vested in me by the State of New York, I now pronounce you man and wife; and what God hath joined together, let no man or woman put asunder. You may kiss the bride."

Henry wraps his arms around me, and I return the love with a long, warm kiss. I lift my left leg as the adrenalin boils within me. My other leg is wobbly, but I want to stay like this forever.

Everyone in the small sanctuary stands and applauds. Henry pulls me to his side, and we turn to look out at our guests. Everything is so calm and serene. I don't want it to break.

"Please remain in your places until the bride and groom leave the room," The Reverend Roy says. "They will greet you all as you leave the chapel."

The organist plays a tune we never heard of, but it tells the bridal party to move on out. The smile is still glued to my face as I nod at the guests.

Henry tugs on my hand and motions for me to look to my left. My watery eyes meet the dark brown eyes of my aging papa who is standing in the last row. He's dressed in a black shapeless suit with a crisp white shirt underneath. He nods at Henry and smirks at me.

I want to hug him, but instead I keep right on going. He has hurt me enough, and I won't let him spoil my wedding day any more than he has.

"Burr. It sure is cold with these doors wide open," Henry comments as we stop on the stoop and begin greeting everyone.

Hugs, pecks on the cheeks, and tears of joy are abundant as the guests congratulate us.

"Well, you two. Congratulations. Everything went perfectly, didn't it?" Auntie says as she hugs me.

"You did it all, Flossie. Thank you so much for everything." Henry says.

Daisy follows with a big bear hug, and I'm tickled pink to see how grown up she has become over the past months.

"I love you, my beautiful sister and handsome brother-in-law," she says.

"Come on, Daisy," Auntie says. "We have to get to the house to let our guests in."

Moments later, Henry and I find ourselves standing in an empty foyer. *My father must have gone out of the side door.*

The church janitor comes out of the dark sanctuary. "Well folks, I have to lock up now. Congratulations to you Mr. and Mrs. Funk."

"Thank you, kind sir." Henry nods with a smile.

Stepping down the four cement steps on to the snowy walkway, we walk hand in hand toward the car.

"Violet Pearl," a familiar voice from behind calls out.

My heart pounds inside my chest. The only instinct I have is to drop my husband's hand and run into my father's arms. My body quivers and hot tears roll down my face as I melt into my papa's large, warm body. He places one arm around me.

"Oh, Papa. I missed you so much. I'm glad you're here."

"It was hard for me, Violet Pearl, but I felt it only right to make an appearance."

I pull away and look at him, "I needed you to walk me down the aisle. You're my father. Do you know how humiliating it was to walk alone?"

He drops his arms, "I have a gift for you."

The joy I felt for a few fleeting moments escapes as trembling and sadness takes over. Henry comes to my side, grabs my waist, "We need to get to the reception, honey. Will you be joining us, Mr. Moretti?"

"I hope the two of you will be very happy." Papa hands me an envelope, kisses me on the cheek, and walks away.

I should be angry with his cold demeanor, but I'm overwhelmed with hopelessness. "Papa," I yell, but he doesn't look back. "Papa!"

Chapter 46

It's a cool, crisp Sunday morning as we travel down the New Jersey Turnpike around noon amid little traffic. Seagulls are flying in all directions trying to find a warm place to land.

"So, Mrs. Funk, how does it feel being an old married lady?" Henry chuckles as he grabs my hand with a squeeze.

I pull my hand away and stare out of the window. Thoughts about my father are whirling around in my mind and the word *married* causes my heart to skip several beats. "We haven't even been hitched for more than twenty-four hours yet, Henry." I shout.

"What's wrong with you? You all but snapped my head off. Whatever happened to the sweet lady who woke up in my bed a few hours ago?"

I fold my arms in front of me. "Just drive the car, Henry. I need time to think."

All I wanted was my father's blessing and acceptance of this marriage. Marriage? I'm not good enough for this man I married. What will he expect of me? Will I be able to be the wife he deserves? Our first night together was magical and more than I ever dreamed it would be. Why am I overwhelmed with negative thoughts today?

After a few minutes of silence with the whirring of the tires hitting the road, Henry glances my way for an instant. "Why don't you open that box with all of the wedding cards in it and read some of them to me."

We're twelve years apart, and I will be living so far from Auntie. I hope I didn't make a mistake. My heart's pounding, and my mind is rambling all over the place. *Maybe, Henry's too old for me. Was Papa right?* My cheeks are flaming.

"Violet. Did you hear me?" my husband asks.

"Yes. I did."

"Maybe you have to use the bathroom or maybe hunger pains are taking over your loving disposition. Talk to me, my dear wife. What in the world is bothering you?"

"Alright, alright. I am thinking about my father. He really upset me yesterday. I woke up several times thinking about it."

"Listen, sweetheart. Don't let him spoil our honeymoon. He'll come around in due time. Let him be for now." *He's right. I must pull myself together and move on.*

I lean into Henry and kiss him on the cheek. "You're right. I'm sorry for being sore."

"We should be at our hotel in a little over an hour, but in the meantime, open up some cards, okay?"

I pick up the tin box from the floor, lift off the lid, and find the first card that has familiar handwriting. I read the words slowly on the handwritten, gold-gilded Rust Craft card with a Victorian-era bride and groom etched on the front.

"That looks interesting. Read it to me, Violet."

Emotions from deep in my soul erupt as I read it silently. *That coldhearted snake.* I proceed to read it to Henry in a loud, obnoxious voice.

"Wedding Congratulations. May cheer and hope and happiness and all things good and true, be woven in the pattern of the future years for you, Violet Pearl. *Why, is my father so cold and distant?*

He didn't even mention you, Henry. In my eyes, he still doesn't see us married. What's wrong with him?"

I begin to tremble as the waterworks fill up in my tear ducts. I start to rip the card up.

"Violet, you didn't read all of it to me, did you? Who is the card from?"

Blowing my nose, I manage to create a false smile. "It's from my father."

"Is that all he said?"

"I don't want to hurt you, Henry. I love you."

"It's no secret that your father doesn't like me, but you're my wife now. We can stand up to him together."

"I don't want to, but I will since you're so persistent."

"To Violet Pearl, I hope you will be very happy in your new life with Mr. Funk. I enrolled Daisy in a private boarding school, so I can be free to travel with the band. I don't know when you'll see me again. Fondly, Your father. Now, you know why I wanted to keep this from you, Henry."

"Yes, he's a very a cold man. Maybe, he has trouble seeing you as a grown woman. Now, put that card away, honey. It's time to make beautiful memories."

Solemnly, I start opening the envelope to put the card inside when a ten-dollar bill falls out. "He's a cheapskate too. Darn him anyway."

I bury the card on the bottom of the pile of cards and stuff the ten-dollar bill in my coat pocket. I continue opening the rest. Soon we're laughing as we're reminded of the guests who really love us. Their words are filled with joy, best wishes, and a few generous gifts for both of us.

The Hotel Willard stands in gray glory as we pull up in front to allow the valet to do his job. A bellhop dressed in gold and purple grabs our suitcases, and we follow him into a large lobby decorated in marble. I feel like a princess being led to her chambers.

"Reservation for Mr. and Mrs. Henry Funk, please," my husband announces as we approach the counter.

"Yes, Sir. Room 604. Here's your key." The bellhop leads us to the elevator, and we continue our journey to the sixth floor.

"Here's your room, Sir. Would you like me to open the door?" Smiles the bellman.

"No, thank you. You can leave our suitcases right here. I have something special planned for my bride." Henry says as he hands the bellhop a couple of dollars.

I begin to step inside. All at once, I'm lifted into my husband's arms. "Now is the time to carry you over the threshold, even if it is one day too late."

I throw my arms around his neck as my heart beats fast, and a huge tingling sensation embraces me from head to toe. We kiss passionately as he kicks the suitcases into the room and closes the door behind us. We're in a world of our own now.

The next two days go fast because we pack a lot into our sightseeing itinerary. Day one consists of a quick breakfast in the hotel restaurant, a walking tour of the United States Capital building, the Washington monument, the Lincoln Memorial, and a romantic dinner at the Occidental Grill on Pennsylvania Avenue.

Day two, we walk a crooked mile all around the Smithsonian and the National Museum of American History. My feet ache. I can hardly stand up. *Good grief, we have three more blocks to walk.* I grab Henry's arm for support. Tears escape from the corners of my eyes and weave jagged paths down my cheeks.

He rubs my hand. "Are you alright, dear?"

"My feet are killing me, Henry."

"Just hang on to me. We're almost to the hotel. You can soak in a nice hot bath, while I order room service for dinner."

I can't get my shoes and clothes off quick enough when I get into the bathroom. Fortunately, I remembered to pack some bubble bath crystals. I sink into the warm, sudsy water and close my eyes. Ah, this is what Doctor Henry ordered, for sure.

The light flickers as a coolness passes over me. "Go ahead; relax completely. Let love radiate from your presence. Consult me about all things, however insignificant." The keeper whispers.

My heart's pounding, my head swimming as I shudder a sigh. I try covering myself, because the bubbles have dispersed. "Get out of here, keeper. I'm on my honeymoon for goodness sake, and this is my private place."

"Yes, yes, yes. You're right again. I am. I don't want you to forget I exist, Violet Pearl."

I'm shivering. I don't like this. Not real. Not Real.

"Not Real." I scream at the top of my lungs.

Henry propels through the door, "What's the matter? Are you alright?"

Chapter 47

The aroma of freshly brewed coffee wakes me up, and I roll over to give my husband a morning kiss. Still struggling to open my eyes, I move my hand over the cold sheet next to me and realize I'm alone.

I leap out of bed, grab my robe, and sprint into the empty kitchen. Everything feels so cold and deserted.

"Henry. Honey. Henry?"

Turning in all directions, I look over the small apartment and then yell out, "Henry!"

The bathroom door is shut. He must be in there.

I knock and then knock again.

No answer.

I turn the knob and slowly open the door. "Henry?"

The room is dark and empty.

He left me without saying a word. *Now I'm alone in this lonesome place all day long. I like people around me. I don't know anyone around here.* I'm not sure what it means to be hysterical, but I'm shaking uncontrollably and can't find an end to it. Somehow, I manage to get myself a cup of coffee and plop down in a chair at the table. I must have needed something hot.

Mother. My dear mother. I wish you were at my wedding. I look at the empty chair across the table and visualize her sitting there. She's in a pink chenille robe, and her long, dark, curly hair is hanging in her face. The shaking subsides, but an eerie feeling fills the dwelling.

This is ridiculous. *Really, Violet. Get yourself together.*

I take a few swigs of the cooled coffee in front of me and then move over to the couch. Slumping down deep into the cushions, I see a newspaper with a note attached to it on the coffee table. I detach the note and read it.

My sweet Violet, I didn't want to wake my sleeping beauty. I hope the coffee was still hot when you got up. I left the paper for you. If you want to come into the city, I left a few dollars on the end table next to the bed. I'll be home at 5:30 for supper. I love you. Your husband.

I wish he woke me up, so I could go to the city with him. I'm not ready to be alone in this place. I smirk at the note my handsome husband left me. *I guess he meant well.* The day will fly by if I find something to do to fill it. Maybe, I should look for a job or sew a project? Instead, I flip through a *Life* magazine.

It's a dreary morning with little light peeking through the three small windows. All I want to do is go back to sleep and let the day roll on by. I fling the magazine to the floor and curl up on the couch. *Maybe, I need to sleep more.* I close my eyes thinking fond thoughts of Henry and I dancing across an empty ballroom floor. During this fleeting moment, my eyes pop open as the fear of being alone takes over me.

Someone was always with me, at least in the same house or place of work. This is a positively weird situation for me to be entirely isolated with no one to talk to. Slowly I get off the couch to check the time. *Maybe I can catch Auntie before she goes to work.*

I turn on the kitchen light, so I can see the clock" 10:00.

The doorknob to the apartment jiggles, and I creep to the short, dark hallway so I can get a better view. I wait a moment and then open the door a crack, leaving the chain across the door, and peer out. I breathe a sigh of relief when I see an empty hallway.

I must have been imagining things. Turning on my bare feet, I stare into my new home and suddenly remember the extra-large closet Henry uses for a place to develop his film.

Is someone hiding in there? I could have sworn I heard a door jiggle.

My limbs quiver as I move on tiptoes and turn the knob. Maybe I better get a knife or an iron pan for protection.

I'm sweating with fear, not knowing what I'll find on the other side.

The keeper from somewhere shouts out, "What are you afraid of? I will protect you."

With wrinkled brow and a confused state of mind, I pull open the door and stand on the threshold of the shadowy room.

Okay, Violet, take one giant step and grab the chain for the light.

"Go ahead." The keeper murmurs.

I close my eyes, lunge forward, and pull the chain.

Scared stiff in place, I slowly open my eyes. "Oh, come on, keeper, I can't believe you tracked me down again."

A counter to my left is used for developing with a clothesline of pictures hanging over it. The workbench to my right is storage for cameras, photo albums, and a few wedding gifts. Crouching down a bit to see under these counters, I realize the shallow shelves are too close together for anyone to hide in them.

Spine chilling laughter fills the space around me, "I'm invisible, so why are you looking for me?"

Disappointment wells up in my throat as I breathe a sigh of a relief. But in doing so, I'm drawn to a few pictures of me. I yank them off the clothespins, turn off the light, and close the door behind me.

"What's he going to do with these pictures of you in the bathtub? That flimsy negligee is so sheer that one can see your naked body as clear as clear can be," mutters the keeper in my ear.

Still in my bathrobe at noon, I spread the photographs on the table and slowly realize I have what it takes to be a model of some sort.

"You are beautiful. Go ahead and look for a place to flaunt that body of yours," the keeper whispers.

I ignore it.

Sudden energy bolts me to the coffee table where the *Daily News* lays. I start flipping through the pages until I finally see the classified section. *The keeper finds me all the time, it seems.* Shrugging my shoulders, I scan the help-wanted ads, scrolling down with my index finger.

Babysitters, cashiers, hairdressers. No. What's the use? Not a thing. *I wish Alex Murphy's place wasn't so far away. I loved my job there.* The only dance jobs I see are for floozies that work on Forty-Second Street for the peep shows. Seamstresses. Waitresses. What happened to the model search?

I fling the paper across the floor, and I don't even care that it's askew everywhere either.

The phone on the kitchen wall rings.

I stare at it until it stops. I don't feel like talking anyway.

After scrambling an egg and making the bed, I manage to get out of my robe and get dressed at 2:00.

On all fours, I crawl around, picking up the paper and putting it back into its orderly fashion when my eyes catch a huge advertisement on the front page of section two.

Hat models wanted at Gimbel's department store.

Apply in person on the third floor in the Millenary section.

Applications available until Friday, noon.

Today's Thursday. Ye gads! I don't even know how to get from here to there.

"Are you stupid?" The keeper asks.

Maybe if I ignore him, he'll vanish.

Looking around the place, I peer out of the window at the street below and see a few folks getting into a bus. I pick up the newspaper, stare at the advertisement, and soon realize I would be wasting my time to even consider going into the city today.

"You have it all over those girls who will be applying for that modeling job." The keeper shouts.

I jump up and shout back, "Leave me alone!"

"I am a spirit. I live within. Listen to me for once."

Running to my bed, I fling myself facedown and pound my fists into the bedspread, mumbling as I burst into tears of panic. "This is not happening to me. I won't let it!"

The telephone rings again. Instead of answering it, I roll on my back and stare at the light-blue ceiling.

I leap off the bed, grab my coat off the hook, and proceed to the front door.

I must get out of here right now. Besides, I must go to the market, so I can shop for dinner. I flit nervously down the hall to grab my shawl and knock down a small, old, white book. When I pick it up and realize it's my mother's! *The Shepherd Psalm.*

I open it and verse four leaps off the page at me.

I read it out loud. "Even though I walk through the valley of the shadow of death, I will not be afraid for you are close beside me." *I don't want the keeper close by me. What does this really mean?*

As I descend the three flights of stairs, I look back quickly with a shallow feeling of peace because I'm by myself. For the moment anyway.

I stop the first person I see. "Excuse me, Sir, but can you give me directions to the nearest market?"

The tall, slender, older man smiles. "Certainly, Miss. If you walk three blocks that way and turn right, you will come to a few stores, one of which is a general store. Good place to shop. Lots of bargains."

Oh me. I forgot my pocketbook. I turn to go back and get it.

No. The keeper's there. I start to tremble in fear and reach into my coat pockets.

One hand pulls out the ten-dollar bill from my father and the other, a few pennies and a wrinkled handkerchief. I breathe a sigh of relief and head to the store. As I walk along taking in the different kinds of architecture, I tell myself over and over that I have one big imagination, and I was indeed alone in my new place just a little while ago.

Soon, I'm standing in the middle of a market filled with every different kind of smell. This place has a fresh fish counter, a butcher, home-baked bread, some overripe produce, and four aisles of canned or packaged goods.

A lady with gray curly hair is stocking shelves and smiles at me. "Can I help you, Miss?"

I hold the ten-dollar bill up, "What can I buy with this, so I can make supper for my husband?"

She grabs my hand. "Come with me, honey. You must be a newly-wed, huh? Although, you look like a kid."

"My husband will be home at five thirty. This will be the first meal I cook for him. It has to be something good but simple to make."

"We have fresh green beans for ten cents a pound. Here's a basket. Let's load it up."

"I only have ten dollars, though."

"Don't you fret, young lady, you'll be going home with some change at that." She chuckles and leads me on an adventure in shopping for groceries. I make my purchase, pay for everything, and head back outside with two loaded paper bags.

The cool air hits my face as I walk swiftly back to the apartment building. Henry will be home in two hours. I have some housework to do and a meal to prepare.

I can't believe I have three dollars left after buying all this food.

I hike up the steps and put down the two bags to open the door. Wait a minute. I never locked it. Looking around the quiet hallway, I make the decision to open the door, pick up the bags, hold my head high, and go inside.

Music's always good for what ails me. I'm so glad that Henry has a phonograph, and I brought a few of Mama's favorite records with me. Cleaning and cooking are delightful tasks now.

Tomorrow, I'll go into the city with Henry and apply for the modeling job.

The smell of chocolate cake and onions frying fills the small living quarters as I set the table.

I decide to change into a low-cut light-blue cashmere sweater and black trousers at 5:00 so I am ready when Henry comes home.

Ah, Peaceful bliss.

That silly so-called keeper spirit is totally make-believe. Once I get a job, I'll be fine. Keeping busy is the name of the game. *I'm normal. Normal. Normal.*

Chapter 48

"You sure outdid yourself, my love," Henry says as he lays down his fork. "This meal is fit for a king. The aroma of the fried onions and garlic made my stomach grumble when I came home tonight. What else did you do to the Salisbury steak? The beans are cooked just right, and how did you know that mashed potatoes with gravy is my favorite? Are you going to join me?"

"I'm serving up my plate now. The secret is garlic, garlic, garlic. That was always a mainstay at our house," I mutter from the kitchen.

"Sounds good to me."

I plant a kiss on his cheek, before I sit down. "So, am I hired as your personal cook?"

He pulls me down onto his lap and gives me a huge bear hug. "You're a keeper. I love you. Onions, garlic. Who cares?"

Time seems to stand still as we kiss and caress each other on the spindly chair.

"Honey. I made you a chocolate cake. Do you want it now or later?"

"Yum. Later, if that's alright with you. I'm stuffed right now. You need to eat something though. Why didn't you answer the telephone today? You were here, weren't you?"

With reservation, I remove myself from his lap and head into the kitchen to dish up a plate for myself. "I was here." *Henry doesn't need to know about the keeper.*

"I was worried and wanted to tell you I love you. You should have answered."

"I took a long hot bath and went shopping. You probably called then."

In bed that night, Henry wraps his arms around me. "I'm so glad that you're going into the city with me tomorrow, Violet. I'm certain the modeling job is yours."

"If that doesn't pan out then at least I will be in the right vicinity to apply for other jobs. Besides, I love to walk around the city, but you already know that."

He kisses me and turns over. "Seven comes quickly. Good night, sweetheart."

"See you in the morning."

I stare at the ceiling for at least an hour while my dear husband snores to beat the band. Every time I close my eyes, he bellows out another roar.

Count sheep. Mama always told me to do that if I couldn't sleep. *One, two, three, four, five....* The numbers fade away.

It's dark in here. I can't see anything.

I reach for the lamp, but it isn't there. I start to tremble with fear and worry. "Daisy? Where are you?"

No answer.

"Violet Pearl, wake up. We have to leave now." Mama's voice is so weak, but I know it's her. My heart's pounding, and sweat's dripping down my face.

"Mama?"

I can see her. Mama with little Daisy in her arms. "Violet, come with us now."

Looking down at her feet, I see she is shoeless and wearing only a slip.

I scream as loud as my larynx will allow me too. She's tugging on my arm, and Daisy's crying hysterically.

"No. Mama. I can't go." I pull away and fall back into bed.

Tossing and turning with the sheet wrapped tightly around me, I find no route of escape. "Help me!" I scream out as I gasp for air in between.

Someone or something is rubbing my arm. My heart soars straight into my throat.

"Sweetheart, wake up. You're having a nightmare."

I can hear screams of terror from a short distance away, and I want so much to flee. I try to open my eyes, but they're stuck shut.

"It's me—Henry. Wake up."

My eyes slowly open. His arms are wrapped around me. I glare at him as though he's a stranger. He rustles my hair and leans in to kiss me.

I push myself away from him, leap off the bed, and somehow find my way in the dark to the cold bathroom.

Slamming the door, I flick on the light and sit on the toilet. "I'm so afraid I'll snap," I scream out in rage, "and come apart like my mother." I sob uncontrollably far into the night. Henry knocks on the door several times. I don't answer.

Chapter 49

Modeling hats for a career is very interesting, but I know I could make them myself and make more money at it. Hats are all the rage right now, and a millinery shop in Greenwich Village would be a big hit. Another one of my pipe dreams, I guess.

Where else can I get a discount on the latest fashions while taking center stage on the small runway in the woman's department at Gimbel's? I do this five days each week from nine to three, with a half-hour lunch break when the college girl comes in to replace me. The most enjoyable thing is that Henry and I ride the bus together every day. Once a week he brings me a tuna salad sandwich on rye for lunch. My favorite.

"Well, Mrs. Funk. You have been working here for three months now. We have doubled our sales since you came aboard," Mrs. Reed, the department manager, tells me one day when I return from lunch.

"I had no idea. Really?"

"You have a beautiful face and figure too. I can put you in a slip and it would sell, dear."

Mrs. Reed has great potential to be attractive if she would take off a few pounds and put on a little makeup.

Nausea again? What time is it? I have another twenty minutes until my shift ends. Oh, Druthers. There are three ladies watching my every move. I can't walk away without telling someone I'm not feeling well. Keep the grin on that face of yours, Violet.

I sashay forward, pivot, and walk back and repeat my efforts several times.

Good. Mrs. Reed's close now. Let's see if I can get her attention. I feel like I'm going to throw up my lunch right here. I must talk to her now.

I touch her arm lightly. "Mrs. Reed. I feel sick to my stomach."

"Oh, dear." She looks at me with a wrinkled brow and a slight smile. "Go. Go to the ladies' room. I'll explain to the customers if they should ask about you."

The Gimbel's ladies' lavatory is on this floor which is a good thing, but it's on the opposite end of the woman's department. Holding my hand over my mouth, I sprint between customers and displays, hoping that I will make it in time.

Once inside the stall, I let it all out in the toilet in front of me. My face is burning up, and I feel like I'm coming down with a cold. I fix my dress and flush the toilet.

I better sit in the lounge for a few minutes.

Looking at my watch, I realize my shift is officially over. I lean over the sink and wash my hands. I glance up at myself in the mirror and appalled at how pale I look.

"Violet, are you alright? You look rather peeked," Marion, a sales-clerk friend says when she comes into the bathroom.

I describe all my symptoms in detail.

"Honey, I think you're pregnant."

"No, no. I'm getting a cold." I look at her in dismay.

She laughs in a most jolly manner. "Listen, everyone goes through this in the early months of pregnancy. It's called morning sickness."

"Well, actually, I'm feeling better already. Time to go home and think about making supper. See you tomorrow, Marion."

"Bye, Vi. I still think there will be a little one in six months or so." She chuckles as I leave.

"Thanks for covering for me, Mrs. Reed," I say to her as I pass her on the sales floor. I couldn't smile any longer, but I feel fine now.

"You are more than welcome. Didn't this happen yesterday too?"

"Yes. It comes and goes though."

"Good thing tomorrow's Friday. You can rest up over the weekend for sure."

"See you in the morning, Mrs. Reed."

"Please call in the morning if you're ill."

"Sure thing."

All this talk about how one feels when pregnant is ridiculous. I'm not ready to have baby. Certainly not.

"Mrs. Funk. You're clearly four months along." Dr. Seagrave smiles at me from behind her desk. "There will be a new baby around February, if my calculations are right."

"Are you absolutely certain?"

"Of course. I hope you're not still having a monthly period cycle?" she asks with a smirk.

"Not in three months. Oh, I get it now."

She scrawls out something on a piece of paper and hands it to me. "I'll see you back here in one month."

Rising from my chair and taking the note, I mutter, "Thank you, Doctor."

I'm in a daze as I walk through the busy waiting room and down one flight of stairs to the traffic-infested street. *Henry and I are still newlyweds for crying out loud. I'm not ready for a family yet.* My brain is working over-time, as I try to understand what's happening inside of me.

Arriving back at the tiny apartment, I glance around the small place and stamp my feet, not caring one bit if anyone is home on the floor below me. There's absolutely no room in here for a crib, much less a nursery. *How will Henry take this news?*

I'm so relieved Aunt Flossie will be here for supper. *Yikes, supper! What am I going to make?* It's 4:00 p.m., and supper is at 5:30 p.m. I feel hot and shaky.

Peering into the iced-up miniature freezer, I shuffle around a few packages of sausage and canisters of orange juice, and way in the back I find a small whole chicken. I pull it out and run it under some warm water, so I can remove the plastic wrap. The hands on the clock above keep mov-ing, but time seems to be on my side when the wrap slowly peels off.

I plop it into a large pot with water. Onion? Celery? I hope so.

Mama's famous chicken soup recipe. Good. One onion left. The cel-ery is kind of wilted, but I can salvage one stalk anyway.

Watched pot never boils. Once it does boil, it will be cooked in an hour.

I stand on my tiptoes and reach into the cabinet over the refrigera-tor. Noodles, rice? Something. Please. Ugh. I grab the broom and whisk it around in hopes of finding a box that I can use. Crash. A flimsy package of noodles falls on the floor and bursts open as it lands.

I grab a dustpan and begin sweeping. At that moment, the water bubbles out of the pot.

The doorbell rings.

"The doorbell. Now? It's only four thirty." I say, annoyed and rush to the stove to pull the pot off the burner.

The doorbell rings again.

I turn the gas down and replace the pot and then run to the door.

The bell rings again.

"Coming. Just a minute!" I scream. I'm in a bad mood by the time I open the door.

"Violet Pearl, you look a shamble. Are you alright?" Aunt Flossie says as she flutters past me carrying a large cardboard box labeled Entenmanns Family Bakery.

"I'm having a lousy day, Auntie. Supper is nowhere near ready, and I have a huge mess in the kitchen." The bottled-up tears from before, sting my eyes again.

She raises her eyebrows. "Well, at least you have desert and a loaf of rye bread."

"Thanks." My temples are throbbing.

Taking off her sweater, she hangs it on the back of a chair. She pulls a clean, folded hankie out of her purse. "Here, wipe your eyes. Now, now. Your aunt is here. Don't fret."

I fling myself at her and wrap my arms around her thin body "I love you so much, and I don't know what I would do without you in my life."

Uncontrollable tears flow out of my eyes, and my nose is dripping into the hankie.

"I'm going to have a baby," I mumble enough for her to hear.

She pushes me gently away. "Oh, Toots. That's wonderful news."

Bubbling and sputtering sounds from the kitchen distract us.

"The soup!" I scream.

Rushing to the stove and turning off the gas, Auntie says, "Smells good. Are you making your mother's chicken soup?"

"Trying to."

"Alright, dear. Get another pot and try to salvage all the noodles you can. Then throw away the rest. I'll see if this chicken is done."

I fall to my knees on the cold linoleum floor. "I'm a mess, Auntie."

"Don't fret, child. The chicken's cooked. Do you have milk and flour?"

I pull myself up and fill the pot with water. "Let me finish what I started. Can you please set the table for me?" I breathe a sigh of relief as I carefully lift the cooked chicken out of the pot with tongs too hot to handle at this point.

"What smells so good in here?" Henry announces moments later as he hangs up his suit jacket.

I give him a kiss and pull out his chair. "Homemade chicken soup."

"It sure smells swell."

"I'm sure it's delicious too," Auntie comments as she sits down, giving me a wink.

A sudden feeling of nausea overwhelms me, and the urge to go to the toilet thrusts me in that direction.

"You two go ahead and eat," I say on the fly.

Falling to my knees in front of the bowl, I heave up everything I had for lunch and then some. So much for a peaceful dinner with my husband and aunt.

Chapter 50

Two months roll by, and I'm getting bigger and bigger. No more morning sickness; instead, I find myself eating all the time. Henry moved furniture around, and to my surprise, a nursery corner was instantly created. He's so excited about the birth of our first baby.

I can't model hats until after the baby is born, which by the doctor's calculations is in three to four months.

Henry surprised me with a Singer sewing machine for my twentieth birthday, and I've been stitching up a storm since then. New slipcovers for the sofa, curtains for the nursery, and a baby blanket are my favorite accomplishments.

Rubbing my hands over my enlarged tummy, I smile when I feel a tiny flutter from within. *Will there be a boy or a girl in the cold month of February?*

The telephone rings. Slowly I rise to grab the receiver off its hook.

"Hello?"

"This is your father."

"Papa?"

"I'm in the neighborhood and thought I would stop in and see you, if that's alright?"

Taking in a huge breath and sighing, I say, "Now?"

"Violet Pearl, I don't know when I'll be in Greenwich Village again. I seldom come this way."

"Is Daisy with you?"

"No, she's not. Look, maybe this is not a good time."

"It's alright, Papa." I roll my eyes. "Do you know where we live?"

"Your aunt Flossie gave me the address and phone number. I'm actually a few blocks away."

"See you soon." My stomach hardens into a block of ice.

I guess I'm happy he's coming for a long overdue visit, but I hope it goes alright.

Coffee's perking, and the last batch of oatmeal cookies are baked. *I wasn't even expecting any company, but Henry loves my cookies. Hopefully, my father will too.*

When the doorbell rings a few minutes later, I compose myself and prepare to meet my long-lost papa.

I open the door and smile. "Papa, it's so good to see you. Come, sit down, and have a cup of coffee."

Hanging his fedora on a coat hook in the hallway, he looks me over. "You have gained some weight, haven't you, Violet."

Looking down at my oversized red plaid larger-than-life smock, I say, "Didn't Auntie tell you the news?"

I watch him as he flits through the apartment, looking everything over with a scowl. "What news?"

"You're going to be a grandfather."

Stopping dead in his tracks right next to the crib, he scowls. "You're too young to be a mother, my daughter."

I take a deep breath before I speak. "I can't turn back the clock, Papa. There will be a baby in a few months."

Papa bolts from the nursery area; he heads for the table. "How about that coffee and homemade oatmeal cookies? Your sister's so intelligent and always at the top of her class. Could not let her stay in that school another day."

"What are you talking about, Papa?"

"Flossie didn't tell you that Daisy's in a different school now?"

"No. She didn't."

"I put her in a prestigious boarding school in Tarrytown, New York."

"Isn't that extremely costly? Honestly, you've always favored Daisy over me, and she's becoming a spoiled brat. You knew I had a heart for the dance and dreamed of becoming a ballerina. My dream was shattered because of you interfering. What kind of father doesn't walk their daughter down the aisle on her wedding day?"

He ignores me. "I took out a small loan, and the entertainment industry is really picking up now. I'm busy every weekend with the band. She's worth every nickel. Do you know that your sister wants to be a doctor?"

"Good for her. How far is Tarrytown anyway?" Suddenly, I'm tired and everything hurts. I just can't fight anymore.

"Just over the Hudson River. Not far."

"I haven't heard from her in a while. She could at least send me a postcard."

He squints his eyes. "Are you happy, Violet Pearl?"

Anger's rising within me, and all I want to do is kick him out of my home. "Of course, I am. Why do you ask such a question anyway?"

"Look at you. You are confined to this tiny place and so far from family and friends. How can you tolerate living like this?"

I shrug my shoulders. "I keep busy, Papa. I made all the curtains and a slipcover for that old couch. I love to cook too."

"But you're not Suzy Homemaker, Violet Pearl." He studies me with his big brown eyes. "You should have gone for that audition on Broadway when you had the chance. Now look where you are."

I pound my fists on the table and stand. "I think you better leave now. I've heard just about enough."

He makes no attempt to move. "I think you're jealous of your kid sister."

I grit my teeth and frown, as my blood pressure rises. "You certainly know how to upset me, don't you? Can't you be pleased with anything I do?"

He lets out a grotesque laugh. "Oh, come on. Lighten up. Laugh, clown, laugh!"

I scream with my eyes shut. "Please get out of here, now."

With a light tap on my shoulder and a nod, he puts on his hat. "Take care of yourself, Violet Pearl." He slams the door.

I pick up the Shepherd Psalm off the little table, open it, and read the first thing that pops out at me. "Your rod and your staff comfort me." *Oh, for crying out loud. How can this console anybody?* I fling the book against the wall.

The following Saturday after a breakfast of bacon, eggs, and a second cup of coffee, we venture to the couch to read *The Daily News*. I decided not to mention anything about my father's visit to Henry.

"I'll do the dishes in a bit, honey," Henry announces to my surprise.

With a quick look in his direction, I say, "Of course, you're joking, right?"

He pats me on my knee. "You need to relax on the weekends, Sweetheart. I must admit that housework has never been my strong point, but I lived alone for a few months. Had to take care of my place by myself."

Henry opens the sports pages, and I browse through the pages of advertising and news articles until I reach the classified section.

"Do you want to go to the movie house today?" he asks as he peers over the top of the paper.

Help wanted. No.

Puppies for sale. No. My eyes scan down the page and over to the next.

Apartments for rent. No.

"Hey there, brown eyes." Henry pushes the paper out of my hands.

"Now, why did you do that?"

Laughing, he grabs me. "Oh, come on. What can possibly be important in the classified anyway?"

"A bigger apartment might be one thing to look for."

"We'll be fine living here for at least a year after the baby arrives. Gives me a chance to save money for a house."

Picking the paper back up, I move my finger down the flats and apartment rentals, and as if it is the only thing on the page, I read *Store Front Space for rent/Greenwich Village.* Now is the time for a millinery shop filled with my creations right here in Greenwich Village.

"There's a matinee at the movie house. Do you want to go?" he shouts as if I were deaf.

"No. I want you to come with me and look at this place." I give him the paper with my finger held on the ad.

"We're staying in this place for another year at least. I don't want to look at anything."

"Please read this ad and then give your opinion."

He looks and reads, "Store front for rent. What?"

"Listen, Henry. I love to sew and have become quite good at it, plus you know how creative I can be when it comes to fashion. A millinery shop in this neighborhood would be a big hit."

"You would make the hats?"

"Most of them."

"You need money to open a store. It just doesn't happen, you know?"

"Aunt Flossie would help me. I know she would."

Wrapping his arms around me, the paper crumbles in his lap. "Okay. Go get dressed, and I'll clean the kitchen. Let's see. There's a telephone number and address. We should call first to be sure someone is there to show us the place."

For the first time since I can remember, I'm excited about my prospects.

Good ole Eleanor, Auntie, and Henry came through again. They cleaned and painted the place while I ordered new hats at wholesale prices over the telephone. I made a three dozen hats at night while Henry listened to his favorite radio programs. Violette's Millenary Shop opened the door on December 1—just in time for the Christmas shopping season. Henry worked at the store on the weekends to put a wall and door so there could be a small nursery with additional storage if need be. The once-exposed bathroom is now an enclosed room. I'm experiencing a fulfilled dream. Joy's coming back in bits and pieces.

Our apartment is four blocks away, and it's wonderful to have city lights to guide me home.

Glancing at my watch, I realize it's time to lock the door, turn off the lights, and head home. Henry's bringing Chinese food home for supper. Good.

I bundle up and pack my tote bag; then I head to the door in the dark as I do every Friday night. The street light outside twinkles lightly.

"You're a success now. Aren't you?" The keeper whispers from behind.

My heart stops, and I'm afraid to take a breath. I drop my bag and freeze in place.

"I'll always make you successful, Violet."

My heart's beating rapidly, and chills are running up my back. I reach for the doorknob. I'm lost for words. *Why must he be in my life now?*

"Take your rightful place with successful people. I'll present more opportunities when you're ready."

Somehow, I'm able to flee to the light switch.

"Alright, show yourself!" I shout at the top of my lungs.

Nothing.

I move behind the counter and open the stockroom door. "Where are you now?"

No one. Not a sound.

Turning on my heels, I contemplate leaving the light on all weekend as I head to the switch. I see a few people talking on the sidewalk outside.

I'm alone. I'm alone in this place. It was just my imagination going crazy again. The keeper isn't real. Somehow, the words bring peace.

I shut off the light, close the door, and hurry home.

Chapter 51

"Hush. Hush. Little Man." I mutter quietly as I pop a bottle into my three-month-old son's mouth. He has the bluest eyes I've ever seen, but he is one wiggly baby until his belly is full. I'm so grateful for my wonderful in-laws because they gave me this great rocking chair, and a wooden play-pen for the shop. Once little Peter goes down for a nap, I can create new hats and hair decorations in a most efficient manner.

"Thank you, Mrs. Funk, for another fabulous creation," Carolyn Smith comments with a smile.

"The red feather adds just enough color to the black, I think."

"I went to Macy's spring sale and found a blazer that's the same red as the feather."

"Please come back and show me the ensemble together," I tell her.

"Little Peter must be sleeping because it's so quiet in here now."

I chuckle, "Once his tummy's full, he's one content baby."

"I'll be back next week to peek at your spring line."

Later that day when we arrive home, I'm welcomed by a kitchen sink full of dirty bottles and a bathroom basin filled to the brim with soiled diapers. The bedspread's in a heap on the floor, and the baby's clothes are scattered around his little nursery. A foul odor flows from the kitchen as I proceed to take Peter's hand crocheted sweater and hat off.

What's that horrid smell?

"Here, Little Man, play in your crib for a while. Daddy will be home in one hour, and I have no idea what to cook for supper."

I dash over to the kitchen. I have an overwhelming urge to curl into a ball and cry.

Peter's cries are piercing my eardrums. "It's too bad, my son. I have to clean this mess up," I call over to him, but he continues to cry. My body, mind, and soul are pulling me elsewhere.

The garbage can's overflowing with debris, and the stench is almost too disgusting to deal with. Wishing I had a clothespin for my nose, I hold my breath and push the trash down into the can with my foot. I close the lid, lug it to the door, and place it in the hallway by the door. *Henry will have to take care of it tonight. It's time he helped around here.*

I take the plug out of the sink and drain it. Peter appears to have settled down to mere gurgles.

I open the refrigerator and fumble with the contents. What can I make? Cheese, beer, milk, and butter. I know I have dry mustard. Good. I can make Welsh rarebit.

Setting everything on the small counter space, I tiptoe to the crib and find Peter playing with his feet and smiling. I breathe a sigh of relief.

Twenty minutes later, after cleaning the place up, setting the table, and stirring the rarebit, I plop down on the couch for a quick rest. I feel so frazzled and strained. This apartment is too small for a family of three, and this motherhood thing is wearing me down.

Leaning my head on the back of the couch, I close my eyes. *If I wasn't married or a mother, I would be a famous designer of my own clothing line. Hats and dresses that match. Where could I go, if I was by myself? Marriage and a family are a roadblock in the way of my success.* Breathing a huge sigh, I close my teary eyes, and let my thoughts drift someplace far away.

"Violet. Wake up. Violet." Strong hands are pushing down on my shoulders.

"Honey. Peter's hungry. Wake up."

I slowly open my sticky, swollen eyes. "Henry? What time is it?"

"Five thirty. Do you have something cooking? Peter needs a bottle." He moves around in front of me with the baby in his arms.

Looking at his furrowed brow and scowling face, I jump to my feet. "Hold him for one minute. Honestly, Henry."

A slight burning smell hits me in the face as I rush to the stove. Since I'm out of my husband's eyesight, I quickly scrape the good part of the rarebit off the top of the destroyed portion, grab some fresh asparagus out of the refrigerator, and place in a pan of shallow water to steam.

Once Peter is down for the night, we decide to call it a day too. Sometimes we whisper sweet nothings in each other's ears, and other times, we kiss and say good night. Henry always falls asleep as soon as his head hits the pillow, but tonight my tossing and turning keeps him awake.

"What's wrong with you?" he asks.

"Our son's going on four months old; I have no place to hang diapers to dry other than the bathroom; the laundry's out of control, and the garbage constantly stinks."

He rolls on his side and pulls me to him. "Do you want to move?"

I'm glad it's dark, so my facial expressions are my own. "Where can we afford to go?" I sniffle.

"Your aunt Flossie told me about a few houses for sale in Richmond Hill."

"What about Violette's Millenary Shop? Do you really think I could give that up? We couldn't afford to move without my income."

"Hush. You'll wake the baby. You know how hard it is to get him back to sleep when that happens."

"There must be larger apartments than this for rent around here," I whisper right in his face.

"Sure, there is…for double the rent. We might as well purchase a small house and then it's ours."

Feeling like my mind is going to explode due to utter confusion, I leap out of bed and creep around the dimly lit dwelling in hopes of calming down.

My husband does not follow me, and I'm fine with that. The little night light in the corner of Peter's quarters guides a way for me to check on the little guy. Staring down at the small body, I gently pull the blanket away from his face and can see he's fast asleep.

Henry's snoring is a fabulous source of free entertainment as I heat up a small pan of milk. Mama told me that a cup of warm milk relaxes the soul, and soon after, you'll drift into a deep sleep.

Sitting on the couch an hour later, I find my emotions are racing more than ever. My heart's beating wildly, and my thoughts are racing all over the place with no consistency.

Move away from my successful business? I don't think so. Who's working at Woolworths now? Filthy diapers. I wonder what happened to Tamara. Hmmm, what should I cook for supper tomorrow? I better try to sleep on the couch tonight, so if I must get up, I won't wake Henry.

I close my eyes, and soon I'm dreaming of running barefoot through a field of giant sunflowers. I push my way through the green leaves and pull a petal or two off the yellow flower as I leap. I laugh and twirl for so long that I lose track of time. The beautiful blue sky is gone, and it's getting dark.

I turn around to go in the direction I came from. The wind is blowing ferociously, and the once-beautiful flowers are wilting over the path behind me.

I start to panic and run in circles, screaming for help at the top of my lungs.

No one answers.

I stub my toe on a big rock and tumble to the wet cold ground.

"Why doesn't anyone help me? I can't find my way home!" I screech as I curl up in hope of finding some warmth.

"Now you call for my assistance, Violet." The keeper whispers over me.

I keep in the same fetal position and remain quiet. I try to open my eyes, but they're shut tighter than a glued stamp. I try screaming but nothing comes out. I must wake up from this nightmare.

"I know the way. You must believe in me. That's all." He yelps. The wind continues to howl above, allowing the leaves on the plants a chance to make a noise of their own.

"Violet Pearl, you cannot stay in this place for ever. You have to achieve all your goals in life."

"I'm dreaming for goodness' sake, keeper. Fly off to some other place?" I manage to get out.

A roaring, ugly laughter fills the entire area. "I'm a spirit, but the name *keeper* works."

Crying out hysterically, "No, no, no. You're not real." I shout.

"You said that before. Don't you remember?"

I'm afraid to open my eyes. "Get out of here!" I scream. "I don't need you to find my way out of here."

"I live with you. All is mine. Listen," he whispers. Now the fear turns into anger as I rise to my feet and start swinging my arms like a seasoned boxer. "That's what you think. You're not my keeper. Take this."

I keep on punching, but my hands are not feeling a thing. "Come on. Get closer so I can knock you down."

Silence.

I open my eyes and see total darkness. No flowers. Nothing.

I fall flat on my face as overpowering panic moves me to howl like a wounded coyote.

Something or someone is holding me tight. "Violet. Wake up. You're having a bad dream again."

My mouth is dry, but I try to speak. I kick and thrash my body. I must get away.

"Honey. It's me, your husband."

My eyes are fastened shut, and I realize I wet my pants again. "Help me."

I feel a warm kiss on my cheek. "Try to whisper, okay? Peter made a few sounds moments ago."

Breathing in a sigh of relief that I had a nightmare and nothing in it was real, I open my eyes.

"That was an awful dream," I whisper as I give him a kiss.

"It's three o'clock in the morning. Let's try and get some sleep before the little one wakes up."

"You go ahead. I must go to the bathroom and change out of these wet clothes. I'll be there in a few minutes."

Placing his hand on the cushion of the couch, "This is drenched. I better wash this in the morning."

Chapter 52

I couldn't take the pressure any more. The keeper, the so-called spirit, would not leave me alone; the stench of dirty diapers became unbearable; working at the shop was no longer enjoyable; and stress held a tight grip on me. I'm trapped inside my body. I feel crushed and beaten down by unhappiness. The mental issues that grabbed my mother are nipping at my heels, and in a matter of time, I too will fall into a deep dark hole with no way out.

This clown is not laughing anymore. The mask is slipping.

I had to do it. I saved enough money for a small room at a boarding house several blocks away from the shop. The key sat in my purse for one week before I gained the courage to flee from motherhood and the dramatic role of the doting wife. I must close the shop for a while. I don't want anyone to know where I am. No time like the present. I look around my small room and shrug my shoulders, "I have everything I need right here." I say out loud.

Moments later, I am struggling to open the shop door at 2:00 in the morning.

I sprint into the almost-black space and flick on the light. Dressed in my nightclothes and slippers, I peer around the room hoping that the keeper is *not* here. I breathe a sigh of relief and grab a piece of sketch paper, a paintbrush, and black paint.

I scrawl out the letters, "Closed until further notice." I hope the paint dries quickly.

This will be the first place Henry looks for me. Darn it all anyway.

"Oh, my dear girl. No need to panic. I won't harm you." The familiar voice mutters from somewhere. Scowling with worry, I look out of the window to the dimly lit sidewalk. "Come on, paper, dry," I say as I shake it profusely.

The familiar hair-raising chill runs over my body as I touch the black paint with my fingertip. Still too wet.

Turning quickly on my heels, I fly around the small open space holding the paper, waving the paper in every direction.

"Violet Pearl. You were never cut out to be a mother or a wife. Fame and fortune await those who are alone."

"Leave me alone," I screech as I place the note in the window of the door.

A policeman walking his beat knocks on the door as he passes by.

Fumbling with the lock, I open the door. "Hello, Sir."

When one is falling fast like me, everything in your head gets all muddled up.

Peering over my shoulder and with a squint of his eyes, he asks, "Are you alone in here, Miss? I heard you scream."

Chuckling with a bogus laugh, I respond, "Oh, I came to my shop to practice for a play I'm in. Hard to do that with a one-year-old son."

"Do you want me to escort you home, my dear?"

"Thank you, Sir, but I plan on staying here for a few hours."

He looks me over from head to toe. "Well, alright, but I'll pass by this way again in one hour to check on you. Be sure to keep this door locked at all times."

"Thank you, officer."

I count to one hundred, turn off the light, and lock the door behind me. The dark, cold, barren street greets me as I run full throttle to the boarding house and fiddle with the key. Good thing the long stairwell is well lit because I'm scared out of my wits right now.

Darn stairs are squeaky. I hope no one wakes up.

I close and lock the door behind me with a sigh of relief. The light switch is right by the door for convenience. Not much in here but a twin bed, a night stand, lamp, one old high-back chair, a sink with a dingy mirror, a very old five-drawer dresser, a dilapidated wooden table, and chair. It will have to do.

I fling myself onto the bed and close my eyes in hopes of erasing my life up to this point.

The minutes drift into days and the days into nights. Looking down at the same pajamas I wore when I first got here, I slump down in the chair and pick up the only *Life* magazine I have.

My eyes are so sore from the constant crying that I find it impossible to see the pictures.

I feel like an empty vessel without a destination. There's no hope for me.

Sniffing and blowing my nose on the same hankie I have used for a week, I pick up the only picture I brought with me of little Peter. Anger overcomes me, and I rip it up and throw the remains on the floor. How could I leave my little baby boy? He's so innocent and in need of his mother. *I'm a self-centered fool.*

I shuffle over to the sink and pour a glass of water from the tap. I grab the opened box of Wheaties from the table and chomp on the remaining flakes. I'm so glad I bought some crackers, cereal, and cookies here before I moved.

A knock sounds on the door.

I stop mid-chew and stare at the door. *This is the first knock on my door since I moved in. Who can be out there? No one knows where I am.*

The knock sounds again.

I fall on the only rug in the small room and fold up into a cocoon. I rock back and forth, biting my lip in the process. My long stringy hair falls around my head, and now I'm getting a strong whiff of my own body odor. My palms are springing geysers.

"Miss? Are you in there?"

I get up slowly and quietly. My mouth is dry, but I manage to say, "Yes. I'm resting."

"I haven't seen you in a week. I was getting worried about you, Miss Smith."

Realizing who it is now, I reply, "I'm fine, Mrs. Jackson. Do I owe you any money for rent?" My voice trembles with emotion.

"No, my dear. You're paid for a month. Don't you remember? I made an extra loaf of bread for you, and I would like to give it to you in person."

I clear my throat and wipe my sweaty hands on my soiled sleepwear. "Can you leave it by the door? I'm in the middle of something."

"Alright, but it would be nice to see your pretty face again."

"Thank you, Mrs. Jackson."

I glance around the room. The bed coverings are all a shamble; the lampshade is tipped sideways; and my white panties are hanging everywhere to dry. The open suitcase is still filled with the same contents it came with over two weeks ago. The only way I'm keeping track of time is by the makeshift calendar I made. I strike off the days when the dark of night covers the window. I slump into the rickety wooden chair.

Sipping on some water and a dry saltine, I try to remember the last time I had an actual meal. My tummy grumbles, and hunger pains are becoming more frequent. Looking at the overfilled trashcan by the door, I realize I'm almost out of food. I open the door and grab the loaf of baked bread. I pull pieces from the warm loaf and savor each bite. *This is so good.*

I pace back and forth, pondering whether I should get to the shared bathroom now to take a long-overdue bath. Using the toilet during the day has always proven to be successful because most everyone works a full-time job. Looking at myself in the mirror, I sweep the matted hair away from my eyes. I'm a disaster.

After a nice hot bath and soaking my hair in lavender soap that I confiscated from the shop, I pull on corduroy trousers, a white cashmere sweater, and the pink pearl necklace Papa gave me years ago. I apply a little rouge, brush my hair, and secure it with bows. I fly down the stairs and knock on Mrs. Jackson's door.

"Miss Smith. Do come in, dear."

Her little apartment reminds me of my aunt Flossie's house, mostly because of the heavenly aroma of homemade bread baking in the oven. There's a tall cherrywood curio cabinet in the parlor filled with adorable white bisque figurines, and the high-back chairs are almost identical to Auntie's.

"Sit down right here, honey. Are you hungry?" She motions to me to take a chair at her kitchen table.

"I could eat something, Mrs. Jackson."

I watch her take oatmeal cookies out of the oven, and my mouth waters as she places the pan on a rack to cool. Opening her well-stocked refrigerator, she says, "Do you like liverwurst? Or, I have some leftover beef stew?"

I just want some food. Anything. But then as quick as I can snap my fingers, she puts the stew in front of me. The teakettle is singing away and so is she. I dig into the stew, trying to maintain a dignified manner, but I'd rather lift the bowl to my lips and gulp it all down. She tells me about her Irish heritage, but I politely nod. She doesn't need to know anything about me. I'll have to fabricate a story, if she asks.

The grandfather clock chimes out four, and I leap to my feet. "I have to go."

"We're just getting to know each other, though. Why are you in such a hurry?"

I know the other tenants will be coming home from work any minute. I don't want anyone to see me. Someone may recognize me.

"The room is a mess. I have a test tomorrow that I have to study for."

"Well, okay, but maybe we can go shopping sometime," she says with a smile.

"You're so kind. Thank you for the nice lunch."

She hands me a basket filled with apples, oatmeal cookies, and a box of crackers.

Back in my room, the reality of where I am hits me hard. I pace back and forth as I mull over and over in my mind, was leaving my family, the right thing to do? Poor little Peter. Innocent Henry. I plop face down on the bed and cry my heart out until darkness overwhelms me.

Two days pass since my time with Mrs. Jackson, and I still haven't done one thing to clean up this disorganized place. I move from bed to floor, from floor to chair, chair to floor, and back through the sequence.

"Ms. Smith. Are you alright?" Mrs. Jackson calls through the door.

"Go away," I mumble.

"Please let me help you, dear. Everyone has gone to work."

Sitting on my bed all wrapped up in the patchwork quilt, my only thought is to get rid of her. "I'm not feeling well today."

"Oh, I see."

"Can you come back tomorrow?"

"I had a visitor today. Someone looking for you."

I start to tremble with worry. *No one knows where I am.*

"Ms. Smith? Is your first name Violet?"

My heart pounds profusely as I make my way to the door, but I don't open it. I hesitate. "Yes. That's my first name."

"The handsome gentleman claims he was looking for his wife. He described her to me and you fit the description to a tee."

I open the door just a crack. "What did you tell him, Mrs. Jackson?"

"There isn't any young lady that looks like that here."

With tears in my eyes, I manage to say, "Thank you."

"You know where I live if you need someone to talk to."

I don't know what happened to me, but after a month of living in despair, I decided living like this is utterly ridiculous. If it wasn't for Mrs. Smith, I would be a skeleton. So, I bathe and get dressed. I clean the room until it sparkles and grab my organized pocketbook before I leave for the day. I wait until it is quiet and then proceed to Mrs. Jackson's. I knock on her door, and she answers quickly.

"Please get your hat and coat, Mrs. Jackson. I want to show you something."

"Now?" She asks with a bit of a surprised look on her face.

"Yes. It's time you know who I really am."

She peers into the window of the hat shop. "I always love to look at the hats in the window here, but I could never afford to buy one."

I smile at her and open the door. "Never say never, Mrs. Jackson."

She gasps, "You must work here, dear?"

The store is chilly and smells a bit musty as we step in. I turn on the light and sprinkle a little lavender fragrance around. I'm so glad, I purchased a few bottles to sell. It comes in handy, and the customers love it.

Mrs. Jackson stands in awe of all the hats, with her mouth open as she takes one hat after the other to try on.

"Violette's, Violet, are you the owner of this shop?"

Grabbing a dustcloth from behind the counter, I chuckle. "Yes. I am. I like the red felt hat with the rose on it for you."

Looking at the price tag, she puts it back. "No, that is too expensive. I can't afford that."

"It's a gift for all that you have done for me."

She places it on her head and looks in a mirror. "I love it. It's the most beautiful hat I've ever owned."

"Feel free to stay as long as you want to, Mrs. Jackson. I might hang around for an hour or so, to clean and see if there are any back orders to fill."

"I'm so glad you're feeling better, but what if your husband comes looking for you?"

"I'll be polite, but I am not going back there."

She moves around the shop as if she doesn't hear me.

This is where I belong—creating fantastic creations for the rich and famous. I fetch the key to the mailbox, on the outside of the building. *Wow. There's a lot of mail.*

I sift through the stack of mail and come across three orders from New York socialites.

"I'll see you at the house later. Can I call you Violet?" she says as she opens the door.

With a smile, I nod. "Of course."

After an hour of organizing the back room and pushing Peter's stuff into a corner, I hear the front door bell ring.

A customer. Good.

Looking down at my shoes and making my way through the curtain, I say, "Hello, can I help you with something today?"

"Violet Pearl. I'm here to bring you back to your husband and son."

I look up from behind the counter "Aunt Flossie!"

"What do you think you are doing anyway, young lady?" She scowls.

I take new stock out of an old shipment. "I needed some time to think about things."

"You're a wife and mother. It's your responsibility to do the best job you can in making those who love you happy."

Pounding my hands on the counter in anger, "What about *my* happiness? Don't you care about how I feel?"

"Listen here, niece of mine! You signed on the dotted line and said I do. You were beaming from ear to ear when you walked down the aisle and when I first saw you holding little Peter. That's a true picture of happiness."

A well-dressed lady enters the shop and tries on a hat from the sale rack.

Leaning across the counter in a whispering demand, I look Auntie in the eyes and say, "Please leave this instant, Aunt Flossie."

She hands me a white envelope with disapproval on her face and walks out of the door.

Chapter 53

Auntie never returned to the shop after that day. She must not have told Henry where I was, because he never darkened the door of the shop. I press forward on the stage of life with a stunning performance that made anyone near me smile. The shop is busier than ever, and I have an adorable new assistant whose name is Tilly.

We laugh, shop, and have lunch in interesting places. Tilly has the reddest hair I've ever seen and fair skin with lots of freckles. The cutest thing about her is her Irish accent. Her family moved here from Ireland when she was five years old.

"Tilly, will you lock up tonight? I'm taking Mrs. Jackson out to dinner, and I like to get her home before dark if I can."

"Sure. Now get out of here and have a wonderful time. You certainly deserve it," she says with a big smile.

I give her a big bear hug, "Thank you so much. I'm so glad I hired you."

Mrs. Jackson and I had a delightful meal of roasted chicken, scalloped potatoes, and sautéed green beans with onions. This restaurant is within walking distance of the house and serves the best home-style meals in all of Greenwich.

"It thrills me to no end that things are going so well for you, Violet."

When I look at her sweet face, something inside me urges me to get off the stage and take off the mask. Looking down at the plate that holds a few alien beans, I say, "Thank you, but sometimes at night I can't help but think about my little boy. It's been three months now."

"Oh, honey. Look at me. Maybe, it is time to go home?"

"I can't." I look at her with tears in my eyes. "Not now. Everything is going so well. Going back to that life as mother and wife will destroy this profitable life. Henry will never take me back anyway."

"You're hurting, my dear. I can see that you're not sure who you really are. Do you believe in God?"

"My mama took me to church when I was little."

"God can guide you if you believe in Him and ask."

Twitching in my seat and not knowing what to say to that, I finally change the subject. "How about a piece of that apple strudel?"

A half hour later, I open the door to my room and find a soiled white envelope on the floor. I pick it up and remember that Auntie gave it to me a month ago. Tilly must have found it on the floor and slipped it under my door.

I drop my belongings on the new scatter rug and fall into my plush new chair.

Holding the envelope in my hands, I immediately recognize Henry's flawless handwriting.

My Beautiful Wife,

I miss you and love you so much. My life is meaningless without you. I saw you enter your shop several times. I didn't know what to say. Peter's nine months old now, and he spends a lot of time with my mother since she's retired. I manage to take care of him at night. He's such a good boy, but he misses his mama. Aunt Flossie and I have been looking at houses in Richmond Hill. I saw one with a garden and nice backyard. I know how much you like flowers. Come home. Come home, please. I need you, and Peter needs you more.

With much love always, Your husband, Henry

PART FIVE

1947

Chapter 54

I really didn't think I could make this drastic change, but with so many people prodding me forward, I had no other recourse but to go back to my family. This house in Richmond Hill is only a few blocks from Aunt Flossie's so she helped me with getting it decorated. The best thing about the place is the big, enclosed front porch, a perfect place for toys. A fair-size parlor, small dining room, and large kitchen make up the first floor. I'm amazed how much Henry loves me, despite leaving him. He's truly an amazing man.

Peter's finishing kindergarten in two weeks, and my little daughter, Jane is a very demanding baby of a year and a half. Tilly bought the business from me, but I still make hats for her.

The sewing machine sings as I finish the last of the light-blue curtains for the parlor. I glance at my curly-top little girl playing in the wooden playpen. She's much more demanding than Peter was at this age. I can get about a half-hour reprieve when she's in there, but then she expects my undivided attention.

"Ma-ma," she says loudly with a frown on her face.

"I'm right here, Jane."

Her lower lip trembles as she plops down and cries loudly.

Looking at my watch, I see that it's only 10:30 in the morning. Too early for lunch and a nap. I must get these curtains finished, and that's all there is to it.

She keeps crying.

I leap up and fool around with the dial on the big floor radio in hopes of finding some music. Ah, the sound of the big bands of the twenties.

She cries louder.

I flit over to her, pat her head, pick up a few toys off the floor, and put them back in the pen.

The cries have turned into screams for attention.

"Stop it this instant!" I scream back and return to my work. I close my eyes and try to make the knot of anxiety disappear. I'm having a tough time, and my skin is covered in sweat.

After a half hour of this deplorable sequence, I decide she's safe, and I must get out for some fresh air. *I can't tolerate the crying. What does this child possibly need?*

I storm through the front porch and slam the door on my way out into the spring air. I breathe a sigh of relief. The street's very quiet during this time of day due to people at work and children in school. I sniff the beautiful lilacs on the huge bush by the corner of the house.

Suddenly, I feel free as a bird—alone with the wide-open sky to fly wherever I want to.

How in the world did I get here anyway? I spread my arms and dance all around the outside of the house several times. After a while, I sit on the back steps and fold up like a morning glory at night. This thing called motherhood has taken over my entire life. My dreams of success are completely shattered.

"Ye gads. I have been out here for a long time. Jane, my baby."

I try to open the back door. Locked.

Moving around to the side of the house, I stand under the window where I left her. Not a peep.

Racing as fast as I can and jumping up the five steps to the front door. I turn the knob every way. It won't open. I pull and prod. *How can the door be locked?* A state of panic covers me like a veil. Should I break a window? Should I scream until someone hears me? My heart's palpitating as big crocodile tears pour down my face.

I must smash the glass in the door; that's all there is to it. Which door? I run to the sidewalk and glance to the left and right in hopes of spotting a policeman. No one's in sight, not even a car or bus.

In a few minutes, I rummage through the dilapidated garage where Henry keeps some of his tools. Ah, a hammer. I smash the glass from the lower panel of the back door. It shatters, and I manage to slip my hand through the remaining sharp pieces to turn the lock. The blood's dripping down my arms, and trickling droplets everywhere. I burst into the kitchen and over to the playpen. I try to swallow, but I can't.

Jane is laying lifeless on the floor. She must have figured a way to climb out.

"Oh God. Help my baby!" I scream out as I fall beside her.

I'm afraid to touch her for fear that she's not breathing. I rock myself back and forth.

Call someone. Get her to a doctor.

I reach out to touch her and pull back.

If I hadn't come back to Henry, I would be a successful entrepreneur, and he would be married to someone else. I glance down at my daughter with feelings of regret.

Whimper sounds rise from my baby girl. I pull her to my lap as I turn her to face me. She has a bump on her head and a scrape on her chin.

"Jane, oh Jane. Oh, my baby. I'm so sorry." I rock her tenderly with new tears forming in the corner of my eyes.

"Mama. I lub you." She raises her hand up and grabs my hair.

Fiddling with her brown curly hair, I croon, "Your mama better get you to a doctor to check out that bump."

Still holding her in my arms, I succeed in getting to the phone in the kitchen.

"Eleanor, I'm so glad you're home. Jane had an accident. Can you come and take us to the doctor?"

"Can you wait outside for me?"

"Sure. I'll wait on the front porch. Hurry."

Looking down at my soiled dress, I race up the stairs with Jane in tow. "Eleanor will be here any minute, but I simply have to change out of this bloody dress. Here, sit on the floor and play with my necklaces." I flee into the bathroom, across the hall, and grab a wet towel to clean off the blood on my arm. Good, Jane is occupied with the jewelry. I slap a few Band-Aids over the oozing sores. Within minutes, we're waiting on the front porch.

That night after the children are in bed I sit at the kitchen table with a cup of cold tea. I'm staring at my scarred arm and mumbling to myself about my behavior for the last few weeks—but especially today's incident. My daughter could have died from that fall.

Henry wraps his arms around me. "You have to go see a psychiatrist, Violet. I'm very worried about you."

I try shrugging him away, but his grip is firm. "I should have never come back to you, Henry."

"Stop talking like that. Please. You need medical help."

I push the cup over, and it spills all over me. "Now, look what happened? I need to get out of this place." I leap off the wet chair and fly into the parlor and collapse on the couch. I'm so tired and mentally drained. It feels like the whole world is crashing down on me, and I don't know how to save it. I hear voices but can't make out who they are. My eyes flicker shut.

I'm being torn apart inside. Darkness is surrounding me, and there's no escape route. The battle within my heart intensifies as the demons from another world attack me with strange noises. My heart is racing like a thoroughbred trying as hard as it can to get to the finish line. I hear the keeper's horrifying laughter. I'm petrified.

Shattered thoughts like glass breaking on the floor rummage through my mind. I could have been a prima ballerina with audiences all over the world, a budding star on Broadway, a famous fashion model, or the entrepreneur of several millenary shops across the country. I have no business being a mother. None.

I'm a failure and frightened beyond description.

The only way to fix this is to exit this world. *How should I do it?*

"Violet, Violet Pearl?" my mama is calling, but she sounds so far away.

My arms are thrashing in front of me trying to find a way out of this deep dark hole. "Where is the light, Mama?"

"Keep searching for it, Violet," I barely hear her say.

I'm freezing. My mouth is dry. I keep smacking the air and shuffle along to somewhere. Anywhere.

It's useless. There's no way out of here. I'm in the pit of despair. Is the world collapsing on top of me? A wave of dizziness passes over me; the world is spinning. I'm suffocating and sick to my stomach.

Everyone will be better off without me.

There isn't any strength left to run any further. I'm in a tunnel.

My body's shutting down.

Chapter 55

"Mrs. Funk? Hello. Mrs. Funk. Welcome back." A pale unfamiliar face stares down at me.

I try to move, but it's impossible. My arms. Why won't they move? Where am I?

"Doctor. She's awake."

The man must be older than Methuselah, but he looks like a doctor all dressed in white.

Wiggling every which way to try to get up, I cry out, "Help me, please."

"We must keep you confined for now. You had a nervous breakdown, Mrs. Funk," he comments softly.

Looking around at the white walls, I start to worry. "What hospital is this?"

"Bellevue," the nurse on the other side of me murmurs.

"No! No! No! Not this place! I can't stay here."

"Sedate her, Nurse Carlisle," the doctor says.

I try to move my arms once again. I can't. They're in a straightjacket. I feel trapped, waiting for everything to cave in.

For days, I feel helpless.

After twenty grueling shock treatments and a drawn-out recovery, I'm finally released to a sanitarium to rest. I have no idea what day it is, let alone what year. It's a beautiful, peaceful place surrounded by perfectly uniformed white birch trees. The rose garden is in full bloom with a bubbling water fountain in the center. Several Adirondack chairs dot the lawn and line the porches. I love to sit on them and let the fresh air clear out the cobwebs of my mind these sunny days.

Henry comes regularly with the children, and he constantly reminds me that I will be able to come home soon. *I've put this sweet man through a living nightmare, and he still loves me? Why?*

Aunt Flossie came once. She did tell Papa and Daisy about my circumstance, but they never showed up. They all think I'm crazy, of course. I'm feeling better, but I still have an emptiness in my heart. *What will make me truly happy and content?*

One day, the psychiatrist pats my hand. "Do something with your hands to get your mind on something else. We call this occupational therapy."

"I've always had an interest in art."

"That's a start. I've been meaning to ask you a question, Mrs. Funk."

"What, doctor?"

"Do still hear the voice of the keeper? You screamed out that name several times when you first came here."

"He is no more. Gone completely." *I sure hope this is the truth.*

So, I ask my nurse for some plain paper and a pencil. I draw pictures of boats at the seashore, the rose garden, and funny sketches of people. I never dreamed I could draw like this. Henry surprises me with a set of pastel paints, artist pencils, and several sketch pads. I really enjoy drawing pictures of my children when they visit. I hope they understand and forgive me someday. Peter hugs me often, but Jane is always hanging on to her father for dear life. She gazes at me, like I'm a monster.

Normal, normal, be normal.

Two months roll by before I know it, and it's time to return home. The doctor was right about keeping my hands busy. Everything in my life is brighter, and I'm enjoying this crazy thing called motherhood.

I find anything to paint Pennsylvania Dutch designs on. There's a gift shop a few streets over that let me put my creations on consignment. Tilly set up a small area in the millinery shop for me too. People are paying for my artwork.

Now that we have a television set in the parlor, I find it's easy entertainment for all of us when I'm working and wanting children out of my hair. As young as they are, they love to watch a man called Arthur Godfrey. This man loves tea, and Lipton Tea is his sponsor.

"Violet, why don't you paint something for him?" Eleanor suggests one day.

I laugh at her as I paint. "Oh, he probably gets a ton of gifts every day."

"But your designs are so unique. I'm sure he'll be impressed."

"I don't know, Eleanor. I'm so busy with the children, the house, and all this painting. I don't know how I can fit one more thing into my life." I grimace at the thought.

Later that night when the children are in bed, and Henry and I clean the first floor of the house. I pick up a nursery rhyme picture book of my daughters to return it to the bookshelf. My eyes focus on the words *I'm a little teapot.*

The kitchen floor is swept, and the dishes are washed and put away. "How are you doing in here?" Henry asks.

"I think I found a gift idea for Mr. Godfrey. He loves tea, you know."

"You what? He's one busy man, Vi. Don't you have enough to do?"

"Oh, fiddlesticks. You know how much I love a challenge. I saw an article in the newspaper about a special kind of paint that if baked in a kiln, the design is permanent." I'm ecstatic about the idea, but I ignore Henry's agitated look.

Since Peter's in school, I drag Jane with me to purchase the special paints and a few plain ceramic tiles to practice on.

After wiping off the original design three times, I finally achieve a creative finished product, but it's still wet. I place it in a cardboard box with special care, grab sweaters for daughter and me, and head to an art studio in Jamaica that has a kiln I can use. Fortunately, I'm able to load everything, in Jane's wagon. I'm so excited about my artwork, I barely pay attention to the sixteen blocks I hike past.

We wait patiently for it to fire. Jane's fast asleep in my arms as I wait.

"Mrs. Funk," an art instructor whispers, when he comes out of the back room. "The tile looks great, and it is cool enough to take with you."

"Do you have any suggestions for a backing on it?"

"How about a strong piece of cardboard?"

"It's a hot plate for a teapot. That should work."

He cuts a perfect piece and glues it on the back of the tile. "The glue will take several hours to dry, but I will be happy to drop this off for you," he offers with a wink.

"That's nice of you, but I want to wrap it up as a gift first. The backing will need time to dry anyway."

"Mom! Look! Arthur Godfrey just mentioned you on the show!" Peter says excitedly.

I run into the living room to watch.

"Thank you again, Violet Funk of Richmond Hill, New York, for this hot plate. I love what it says."

I stand in awe of the talk show host holding up my hand-painted tile.

I'm a little tea tile

Happy and hot

Because I'm where

Arthur Godfrey puts his pot!

I'm breathless with joy as I see a celebrity hold up my artwork on television. I'm really going places now.

I became an overnight success. Orders from big tile contractors, gift shops, and individuals arrive by mail or telephone. I'm so busy, the days go flying by. I don't have enough room in our little house to paint and keep up with the orders. Tiles are everywhere. Heavy cookie sheets come in handy to transport unfired work across town to be fired after Henry comes home at night. Mr. Winkles, the owner, charges me ten dollars to load up the kiln. I'm feeling on top of the world because the sales are paying all my expenses. I have money in my wallet. Life couldn't be better.

"I've been thinking, I'd like to take a drive out to a little town on Long Island, Violet." Henry announces one night after the kids are in bed.

"What for?"

"I've been thinking, it would be nice to look for a small piece of property and eventually build a house. The children could grow up in a quiet community, and I could commute into the city by Long Island Railroad."

"It seems like you've been thinking about this for a while, Henry. I don't know. What about my potential tile business? All of our friends are in Queens, the children are content, my garden's beautiful, and I feel wonderful." I wince internally.

"Oh, I only want to look, honey. We can't afford anything extra anyway. It'll be a nice day trip for us. We can find a public beach to go to. The children will love it."

"I refuse to move again. I'm so comfortable here. However, I've never been past Jones beach, and it would be fun to explore the rest of Long Island." I fold my arms and force a smile, "I guess it won't hurt to look, but that's all."

He wraps me in his arms and plants a warm kiss on my lips, "How does this Saturday sound to you?"

Chapter 56

Long Island
1951

"Peter, please watch your sister so she doesn't fall down that cliff," I call out to my son as I help move the furniture into our new house.

"Miller Place Park. It will be a nice community when they sell all the parcels of land. I know you have to do without some things for now, but this is our home, and look how happy the children are." Henry says as he wipes his forehead.

"It will be nice when the grass grows," I reply. "Right now, it is a huge sandbox. Hard to keep the kids clean."

I grab and hug him with all my might. "Moving out here is the best decision we ever made. By next Saturday, my art studio will be all set up in the basement. It's a bit dingy down there, but at least there's electricity."

"You'll have extra time in September when both children are in school. Since I am taking the train to and from work, you can take the car and make sales calls to area gift shops."

Looking out of the back door of the little bungalow, I can see brother and sister playing tag with the beautiful blue Long Island sound as the background. "Oh Henry. It is lovely here and you're right. They're so happy." *I'm trying so hard to be at peace with myself.*

"A few more things off the truck and then let's have some lunch," he calls over his shoulder as he heads out of the door.

We were able to afford built-in bunk beds on one wall with stationary dressers and a desk on the opposite wall of both bedrooms in the house. Peter shares with Henry and Jane with me. Very tight but cozy.

One bathroom, a small kitchen that has the beautiful water as a background, a combination of living room and dining room complimented by a red brick fireplace. We eat all our meals on a redwood picnic table, situated by the fireplace. My furniture is far from elegant, but I'm not going to let that bother me. The children are so happy, and the view is priceless. *I guess I can handle living in this little place, if it brings us happiness. Simplicity will surely bring us together as a family.*

It's three months later and a warm fall day when I drop Henry off at the Port Jefferson train station at seven o'clock in the morning with the kids in the back seat. The train ride to Manhattan with all the stops along the way takes about two hours.

"Kiss, Daddy. Please," Jane squeals.

Henry pops out of the car and gives his daughter a kiss on the top of her curly head. He smiles at both children. "You kids have a good day at school, okay?"

I get out and give him a hug as he runs to the platform to board the train. *I can't believe I'll be alone at last.*

As I pull up into the driveway, I smile at the green grass that covers the front lawn, the evergreen shrubs, and flower laden window boxes under the bedroom windows. I walk up the slate walkway to the front steps but continue to the side of the house instead. I lift the cellar door and venture down the dark cement stairwell. Fortunately, we asked the builder to put a nice wood door with a window in it, so some light would shine through. *It still creeps me out to come down here.*

Flicking the light switch on, I can see most of the basement, but it's still dreary.

I purchased a small, used kiln from the high school, which is perfect for the volume of orders I have at this time. Henry promises to put a telephone down here for me in the future. I'm always careful to lock the door before I sit down to paint. I get to work and soon finish a dozen tiles with calico cats painted on them. They're best sellers for baby gifts.

Dumping the dirty turpentine into the coffee can and replacing it with clean, I suddenly feel like I'm not alone. *The keeper hasn't bothered me in a long time, so why am I concerned?*

I quiver with worry and place my hands over my face as though I want to hide from someone or something. "What do you want from me?" I shout out from the depth of my lungs.

A Spine-chilling draft sweeps over me, and the hair on my arms stands on end.

There's a new composition book at my fingertips and a pencil that is used for sketching new designs. Maybe, I'll record the conversation as it happens. If the keeper's creeping around, I must be prepared. Hesitating, I fold back the notebook to the first page and wait.

"How shall I begin?" I cry out.

"You ask too many questions. I told you there is a spirit inside. We can help you if you have faith. You talk too much."

My face is burning, even though my body's trembling. Scrawling words as the exchange progresses, I ask, "How can I stop talking? Where have you been, keeper?"

"I lurk around always. Sometimes quietly. It's enough that you have discovered me. You need discipline and concentration. Focus. Listening is enough."

I write.

"Why can't others hear you? Why are you singling me out? Why?"

"They look for superficial things to find peace. Peace comes from within. They do not listen. I come in the silence. You hate your mortal mind, you crazy mixed up kid. If you would listen to me, you would not hate at all. I am the spirit inside you. I am that I am."

"You seem to know my questions before I have time to write them."

"Good. You are catching on. One day you will show these writings to the proper people. They will be convinced. As you complete each book, you must put it in an envelope and mail it to yourself. Seal it, never to open again. Write. Write when I tell you. The more you listen, the less you talk."

"I have so many dreams of being famous in this area. Can you help me?" *I don't seem frightened anymore.*

"Of course, you are the leading actress in the play of life. You were always stubborn and would not take less than a leading role."

"Enough. Enough. Enough! You're playing with my mind. I have a family, a new house with the beautiful Long Island sound at my fingertips."

"Alright, but remember, I come in the silence. Maybe, in a dream."

I wrap my arms around my head and groan in frustration. *This doesn't make any sense.*

"I'm fine by myself, keeper. Go find someone else to hover over. Months have passed and no sign of you. I'm capable of taking care of myself without you interfering."

"Ah, you may think you don't need me, but I will make your life so much better. It will require you to have discipline and concentration. Listen. Write. Enough."

Prickles of wetness break out on my neck. I turn the radio on full blast.

Chapter 57

I invest in a bigger kiln, but it's a beast to get down the basement stairs. Henry enlists the help of two teenage neighbors to help with the task.

"How in the world can you keep up with these orders, Violet?" Henry asks one night.

"I've been racking my brains with a way to do them in a quicker, more efficient manner."

"If we could come up with something to copy the outline of each design and then imprint the design onto each tile, I think that would save a tremendous amount of time, Vi."

Instantly my mind clicks. "Maybe silk-screening is something to consider."

"Fabulous idea. I'll see if the library has any books about that. Meanwhile, you keep that creative mind of yours going, okay?"

He didn't need to tell me that. My mind never stops thinking of new designs and ideas.

Over the next few weeks, my husband learns a lot through researching and reading about this unique way of imprinting designs. Henry created a manual silk-screen system and found black ceramic paint to squeegee onto the embossed design. After numerous times of trying to get the right consistency to the smelly concoction, he's now able to duplicate twelve designs in ten minutes. He built a drying rack with twenty trays holding a dozen tiles on each tray.

The tiles must dry for at least twenty-four hours before I can fill in the colors. It's a process that helps me create almost three times the number of tiles in half the time.

Music keeps me motivated, as well as my mind occupied. Good thing.

My new friend Astrid, who lives around the corner from us, is fascinated with the tiles and when she showed me a few of her personal art projects, I grabbed her as a helper. She fills in several colors of each tile before I check, complete, and fire.

During the day, I'm a cheerful person telling jokes or simply clowning around. Once again, the mask is on tight. At night, the old battle within my heart resurfaces. The keeper visits through my writing. I sneak into the bathroom and close the door. I write until there's no more from him.

I hide the notebooks under the mattress.

I desperately want to be happy, but my past keeps haunting me. I have a wonderful husband, two beautiful children, a successful business, and my own gift shop in Port Jefferson, ten miles away.

Yet, tension, frustrations, and temptations of all kinds are mounting in my life, and my disposition is suffering. I'm an outward success, but an inward failure. I'm miserable and depressed when the gloominess of night settles around me. "You can search and search for happiness, but in the end, I am who you will turn to." The keeper reminds me of this often. I'm trying to be stronger than my fear.

One day, a tall, very distinguished-looking gentleman enters the shop. I can guess by the way he carries himself and his expensive Italian shoes that he's very wealthy.

He winks at me and smiles.

I blush. "May I help you, Sir?"

He glances at the tiles and then back at me. "Yes, my dear. I'm building a brand-new house in Belle Terre, and I would like you to design and paint a mural on a fireplace facing for me. Is that something you would be interested in doing?"

Knowing in my mind that the neighborhood he's talking about is for the rich and famous, I'm uncertain. "I don't know. I must see the space, measure it, and get back to you with an estimate. My name is Violet Funk. What's yours?"

He reaches out to shake my hand. "My name is Irving Kahn. Here's my business card with telephone number." *Could this be the Kahn who is a millionaire?*

The dollar signs rush through my psyche. I shift from one foot to the other. "I close the shop in an hour. If you give me directions, I can check it out today." I shudder a bit after I say that because I don't know this fella at all.

A while later, I'm standing in the vast, unfinished space designated as the living room for the sole purpose of entertaining guests. I sink inside with despair. Without uttering a word but with a smile on my face, I wonder how in the world I can do this. It's a monumental task.

Workers are hammering on the roof, and gardeners are fast at work directly outside the floor-to-ceiling picture windows. I find a milk crate and sit down on it while Mr. Kahn chats with the contractor.

Looking at the area designated for the fireplace and the wall around it, I realize this could be my most challenging job offer.

"So, what do you think, Violet?" Mr. Kahn asks from behind me.

I pop up in a most clumsy way. "Um, uh, I have to measure it and then get back to you, Mr. Kahn. It's a huge space. Do you have any idea what you envision there?"

"A garden theme of some sort would be interesting. Jack, can you grab a couple of men and get this space measured for me?" he says to the contractor.

"Of course, Sir."

Within minutes, I have the measurements in my hands and head out of the door. "I'll get back to you in a few days with an estimate. Just out of curiosity, when would you like this completed, Sir?"

"Take as long as you need. We don't plan on moving here until next year." I suddenly feel less intimidated. If I could take my time and not rush, perhaps this is within my scope of creativity. I drive home in a daze.

Henry erects a huge makeshift table in the far corner of our basement. A few new outlets and floodlights help illuminate my working space. The tiles are laid out facedown exactly how they would be on the fourteen-by-eight-foot wall, all numbered in sequence to my design sketch.

In between the children's demands and filling other orders, I manage to put at least five hours a day on the project. Once a week, Astrid joins me at night to paint other orders.

"Here's an old phonograph, my friend. There are a few records in this box, but I'm sure you have your own favorites," she comments as she sets the box down.

Shelves separate the two working areas. "Thanks, Astrid. If the music is quiet, feel free to play anything."

Henry snores loudly most nights, and since I'm such a light sleeper, I usually toss and turn. Of course, the keeper uses this time to attack me.

I write.

I had no idea what to paint on this mural for Mr. Kahn until I found out that he's Jewish. I purchased an old Bible at the used book sale a few months ago, and after searching the Old Testament, I envisioned my creation. I see a beautiful maiden in authentic Jewish dress, standing under a fig tree.

The keeper retaliates. "I am the one who brought Irving Kahn to you. I am yours, you are mine. I told you not to paint a picture of a maiden from the Bible, but you did anyway. You will fail. He will make you do it all over again."

I cringe as I scrawl out the words on the page. It's almost done. I must paint her face. I will search for the right countenance on her face, but where? I've read, painted, and spent countless hours sketching. I want this lady to have a facial expression that shows contentment, from the inside out.

"I am success. Relax. Peace. Fret not yourself. Be strong. Take the woman out of the painting and replace her with mountains," the keeper dictates. I respond in writing and out loud.

"It's all in the face. It's about the face in the mural."

I close the book, place it in the safe place, and finally drift off to sleep.

Months pass by, and the mural looks flawless, but I can't paint the face. I search high and low for an answer to my inner turmoil, so I can paint the features. It's been almost a year. They can't finish the room until the mural is up.

"In three weeks, the tile contractor will install the mural, Violet. I hope you're almost finished with it," Mr. Kahn says on the phone.

"It'll be done, Mr. Kahn. I promise." Doubts and fear encompass me as I attempt to paint the face. I throw the paintbrushes against the cement wall, walk away from the project, and cry my eyes out in despair, as I venture up the stairs into the fresh air. Keeper's grotesque laugh haunts me.

What am I looking for? Is there a higher power? I'm not at peace with myself. How can I paint contentment on the woman in the painting, if my heart's in agony?

I visit a Jewish Rabbi and spend countless hours asking questions about the Old Testament. I paw over pictures of fine Italian art and spent a weekend in a Catholic convent. The nuns exhibit a beautiful love for God. I know God is real, but how do I find him?

I spend an hour a day for five days at the library glancing through the philosophy and religion section.

Every night, I pick up a sketch pad and struggle to invent the face, but it's never right.

"Tell him, you need more time. Get rid of the girl in the painting. You will be happier and so will he," shouts the keeper.

I get up the courage to react, but fear overwhelms me. I continue to write down my retaliation. "No. No. No. You're wrong, keeper. I know I'll be able to finish this mural by the deadline. Leave me alone. You're playing around with my head."

"Okay, little Girl. You will come back to me. Look, you searched and searched for something greater, but what happened? Ah, you are right back under my control."

This same spirit, the keeper, has been haunting me for years now. I wish there were a way to get rid of it, once and for all. I close my eyes and scream, "*Please stop!*"

Chapter 58

Summer 1954

Relaxing with a cup of coffee on a sunny morning, I leaf through a *Family Circle* magazine and discover a small advertisement. *Order this book today.* The Secret of Happiness *by Billy Graham.*

I order the book and read through it several times, underlining key phrases, and I weep tears of unspeakable joy. The title of this book intrigued me because happiness is the biggest thing that has been eluding my life. I learned the longing in my heart is for God, and my sins are responsible for discontent. My history of mental issues separated me from the security of knowing Jesus personally. I read that God is three in one. God the Father, Jesus the Savior, and the Holy Spirit. The one and only Holy Spirit. Mr. Graham emphasizes that the secret to happiness is a full surrender to the living God through a personal relationship with Jesus Christ.

Falling to my knees, I cry out loud. "Living God, I don't want to cause my family any more trauma, and I need to put my past at your feet. Lord God, I need your help. Please forgive me of my sinful past, and for trusting in an evil spirit. I ask you Lord God, to take this demonic being out of my life for good. Please make me the woman you want me to be. I give my life to you, oh Lord, my God. Amen."

In an instant, peace fills my soul and mind. I'm experiencing joy from within my heart, and contentment embraces me. I surrendered my life to Jesus. It's a relationship, not a religion. For the first time in my life, I feel God's presence. I must open the pages of the Bible, so I can learn more about how to live a Christian life.

Daylight breaks as I get up with tears of delight rolling down my face. My eyes are swollen from weeping. I make my way quietly through the front door, around to the side of the house, down the cellar stairs, flick on the light, and head to the mural. I moisten the pallet with turpentine, and instantly paint the face. *That's it. She's looking for Jesus, the Messiah.*

Three weeks later, I'm standing in front of my completed work of art on the fireplace facing of this magnificent house.

"Absolutely stunning, Violet." Mr. Kahn remarks.

"Thank you. Her face was the most challenging part of this task. The maiden has an expression of noticeable joy, peace, hope, happiness, and security now."

"I can see that. She'll be a conversation piece for years to come. She looks so peaceful but looking at something," he says.

Lord, give me the words to say, "She's looking at the Messiah."

In my heart, I know this picture reflects that which is evident in my life. The maiden is my symbol of all the people who are waiting to hear the good news about Jesus, the only Savior and Lord.

I'm a work in progress, and I know God is not finished with me yet. As for the keeper, it's gone, by the grace of God. Do I still have moments of despair? Of course, I do. Do I lead a flawless life? Not by a long shot. The living God is who I turn to every day, and I believe the Bible to be the inspired Word of God. I opened the gates of my heart and let the Savior in. My tiles are breakable things with no eternal value. I no longer fear the past, present, or future. Jesus healed my emotional scars by giving me a new life in Him.

Psalm 23

The Lord is my shepherd to feed, guide, and shield me. I shall lack nothing.

2 He leads me to lie down in fresh, tender, green pastures; He leads besides the still and restful waters.

3 He refreshes and restores my life. He leads me into the paths of righteousness for his name's sake.

4 Yes, though I walk through the valley of the shadow of death, I will fear or dread no evil, for you are with me. Your rod of protection and your staff of guidance comfort me.

5 You prepare a table before me in the presence of my enemies. You anoint myhead with oil; my cup runs over.

6 Only goodness, mercy, and unfailing love shall follow me all the days of my life, and through the length of my days, the house of the Lord shall be my dwelling place.

Epilogue

"Oddballs matter (to God)"

1954

My story continues as physical and emotional storms of all magnitudes encompass my life. Hurricane Carol shakes the house with her fierce winds. Henry and Peter can't make it home. The shutters are flapping against the windows, the lights are flickering, as I search for the oil lamp. Where is it? I'm alone in the darkness. Jane, where are you? I make my way to her room, but as I open the door, I shiver with fear thinking someone's right behind me. Goosebumps creep up my arms, and I begin to get sick to my stomach. I must get my daughter and fight for our lives.

I'm trying to balance marriage, motherhood and a successful ceramic tile business, but juggling was never my forte. I'm so busy. Too busy. A popular crooner wants me to paint a tile mural for his kitchen. I'm modeling in a swimsuit for a post card. Will these things lure me away from Godly things? Lost people matter to God, my creator, and to me. I must keep my head on somewhat straight. I'm a little odd, but most of us are a little odd. So what.

It's my mission to tell folks from either side of the track how to have peace with themselves and God. Papa still thinks I have a screw missing, but that doesn't stop me from praying for him. Aunt Flossie reads biblically based material and my Holy spirit-filled letters. Yet, she's still doubtful. Daisy says she doesn't believe there's a God. I fall to my knees in prayer often and pray for my husband and children. I want those I love to experience the peace I find in knowing the Lord God.

There's no question about it, *Oddballs do matter to God.*

There's nothing wrong with me, wrong with me, wrong with me!

Acknowledgements

"Faithful is He who is calling you, He will fulfill His call"
Thessalonians 5:24

Thanks be to God for turning on the green light and keeping me focused on writing.

I would like to thank my handsome, patient, loving, faithful husband Tom for his support of me and my writing habit. His encouragement kept me moving forward on this incredible journey.

To my beautiful daughters, Tiffany and Tonia, I thank God for you every day. The years have rolled by, and the miles separate us, but you have blessed me with precious grandchildren. My love for you reaches higher than the heavens.

In devoted tribute to my gorgeous mother, Violet Munro. "Laugh, clown laugh" and "Oddballs Matter" are based on her incredible life. Her words of wisdom and guidance in her Bibles, and on the hand painted tiles still move me deeply.

I celebrate the memory of my father, Henry Munro, and his incredible love for my mother.

In loving memory of my late husband, Guy Nadeau, whom I shared thirty wonderful years of my life with. His gentle spirit lives on.

To my one and only BIG brother, Peter Munro who is only a phone call away, and who couldn't separate fiction from fact. Cathy, my sister-in-law who encouraged me from the start. I love you both. For the first readers of the first draft of *Laugh, clown laugh*, Shirley McCoy, Linda Pollino, Darlene Truax, and Nancy Determan. Thank you all for taking the time. Your support and encouragement go beyond words.

Thank you Susan May Warren, author for igniting the flame over five years ago. I learned so much from you. I'm grateful for Jeanne Leach who did the best developmental edit of this novel. I'm convinced her efforts made for a much better read.

I thank all those associated with American Christian Fiction Writers conferences. I'm still learning novelist tricks of the trade from all of you. Appreciation goes out to Linda Brooks Davis for hosting my first interview without a book. Hats off to my friend Jean Steiger, who edited the back cover at the last minute.

I salute everyone on my *Amazing Dream Team*. Thank you for your willingness to be on my squad. I hope you enjoy every chapter of *Laugh, clown laugh*. There are sixteen in this stunning group, so too many to mention by name. May God bless you many times over.

I appreciate the prayers and support from my friends at Koffee and Kare of Alexandria Covenant church and The Bible Babes, of Glenwood. Thank you for walking along side me during this long journey. "If you believe, you will receive whatever you ask for in prayer." Matthew 21:22

Thank you Jesus! Hallelujah! May All the honor and glory always be yours.

About the Author

Penny N Haavig is a native of New York, with vaudeville roots. She's a retired preschool teacher but can be found "clowning" around in area senior living facilities, as Dancing Dot. Her volunteer endeavor is at Love Inc., a non-profit organization helping those needing physical, relational, emotional and spiritual assistance. Penny lives in Minnesota with her husband, Tom and loveable horse Kammy. *Laugh, clown laugh* is based on her mother's life, and is her first novel. She can be contacted at pennynhaavig. com

Laughter can conceal a heavy heart. Proverbs 14:13